DELIRIUM

Praise for *Fever*:

'Full of twists, immaculately researched, it is very exciting and unpredictable' *Independent on Sunday*

'It's a great ride with evocative settings and intense emotion ★★★★' *SFX*

'WOW . . . that rare gem of a book that I can't stop thinking about and will read again and again . . . Outstanding! It's 10 times better than *Twilight*' Waterstones, Cardiff

'Vivid . . . captivating and passionate' London and South East Libraries

'It's a page-turning intellectual teen read that ANY adult would enjoy. Open the page, open your mind and go with the flow. TIP TOP TERRIFIC!' Waterstones, Thanet

'Completely addictive and if I could have read it in one sitting I would have done . . . an excellent and compulsive read which has left me wanting more ★★★★' goodreads.com

'Oh my god! What a book . . . This is one of the best love stories I have read . . . If you like your love stories with a twist I recommend you read this ★★★★★' *Best Books*

DEE SHULMAN has a degree in English from York University and went on to study Illustration at Harrow School of Art. She has written and/or illustrated about fifty books, but the Parallon trilogy is her first series for teenagers, which is surprising considering she lives on a campus with about 760 of them.

feverbook.co.uk

Books by Dee Shulman

The Parallon series

FEVER

DELIRIUM

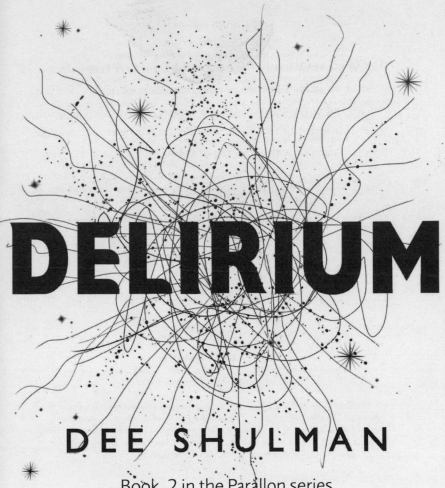

DELIRIUM

DEE SHULMAN

Book 2 in the Parallon series

PENGUIN BOOKS

PENGUIN BOOKS

Published by the Penguin Group
Penguin Books Ltd, 80 Strand, London WC2R ORL, England
Penguin Group (USA) Inc., 375 Hudson Street, New York, New York 10014, USA
Penguin Group (Canada), 90 Eglinton Avenue East, Suite 700, Toronto, Ontario,
Canada M4P 2Y3 (a division of Pearson Penguin Canada Inc.)
Penguin Ireland, 25 St Stephen's Green, Dublin 2, Ireland (a division of Penguin Books Ltd)
Penguin Group (Australia), 707 Collins Street, Melbourne, Victoria 3008, Australia
(a division of Pearson Australia Group Pty Ltd)
Penguin Books India Pvt Ltd, 11 Community Centre, Panchsheel Park,
New Delhi – 110 017, India
Penguin Group (NZ), 67 Apollo Drive, Rosedale, Auckland 0632, New Zealand
(a division of Pearson New Zealand Ltd)
Penguin Books (South Africa) (Pty) Ltd, Block D, Rosebank Office Park, 181 Jan Smuts
Avenue, Parktown North, Gauteng 2193, South Africa

Penguin Books Ltd, Registered Offices: 80 Strand, London WC2R ORL, England

penguin.com

First published 2013
001

Set in Sabon MT 10.5/15.5 pt
Typeset by Palimpsest Book Production Limited, Falkirk, Stirlingshire
Printed in Great Britain by Clays Ltd, St Ives plc

British Library Cataloguing in Publication Data
A CIP catalogue record for this book is available from the British Library

ISBN: 978-0-141-34027-2

www.greenpenguin.co.uk

Penguin Books is committed to a sustainable
future for our business, our readers and our planet.
This book is made from Forest Stewardship
Council™ certified paper.

ALWAYS LEARNING   **PEARSON**

For Axie

In Book 1, *Fever*: the story so far . . .

London AD 2012: After two expulsions, sixteen-year-old rebel misfit **Eva Koretsky** unexpectedly wins a place at St Magdalene's, a school for the highly gifted. When virologist Professor Ambrose shows her some unusual slides, she can't resist exploring further, and accidentally becomes infected by a deadly virus. Defying all medical predictions, Eva survives, but is severely weakened and plagued by vivid nightmares.

Londinium AD 152: When eighteen-year-old gladiator **Sethos Leontis** is dangerously injured in the arena, he is taken to the house of his patrons to recover. There, he falls in love with Livia, their adopted daughter. But she is betrothed to Cassius, the ruthless Londinium procurator. Seth and Livia plan to flee, but Cassius and his guards intercept them. Seth is forced to watch Cassius cutting Livia's throat before they turn on him.

Parallon: Seth wakes up miraculously healed in a shimmering world where he has the power to invent his own environment. But he is alone – and Parallon without Livia is an empty prison. When he inadvertently discovers the vortex, a fiercely guarded time corridor, and survives the experience, he becomes the reluctant protégé of Zackary, the vortex's mysterious guardian. Meanwhile fellow slave Matthias has arrived in Parallon, and as more and more people follow, Seth discovers that all the inhabitants are connected by a devastating fever. Zackary finally agrees to help Seth track the fever by sending him through the vortex to begin research in the formidably equipped St Magdalene's School.

London AD 2013: Seth walks into the St Mag's biology lab and finds himself face to face with Livia. Except she calls herself Eva. And she doesn't know him.

When Eva sees Seth for the first time, some buried memory is triggered, but she doesn't trust it, especially as his presence seems to be exacerbating her nightmares, and his touch is almost overwhelming. Despite every effort to avoid him, she continues to be magnetically drawn to him, until she can resist no longer. He finally convinces her that she somehow shares a past with Livia and helps her remember their passion, and Cassius's vicious revenge.

But the rediscovery of their love is marred by the knowledge that Seth believes he carries a deadly virus, and one kiss from him could kill her. Having already lost her in one life, Seth decides, to Eva's dismay, that he is not prepared to take that risk.

The rift this causes almost breaks them both, and finally, unable to hold back any longer, Eva reaches up to kiss him, determined that wherever their love takes her it is a place she wants to go . . .

Significant Characters from Book 1, *Fever*

London 2012/13

St Magdalene's School

Eva Koretsky, sixteen, misfit, genius, hacker, singer. Daughter of Jane and stepdad Colin Brewer. Stepsister to Ted.

Sethos Leontis, eighteen, originally first-century AD gladiator slave in Londinium. Travels to London 2013 via a time corridor.

Astrid Rettfar, seventeen, bass player, band leader

Rob Wilmer, seventeen, in love with Eva, plays keys in the band

Sadie Bekant, eighteen, drummer in the band

Ruby Garcia, seventeen, formerly Eva's best friend, now her sworn enemy

Rose Marley, school matron

Dr Crispin, headteacher

Dr Franklin, biology teacher

Dr Drury, music teacher

Professor Ambrose, visiting pathogenic virologist

Guy's Hospital

Dr Falana, consultant haematologist, grappling with Eva's mystifying symptoms

Londinium AD 152

Cassius Malchus, procurator, husband to the missing Livia

Otho, Cassius's elite guard

Rufus, Cassius's elite guard

Pontius, Cassius's elite guard

Blandus, Cassius's accountant

Sabina, Cassius's house-slave (helped with Seth and Livia's escape attempt)

Domitus and Flavia Natalis, adopted parents to Livia

Vibia, Natalis's house-slave (helped with Seth and Livia's escape attempt)

Ochira, Natalis's house-slave

Tertius, lanista (manager and trainer) of the gladiatorial barracks

Parallon

Zackary, enigmatic figure who lives near the river and the vortex

Matthias, formerly Seth's best friend and fellow slave (physician) in the AD 152 gladiatorial barracks

Georgia, one of Matthias's girlfriends

Clare, friend of Georgia, in love with Seth

Elena Galanis, a café waitress that Matthias infected in 2013 London and brought over to Parallon

Winston Grey, a motorcyclist Matthias infected in 2013 London and brought over to Parallon

Emerson, Blake, Tamara, other friends living in Matthias's house

Prologue

Londinium

AD 152

There was a loud hammering on the front door. Ochira, one of the Natalis family house-slaves, paused in her vegetable chopping. Both porter slaves were currently in the cellar, mopping up water from a leaking drainage pipe, and all the other house-slaves were out on errands. Ochira had no choice.

She walked quickly across the atrium to the door. A tall, angular man wearing a richly woven toga stood leaning against one of the marble pillars.

'Greetings,' he began.

Ochira bowed low.

'My name is Ambrosius. I have come to visit the lady Livia. Is she at home?'

Ochira's face paled, and her hands began to tremble. 'The – the l-lady Livia is n-not here.'

'Then I'll wait,' he said, pushing past her towards the atrium.

Ochira stumbled backwards, overpowered by his unexpected

entry. She darted quickly after him, wringing her hands. 'The lady Livia was married three months ago –'

The stranger instantly froze, then slowly turned back to face her, his dark eyes narrowing dangerously. 'Impossible!' he hissed, taking hold of Ochira by the shoulders and shaking her. Ochira gasped in pain.

'Forgive me,' he said quickly, dropping his hands. Then he massaged his temples wearily. 'Was she willing?' he asked evenly.

Ochira bit the inside of her cheek and stared at the ground.

'Who is he?' the stranger spat.

'C-C-Cassius Malchus . . . the procurator himself.'

'And Livia is at his house now?' he asked, striding back towards the door.

Ochira was too afraid to answer.

The stranger suddenly swung round and fixed her with his black eyes. 'Is – the – lady – Livia – at – Cassius's – house – now?' The chilling restraint of his voice served only to amplify the slave girl's fear.

She trembled and shook her head. 'No, sir! Th-the l-lady Livia has disappeared.'

'Gone?' he choked.

Ochira bit her thumbnail nervously. She had been absolutely forbidden to talk on the subject, but there was something so powerful about the stranger that she was unable to resist the overwhelming compulsion to confide.

'Some say she r-ran away . . . but –'

'But?' he hissed impatiently.

'Others think . . . she was . . . m-murdered . . .'

The stranger's sudden stillness was terrifying. Ochira didn't dare meet his eyes. She stood staring at her shoes until he turned and strode from the house.

With a shaking hand she shut the heavy wooden door and slumped against it, a deep sense of foreboding tightening in her chest.

1

Survival

St Magdalene's School, London

Thursday 14 March AD *2013*

I watched in horror as his lips suddenly curved into a sadistic smile. I knew that the moment had come. He would offer no mercy. His eyes were filled with savage pleasure.

How did he find out about us? Who betrayed us? I tried to see past him, tried to find Seth. But Cassius's vicious face filled my vision . . .

And then the flash of silver . . . the knife glinting in the moonlight. The knife he'd brought to kill me. He laughed, relishing the moment. I would not show fear. I refused to give him that satisfaction.

And then I felt the heat of the blade as it sliced along my throat.

I couldn't even scream . . .

'Eva! Wake up! Eva . . . can you hear me?'

Rose Marley, the school matron, stood over me. I tried to catch my breath, but I was looking around the room frantically.

'Seth?' I choked. 'Where's Seth?'

'I sent Seth back to his room to get some sleep, Eva. He hasn't left your side for hours! I've never seen such stamina! I don't know why, but he seemed convinced that we were about to lose you!'

Oh, Rose. If only you knew how close to the truth you were. Seth had been so sure that I wouldn't survive his kiss. Yet here I was. His virus hadn't claimed me. I was still at St Magdalene's. Still alive.

'How long have I been asleep?'

'Hmmm . . .' Rose consulted her watch. 'About fourteen hours. Must be your record!'

So that's why Seth had felt able to leave. If he was as lethal as he thought, I would be dead by now.

Suddenly the sheer joy of this realization made me want to laugh out loud. And if that wasn't reason enough, Rose Marley's expression was priceless – a mixture of bewilderment and exasperation.

'Honestly, girl,' she muttered. 'One minute you're screaming, the next you're laughing. What am I to do with you?'

'Nothing, Rose!' I grinned. 'Everything's going to be fine now, I'm sure of it.'

Rose shook her head, straightened up and walked over to the window. The light was seeping through the curtains.

'What time is it?' I asked.

'About twelve. Nearly lunchtime.'

'What day?'

'Thursday.'

I groaned. 'I should be in biology.'

'We'll talk about you going back to classes after lunch.'

'Aw, Rose!' I whined. 'You're treating me like an invalid again!'

'Oh, excuse me!' snorted Rose. 'I must be mixing you up with the girl who stopped breathing a couple of weeks ago!'

I rolled my eyes. 'OK if the invalid takes a shower?' I asked in the sweetest voice I could muster.

She reached over and checked my blood pressure. 'Fine. Just don't lock the door.'

Throwing back the duvet, I pulled myself out of bed. Hmm. No dizziness. Definitely feeling better.

'Lunch is ready, so come down as soon as you're done,' she called, making her way downstairs. I grabbed my towel and headed for the bathroom.

As I stood under the water, all my fears seemed to evaporate into its steamy comfort. I closed my eyes and deepened my contentment by thinking of Seth: his beautiful face; his strong body; and the perfect kiss we had just shared – and survived. The headiness of the physical sensations came flooding back . . . the smell of him; the sweetness of his breath; the softness of his mouth; the familiar warmth of his arms as they curled round me. And then I was overwhelmed once more by the mind-blowing knowledge that I was still here. I'd got to live. And to keep Seth! How cool was that?

I wrapped myself in a warm fluffy towel and padded back to my room. After quickly slipping on jeans and a T-shirt, I was just combing out my wet hair when there was a quiet knock on the door.

'Eva?' whispered a familiar voice. A moment later I was smiling into those clear blue eyes. His arms enveloped me and I was back where I belonged.

'Oh, Eva,' he breathed into my hair, 'I just had to come and make sure you were still here.'

I grinned up at him. 'Can't get rid of me that easily!'

Then his mouth was suddenly on mine and I was transported. The St Magdalene's medical block slipped away and we were back in our green meadow, insects buzzing, birds singing, the fragrance of grass and wild flowers filling the air.

'Eva!' a voice called from the distance.

The meadow disappeared. I was once more in my room, Seth standing warily in front of me . . . Rose calling from the bottom of the stairs. 'Are you ever coming down?'

Seth grinned and put a finger to his lips.

'How did you get past her?'

He shrugged enigmatically.

'I'll engineer a diversion downstairs so you can slip out!'

'Don't worry,' he smiled, 'I can manage my escape without any tactical manoeuvres.'

'Will I see you in art history this afternoon?' I still couldn't quite believe he was real.

'Will Rose let you out?'

'She'd better not try stopping me,' I pronounced. He turned to leave again, but I couldn't bear to let him go. I gripped on to his shirt and reached up to touch his face. So perfect.

'*EVA! Are you all right?*' called Rose from downstairs. I heard her feet begin to mount the steps.

'Just coming, Rose,' I called back quickly, reluctantly releasing him and heading slowly for the door. The last thing I needed was her catching Seth in my bedroom. I turned my head to snatch one final glimpse of him and again almost lost my resolve. How could I leave him? I'd only just found him. He seemed to be feeling the same way, because within moments I was back in his arms.

'I can't let you go,' he murmured against my lips.

'You have to,' I smiled, but continued to hold him tight.

'*Eva Koretsky! Do I have to come up there and get you?*'

I sighed, as Seth's arms fell reluctantly away.

'I'll get out of here as soon as I can,' I muttered, and headed downstairs.

An hour later I was triumphantly crossing the quad to art history. Before I got halfway, Rob Wilmer stepped in beside me.

'Eva, you're looking great!' he said with a grin. 'How're you doing?'

I nodded happily. 'Good, thanks. Really good!'

'Brilliant!' he said, squeezing my arm – and leaving his hand attached. I shot him an uneasy glance.

'I could have done with you in biology this morning,' he chatted on obliviously. 'I'm not getting bacterial cell polarity at all.'

We'd nearly reached the art history room when I felt the familiar warm presence behind me. I turned round delightedly, but Seth's face was like thunder, his eyes entirely focused on Rob's hand hooked round my arm.

An instant later, Rob, barely aware yet that Seth was there, dropped his hand as though it had been scalded.

Weird.

Rob stood looking down at his hand in confusion. I glanced up at Seth's face, but it was inscrutable. And then Seth's arm was round me and my world tipped back into balance. He propelled us to seats near the front and I settled comfortably into his warmth.

When Dr Lofts turned out the lights, I did my best to concentrate on the amazing colour of the Fauve paintings she was introducing. It might have been an easier task if Seth hadn't been sitting so close. I was just about managing to keep my eyes on the screen, when our hands accidentally touched – and suddenly another set of images superimposed themselves on to the darkened room . . . A Roman forum . . . Seth standing in front of me, a big cloak slung round his shoulders, the glimpse of white toga underneath.

When the noises of the forum began to overpower the sound of Dr Lofts's lesson, I knew I was in real danger of slipping. I could feel my breath coming too quick and shallow, my pulse too fast. I grabbed on to the seat, willing myself back in the room. But the seat wasn't there.

'Eva?' Seth was holding me by my shoulders. But which Seth? I didn't know where I was now. I began to panic.

'Eva, breathe. Slow deep breaths. Can you hear me?'

I tried to do as the voice instructed. Deep breaths. In. Out. I didn't want to be in the forum, something terrifying waited for me there . . . Slow deep breaths . . . Slow deep breaths . . . To my relief the market place started to dissipate and the sounds of the classroom regained supremacy. I opened my eyes and Seth was right there. My Seth. My *now* Seth. Unfortunately, so were a few other people. Including Dr Lofts.

'Everything all right?' She'd stopped her presentation and was looming over us.

'Everything's fine, Dr Lofts,' Seth answered quickly.

'Perhaps you should take Eva outside for a breath of air.'

'Are you OK to walk, baby?' Seth murmured.

I nodded shakily, and with his support I made my undignified exit. Seth led me over to a bench, sat me down and then squat-ted in front of me. 'Eva – where did you go?'

'The forum . . . I was meeting you. But everything hurt . . . and I was s-so scared . . .'

Seth's eyes narrowed furiously. 'Cassius!' he spat.

Dark images began flooding my brain. Cassius – his hot stinking breath against my face – his heavily ringed hand smash-ing into my jaw . . . the impact throwing me back against the wall . . .

'Eva –' That compelling voice – but too far away . . . and Cassius's grasp so tight – now wielding his silver-studded stick, his eyes glinting with ruthless purpose.

'Eva – don't let him take you back . . . Listen to me, baby . . . You're safe. Can you hear me?'

Seth. Slamming through the darkness, pushing away the vicious laughter . . . His warm arms round me, his body still and strong.

I was shivering, but his hands softly rubbed my back while his voice whispered sweet, familiar Greek words – a comforting combination that gently hauled me back to my life. My happy life.

'Hi!' he smiled when I finally stopped shaking.

I reached up and kissed him. 'Thank you,' I whispered.

'Hey, Eva – you did really well this time.'

I snorted. 'In what possible way did I just do really well?'

'No ambulance, no blackout! You found your way back from one of the bad places,' he said. 'That's the first time, I think.'

I blinked up at him. It hadn't felt like much of a victory.

'It may mean you're gaining control over that life.'

I squeezed his hands. 'It's going to be OK, isn't it?'

'We're together – of course it's going to be OK!'

'I just wish I understood what's happening – what happened to me.'

'Me too. But we do know one thing. The fever is the key. Once we understand that, we'll understand it all.'

'There is something we know about it . . .' I smiled, laying my head on his shoulder.

'What's that?' he asked, touching my temple with his lips.

'. . . It isn't as lethal as you thought!'

'You mean the kiss?' he murmured, gazing out across the quad. 'I don't really understand quite how you survived that,' he admitted, squeezing my hand. 'Unless I misunderstood what Matthias told me . . .'

'Matthias?' I queried. The name rang a bell.

Seth's face hardened. 'Er – nobody,' he sighed. 'Just someone I used to –' Then he shook his head and shrugged. 'Anyway, he led me to believe that the infection wasn't only transmitted by blood.'

'Which is what you'd previously thought?'

Seth shrugged. 'I know very little . . .' he admitted.

I sighed. 'And I've done everything I can to find out about my illness, but I just keep drawing blanks.'

'Drawing blanks?'

I grinned. It was so easy to forget English wasn't his first language. 'Coming up against dead ends?'

He blinked, bewildered.

'Hitting walls?'

He shook his head and laughed. 'I'm guessing that you're trying to find an elegant way of saying you haven't found the answer yet either?'

I play-punched him on the shoulder. 'OK, Mr Brilliant. Any suggestions?'

'Of course – we need to work together. Two perspectives. Two journeys. Two heads. Together we'll crack this thing.'

'Crack this thing?' I mocked, but that was all I got to say, because he had decided to shut me up with a kiss and I wasn't going to argue with that.

2

Celebration

Parallon

Matthias was creating vase after vase of fragrant roses. In shades of pink. Because pink was Georgia's favourite colour. And he was trying to get this right. He surveyed the room with satisfaction. The walls were festooned with swathes of ribbon and flowers. The table creaked under the weight of the sumptuous banquet. It was nearly time.

According to Georgia's calculations it was now 25 July – her nineteenth birthday. Of course her dates didn't tally with anyone else's in Parallon, but she really didn't care. Neither did Matthias. He was always ready to celebrate. Celebrations were fun and they were a good distraction. And he was after distraction.

'Oh, they're beautiful!' gasped Georgia, as she clunked a large jug of punch on to the table.

Matthias smiled, then frowned as he noticed that she'd also added two plates of sausages on sticks and several bowls of crisps.

'I can't get used to the disgusting eating habits of your century,' he sighed, kissing the top of her head.

'Are you planning to get changed?' she asked, looking pointedly at his tunic. She couldn't believe he still preferred to walk around in his weird Roman clothes.

'It's your birthday – what would you have me wear?'

'You may regret that question!' she laughed, as Matthias's tunic was suddenly replaced by a blue shirt and chinos. He raised his eyebrows, but she was shaking her head. 'No – not right. Too conservative.'

He looked down to find he now wore a white T-shirt and jeans.

'Are we done?' he groaned. Her head was cocked ominously to one side. She was still considering. A moment later he was sporting a dinner suit and black tie.

Georgia surveyed him with approval. 'Perfect! Now hold the fort while I get myself dressed.' And she swept out again.

Matthias was just about to pour himself a drink when Clare crept in.

'Has she gone?' she hissed. 'I need to do the cake!'

'What cake?'

'Duh! Matt! The birthday cake!'

Matt gazed in fascination as Clare experimented with options.

'Too much?' she asked, as a huge, white, three-tiered, sugar-frosted confection appeared in the middle of the table. 'I've been designing it for days!'

'That can't be edible,' breathed Matthias. 'What are all those little flowers made of?'

'Sugar! Now hands off!'

He'd never seen anything like it, and just couldn't resist grabbing a corner flower and popping it into his mouth, but instead of slapping his fingers, as he'd expected, Clare stood frowning at the cake distractedly.

'Matt – d-do you think Seth might put in an appearance tonight?'

'No, Clare, I don't.' He tried to walk away, but she grabbed his arm.

'Why did he go, Matt? W-was it me? Was it something I said? He's been away so long . . . and I've looked everywhere for him. You must know – y-you're his b-best f-friend . . .'

Was, thought Matt bitterly. He hadn't told anyone why Seth had left. How could he? It would mean admitting that *he* was to blame. And the infuriating part was that he hadn't done anything wrong. Matt hadn't *abused* the vortex as Seth claimed. He'd made use of it. In the best possible way. He'd given Winston, Elena and all the others a great gift – the gift of immortality – in an incredible, magical place where everything was possible. The fact that he'd had to kill them in their original world and time was immaterial. They would, after all, have died sooner or later.

I bet if I told Clare about the stupid argument, she'd agree with me, thought Matt bitterly, but he was unable to test that theory because it would mean exposing the vortex, and Seth had made him swear *never* to reveal the nature or whereabouts of the unique doorway. And, despite everything, Matt didn't want to break his word. Not to Seth. Even though Seth had made it absolutely clear their friendship was irrevocably over. Which was why Matt knew that Seth was never going to walk back through that door.

But he had no intention of sharing that information with Clare. Why in Apollo's name hadn't she got over her crush on him yet? Most girls fell for Seth, but they moved on. Especially as he never gave them any cause for hope. His heart had been won and lost to Livia. And when Livia died, all his love had gone with her.

Except that now he was fixated on some girl who looked like Livia. At some twenty-first-century London school. Matt glanced helplessly at Clare. He had neither the vocabulary nor the will to comfort her. She was sweet. He liked her – would have *really* liked her if Georgia wasn't so possessive – but *all this emotion*! Girls! Why did every little thing seem to mean so much to them?

'Hey! I thought this was supposed to be a party!' declared Elena, breezing into the room in a stunning black silk sheath dress.

Matt smiled appreciatively.

Elena moved gracefully over to the punch and poured herself a glass. 'Goodness!' she smirked, staring at the table. 'Who's brilliant contribution was the *wedding* cake?'

Clare turned on her furiously, stood for a moment in spluttering silence and stormed out.

'What did I say?' shrugged Elena, padding towards Matt and kissing him hard on the mouth.

'Elena,' he murmured into her lips, 'please give Clare a break!'

'I'd sooner give Georgia a break – from you . . .' she smirked.

'Be good,' he hissed. 'It's Georgia's birthday.' Matt reluctantly pulled himself out of Elena's embrace, and straightened his tie – just in time.

'Well? How do I look?' smiled Georgia, striding into the room, resplendent in a gold leather jacket and leopard-skin minidress.

'Gorgeous,' smiled Matthias, shooting a warning glance at Elena. Georgia frowned, sensing the taut atmosphere, and was on the point of commenting when the doorbell rang and Matt leaped gratefully to answer it.

It wasn't long before the entire villa was filled with people. Matt glided between them happily, refilling glasses, joking about the music playing and generally fulfilling his role as host. He was just spooning chicken and coriander on to Elena's plate when his hand suddenly froze. A man in a Roman tunic had just edged past.

Seth?

The flash of elation was instantly crushed by the realization that it wasn't Seth. This man was too broad and heavy. Matthias watched him settle into a corner next to one of the speakers, his heart racing. But it was no longer excitement coursing through his veins; it was fear.

3

Breaking News

Jennifer Linden looked around the office desperately. It was 6.45 p.m. and unless she left right now she was going to be late.

Although the programme she worked on had finished airing nearly an hour ago, most of the other desk assistants, producers and fixers were still hard at work – as she would normally be. There was an unspoken rule that unless you were suicidal you didn't leave work before the reporter. Especially when she happened to be Amanda Pilkington. And despite the sounds of murmured desk conversations, the tapping of keyboards and whirring of fans and printouts, Jennifer could still hear the production meeting going on next door. A crucial live link hadn't come through on tonight's programme and they were doing a major inquest. How long was it going to go on? Her eyes flicked towards the meeting-room door and glimpsed the line of digital wall clocks . . . Oh God – the UK clock was reading nearly 7 p.m.! If only

19

she was in Buenos Aires – she'd still have a couple of hours to play with.

Maybe if she left her jacket on the back of the chair and snuck out now, Amanda, her boss, might just think she'd popped to the loo. But it would mean going the whole evening without a coat, and it was freezing.

Small price to pay, she decided.

So, taking a deep breath, Jennifer saved and closed the 'Eurozone Deficits' document she'd been working on, and was on the point of shutting down her PC when an ominous shadow loomed over her desk.

Amanda.

Jen's heart sank. How'd she managed to sneak up on her *this* time?

'I need these read, analyzed and prioritized by the morning,' said Amanda, sliding a disk on to Jen's desk.

Jen nodded mutely. She didn't bother mentioning that it was Friday night. That she was supposed to be meeting someone on the other side of London in exactly twenty-nine minutes. That they had gold-dust tickets for the Livid Turkey gig at Wembley. There was no point. Around here Amanda was God, and if she wanted something done – it got done; if she wanted you to stay in the newsroom all night and all weekend – you stayed.

Jennifer glanced at the door as Amanda closed it deliberately behind her. She could hear Amanda's heels as they clipped along the corridor to the lift. Jen ground her teeth. She'd be here till morning. With a deep sigh, she pulled out her mobile and started texting.

Hi Nick, won't be able to make it. Gotta stay and work.

Gutted

Her finger hovered over the send key.

How could she bail now? What would he think? It sounded so lame. Like she didn't want to go. And she did – she really did. They'd only been together five weeks, and she liked him. A lot. Not to mention Livid Turkey, of course, her favourite band. She glanced at the time and, with a sudden resolve, made her decision.

A couple of minutes later she'd shut down her computer, slid the disk into her pocket and was slipping out of the door. She paused for a moment to steal one last guilty look at all the others still at their desks. Then she ran.

As she sprinted towards Leicester Square tube station she promised herself that she'd get the job done on her laptop at home as soon as she got back from the gig.

She arrived at Wembley twenty-four minutes late. Nick was standing near the entrance, talking on his phone, frowning. He grinned briefly at her, but then his eyes shifted away as he nodded to the person at the other end.

She touched his arm briefly and stood waiting for him to wind up the conversation, but he turned fractionally away from her, clearly indicating he wanted privacy.

Jen suddenly regretted not sending the text. She'd just compromised her position at Channel 7, bust a gut to get here, run all the way from the station, and now he was turning his back on her. Fuming, she wandered into the crowded entrance lobby and began rifling through the merch table. They were charging a fortune for band T-shirts, but – what the hell?

She was just handing over a wad of cash when she felt a pair of strong arms round her waist.

'Hey, sweetheart,' he murmured into her neck. 'What happened to you? I thought I'd been stood up.'

She felt her shoulders involuntarily relax – all the day's tensions suddenly dissolving at his touch, and her fury forgotten. 'Sorry, Nick. Got stuck at work.'

'Honestly, Jen, your work sounds worse than mine. Come on – let's go in!'

Jen stuffed the new T-shirt into her bag and allowed herself to be pulled through the rammed auditorium. They had arranged to meet early to get a good spot near the stage and though they'd now missed any hope of being right at the front, they still managed to get reasonably close.

'So who were you talking to?' She had to shout to be heard above the warm-up soundtrack.

'Work call,' he shouted back non-committally.

And that was probably the last bit of conversation they succeeded in making for the next three hours. Soon the support act (Underground Pirates) were thrashing through their set and at last Livid Turkey erupted on to the stage, claiming undivided attention.

When the pounding rhythms and screaming applause had finally died down, Jen and Nick emerged, hoarse but elated, their ears ringing, their legs aching and their heads buzzing. Nick had brought his car, and though it took them ages to get out of the car park, Jen wallowed in the bliss of not having to fight through the swarm of fans to the tube.

She sat next to him, trying not to spoil the moment with thoughts of the disk sitting in her pocket. Instead she considered his impressive profile as it flashed into life each time a car head-light swerved past: strong nose and chin, sensitive mouth . . . unexpectedly sensitive – for a policeman. She shook her head in bewilderment. What on earth was she doing with a police-man? How'd that happened?

She hadn't told her flatmate, Debs, yet. And she definitely hadn't mentioned it to her parents. Why not? Why was she so weirded out by it? She knew why. Because people like her didn't go out with policemen. They went out with other journalists. Photographers. Film-makers. She did have one friend who had briefly dated a lawyer, but that was as near to the blue line as any of them had got.

'You're very quiet,' he said suddenly. 'Had a tough day?'

'Not nearly as tough as the night's going to be,' she sighed. 'I've got a massive pile of work to do when I get back.'

'Ah well – that makes me feel better. I have to head off to the station when I've dropped you.'

'I thought you had the night off?'

'Yeah – so did I,' he muttered.

'Trouble?' she asked.

He turned and grinned at her. 'I can see your antennae twitching, Jen. You don't honestly think you'll get me to spill my guts to a news journalist, do you? However seductive she is,' he added, running his finger along her thigh.

'I wasn't fishing for a story,' she humphed indignantly. But that wasn't strictly true. She was always fishing for a story. And she'd known when she'd met him tonight that something was up.

She snuggled into his shoulder. 'Anyway, I don't want to think about work. Have you got any time off this weekend?'

He shrugged. 'I'll call you as soon as I know. Why? Is her ladyship letting you out to play?'

'Who knows?' groaned Jen. 'Do you know something, Nick? Sometimes I just feel like chucking it all in and getting a decent job with sensible hours, working with nice people who let you out of the office occasionally to have a life.'

'No you don't,' he smirked, and pulled into her street.

She watched him from the doorway as he drove off, wondering whether she was still so interested in him because she never got to spend enough time with him. Turning reluctantly back into her hallway, she started climbing the four flights to her flat.

Debs was sprawled on the sofa, channel-hopping.

'All alone?' she frowned, as Jen slumped down next to her.

'We've both got to work,' growled Jen bitterly.

'So – who is this guy?'

'I told you . . . his name's Nick,' Jen snapped, getting up from the sofa to retrieve her laptop.

But Debs refused to be stonewalled. 'And what is it Nick does that he has to go back to work on a Friday night?'

Jen opened her laptop and slipped the disk inside. She tried to look engrossed in her login screen.

'Jen! We've known each other for seven years – we don't have secrets. Now tell me – or I'll start to worry you're dating a psycho – or . . .'

The sudden silence forced Jen to look up.

Debs was staring at her friend, her eyes wide.

'Or what? Spit it out, Debs.'

'He's not married, is he?'

'Of course not!'

'So what's wrong with him?'

'There's nothing wrong with him.'

'Well, what's the big secret, then?'

'There's no big secret.' Jen knew it was hopeless. She couldn't hold out against this level of attack. 'OK – he's a policeman . . . Well – a detective. A detective inspector, in fact.'

'You're kidding, right?' Debs didn't need to say more.

Jen instantly bristled. 'What's wrong with that?'

'Well – nothing, I guess. Just – a bit unexpected . . . How'd you meet?'

'We actually first met about three months ago. Through work.'

'What work?'

'A shoot.'

Debs was sensing a certain reluctance in her friend. So she persisted relentlessly. 'What shoot?'

'Oh – you probably won't remember the story . . .'

'Try me.'

'OK,' sighed Jen. 'The one with the weird disappearing motorcyclist.'

'Oh? You mean the humiliating story you nearly lost your job over? Hmmm . . . I think I may just about remember that one.'

Jen shuffled uncomfortably. 'I didn't exactly nearly lose my job.'

Debs shook her head and snorted.

Jen was so regretting this conversation. 'Look – I still believe something very weird happened that day . . .'

'Just don't say that out loud anywhere else. They'll have you in a straitjacket.'

'Debs – there were *nine* eyewitnesses.'

'Er – for about an hour . . .'

'No. They stuck to their story for ages.'

'I think – if you consult your notes – you'll recollect that they stuck to their story just long enough to get you and the TV crew drooling over them and broadcasting it, yet – uncannily – their conviction disappeared the moment the police started to question them,' pressed Debs ruthlessly.

'Well – I still think they just lost confidence,' protested Jen.

'Ha!' exploded Debs. 'They lost confidence in the story that they had witnessed the complete *evaporation* of a bleeding, dying motorcyclist! Er – I wonder why? . . . Oh my God!' she suddenly gasped. 'Nick was one of those detectives?'

Jen's expression confirmed it.

'He was the one that completely rubbished your *X-Files* wooo-wooo paranormal explanation. Am I right?'

'It wasn't quite like that –'

Well, not exactly. Jen cringed at the memory of that day. Damn Debs for bringing it up.

It had all started out so promising. Exciting. Amanda had been away in Abu Dhabi covering the Future Energy Summit and most of the other reporters were out filming the Docklands warehouse fire. So when the call came in about this strange little story, Hugo (head of Home News) had said Jen could cover it. She'd been thrilled. It was the first report at Channel 7 she'd been assigned lead position on.

'I'll put Kishoor on filming and streambox,' he added.

Jen had breathed a sigh of relief. At least there'd be someone around with some experience. They'd set off almost immediately and were the first news team there. The police had already closed the road and cordoned off the smashed-up bike. Nicholas Mullard – the detective in charge – was standing inside the taped area, wearing a pair of latex gloves and talking to the forensics team.

Crowds were beginning to gather, so while Kishoor set up the tripod and live feed links, Jen had to quickly work out who were actual witnesses and who weren't. When she'd located the key bystanders, she began asking them what they'd seen. They were pretty shaken, but keen enough to share. Only one man had seen the impact itself: the biker had hit a pedestrian, violently swerved and been thrown clear of his motorbike. But the bike had then followed his trajectory and ploughed straight into him.

When Jen had asked about the pedestrian, the witness was sure he'd seen him get up. Someone else thought it was the pedestrian who had gone over to help the motorcyclist. Nobody was quite certain about that. But they were all consistent about what happened next. Two separate calls went out for an ambulance, which took ages to arrive, though there'd been some sort of medic around to administer emergency first aid.

Jen had looked everywhere for him, but he too had disappeared. Someone said she'd seen him run off when the ambulance got there. Another thought he'd gone before the ambulance arrived. Nobody was very sure.

The only thing all nine were completely, unequivocally unanimous about was that they had seen the biker's body dematerialize before their eyes. Their conviction was unnerving and utterly compelling.

As the story had broken just an hour before their programme aired, Hugo had taken Kishoor's footage straight through to the studio. They filmed the smashed-up bike and the pile of clothes lying in a man-shaped heap by the side of the road. Whichever way you looked at it, the images were bizarre and sinister.

Jen had stuck the microphone towards Nick Mullard as he scoured the site, asking him what he thought. He had simply shaken his head and refused to comment.

'How can I express an opinion before I've collected evidence or statements?' he'd asked, reasonably enough. So she'd followed the procession to the police station and, while statements were being taken, had begun her live broadcast just outside, speculating into camera about possible explanations for the biker's disappearance. The problem was that once she'd lost the compelling, bewildered faces of the witnesses it was impossible to come up with anything that sounded even half credible.

So although she was pretty sure she'd stumbled on to something genuinely uncanny – possibly the major story of her career – she found herself standing in front of a live TV camera with nothing convincing to say. But the studio presenter was asking her to come up with a theory, so she ploughed on.

Probably her speculations along the alien abduction line (a witness theory that hadn't sounded nearly so ludicrous at the roadside) hadn't helped. Neither had the spontaneous combustion theory she moved on to next. But the final nail in the coffin came when the first witness emerged from the interview room.

With overwhelming relief, Jen and her microphone had pounced on him. But instead of rescuing her and reaffirming the events, he categorically refused to comment, wouldn't make eye contact and scurried quickly away. When exactly the same pattern repeated with witness two, the editor cut Jen off, and she knew that her story had collapsed and she'd successfully committed reporter-suicide on live TV. Her first (and last) stab at leading a story had ended in catastrophic humiliation.

'God – I can't believe you two got together – from across the barricades! How did *that* happen?'

Jen blinked. Damn, Debs was still there, smirking.

'I don't want to talk about it,' hissed Jen furiously.

'Oh, come on, hun, I'm your best friend!'

Jen wondered briefly whether having a best friend was such a privilege.

'I've got work to do,' she sniffed. Her disk had loaded and the Eurozone currency statistics she was supposed to be reading were blinking at her in alphabetical order.

Suddenly Debs's hand shot across the keyboard and the screen went black.

'Bloody hell, Debs – what do you think you're doing?'

'I'm patiently waiting to hear how my friend Jennifer Linden – TV reporter and believer in all things paranormal – hooked up with a cynical, rational, hard-nosed police detective.'

Jen snorted with fury. 'I am NOT a believer in all things paranormal – you make me sound like a complete moron – I am just as rational as Nick bloody Mullard. I simply happen to know that something inexplicable happened that day.'

'So what's Nick's take on it?'

Jen looked down at her laptop longingly. Even currency stats were more appealing than this conversation.

'We haven't discussed it.'

Debs blinked at her in silence. Waiting.

'Well – it just hasn't come up.'

Debs continued to stare in disbelief.

How could she tell Debs that she wasn't even sure Nick realized that she was the idiot reporter on that story? She hadn't dared remind him.

When she'd met Nick five weeks ago – at the big One Earth demo in Parliament Square – she had accidentally smiled at him. She'd remembered his face but had momentarily forgotten where from. He had smiled back (she thought probably for the same reason) and they had somehow got talking. And that was that. The longer it went on, the more awkward it was to bring up.

She hauled her laptop out from under Debs's hands and took it off to her bedroom. At least she knew where she was with the currency crisis.

4

Stranger

Londinium

AD 152

Cassius Malchus's palace was magnificent. It boasted beautifully proportioned rooms, magnificent mosaics and exquisite sculptures in gardens filled with rare and exotic plants and trees. Honoured guests would dine sumptuously and drink the finest wine. But hovering behind the elegant facade pulsed a repressed and terrified household. No slave felt safe. Their days were long, the work relentless, the punishments savage. Cassius employed a team of ruthless guards who were briefed to implement his will and to mete out whatever discipline they chose. This gave them immense power over the weak and helpless battery of slaves at their mercy. Only the toughest survived, and few lasted long.

Sabina's fate was sealed the moment she delivered Livia's first secret letter. Spies watched as she slipped it to her aunt Vibia, the kitchen slave at the Natalis house. They knew the intended recipient: Sethos Leontis. They continued their watch and witnessed Vibia returning Seth's answer to Sabina by a stall in the forum.

The moment the escape plan was in motion, Vibia had met with a fatal wagon accident, and Sabina had been soundlessly taken and tortured until she'd relinquished every piece of outstanding information. Then, two days after Livia's 'disappearance', Sabina was publicly crucified. Four months later, the cross was still standing in front of Cassius Malchus's house.

When the stranger approached and saw the crucifix, his lip curled in disgust. His eyes swept over the opulent villa front: the golden eagles; the huge pillared portico; the carved double doors and the four guards eyeing him suspiciously. But as he neared, not one of them made a move towards him. His richly decorated cloak afforded him unquestionable status.

He climbed the front steps and knocked firmly on the heavy door. A couple of moments later, it was opened by a pale, sturdy-looking house-slave. Her eyes darted beyond him, checking for hidden dangers.

'My name is Ambrosius and I've come to see Cassius,' the stranger announced quietly.

'Are you the new physician?'

The stranger tilted his head a fraction.

She frowned, unsure what to make of him. 'Follow me.'

She led him along glinting mosaicked floors, through a breathtaking atrium towards the rear of the house. As they walked he noted that guards stood in attendance along every corridor.

At last they arrived at a door flanked by three particularly lethal-looking men. The slave girl melted away and the stranger found himself alone to face Cassius's elite guard, Otho, Pontius and Rufus. He lifted his face to speak, and as Pontius stared lazily back at him, Ambrosius flinched, recognition briefly tightening his neutral expression. The moment passed so quickly that Pontius registered nothing.

'I have come to see the procurator.'

Just as Rufus was about to question him further, the stranger raised his eyebrows, fixed him with his eyes and added, 'Tell Cassius that Ambrosius is here.'

All three guards nodded simultaneously. Otho opened the door and led him inside. Cassius was sprawled across a sofa. He did not look well. He was feverish, pale and, judging by the bowl on the floor beside him, vomiting regularly.

Ambrosius grimaced and gestured for Otho to get the bowl emptied.

Cassius's heavily hooded eyes rolled up to look at the visitor.

Ambrosius strode over to the man lying on the sofa and regarded him dispassionately.

'How long have you been sick?'

'I don't know – about four months.'

'And your symptoms?'

'Fever, headache, weakness, vomiting . . .' gasped Cassius, looking round for the bowl. Otho arrived with it just in time.

'All the physicians have treated the imbalance of black bile and blood,' spat Otho. 'But they have failed him.'

Ambrosius nodded. 'Leave us,' he said.

Otho, who obeyed nobody but Cassius, wanted to argue, but found himself walking obediently out of the door.

Ambrosius squatted in front of Cassius and stared into his eyes.

'Cassius, I want you to tell me where Livia is.'

Cassius tried to shrug. When Ambrosius continued to stare, he said at last, 'Gone.'

'Where has she gone?'

Cassius turned his face away, but Ambrosius put both his hands under the procurator's chin and pulled his face back round.

'Is Livia still living?'

Cassius tried to flick his eyes away, but couldn't. He felt the pressure of the stranger's hand on his neck.

'Did you kill her?'

'She deserved to die,' Cassius rasped finally.

Ambrosius's hand tightened and he watched coolly as Cassius's eyes bulged. Then he deliberately dropped his hand and looked down at the gasping man.

'You are not worthy of a speedy end.'

'You have not come to offer me a cure?'

Ambrosius laughed derisively and turned briskly away. Then he walked back through the chamber door, past the elite guard and out of the villa.

Cassius stared after him, vomited, and then sent an armed patrol to arrest him. Despite their meticulous methods, they could find no sign of the man.

5

Release

I couldn't wipe the grin off my face. I was moving back to my own room. Freedom at last. Nobody checking how well I slept, how much I ate, how long I spent working. Of course, Rose forced me to make a million promises, but it was worth it.

The last book was packed and I was just zipping up my laptop case when I heard Seth arrive downstairs . . . My happiness was complete. He was here to help me carry my stuff over. I'd no idea what he'd done to get round Rose Marley, but he'd not only managed to swing visitation rights in the medical block – something *nobody* else got – he'd somehow become the only person beside herself she trusted to look after me.

As soon as I heard his feet on the stairs, I ran to the door. He was through it and pulling me towards him before I could take a breath, and we were back in each other's arms. Exactly where we belonged. But he pulled quickly away.

Before I had a chance to register my disappointment, Rose had bustled through the door. 'Eva! You look a little flushed.

Are you sure you're ready to leave?' Her hand was instantly on my forehead.

'I'm fine, Rose. I promise.'

She raised an eyebrow and placed a bottle firmly in my hands. 'These are multi-mineral and vitamin pills. You need to take one daily. Without fail.'

'No problem.'

'And I want your word of honour that you will get to bed early, you will eat regularly and you won't work for too long at a time.'

'I've promised a million times, Rose,' I started to whine, but Seth interrupted –

'I'll make sure, Rose.'

And instead of getting annoyed that he was butting in, she just smiled up at him and nodded. 'I know you will, Seth. OK, you two, get along with you!'

Seth picked up all my stuff, leaving me with the arduous task of carrying the vitamin bottle. I took one last look around, then hugged Rose – totally surprising myself. I was *not* a hugger by any stretch of the imagination. But I realized suddenly that Rose was much more to me than the school matron. She had become someone I cared about . . . maybe even trusted. She probably had no idea what an exclusive club she was in. I tried not to dwell on just how exclusive as I followed Seth out.

Moments later I was braving the excruciating curiosity of about fifty pairs of eyes as we crossed the thrumming quad. I stalled for a second, considering retreat, but Seth deftly transferred everything he was carrying across to one arm and pulled me towards him with the other. Suddenly I felt bathed in his warm protective glow, and my discomfort just dissolved. I stared up at him, mystified, but he was focused on steering me through the arched entrance to Isaac Newton, my boarding house. The heavy wooden door slammed shut behind us and we were instantly enveloped in the cool, shady peace of the ancient stone vestibule.

'Home,' I murmured, as I slumped contentedly against him.

'Nearly,' he whispered, gently urging me forward along the narrow vaulted corridor to my own little room. I unlocked the door and threw myself on to the bed. Seth carefully stashed all my stuff against the wall, then closed the door, turned the key and followed me over, stretching out next to me.

He lay propped up on one elbow, one finger tracing along my cheek. I sighed and reached my arms round his neck to pull him closer.

We were alone in a locked room. My heart began to race as his lips brushed mine, the warmth of his touch sparking a bright heat inside me. I closed my eyes as my shaking fingers began moving tentatively down his neck, along his shoulder and across his chest. Suddenly they were tracing the ridged line of his arena scar. My whole body shuddered at the memory and I froze.

'It's OK, baby,' he breathed. 'It doesn't hurt.'

And then his mouth claimed mine and I could feel his heart pounding under my fingertips, but it was the sound of his breath, so shallow and hoarse, that made me want to obliterate any distance between us. I edged closer so that our bodies were touching, and instantly his arms were round me, enclosing me. And this closeness felt so right. Like we were two halves of the same whole. My heart was thudding so hard I knew he must be able to hear it, but I really didn't care. And then as my fingers ran further round his back, he moaned, which sent a shiver of joy through me, and my own breath caught in my throat. His mouth broke away from mine and he began kissing my face, my eyelids, my neck, while I ran my hands through his hair. I loved the taste of him, the smell of him, the feel of him. His mouth found mine again and we breathed heavily into each other as our hands began to explore further.

And suddenly he jerked to a stop and pulled away.

'Seth? W-what's wrong?' I choked.

He groaned and rolled over on to his back, where he lay with one arm across his eyes, trying to get his breathing under control.

'You know we can't do this, Eva,' he gasped.

'No, I really don't,' I said shakily, running my hand across his shuddering chest.

He laughed hollowly. 'That is not helping,' he moaned, lifting my fingers and kissing them.

'Seth, please!'

He shook his head, skimmed a finger along my arm and gazed down at me.

'Eva, I want us to have time in this life. We were cheated in the last one. I couldn't bear to lose you again.'

'You'll never lose me. I won't let it happen,' I murmured.

'Neither will I,' he said, and with a sudden determination he pulled himself up to a sitting position and swung his legs over the side of the bed. I leaned my head against his back and locked my arms round his waist. I felt his resolve weaken again. I kissed the back of his neck, loving the scent of his skin.

'Eva,' he rasped, 'I was famous in Londinium for my strength and control. And now I don't even have the power to stand up.'

'I'm glad,' I whispered.

But he was clearly working on himself, because I suddenly saw his knuckles whiten as he gripped the side of the bed and wrenched himself off it. Then he put his hand out and hauled me upright too. I felt a little shaky.

'I am now about to fulfil promise number one,' he said firmly.

'Promise number one?' I grumbled.

'School dining room. It's suppertime. And I am tasked to make sure the girl eats.'

6

Impatience

St Magdalene's

Early Thursday Morning, 21 March AD *2013*

'Seth?' I gasped into the darkness, my heart pounding.

'Sorry,' he murmured into my hair. 'I didn't mean to wake you. I was just missing you.'

He sat on the side of the bed and I wrapped my arms round him. 'What time is it?' I asked sleepily.

He squinted at his watch. '4.30 a.m.'

I didn't bother to ask how he'd managed to sneak along the creaky corridor past the housemaster's door. I'd witnessed his clandestine skills in the medical block.

'Couldn't you sleep?'

'Oh – I've just been out . . . doing a bit of – er – private lab work.'

I sat up. I was fully awake now. 'What kind of work?'

'Virus research,' he answered quietly.

'Where?'

'Biology lab.'

'How d'you get in?'

He plunged his hand into his jacket pocket and dropped a set of keys on to my pillow.

'Dr Franklin's keys?' I gasped.

'She lent them to me,' he said, blinking innocently.

'Impossible,' I hissed. '*Nobody* gets permission to borrow Dr Franklin's keys. She's obsessive about them.'

He shrugged and untied his shoes. He clearly wasn't going to give me any more info on that subject.

'So what research were you doing there?' I pressed.

'Some blood analysis . . .'

'Without me?' I choked. 'I thought we had a deal!'

'I'll show you tomorrow, I promise,' he said, kissing the top of my head.

'When?'

'When everyone else is asleep,' he grinned. 'So you'd better get some sleep now.' He pushed me back on to the pillow, threw his jacket on to the chair and climbed in beside me.

'How am I supposed to go to sleep now?' I moaned. 'Aw, tell me, Seth,' I pleaded, twining myself round him.

He chuckled. 'I will – tomorrow.'

'*Please* – just give me something to go on!'

He rolled his eyes. 'OK. It's really a continuation of the research I started in Parallon.'

'*Parallon?*' I whispered. Had I heard that name before?

'Oh, Eva,' he breathed. 'There is so much I have to tell you . . . but it's late. You need to get some sleep.'

'I am *so* not tired, Seth,' I said firmly, propping myself on to an elbow. 'Now tell me – where the hell's Parallon and what exactly were you doing there?'

Seth pushed out a breath, sat up, arranged the pillows against the wall and leaned back. Then he stared broodingly into the shadowy darkness of my room for what felt like a century.

'*Seth!*' I wailed.

'Sorry, Eva . . . I'm just not sure where to begin – how to begin.'

I held his gaze and waited.

'All right, then,' he sighed. 'But I warn you – you'll need an open mind.'

'First rule of science,' I murmured, snuggling into his chest.

'Parallon is where I went after Londinium.'

'You mean – after you d-died?'

He nodded.

'So –' I couldn't even begin to frame the question.

'I mean – I died in Londinium and woke up in Parallon . . . But it wasn't anything like the afterlife I expected . . . No fields of nymphs or shades of all the people I'd lost. It was more like Londinium . . . only emptier . . .'

'Londinium?'

He nodded, his eyes staring bleakly ahead.

'But we *both* died in Londinium, Seth . . . Cassius k-killed both of us – we were together.'

Seth grabbed my hands. 'Exactly,' he rasped. 'I couldn't understand how I came to be in Parallon without you either. Every day I searched for you. Every day I prayed I would find you. And every day the heaviness of an existence without you sat on my chest like – like the weight of rock.' His voice cracked and his eyes burned. '*You* were the reason I began researching the fever. I had to find out why I was there and you weren't. And the only difference I could see between our deaths was just that: the fever. You died instantly . . . I didn't.

So the fever had to be the key. It was the fever that took me to Parallon.'

'But – what happened to me then? How did I get from there to here?'

He shook his head. 'I have no idea. When I first saw you here, I just couldn't believe it . . . after so many years of searching. But your journey was different. You've had a whole lifetime here . . . maybe others . . . I've no idea. I had to travel here.'

'From Parallon?'

He nodded.

'How?'

'Through a tunnel of water – a wormhole. Zackary calls it the vortex,' he said.

'Who's Zackary?'

'I wish I knew.'

'He lives in Parallon?'

'Some of the time. It was Zackary who taught me how to use the vortex. And I can think of several more comfortable ways to travel,' he added wryly.

I tried to imagine a tunnel of water – and maybe his description was just so evocative, or my proximity to him triggered some kind of telepathic communication, but I could suddenly feel a terrifying, roaring pull . . . a claustrophobic panic as water swirled around me. I clung on to him, waiting for the sensation to end.

'Eva?' He was frowning into my face. 'Eva, what is it?'

I breathed out shakily. 'The vortex,' I panted. 'It just sounded . . . fairly unpleasant.'

He was staring at me. 'Come on – I think it's time we went to sleep. I can tell you more another time.'

'No! I need to hear this, Seth. Please tell me.'

He studied my face carefully. 'Are you sure you're not too tired?'

When I finally stopped plying Seth with questions and let him sleep, I lay staring into the darkness of my room, listening to his comforting rhythmic breathing and trying to picture the impossible world of Parallon.

I knew enough about String Theory to accept the theoretical proposition of alternative dimensions, and I ran through the Metastable Vacua hypothesis in the hope of making some logical sense of the strange world Seth described. But the weirdest thing about it was that my natural scepticism seemed to be on some kind of shutdown. I shouldn't have been able to buy into that *Intention–Creation* principle. How was it possible that the physical world was symbiotically linked to the psychological? Yet – for some reason – I did buy it. Maybe because it was easier to believe stuff at night; or because his voice was so hypnotic; or because I just trusted he was telling me the truth . . . but when he finally stopped talking, I could almost imagine myself there. What was harder to understand was his acute sense of dislocation. I considered the vocabulary he used – *endless; interminable; meaningless* – and the casual, almost disdainful way he'd described *willing* stuff into existence – food, clothes, buildings, equipment . . . To me, Parallon sounded completely awesome. You could invent *anything* so long as you had, at some point, experienced it . . . your injuries would magically heal . . . you couldn't die . . .

So why did he hate it there so much? He made Parallon sound more like a prison than a playground. Was it simply because he didn't understand how he'd got there? How the fever worked? And how was his sickness linked to mine? He was convinced there was a connection. Crucial symptoms were very similar – but only he ended up in Parallon.

So what possible research could Seth be doing in the biology lab? I was desperate to check out what he was up to. And how had he managed to get hold of Dr Franklin's keys? I considered grabbing them and running over to the lab right now, but I didn't have a clue what to look for. Surely I could wait? Tomorrow was just a few hours away. I shifted my focus to the sleeping figure next to me. God, he was beautiful. And he looked so peaceful. I moved tighter into the orbit of his warmth, longing to share his tranquillity.

7

Trust

St Magdalene's

Thursday 21 March AD 2013

I groaned. It couldn't be 7.30 already – I'd only just shut my eyes. Blindly, I reached out my arm to switch off the alarm, but it had already stopped ringing. I opened my eyes in surprise and found myself staring into a fierce blue gaze and a warm *hello* smile.

'Seth, you stayed!' I gasped, wriggling into the arc of his arms and resting my head against his shoulder. I closed my eyes contentedly.

'Eva,' he whispered into my hair.

'Mmm?' I murmured, refusing to open my eyes.

'Just wondered if you're planning on going to school this morning?'

'Plenty of time,' I muttered into his chest.

'Er – five minutes, in fact.'

What? He pointed at the clock. Where had the last hour gone? I shot out of bed, the room spinning dangerously around me.

'Oh no!' I moaned, trying to get myself vertical. He put his arms out to steady me and I stood swaying for a second, waiting for the room to stop moving.

'You OK?' he asked, his hand on my forehead. 'You feel a bit hot.'

'I'm fine,' I answered quickly, leaning against the chair I'd dumped my jeans on yesterday. I had to be fine – I had a long day ahead and I was desperate to go to the lab with him later.

'Do you mind if I shower here?' Seth asked, his head cocked to one side, politely waiting for my answer. Like I would have said no!

'Be my guest!' I grinned, completely distracted by the thought of him in there. I watched him move lithely across the room and as soon as the door was shut I did my best to focus on trying to get myself dressed. I refused to notice my shaking hands as I zipped up my jeans, though it made doing up the top button clumsily slow. By the time Seth emerged, dressed but with dripping hair, I was still attempting to tie my laces. My hands were not cooperating.

I didn't want Seth to see, so I tucked the laces into the trainers and stood up.

He was looking at me with narrowed eyes, but he simply put an arm round my shoulders, grabbed my room key and Dr Franklin's set, and steered us out.

Ruby was just locking her door as we emerged. She stood for a moment, open-mouthed, and I swallowed nervously.

'Morning, Ruby,' called Seth breezily. 'Glad to see we're not the only ones running late.'

She blinked . . . and then . . . giggled flirtatiously. 'At least you and me have history first period, Seth. Dr Edwards is pretty cool about punctuality . . .'

I groaned. Dr Isaacs, my philosophy teacher, wasn't. *And* he had a detention addiction – especially for lateness. 'I'd better run,' I sighed, wondering vaguely what my legs would make of that instruction. 'See you at break, Seth.' I ducked out from under his arm, but his hand closed round my shoulder.

'Hey, Eva,' he said lightly. 'You heard Ruby, I've got plenty of time. I'll walk you to philosophy . . . Catch you later, Rubes.'

I shook my head. He was so much better at relationships than me. But then I guess almost everyone was.

'I'll see you at break, baby,' he smiled, touching my lips with his finger as he deposited me at the door of my class. When he took his arm away, I momentarily lost my balance and had to surreptitiously grab the door handle for support. But I think I covered the stumble pretty well. I waited till he was heading back through the quad before I moved. Just in case. To my dismay my legs were still unsteady, so I walked ultra-carefully into the classroom and sat as near to the door as I could get. A second later Astrid clattered into the seat next to mine.

'Eva, babe!' she grinned. 'Thank God you're here. You're the only one who doesn't put up with my bullshit in this class. Dr Isaacs is way too tolerant.'

I laughed, trying not to wince. My head was beginning to ache and the prospect of one of Astrid's heavy metaphysics debates was not exactly restful. But it was still way better than being holed up in the medical block.

Seth was leaning against the wall outside the room at the end of the double period, with two steaming polystyrene cups.

'Wow! That's what I call service,' smirked Astrid. 'Though

this must mean you're not planning to spend break ploughing through the hoards in the dining room with me?'

I shrugged apologetically. 'See you there for lunch?'

'Deal – we have so much stuff to catch up on . . . You will be able to make band practice after school, right?'

I closed my eyes for a moment, gauging the intensity of the headache.

'Aw, please, Eva! We really need you there!'

'Of course I'll be there,' I answered quickly. 'Can't wait.'

'Eva,' frowned Seth, 'Rose doesn't want you –'

'I'll be fine, Seth,' I interrupted quickly. 'See you at lunch, Astrid.'

I avoided Seth's eyes when he handed me my cup of coffee, and then as we walked slowly across to physics I turned a little away from him so he wouldn't see how much my hand was shaking. I hardly dared take a sip, because I knew I'd probably slop the lot down my chin, but the warmth of the cup was comforting.

I spent the next hour drifting in and out of photovoltaics, cursing my now throbbing head. Fortunately Seth made up for my lack of contribution, so I don't think Dr Chad picked up on my waning attention.

By lunchtime all I really wanted to do was lie down some-where quiet . . . my peaceful little room for example. But that wasn't an option. Not if I intended to stay under Rose Marley's radar. If I slipped up now I would never be able to get into the lab with Seth – and nothing was going to stop me doing that.

So I hauled myself through the rest of the day, and at 4 p.m. Seth stood at the door of practice room three looking distinctly uneasy.

'Trust me, Seth, I'll be fine. It's just a headache. Now go for your run,' I urged. 'You'll be climbing the walls if you don't.'

'But –'

'Eva Koretsky! You coming or what?' bellowed Astrid from inside.

I gave Seth a quick goodbye kiss and followed Astrid into the room. The others were already set up. Even my guitar was plugged in and ready to go.

I headed towards it, but Astrid stopped me.

'Hold it, guys! Before we start, we need a short band meeting.'

I frowned. We never did band meetings. Sadie blinked in surprise and put down her sticks.

'There are a couple of things I wanted to sort out.'

I was clearly going to need a chair. I looked around the room. There weren't any.

'First, we have to come up with a band name . . .'

'What, *now*?' I groaned. I was definitely going to need a chair.

'Yes, now. Preferably in the next half hour,' stated Astrid firmly.

'But – bands take months to agree on a name,' argued Rob.

'We don't have months. We have minutes.'

'What's the big rush?'

'It's time to start gigging.'

'Astrid, we gig nearly every Thursday!' I protested.

'Yeah – in the *school common room*, Eva! We need a slightly wider audience.'

Rob was nodding thoughtfully. 'Astrid's right. We're ready.'

'Yay!' whooped Sadie. 'I'm totally up for that!'

'But –' I was so on my own here. And I definitely couldn't argue standing up, so I slid down to the floor and rested my chin on my knees. My head was throbbing. I shut my eyes and tried to concentrate on the conversation drifting on above me. It would be dangerous to lose focus now – Astrid was on one of her missions.

'I was hoping to come up with a name that uses all of our initials,' Astrid continued. 'What do you reckon to Aser?'

The group groan put a swift end to that one.

'Ace would work better . . .' said Rob.

'But that doesn't represent either you or Sadie,' objected Astrid.

'Arse?' snorted Sadie.

'Very funny . . .'

'*Eva!*' Astrid was shaking my shoulder.

I forced my eyes open and gazed blearily around the room. 'Sorry?' I croaked.

'What do you think of the Astronauts?'

I blinked stupidly.

'For the band name, Eva!'

'Er – yeah!' I swallowed. '. . . I like it.'

'Excellent!' grinned Astrid. 'Everyone agrees. Now all we need is a website.'

I suppressed a groan.

'Eva should do it – she's so quick at writing computer code.'

'Oh, come on, Rob, like Eva'll prioritize building a band website when there's some deep astrophysics quandary to ponder. We can just use a template and throw something together. I'll take some photos later.'

'OK, great,' I said quickly, hauling myself to my feet. 'So shall we get on with playing some songs?' There was no way I was giving Astrid the chance to come up with any more big ideas.

By the time we'd finished rehearsing, my head was pounding and my legs could barely carry me across the quad. But I felt alive. Our music did that to me. It was like a medicine, an antidote: playing together, feeling the song grow, become something else – something we were all part of – gave me such a buzz.

Rob kept pace beside me as I made my slow way back to the house. Then he insisted on walking me to my door. I didn't argue – my legs were feeling marginally unreliable. As I turned the key, he pushed the door open and glanced around inside.

'What's up?' I asked, watching him hover.

'Er – nothing,' he answered, nonchalantly pushing open the door to the shower.

'If you're looking for Seth,' I sighed impatiently, 'you'll probably find him on the running track.'

'At this time?' Rob frowned.

I shrugged. 'He has to run – seriously run – for at least two hours a day.'

'*Why?*' Rob's mouth was hanging open.

'Something he's got used to. He needs to expend the energy, keep strong . . . ready . . .'

'Ready for what?'

'Ready for anything life throws at him, I guess.' His enemies. His nightmares . . .

Rob was staring at me, perplexed.

'And then there are the endorphins, of course,' I added quickly. 'You can get addicted to those, you know.'

'He shouldn't need a chemical rush, Eva,' Rob said quietly. 'Not when he's got you –'

I felt Seth's presence before I saw him. The heat radiated off him as he filled the doorway.

'Hey,' I whispered huskily. He was in his running clothes, his hair plastered to his neck, his shoulders glistening, his shirt slick with sweat . . . his eyes completely focused on Rob. The tension in the room was like a physical force.

'Thanks for dropping me back, Rob. Er – see you tomorrow,' I muttered, willing him to leave.

But Rob wasn't listening to me. He was staring blankly at Seth, his mouth slack.

'Rob?'

No answer.

'Seth?' I rasped. What the hell was going on here?

Suddenly Rob's head jerked up, his eyes refocused and he looked around in a daze.

'Night, Eva. Goodnight, Seth,' he breathed, and wandered out.

Seth took a deep breath, then, catching my horrified expression, crossed the room and enveloped me in his arms.

'You're white, Eva. What's wrong?' Gently, he pulled me over to the bed. 'Sit down, I'll get you some water.'

'What did you just do to Rob?' I asked, as he put a glass in my hand.

He went over to the sink and poured himself a glass of water. Then swallowed slowly. Playing for time.

'Seth?' I waited.

He crossed the room and sat down on the bed next to me. 'I am not comfortable with Rob hanging around you,' he said with a shrug.

'I know that. But what did you *do* to him?' I repeated patiently.

He looked down at his hands. 'Nothing serious.'

'Nothing serious?' I choked.

'Look, Eva, all I did was *gently suggest* he leaves you alone,' Seth answered defiantly.

'And you can just *gently suggest* something without having to open your mouth?'

He nodded. 'But Rob needs regular reminders,' he added with irritation.

I stared at him, waiting for a coherent explanation. He sighed.

'OK, it's just a Parallon thing . . .'

I raised my eyebrows. He shifted uneasily.

'I'm not really sure how it works. Zackary calls it the *time amplification syndrome*. Basically, the further away you get from your own time, the more intense your personal strengths and weaknesses become.'

'And you just happened to be good at getting what you wanted?'

'Survival was all I wanted until I met you . . .' He shrugged again.

I wasn't going to be deflected. 'Have you ever *gently suggested* anything to me?'

His eyes widened with shock. '*No*, of course not! How could you even think that? I love you, Eva. I would never try to exert my will over you.'

'But you could?'

'I *wouldn't*.'

I stared down at my hands. The thought of that much power terrified me.

'Eva,' he whispered hoarsely, 'please don't doubt me.'

I glanced up when I heard the rawness in his voice. He was watching my fingers as they twisted in my lap, his shoulders stiff. Catching my movement, he lifted his eyes to mine. And suddenly I saw the unguarded, vulnerable Seth. The one I had watched over, night after night in Londinium as he fought for his life.

I took his face in my hands and kissed him. 'I trust you, Seth,' I breathed. 'But – if you ever try that stunt on me –'

He grinned, pulled me towards him and made damned sure that was the end of the conversation.

8

Lab

Seth was standing by my bed, silhouetted against the soft light of the bedside lamp. I frowned, trying to unscramble my brain.

'What time is it?' I croaked.

'Just after midnight,' he whispered.

I sat up and rubbed my eyes.

'You don't need to come, baby,' he murmured, squatting down on the floor in front of me and tucking a strand of hair behind my ear. 'But I couldn't face your wrath if I didn't wake you.'

The lab. Of course.

I threw the duvet back and jumped up. Too fast.

'Hey, steady,' he warned, waiting by my side until the dizziness passed.

'Are you sure you're OK?' he murmured uneasily, as I leaned against him to cross the quad.

'I'm great,' I answered heartily.

Seth quietly unlocked the lab and we headed straight for the quantum particle microscope.

'So, Eva – this is where we are,' he began, pausing to pull up a stool for me. 'As far as Dr Franklin is concerned, I am conducting a broad research project into immune response times. I need a significant number of subjects – at least a hundred and fifty. And guess what? That just happens to be the number of students at St Mag's.'

'You're trialling *everyone*?'

'I've got consent forms back from all the parents, guardians and students. I'm just waiting on the staff.'

'Consent forms for what?'

'To take blood samples.'

'You're getting blood samples from students and teachers?'

'And technicians and secretaries – well, basically, everyone. I've already collected nearly eighty samples.'

'OK – so what precisely are you testing for?'

'I've told Dr Franklin I'm checking out quantifiable responses to a number of specified stimuli. Which is *nearly* the truth.'

'How nearly?'

'Well, of course, along with the number of *specified* stimuli, there is a non-specified one . . . my blood.'

I stared at him, waiting for the punchline. He gazed mutely back at me.

'Seth,' I said, in my really patient voice, 'you're well. Your infection won't be active. The pathogen won't be replicating. So even if it's still present, there'd be no way to isolate it, especially as we don't know what antibody activity to look for.'

He pressed his lips together, sighed and moved towards the fridge. 'Last night I prepared thirty slides, each with blood from a different student.'

'OK . . .' I said. Where was he going with this?

He opened the fridge door, revealing stacks of test tubes and layered slides. Selecting one of the slides, he placed it on the microscope's stage, switched on the screen and keyed in the magnification.

'This is the blood of Rowan Jackman from Year Ten.'

I nodded.

'Just watch the screen.'

I was seeing normal T-cells bouncing and bobbing as they usually did.

'Now I'm going to add a tiny drop of my own blood to the slide.'

He pricked his finger with a needle and dropped the tiniest speck on to the edge of the slide, leaving a clear gap between the two samples. As soon as the slide was in place he wrapped the needle in paper and threw it into the sealed waste container. Then he carefully put a plaster on his finger.

I giggled. 'Hey – what happened to my tough gladiator?'

Seth's whole face darkened. 'Eva – could you move a little further away? I don't want you anywhere near this slide.'

I frowned. 'Seth –'

'Just watch,' he said quietly, adjusting the tilt gradient so that the samples started to converge.

'Oh my God!' I choked, staring at the screen.

'Eva, are you all right?' Seth immediately stabilized the slide, stopped the transmission and came to stand in front of me.

'The spiky thread-like structures . . .' I gasped. 'They're – *in your blood?*'

'You've seen them before?'

I nodded weakly.

'So do you know what's going to happen when my blood meets Rowan Jackman's?'

I looked up at him and whispered hoarsely, 'His blood cells are going to – to disappear.'

Seth stared at me in confusion.

I walked over to the slide, restored the tilt and resumed the transmission.

We both watched in silence as the two bloods converged and the spiky structures began their cell invasion. Of course, less than a second later the entire screen was clear.

'But how could you have already seen this?'

'Professor Ambrose showed me,' I murmured. 'This is the virus I was infected with. Seth, we need to check what *my* blood looks like under the microscope.'

I went and got a slide and looked around for something to stab myself with. Seth's needle had been discarded – and anyway, I wasn't an idiot. There was nothing suitable around so I ended up grabbing a loose piece of skin by my thumbnail and biting it off. Enough blood oozed out to use on the slide.

My fingers started to tremble as I fitted the slide back into the microscope.

Seth moved next to me and we watched together as the T-cells bounced around.

'No threads,' breathed Seth, but he was peering at the screen. 'Can you raise the magnification, Eva?'

I keyed in another thirty per cent.

'What's that?' he asked, pointing at a tiny smudge in one corner.

'No idea,' I answered and raised the multiplication another fifty per cent.

The smudge looked like a minute cluster of dots bobbing in a little self-contained mass.

'Have you ever seen anything like that before?'

Seth shook his head. 'It's probably nothing. Could be just a slight blemish in the glass. The magnification is huge.'

I nodded.

'We should try with a fresh slide,' I said, but as I reached across the bench to get one, I staggered, and had to lean against the wall to steady myself. Seth's eyes darted to my face and he started packing up the lab.

'Hey – we so haven't finished here,' I protested.

'We so have! For tonight, anyway, Eva. You need to get some sleep. We'll come back tomorrow.'

I really wanted to argue. The old Eva would never have left the lab right in the middle of something so momentous. But the old Eva didn't feel like crap most of the time. Unwillingly, I let him take my arm and lead me back to my room.

'Will you stay?' I breathed, as he helped me unzip my hoody.

'There's only so much *gentle suggestion* my housemaster can take,' he sighed. 'I really should put in an appearance back at the house.'

I nodded reluctantly. I couldn't do much else after my earlier reaction to his *gentle persuasion* of Rob.

He leaned down and kissed me. 'Oh, Eva,' he breathed, resting his forehead against mine, 'how can I leave you?'

His soft breath on my face felt like a healing drug. I kissed his mouth gratefully, longingly, then hungrily. He kissed me back, carefully. As I pressed my body against his, he sighed. 'Eva, I –'

I backed towards the bed, trying to bring him with me.

'Eva, no –'

'I thought boys were meant to be insatiable,' I complained. 'You clearly don't want me as much as I want you.'

'How can you talk about want? Have you any idea how endlessly I've longed for you? I promised myself that if I ever found you, I would never do anything to risk losing you again. And here you are: my own personal miracle – asking me to do exactly that!'

'We don't know for certain! You were scared to kiss me, remember?'

'You saw my blood, Eva . . .'

'I might be immune,' I murmured, running my hands through his hair. He grabbed my wrists, breathing hard.

'Tomorrow,' he said hoarsely. 'Tomorrow we can find out for certain.'

My stomach clenched. 'Y-you mean put our blood together on a slide . . .?'

He nodded.

'Have you found anyone immune yet?'

He didn't need to answer.

9

Late

Shoredicth, London

Friday 22 March AD 2013

'Ha ha! Here's one for you, Jen!' snorted Debs from the sofa. She was watching a *Crimewatch* reconstruction on TV.

'Yeah, yeah,' muttered Jennifer absently. She was bent over her laptop at the table, furiously finishing off her final summit report for Amanda. And as she was already running dangerously late for her date with Nick, she needed a distraction like a hole in the head.

'Another disappearance, Jen. Surely you're interested?'

Jen flashed her a murderous glance and continued typing. But her concentration had been broken and – if she was honest – her interest had been piqued. Her fingers slowed to a standstill as she squinted across at the TV. Less than a minute later she'd abandoned her laptop and was perched on the arm of the sofa.

They were watching the last known movements of a London café waitress, Elena Galanis.

'Oh my God, I know that café,' breathed Jen. 'I've probably bought a cappuccino from the missing girl.'

'Along with hundreds of other punters . . . Weird case, though, don't you think?' mused Debs.

'Abduction, obviously,' said Jen. 'Why else would she be on *Crimewatch*? Damn – look at the time! I'm late for Nick – again. And I still haven't finished my report.'

'I don't know, Jen,' murmured Debs. 'It's not an obvious abduction. No sign of struggle. And, anyway, she wouldn't be that easy to abduct – she's an Aikido black belt.'

Jen stood frowning for a moment, then shrugged, saved her work, shut down her laptop and headed for her bedroom. She was still in her work clothes and had intended to shower and change, but she no longer had time to do either.

'Damn,' she muttered, pulling a comb through her hair. She quickly touched up her mascara and applied a coat of lip-gloss. Staying in her work suit meant she'd have to wear her uncomfortable heels all evening too. She sighed, picked up her phone, keys and jacket, and yelled goodbye to Debs.

Seventeen minutes later she was running out of the station towards the line of taxis. She had just opened the door of the first in line when she remembered she'd left the bottle of wine she'd bought on the kitchen counter. Could this evening get any worse? How could she turn up late *and* empty-handed? She'd have to buy another one. She hit her head with her fist and stepped away from the cab. And then her phone rang.

'Nick!' she wailed. 'I'm so sorry I'm late. I'm at Highbury, but I left the wine at home, so I've just got to –'

'Forget the wine, Jen. I just want you here. Now. Please . . . It's all ready, and we're starving.'

Oh God! Of course. It wasn't just the two of them tonight. He'd invited people she didn't know. Would that make matters better or worse? Worse, she decided immediately. Although they offered the advantage of distraction, that advantage would be completely outweighed by Nick's annoyance.

'Are there any taxis at the rank?'

Her cab was just pulling away, but she put an arm out and the driver stopped, rolled his eyes and opened the passenger door.

'I'll be there in two minutes,' she said.

When Jen got to Nick's building she stood for a moment on the doorstep trying to collect herself. She felt her throat ache in the way it always did when she was about to cry. What was the matter with her? She took a deep breath and rang the bell.

She heard his feet on the stairs. She couldn't tell from the sound of them whether they were angry feet. Her shoulders hunched in preparation. At last the door opened. Nervously, she looked up into his face.

'Hey, Jenny – are you OK? You look . . . shattered.'

'Oh, Nick,' she sniffed, swallowing the big lump in her throat. 'It's so good to see you.'

He hugged her, then took her hand and pulled her upstairs. 'Come and meet the guys.'

'The guys' turned out to be Nick's sister, Amy, her husband, Giorgio, and a couple of mates Nick had known since school, Marios and Jamil.

Jennifer knew that if Nick was introducing her to his sister *and* his oldest friends it had to be significant. She glanced across at him and smiled.

'Be gentle with Jen,' he joked, 'she's had a rough day.' He handed her a glass of red wine and ushered her over to the dining table. 'Sorry, sweetheart, we've got to eat immediately – my sister loses all her charm when she's hungry!'

'Oh, Amy, I feel so bad . . .'

'Hey – no problem, Jen. But the food had better be good – and plentiful, bro – I didn't have time for lunch.'

'Too busy giving the brats detention?' called Nick from the kitchen.

'Had to run netball practice. In case Nick's hint wasn't clear enough,' she grinned, 'I'm a teacher, Jen!'

'Yeah – I kind of gathered!'

'Got loads of bossing-around practice on my baby brother!'

'Oh yeah?' Jen smirked.

'Only had to seriously pull rank once though –'

There was an uncomfortable silence, as Nick came in and deposited a huge platter of tricolore on the table. Jen glanced around. Everyone was studiously staring down at their plates. She frowned up at Nick, questioningly.

'Salad, anyone?' he snapped.

Nobody moved.

'Jen?' He spooned some on to her plate.

'Thanks,' she mumbled uncomfortably.

Nick suddenly huffed out impatiently, and took a long gulp of wine. 'It's no big deal, Jen. Amy's just talking about a stunt she pulled a few years back.'

'What stunt?' asked Jen uneasily.

'I didn't pull a stunt!' Amy exploded. 'Your OC had already given you an honourable discharge, for God's sake!'

'Honourable discharge from what?' Jen whispered.

'Special Forces,' sighed Amy. 'Nick got injured in Afghanistan.'

'Y-you were in the military, Nick?'

'Long story,' he nodded, effectively closing the subject. 'Now, please, guys, eat the damned salad or the pasta's going to dry into a solid lump.'

The evening was back on track. Nobody referred to the topic again, but Jen couldn't stop thinking about it. What was Nick doing in Afghanistan? Weren't Special Forces some kind of elite military unit? She didn't know much about it, but was desperate to find out more. And clearly nobody was going to enlighten her tonight. But they were all warm and friendly to Jen, and made sure they filled her in on any background if the conversation veered too far into their shared pasts. They obviously knew each other really well, and talked in a sort of shorthand, finishing each other's sentences and mocking one another ruthlessly at any opportunity. By the time they'd finished the main course, Jen's cheeks were aching from laughing so much. And Nick seemed pretty relaxed. Especially given the fact that he'd put together such an impressive dinner after a day's work. She'd never have been able to pull off that smoked salmon and asparagus linguine.

'I'm stuffed,' moaned Amy. 'Thanks, bro.'

'Hey – don't give up on me now. I've got some great cheeses,' Nick announced, as he set the board down next to her.

'Aw, Nick! You know I can't resist a ripe brie! How will I keep up with the little darlings at the netball match tomorrow?'

'Lots of protein! It'll give you strength! Here –' He passed her a slice of the French loaf he'd been cutting.

The cheese board had just made its way to Jen, when Amy suddenly asked Nick if he had anything to do with the Elena Galanis investigation.

Jen frowned. The name rang a bell.

Nick just continued slicing bread as though Amy hadn't spoken.

'Nick? Er . . . hello! Earth to DI Mullard . . .'

He turned towards her slowly, his eyes hard.

'Sorry, Amy?'

'Just asking if you were investigating the disappearance of Elena Galanis – you know – the girl from the Bridge Café. Must be on your patch.'

There was a moment's pause.

'No,' he said coolly, 'I'm not.' He moved to the door. 'Coffee anyone?'

Jen watched him take drink requests, wondering if she was the only person there who knew he was lying. Which made her suddenly very interested in the disappearance of Elena Galanis.

But a couple of seconds later it hit her. The reason Nick had lied was because *she* was there. The press. The enemy. And the warmth of the evening suddenly dissolved. She felt sick. How could she possibly kid herself that they could have a relationship?

And he was right not to trust her. She *was* interested in the story . . . She even called it a story, not a case.

Jen had been planning to stay over, but suddenly knew she couldn't. She stood up, heart pounding, and went and found her coat.

'Er – sorry, guys, it's been lovely, but I've just noticed the time – I've got work to finish tonight.'

She pretended not to notice their surprised faces as she breezed past them into the kitchen, where Nick was making coffee.

His eyes took in her coat and bag. 'I thought you were staying?' he whispered.

She shook her head. 'Thanks, Nick. The dinner was lovely. You're a great cook. Sorry I was late. Sorry about the wine.' She gave him a quick kiss on the cheek and walked out. Pretty sure that that was the last time she would ever see him.

10

Plans

'Eva?'

My eyes blinked open. Seth was closing my bedroom door with his elbow, while carefully fielding a tray piled high with food. The delicious scent of coffee filled my room.

I giggled. 'Breakfast in bed! I could get used to this!' Then I glanced at the clock. 'God! 9.30! I'm late for –'

'It's Sunday, baby. No school,' he soothed, perching on the edge of the bed, balancing the tray across his knees. He leaned over and kissed me. He smelled of shower gel and breakfast and . . . Seth. I inhaled deeply.

'You'd better be hungry, Eva! It wasn't easy smuggling this lot out of the dining room.'

'My hero,' I smirked, sitting up and doing my best to ignore the dizzying headache that was playing round my temples. 'You don't suppose the biology lab's free right now, do you?' I murmured, nibbling on a slice of toast.

He shook his head. 'Year Seven photosynthesis seminar.'

'Oh yeah – how long does it go on?'

'All morning.'

'So we can try and get in this afternoon?'

'Theoretically. But you've got a band practice at two.'

I smacked my forehead. 'God, I'd forgotten.'

'We can go tonight, though. It'll be easier once everyone's asleep.'

'So – what can we possibly do with our free morning?' I grinned, shoving the tray on the floor and climbing into his lap. 'I don't have much work this weekend, do you?' I nuzzled my head into his neck and stroked my fingers across his chest. His heartbeat quickened and I felt his hands tightening on my waist.

'Oh, Eva!' he groaned, shaking his head ruefully. 'My self-control isn't infinite!'

'Good,' I murmured against his lips. But I could feel his resolve strengthening. He sighed shakily, lifted me gently off his lap and stood up. 'How do you feel about going for a walk?'

'Sethos Leontis – *walk?*' I laughed. 'Could you persuade your legs to move that slowly?'

He raised an eyebrow. 'I think I can just about manage. Anyway, I'll run while you're at band practice.'

'I'd have to sign out with Rose.' I frowned dubiously.

'Already covered,' he smiled.

I blinked at him in surprise. He was trying not to look smug.

I shook my head. 'So where are we going?' I asked, easing myself carefully off the bed.

'Mystery tour!' he answered enigmatically, gently steadying me as I stood.

'Aw, Seth – I hate surprises . . .'

'That's not true, Eva.'

'For me it's true,' I argued, running through a few from my top-ten list: *Your dad's dead . . . I'm getting married again . . . This is your stepbrother, Ted . . .*

'Hey,' whispered Seth, interrupting my joyous catalogue. 'Do you remember how you used to love the garden at the Natalis house?'

I frowned and glanced up at him.

'I would lie on that damned couch and you'd tell me all about the different plants and flowers that grew there. You'd paint such vivid pictures that the room seemed to fill with their colours and scents. You even described the birds that visited, sometimes singing funny little snatches of their songs . . .'

I tried to remember.

'One day, when it was airless and hot, you were desperate to show me how beautiful the garden was, but I couldn't move. Do you remember pacing around, trying to work out a way to take me out there? You looked like a caged animal!'

Yes, this was beginning to feel familiar. I was suddenly picturing the blue walls, holding us both in, and a door out on to dappled green sunlight.

'And then Vibia stepped into the room with an enormous pot of fragrant white roses, and said, "I brought a piece of the garden in for you both to enjoy, my lady."'

My heart turned over as I suddenly remembered the moment . . . the sweetness of the gift, the surprise that Vibia had cared enough to risk Flavia's wrath to produce it.

'Not all surprises are bad, Eva,' he said quietly, gently lifting my chin and kissing me tenderly.

*

'Are you sure you're OK?' Seth asked, frowning down at me as he steered us off City Road and into a small side street.

'I'm great,' I lied heartily, willing my legs to move with a bit more conviction. The shakiness was not subsiding.

'Not much further,' he smiled tightly.

What was he up to? We crossed the road and turned into an even narrower street.

'Look,' he murmured, pointing out the name of the road as we strolled past. Love Lane. I smiled and squeezed his hand. But he didn't want to stop yet.

'Just along here,' he breathed, leading us through a shady alley. A moment later we were standing at the entrance to a tiny secret garden.

'Wow!' I gasped. How had he found this?

'Good surprise?' he teased.

'Amazing!' I conceded ruefully.

Together we walked along the narrow gravel path, bordered by flowering narcissi and grape hyacinths, until we'd reached the centre of the garden. Tall trees and foliage enclosed it, blocking out all signs of the throbbing city. In this quiet scented green world, it suddenly felt as though we were the only two people alive.

'Look,' he whispered, pointing to a bronze sculpture. I held my breath as I walked round the life-size image of a pair of sleepy lovers enclosed in each other's arms, lifting their heads in surprise, as though we had just disturbed them.

'Do you think we ought to leave them in peace?' I suggested, after gazing at them for a while.

'Maybe it would be polite,' smiled Seth, leading me further along the path to a bower covered in blue twining ceanothus flowers. Underneath the canopy was a carved wooden bench.

'Shall we?' he asked, brushing leaves off the seat and pulling me down next to him. 'Eva, I have something I want to give you.'

I frowned. What more could I possibly want than to have him here beside me? He dug around in his pocket and pulled out a folded piece of cream canvas, and handed it to me.

I slowly unfolded it and stared down at the contents.

'It's the knot of Heracles,' he whispered. 'A Greek love token. I found some silver wire in the art room and made it for you.'

'You m-made me a ring?'

'You don't have to wear it,' he said quickly. 'I just —'

I turned it over in my hands, completely speechless. 'It's beautiful,' I whispered finally. And it was. The thread of silver was so smooth as it curved into the knot at the centre of a flaw-less circle.

'It's supposed to have protective properties,' he said huskily. 'I'd wanted to give you a ring like this in Londinium — to keep you safe. Maybe if I had . . .'

Gently he took the ring from my palm and slid it on to my third finger.

'My people believed there was an artery from this finger straight to your heart,' he smiled. Then he took my hand in both of his and kissed me. And as the warmth of his lips and the heat from his fingers spread through me, my heart hammered against my chest with such intensity, I briefly wondered if maybe his people were right.

The unexpected rustling of a couple of sparrows in the foli-age above our heads reminded us of where we were. Breaking apart, we watched the birds hopping around us, and our breath-ing gradually returned to normal. I gazed at the sparrows, and twisted the ring on my finger. I'd never worn a ring before, so it felt kind of strange. I glanced down. It didn't look strange though. It looked right. But how had he managed to guess the size? Surely everyone's fingers were different?

'I measured it,' he smiled, running his index finger along the ring's surface.

Did I ask that question out loud? I didn't think I had.

'Measured it?'

'When you were asleep. I used a piece of thread.'

'Really?' I giggled, trying to picture the scene.

'You were remarkably compliant, actually,' he murmured into my lips.

'Me, compliant? You must have got the wrong girl.'

'Obviously not,' he argued. 'It's an exact fit.'

The birds had moved away from our bower and were fluttering around a bed of hyacinths. We sat watching them some more.

'However did you find this place?' I whispered.

'I came across it on one of my runs.'

'It's perfect.'

'It's perfect now you're here!' he breathed against my neck.

'Ha! I know a long line of people who'd disagree with that statement!' I snorted.

'Name me one!'

'Just the one? OK – let me see – er – Ruby . . . Omar, Mia, Dominic, Karl, not to mention my mother, my stepfather, my stepbrother, all the teachers at my last school, all the teachers at the school before that, all the pupils at those schools . . . Shall I go on?'

'Impossible!' Seth laughed.

'Oh, Seth, if only you knew,' I sighed. 'One day you'll realize that you're the one seeing me wrong.'

He just rolled his eyes, like I was talking complete rubbish, and I decided I could bear him seeing me wrong for a bit longer. He'd get there himself soon enough.

'Come on, ridiculous girl, there's more I want to show you,' he announced, pulling me to my feet.

'OK, where to now, boss?'

He waggled his eyebrows. 'Wait and see!'

We walked slowly through sleepy Sunday-morning streets on to Bishopsgate. When we reached Marks & Spencer, Seth came to a stop.

'Do you know where we are, Eva?'

I frowned. Clearly the question was loaded. He stood in front of me and put his hands over my eyes. 'Can you *feel* where we are?'

My whole body tensed, fighting against the dizziness that was tugging at my consciousness. I put my hands over his and held on tight as his heat began spreading through my veins, transporting me. I didn't want to leave the world I trusted, but as my fingers held on to his, the rumble of distant traffic started to blend with the rough shouting of traders, the clatter of horses' hooves, the thrum of wheels on stone.

'Oh God – the forum,' I gasped. 'We're in the forum . . . *Seth – go!*' I screamed. 'It isn't safe . . . you have to run . . . Otho is coming –' I tried to push him away, but he gripped my hands.

'No, Eva. He isn't coming. He can't hurt you now.'

'*Seth, you have to run!* Cassius will kill you – please –'

'Shhhh, my love . . . he can't touch us now . . . We're free . . . shhhh –'

Why was he saying that? I could see the guards coming straight for us, their knives glinting at their belts. Why couldn't Seth see? Why wasn't he running? What was wrong with him?

Seth's arms were tight round me, but I was struggling against him, sobbing, screaming. And he just kept dragging me further into the forum.

'*Seth, get out of here!*' I screamed again, my voice sounding wild and hoarse. '*Please!*' I was gasping, gagging, desperately trying to grab air into my lungs. But my throat had seized up; I couldn't breathe. Dark shadows were edging their way across my vision. *Oh God, help me!* I couldn't hold on to him any more. My fingers were numb; I couldn't feel them. Seth was slipping out of my grasp . . . I peered through the darkness for him, but couldn't see anything. *Where are you, Seth?*

'*Eva! Stay with me. Breathe, baby!*'

The last sound I heard was a hostile voice echoing through my clouding brain.

'*Get your hands off the girl!*'

They were here. They'd come for us again.

11

Incident

DI Nick Mullard had a lot on his mind. So he was extremely irritated when the call came through about the incident on Bishopsgate.

'Handle it,' he snapped at DC Williams, who was calling him from the scene.

But DC Williams clearly couldn't handle it. She was babbling. 'You need to come. I've never seen anything like it.'

Nick swore under his breath, saved the file he was working on and scrolled through the duty rota. 'Isn't DS Shah meant to be on duty today?'

'DS Shah's lying on the ground beside me, sir . . .'

'What?'

'O-out cold,' she gulped.

Nick was on his feet and pulling his jacket off the back of the chair. 'Have you called an ambulance? I'm on my way.'

Ten minutes later, he was presiding over the crime scene. The blue lights of three stationary ambulances flashed at the side of the road. Five men lay groaning on the ground. One of them was DS Jamal Shah.

DC Williams had calmed down and was trying to give Nick a coherent account of the incident. 'When we got the call, it sounded like a straightforward breach of the peace,' she began. 'A couple of teenagers . . . lovers' tiff . . . nothing serious. But it turned violent really fast. By the time we got to the scene she was screaming for him to get away, but he was refusing to let go of her.'

'So you intervened?'

'We were just pushing our way through the crowd, when a couple of members of the public started trying to stop him.'

'What did they do?'

'They shouted at him to get his hands off the girl . . .'

'And?' snapped Nick when she tailed off.

DC Williams was gazing blankly ahead of her. 'The – the boy just . . . lifted his head and stared at the pair of them . . .'

Nick let out an irritated snort. 'And?'

'And they just turned round and . . . walked away . . .'

'Which is when DS Shah stepped in?' prompted Nick.

She nodded. 'Jamal pulled out his taser and moved slowly towards the pair of teenagers. The girl had stopped screaming and was lying limply in the boy's arms. I have no idea what he'd done to her. He kept whispering her name – Eva, Livia . . . something like that – but he suddenly seemed to sense Jamal's approach and straightened. As soon as the boy saw the taser he kind of lunged and flipped it out of Jamal's hand – it was almost too fast to really see. Then he just shifted his weight slightly and Jamal was hurtling through the air and crashing into a lamp post.'

DC Williams licked her lips nervously. Nick waited for her to continue.

'Then the boy started to try and run with the girl still in his arms. But he was surrounded. And those big guys there,' she pointed to the men groaning on the ground, 'tried to take him down . . .'

'Completely unsuccessfully, by the looks of things,' observed Nick quietly. 'What kind of weapon was the boy using?'

'I s-saw no sign of a weapon, sir,' whispered DC Williams. 'He just moved so fast . . .' She gulped. 'And as soon as his path was clear, he kind of looked round at us all, and we just stood there watching him head off.'

'No one tried to stop him?'

DC Williams blushed and shook her head.

'Which direction did he go?'

She blinked back at him and frowned. 'I can't seem to remember.'

Nick stared at her in disbelief. He'd thought her to be reasonably competent until today. 'How about the girl he was carrying. Was she alive?'

'I've no idea,' Williams answered bleakly.

12

Encounter

Parallon

Matthias was strolling back from the café the long way round. He was in no hurry to get home. Georgia was being unreasonable again. Her animosity towards Elena was becoming unmanageable.

As he approached the villa, his pace slowed. It stood in solitary splendour, a glorious shimmering vermillion, bathed as it was by the light of the setting sun. For a moment he felt the rippling thrill the house used to give him – the exquisite joy that it was theirs: his and Seth's. How long was it since he had reminded himself of his good fortune? He didn't need to search for the answer.

As if in response to the nostalgic yearning, he suddenly caught sight of a man in a Roman tunic cross the road in front of him and stride swiftly into a small alley.

Matt recognized him immediately as the man he'd glimpsed at Georgia's birthday party. He was tall and well built, and though heavier than he knew Seth to be, there was enough in his bearing and costume to make the pull towards him irresistible. That – and a reluctance to go home.

So Matthias slipped back into the shadows and silently followed until the stranger arrived at a large wooden door.

The building was definitely Roman, but Matt had never seen it before. Had he just missed it, or was it new? The man heaved the door open, but had almost disappeared inside when he suddenly stopped and turned round, his eyes ominously narrowed. Matt shrunk back into the shadows, transfixed. The Roman's eyes scoured the street suspiciously. Matt's heart started to thump, all his slave-fear resurfacing with uncomfortable familiarity. His instinct to run was overwhelming, but there was little chance he'd be able to outrun this man. He emanated power and strength. Better try and stay hidden. He flattened himself tighter into the wall, willing himself invisible.

'I suggest you come out of the shadows, boy, and if you don't tell me why you're skulking there, you'll regret it.'

Matthias's fists clenched. He looked around, desperately hoping the stranger was talking to somebody else. But there was nobody else.

Reluctantly, Matt shuffled into view. He tried to keep his eyes on the ground as the Roman strode towards him, but when they inadvertently flicked up towards the man's face he instantly knew that he was facing a Roman soldier.

Working as an arena physician, Matthias had encountered many men of immense strength and fitness, but they had all worn the hunted look of a gladiator. There was nothing hunted about this man. He was older than any of the gladiators Matt had known, and he wore his strength with a kind of arrogant pride – the pride of a legionary. He had clearly fought for Rome. Matthias could even make out the helmet chin-strap scar – the stigmata of the legions.

Matt's throat was suddenly dry. The last serious encounter he'd had with Roman soldiers was when they had burned down his village, killed his family and clapped him in chains. He cursed himself for not running when he'd had the chance.

'Why were you following me, boy?'

'Y-your t-tunic. Reminded me of . . . er – home . . .'

'You speak my tongue?'

Matthias nodded.

'But you aren't a Roman. Your accent . . . Greek?'

Matthias nodded again.

'And you wear the strange garments of this land . . .'

Matthias looked down at his black T-shirt and jeans, and willed himself into a tunic.

The Roman's eyes widened in shock at the sudden transformation. He clearly hadn't been in Parallon long, and his confusion gave Matthias the confidence to move boldly across the space that still separated them. He was about to introduce himself, when two big hands suddenly crushed his neck in an iron grasp.

'What kind of demon are you?' hissed the Roman, his hot breath stinking of wine and garlic.

'I am no d-demon,' choked Matthias. 'We can all change garments at will here. In Parallon we have the power of the gods!'

The stranger's grip loosened as he tried to absorb Matthias's words. As soon as he had his liberty, Matt willed a couple of stools and a low table with a flask of wine, a bowl of olives and two goblets.

'Sit,' he rasped, pouring them each a cup, 'and let me tell you all about this strange and wonderful world.'

13
Reach

'Don't leave me, Eva. Please.'

His voice was pulling . . . calling to me . . . I had to find him. But I couldn't see anything. It was so dark.

Seth, where are you?

'I'm right here, baby. I'll always be here. Please come back to me.'

He sounded close. I could practically feel his breath on my cheek . . . his warm touch on my hand . . . *Seth?*

I opened my eyes.

'Eva! Oh, thank the gods!'

I blinked. Bright impersonal room, buzzing machines . . . flashing digital displays . . . And staring down at me – his face a mask of pain . . .

'Seth!' I choked. 'What's wrong?'

He frowned, as though he didn't understand the question, but a moment later his mouth arched into a glorious smile. 'Oh, Eva!' he laughed. 'Nothing's wrong . . . not now.'

'Good,' I croaked. 'You had me worried there for a second.'

He sighed heavily, and though his mouth retained its smile, something in his expression darkened and my heart started to pound. 'What happened, Seth?' I reached my fingers out to squeeze his hand, but realized, too late, that there was a cannula embedded in my wrist. I winced as it snagged.

'Careful, baby!' he groaned, as the damn thing started to leak.

'Hey, it's fine, Seth. Nothing to stress about.'

But Seth was staring down at the tiny oozing at my wrist as though it was a river of blood.

'Seth! I'm OK!' Well . . . apart from the grinding headache and the punched-in-the-chest sensation. Why was he overreacting like this? He'd seen me in hospital before.

'Seth, I –' The door suddenly swung open and a large nurse pulling an instruments trolley backed in.

'Oh my goodness! You're *awake*!' she gasped, wheeling the trolley to the bedside. 'I was beginning to think you might never . . .' She suddenly blushed, realizing she was treading the wrong side of tact. 'I mean, um – how are you feeling?'

I glanced at Seth, whose eyes were burning with fury.

'Fine,' I sighed, as she checked my temperature and attached a blood-pressure cuff. 'How long have I been here?'

She consulted her notes. 'Well, you arrived on Sunday. You left intensive care last night. It's now Tuesday afternoon . . .' she said, filling in my results. 'Excellent! Your temperature is down to 38° and your blood pressure has improved. I'll just do a quick ECG and then page Dr Falana . . .' She looked pointedly at Seth, who stared impassively back at her.

'Eva needs some privacy here,' she said firmly. Seth glanced at me, shook his head and went to stand by the window. When he was clearly out of the way, the nurse pulled down my sheet and started plugging cables into the electrodes stuck all over my skin. I was definitely glad Seth wasn't watching this. I glanced nervously at his back, willing him not to turn round.

'Now, just relax, Eva. This will only take a minute,' she murmured, setting the machine to print.

Relax, right!

Seth somehow sensed the moment the cables were removed and my sheet was back in place, and he immediately resumed his seat next to the bed, staring down at the bloody stain on my wrist cannula.

'How's the headache?' asked the nurse, as she attached the heart-trace printout to my notes. 'You're probably due for some analgesic. Is there anything else I can get you? A glass of water? Something to eat?' She was beginning to babble – maybe it was embarrassment over her earlier indiscretion . . . or Seth's smouldering presence. Whatever the reason, she was seriously crowding me.

'Something for my head would be great,' I mumbled, willing her to spend a day searching the meds cupboard.

But she didn't take the hint. Not when there were pillows to plump and drip stands to adjust. I was on the point of jumping out of bed and pushing her out of the door, when she finally gathered everything on the trolley and left.

'Seth, what is it?' I whispered as soon as we were alone.

He stared mutely down at my wrist.

'Please, Seth, speak to me!' I implored.

'What can I say?' he choked, running his hands through his hair. 'I'm so sorry, Eva.'

'What for?' I asked, baffled.

'This!' he groaned, waving his hand around the room impatiently. 'This is all my fault.'

'Oh, Seth,' I sighed in exasperation. 'I've got a *virus*. This is what it does.'

'Oh – right,' he retorted. 'So your collapse had nothing to do with me dragging you to the forum?'

'You didn't drag me to the forum –'

'I thought together we could control your memories . . . exorcise them. I –'

'Look, Seth,' I said quietly. 'I didn't feel great before we set off on our walk. But I'm not going to let a damned virus stop me having a life.'

'Eva, you nearly didn't have a life. They had to use electric pads to get your heart started!'

'Seth, you don't –' I took a sharp intake of breath as the door swung open again. 'Er – hi, Dr Falana . . . Long time no see!'

'Hmm – I was hoping it would be longer, Eva. Of course, I'm delighted you're recovered enough to engage in healthy debate,' he added, glancing across at Seth, 'but I'd rather you were resting! Your body's had quite enough excitement for the time being.'

'I'm feeling fine,' I grumbled petulantly.

'Eva,' he frowned, 'you only have one body. And yours has just taken one hell of a pounding. You have to look after it.'

I so didn't need this little talk right now. Not with Seth sitting next to me blaming himself for everything.

'Dr Falana, I'm better now – really . . .'

'Eva, you're not listening. You had another cardiac arrest. We were extremely worried about you. We called your parents –'

Oh God, not my parents. They were the last people I could handle right now. I looked wildly towards the door.

'Hey, calm down!' he exclaimed. 'They've gone now. They headed back to York as soon as we moved you from critical care.' He was watching me cautiously, clearly troubled by our unusual family relationship.

'We don't exactly get on,' I muttered, as the relief permeated. But I was kind of touched they'd come down. 'They were both here?' I asked, amazed.

Dr Falana nodded. 'I don't think your stepfather wanted your mother travelling alone.'

I was bewildered for a nanosecond. Until I remembered the baby. They were completely obsessed with it.

'She's pregnant,' I explained. 'I'm surprised he let her anywhere near. He's terrified she'll catch something from me.'

Dr Falana nodded. 'That might explain why they spent the whole time hovering in the corridor.'

I smirked.

'I did try telling them that your symptoms are most likely a post-viral auto-immune response, and that there is no sign of infection,' he shrugged.

I couldn't help smiling. Not even a hospital consultant could convince my mum and Colin I was safe to hang around.

I glanced across at Seth. He wasn't smiling. I instinctively moved my hand to touch his before I remembered the damn cannula. Flinching, I gazed hopefully up at Dr Falana. 'Can we get rid of this now, please?' I begged.

'Well, you've managed to make your usual mess of a line, I see!' he tutted, inspecting the mucky, bloodstained bandage. 'All right, then,' he sighed.

He put on a pair of surgical gloves and deftly unwound the bandage, then pulled out the tube and cleaned up the bruised skin.

'That's so much better! Thank you,' I grinned up at him, gratefully.

'Eva,' he said sternly, 'I haven't finished with you yet! We need to talk about health strategies . . . limiting triggers, alternatives to school and so on . . .'

Alternatives to school? What the hell did that mean?

'Please, Dr Falana,' I whispered hoarsely. 'You can't –'

He sighed. 'Eva, you're sick . . .'

'I'm *not* most of the time,' I insisted. 'I   I really need to be at St Mag's, doctor.' I could hear my voice cracking. 'I – I promise I'll take care of myself –' My throat was so dry, the words were sticking there. I tried swallowing, but it wasn't helping.

'Breathe, Eva,' Seth murmured under his breath, his fingers running across my knuckles soothingly. And suddenly his calming presence seemed to charge the whole room.

Even Dr Falana appeared to relax. 'All right, Eva, I understand you need to be at St Mag's,' he nodded. 'Er – I'll talk to your matron. With her help, and a careful management programme, I'm – I'm sure we can keep you out of trouble.'

I stole a sideways glance at Seth, but he blinked innocently back at me.

'Thanks, Dr Falana,' I smiled, heaving a big sigh of relief. I leaned back against the nurse-plumped pillows and gratefully closed my eyes.

14

Companion

Parallon

Matthias had a new friend. His name was Otho. Matt had been right, the Roman he'd followed had at one time been a soldier in the legions, though he'd spent the last five years in Londinium, working as a guard. Otho was a little vague about his job, but Matthias was the last person to be inquisitive. He had his own secrets. He had not, for example, mentioned to Otho that he'd been a slave in Londinium. He'd told nobody in Parallon. The memory humiliated him and had no place in his new carefree life.

And now that Seth was gone, that secret was pretty safe. Seth hadn't cared who knew about his slave past. Matthias recalled with annoyance the moment when Georgia asked Seth about his tattoo. Matt was gesticulating madly behind her head: *Don't tell her!* But Seth simply smiled and shrugged. 'Oh, that's just the mark of Tertius, my lanista,' he said, rubbing the top of his arm ruminatively.

'Lanista?'

Seth lifted his chin. 'Didn't Matt tell you?'

Matthias's heart sank.

'The lanista was my master and trainer. And I was his slave . . . his property.'

'W-what did he train you to do?' Georgia swallowed.

'To fight,' Seth said quietly. 'To entertain the crowds . . . in the arena. I was one of his gladiators.'

'I-is that how you got all those s-scars?' she asked carefully.

'Most of them,' he shrugged.

Georgia was staring at Seth with horror in her eyes – just as Matthias had predicted. Then suddenly she turned to him.

'M-Matthias? What about you – were you –?'

Matthias frowned, his eyes darting to Seth in fury. How could he have allowed this conversation to take place?

But Seth just smiled easily and said, 'Oh, Matt was a physician – much more valuable.'

Matt had breathed a sigh of relief and quickly changed the subject. As far as he knew, Seth never talked about Londinium to her again.

Although Otho's *Romanness* was a constant reminder of those days, which was unsettling, Matt also found it strangely comforting. His presence helped plug the hole that Seth had left. And unlike Seth, Otho took to Parallon life with unbridled enthusiasm. Delighted to have a new protégé, Matthias proudly introduced him to all his favourite haunts and people, tirelessly schooling him in English so that he wouldn't feel disadvantaged.

When Otho's language skills were finally good enough for him to enjoy a visit to the café, Matt knew he had to address one final obstacle.

'Otho, you're going to have to wear jeans eventually. You may as well get on with it now. The women here prefer men in trousers, I assure you.'

Otho found jeans hot and uncomfortable, and couldn't understand why they were so popular. He scowled at Matthias petulantly. But his desire for female company finally triumphed.

Matt inspected his adjusted outfit and nodded. 'Now just remember not to slip into Latin and you'll be fine.'

When they arrived at the café, Matt's eyes widened. It was buzzing with people. The space had been extended again and was now practically the size of a forum. He was surprised by the swathes of faces he didn't recognize. No question – the Parallon population was growing. Fast. He suppressed a niggling worry that he might have contributed to this population rise. But what did it matter? There was plenty of room.

'Matthias, come!' Otho had secured a table and was beckoning over a couple of girls. Although not a handsome man, Otho had an edgy, dangerous quality, which the girls seemed to find attractive. By the time Matt sat down, Otho had already provided himself with a flagon of wine.

'So how long have you been here?' Matt asked the taller of the two, as he conjured cappuccinos for them.

She frowned, blowing distractedly across the rich creamy froth. 'I think we got here the day before yesterday. Is that right, Becky? It's a bit of blur, really.'

'Everyone's been so nice,' Becky added with a nervous laugh. 'But it's all kind of hard to take in. It feels too real to be a dream, and I keep expecting to wake up any minute . . .'

'. . . in a hospital bed,' snorted the taller one.

'Lara and I got taken to the same hospital . . . I thought I was still there when I woke up here –'

Matt nodded. He remembered how that felt.

Both the girls seemed a bit dazed, but were adjusting much

more quickly than Seth and he had done. He assumed that was because there were so many more people around to ease the transition.

'Anyway, where are you two from?' asked Lara shyly. 'You have an accent.'

'Er – I'm originally from Greece,' said Matt, 'and Otho here is from . . . Rome.'

Before the girls were able to delve any further, Matt grinned and, gesturing to the table next to them, said, 'The apple cake they're eating looks good. Shall we get some?'

He was just conjuring four plates when he felt Otho stiffen beside him. Matt followed Otho's gaze. He was frowning at the tall blond boy at the next table.

'Did you want something?' Otho hissed dangerously, rising to his feet.

The boy, who had been grinning flirtatiously at Lara, glanced up at Otho in surprise.

Otho towered over him menacingly, his eyes narrowed, his fists clenched, and held the pose until the boy ran a dry tongue across his lips.

'Er – no, man, we're g-good.'

Otho didn't move. 'I don't agree,' he murmured quietly.

It wasn't until the party at the next table had stood ignominiously and left the café that Otho sat back in his seat. He took a huge bite of apple cake and put his hand over Lara's.

'I don't share,' he announced, his face impassive. She smiled timidly up at him.

Matt watched as Otho brushed a stray cake crumb from Lara's mouth, and sighed. He had missed basking in the aura spill of a charismatic friend. When Seth walked out on him, he had felt so anchorless. And now Otho had come along: just as powerful; just as charismatic. He took a long draft of wine and smiled contentedly.

15

Investigation

Jen's boss, Amanda, would be leaving the office in exactly twenty minutes. She was off to Brussels for the European Sovereign Debt Crisis talks. Jen was doing one final frantic check through her research for the questions Amanda would be putting to the delegates. It would be disastrous if she'd got anything wrong. She'd made it to the bottom of the last page when the unmistakeable click of Amanda's heels on the tiled floor announced her imminent arrival.

Jen uttered a little silent prayer to the god of hapless reporters, shuffled the papers into a neat pile and stapled them. Then she slipped them into a document case and had the folder poppered up and ready to hand to Amanda the instant she breezed by the desk. Amanda was on her mobile, so she didn't even glance at Jen as she took the folder and clicked out of the office and into the lift.

Jen savoured the moment, slowly inhaling the wonderful sense of release. The tyrant was gone. For three whole days!

Her eyes caught Jake's (who had the desk across from hers). He was grinning and silently punching the air.

She got out her phone to text Nick. And then remembered she couldn't. She'd broken up with him nearly a week ago. And he hadn't argued at all. Not one word of protest. Just – 'If that's the way you really feel, Jen . . .'

A wave of misery rumbled in her gut, instantly dampening her Amanda-free euphoria. Typical – she'd finally got some time off, and she had nobody to spend it with. Apart from Debs, of course. Though Debs had been getting on her nerves lately.

But it was 6.15 p.m., and Jen was damn well going to make the most of Amanda's absence. Their broadcast had aired and her work was done. She mouthed a quick goodbye to Jake, grabbed her jacket from the back of the chair and fled.

Forty-five minutes later she was sprawled in front of the TV with a tub of Rocky Road ice cream, spoon in one hand, remote in the other. She knew the drill. This was what girls did when they split up with their boyfriends: watch reruns of *Friends* or (if they were planning a good wallow) *Titanic*. Jen persevered through five full minutes of *Friends*, but then gave up and allowed her fingers to switch to Channel 4 News.

'Loser,' she muttered to herself. 'Only a total geek escapes the Channel 7 newsroom to come home and watch the news all evening.'

But long ago she'd been forced to admit that her passion for news was closer to an addiction. Which was probably why she hadn't managed to keep a boyfriend. She worked such long hours, and – up till now – her work had definitely come first. Men on the whole didn't like that hierarchy much. Well – most men. Nick had been different. He seemed to feel the same way about his own work.

Oh God – she'd started thinking about him again. And now she'd accidentally begun to think about that stupid phone call . . .

'Hey, Jen – just ringing to check you got home OK.'

'Yes, Nick. I'm back. Safe and sound. Er – thanks for the meal. It was great.'

'Jenny? What's wrong?'

Silence.

'Why did you leave?'

'You know why.'

'I honestly don't.'

'Oh, come on, Nick.'

'What? Did I do something? Say something?'

'It's what you didn't say.'

Silence. The penny had finally dropped.

'We can't have a relationship where you won't talk to your friends about your work because I'm there. How can you call it a relationship if you don't trust me at all?'

'I do trust you –'

'No, you don't, Nick. Just admit it to yourself.'

Silence.

'Look – there's no possible future for us, so we might as well end it now – save us the trouble later.'

Silence . . . then, 'If that's really how you feel, Jen . . .'

'Yes, it is. Goodbye, Nick.'

She had half expected him to call back. Well – she'd hoped he would. But he hadn't. There had been continuous silence between them for five days.

Debs had been characteristically unsympathetic.

'Well, what d'ya expect? He's a cop, Jen. Why would he talk to a reporter? He'd be insane to. And as reporters go, you're dangerously relentless – obsessive even.'

'Thanks, Debs. You make me sound so attractive.'

'Anyway, I don't know what you were doing with him in the first place. I mean – what on earth do you have in common?'

Jen had thought about that a lot lately. And she'd decided that, actually, they did have quite a bit in common. They were both crazy about Livid Turkey and had been loyal supporters since the band's early gigs in obscure back rooms in Camden. They were both slightly reluctant workaholics. Both would go to any lengths to dig out the truth. And . . . they'd both fancied each other. Quite a lot. Or so she'd thought.

Jen was miserably scraping the last spoonful from the Rocky Road tub, when the urgency in the newscaster's voice pulled her focus back to the TV. Breaking news – the demonstrations in Westminster had escalated into full-scale riots. She watched in horror as the furious crowd surged forward and began smashing shop windows with hammers and bricks. The camera was jerky and the images kept blurring, but the growing violence was unmistakeable. Jen's first instinct was to get over there, see what was going on first-hand. Then she wondered who Channel 7 would be sending to cover the story . . . Obviously not Amanda, who would be halfway to Brussels by now. Typical! If only she'd been allocated a different reporter, she might be on this story, which was way more exciting than currency stats. Then she suddenly gasped: the camera had panned to a line of police in riot gear, with huge perspex shields, desperately trying to hold their line against the unstoppable wave of rioters. What if Nick was there? Would he be OK? DIs didn't normally get involved in riots, did they? But for some reason he'd been at the One Earth demonstration. She'd met him there . . .

Jen had an overwhelming urge to call him, check he was all right. She glanced at her phone. How could she? They'd broken up. Maybe just a text? As a friend? She picked up her phone and had just typed '*Hi*', when it started to ring. She almost dropped it . . . especially when she saw the caller ID.

Nick.

Should she answer?

Who was she kidding? 'Hello?'

'Jen?'

'Nick. God, are you OK?'

'I'm fine. Jen –'

'It's just – the riots – I was watching them –'

'Are you watching the news right now?'

'Er – yes.' Damn. Now she felt embarrassed. If only she'd been going out on some hot date.

'On Channel 4?'

'Yes –'

'Just keep watching.'

Jen turned her head back to the TV screen and noticed Nick had hung up. Could he be more cryptic?

She sat through the prime minister making a big law and order clamp-down speech, then forced herself to concentrate throughout the next feature on rising eurozone debts, and when they moved on to local news she began to wonder whether she'd misheard Nick's message. She couldn't see anything significant about the feature on an archaeological dig in the City, and glazed over, idly running her finger inside the Rocky Road tub and licking it distractedly.

Then suddenly the screen filled with a photo of that missing waitress, Elena Galanis. This was a news story she wasn't expecting tonight. Oh God – had they found the body? Nobody had mentioned anything at Channel 7.

No. They hadn't found the body. Elena's father had just flown over from Greece and was making an impassioned plea for witnesses. It was clearly an emergency press conference, because Jen could just make out Jody Stevens clamouring for attention in the sea of press faces – and Jody wouldn't normally have been Channel 7's first-choice reporter.

Jen's eyes welled in sympathy at the husky grief of the man now speaking broken English straight into camera . . . *Elena would never just take off without letting them know . . . somebody must have seen her* . . . He broke down and, as he was led away, the editors cut in recent footage (stuff that Jen had already seen) of the café owner, an unhealthy-looking guy in his forties, stating adamantly that Elena had never taken time off without giving notice before. They re-ran the footage of Elena's ex-boyfriend, also equally certain that Elena wasn't the type to just walk out. The report was just winding to a close when the front doorbell buzzed.

Sighing, Jen uncurled and moved to the intercom. 'Forgotten your keys again, Debs?'

'It's me, Jen.'

'*Nick?*' she gulped, glancing down at her crumpled skirt now displaying a small but definite ice-cream stain. She pressed the entry button, calculating that she had about thirty seconds to get herself and the flat looking presentable before he got up the stairs (he was very fit). She hurled the ice-cream pot in the bin, threw the spoon in the sink, kicked her shoes under the sofa, ran her fingers through her hair, and had just turned her skirt round so that the stain was at the back when Nick reached her door. Surely that was less than thirty seconds?

She took a deep breath and pulled the latch.

He filled the doorway. Jen's heart missed a beat, but she tried to view him dispassionately . . . At least three days' beard growth, clearly still in his work clothes . . . and looking as good as ever.

'Can I come in?'

Jen stepped to one side.

'Did you see the piece on the missing girl?'

'Yep.'

'What do you make of it?'

Jen eyed Nick warily. This was totally taboo territory.

'Isn't she one of your cases?'

'Was. MI5 have just taken over.'

'*What?*'

'To be honest, I have no idea what's going on. But I'm sure there's a connection.'

'A connection to what?'

'To the motorbike case.'

Jen felt herself flush. She'd convinced herself that Nick had no idea she'd been that humiliated reporter. Clearly, she'd been wrong.

She swallowed, curiosity trumping embarrassment. 'What kind of connection?'

Nick took a deep breath. 'We didn't release this information because it was considered too dangerous.'

'What information?'

'Well, Elena's jeans and shirt were lying across the bed – still buttoned up. Her underwear was inside, socks, bra, pants . . . as though she had just –'

'Disappeared?'

'The forensic team are convinced it's the abductor's signature, and we decided not to release the details to prevent copycat crimes. But, of course, that particular signature reminded me of another case.'

'The Winston Grey disappearance.'

'You remember how we found his clothes – laid out as though he had literally dematerialized?'

'Yes – the leathers still retained his shape.'

Nick had begun pounding round her very small living room. When his tense pacing had started to make her dizzy, Jen spoke.

'Nick, why are you here? And why – of all people – are you telling *me* this?'

Nick came to a stop, ran a hand through his hair and slumped down on the sofa. He raised his eyes and looked at her.

'I've been a policeman for seven years. And a DI for three. In those three years I have run – I dunno – about forty-seven investigations, of which I'd say eleven have been homicides. To call a crime a homicide you need some sort of evidence of a death. In nine of those eleven cases we have either found a body, the remains of a body or forensic evidence indicating foul play. Only two cases have provided no leads whatsoever . . .'

'The biker and the waitress.'

Nick nodded, pursing his lips. 'I did everything in my power to come up with a credible explanation for Winston Grey's disappearance. I had to – especially after you'd stirred things up with that paranormal body-evaporation stuff. At the time I had you down as a freaky little ingénue – cute, but kooky. And I assumed you'd somehow managed to infect all the witnesses with some weird mass hysteria thing.'

Jen gasped in fury. 'You thought I'd primed them with their stories? What the hell do you take me for?' She stood up and strode out to the kitchen and leaned against the fridge, trying to get her breathing under control.

She felt his hands on her shoulders.

'Jen, Jen . . . I'm sorry. I didn't mean –'

'Didn't mean what?' she hissed, shaking free of his hands. 'Didn't mean to imply that I was dishonest and manipulative? What then exactly, Nick? And why the hell were you going out with me if I'm so *kooky*? Was it some kind of game? Some stupid policeman joke?'

She wanted to flounce out, but her kitchen was tiny and he took up the entire floor space between her and the doorway, so she was trapped. She leaned wearily against the counter.

Nick stood facing her, his fists clenched.

'Jen – when I first saw you at the motorbike scene, I asked around to find out who you were. I wanted to get your phone number right then and there. But, of course, as soon as I saw how the investigation was going, that I was going to have to refute everything you were saying, I knew you'd *never* go out with me. I couldn't believe my luck when you smiled at me during that demo in Westminster.'

'I'd temporarily forgotten who you were.'

'Hmmm, I thought so,' he frowned. 'That's why I never dared mention the Winston Grey thing. I was worried that as soon as you realized you'd leave.'

Jen looked up at him through narrowed eyes.

'But you left anyway,' he whispered.

'Can you blame me?' she asked. 'What did we have? A mutual affection for a couple of bands? We didn't *share* anything – except a few meals and one or two bottles of wine.'

'I couldn't talk about my work with you – or anyone. I've signed the Official Secrets Act. I would be kicked out of the force if I leaked anything – you know that.'

'So why are you talking to me now?'

'I shouldn't be. It's just that MI5 are refusing to see a connection between the two cases. They are convinced Elena's either gone underground or she's the victim of an international spy cull.'

'You've gotta be kidding? Based on what information?'

'Elena studied political sciences at university in Athens.'

'Lots of people study political sciences, are they all spy suspects?'

'She's fluent in four languages.'

'How is that evidence?'

'Well, languages would obviously be an advantage – and one of the languages is Russian . . .'

'So?'

'Her mother, Klara, studied at Leningrad State University at the same time as Vladimir Putin.'

'The Soviet *president*? Interesting company. And because her mother went to the same university as Putin they conclude Elena's a Russian spy! Ha! Come on – we're not in some James Bond movie.'

'Honestly, Jen! You can't have forgotten Anna Chapman and Tracey Lee Ann Foley? Not to mention Litvinenko.'

'So how persuasive is the Putin connection?'

'We don't actually have any concrete evidence that Klara and Putin were friends at all, though it's likely they knew each other as Klara became a member of the Communist Party the same year as Putin. In 1985 she married Petros Galanis, a Greek engineering student, and in 1991 they left St Petersburg with their two-year-old child, Elena.'

'So Elena didn't grow up in Russia?'

'No – Greece. But as soon as she graduated, she travelled back to Moscow, where she spent seven months.'

'Doing what?'

Nick shrugged. 'Part-time jobs, visiting family.'

'And then – she came here?'

'No – she flew to Madrid and travelled around Spain for about four months. She pitched up in London in June last year.'

'And worked as a waitress the whole time?'

'More or less. When she first arrived she picked up a part-time job behind the bar at a music venue in Hackney, and about six weeks later she started waitressing at the Bridge Café. As far as we know she kept the bar job going on Friday and Saturday nights. That's where she met her boyfriend – well, ex-boyfriend.'

'Presumably he's on the suspects list?'

'Of course. They were apparently only together for a couple of months, and allegedly hadn't seen each other for a while. He's a big indie music producer. He looks pretty clean, but his alibi is shaky so we haven't ruled him out. The café owner was at his mother's eightieth birthday party on the night of Elena's disappearance – plenty of witnesses and no obvious motive.

'No sign of a break-in – and it doesn't look to me like she's done a runner – nothing seems to be missing. Purse, phone, credit cards, keys – all in her bag . . . Her toothbrush, contact lens case and fluids, hairbrush, make-up, all neatly arranged on the bathroom shelf . . . A couple of empty suitcases under the bed.

'We've gone through every contact on Elena's phone and combed through all her papers. Everything points to abduction or murder, but nothing we've found has given us any clue to a perpetrator.'

'There must be something specific that's got MI5 so interested?'

'Apart from her background, some – er – unusual forensics . . .'

Jen raised her eyebrows.

'When our team combed her flat we found evidence suggesting she may have been poisoned. DNA confirmed that she had vomited violently – though the lab has been unable to trace any identifiable poison or pathogen.'

'So why assume poisoning?'

'If someone had been deliberately poisoned you might expect to find traces in stomach contents – but not always. Not if the poison was injected, for example. So as far as MI5's concerned, Elena's political background, along with the suggestion of poison, are significant enough for them to get interested.'

'Had they been watching her?'

'Not as far as I know.'

'So what about Winston? They don't think he was a spy, then?'

'No. He was a non-political East Ender, who worked as a mechanic at a South London garage, and had been there since leaving school. Virtually impossible to label him a spy.'

'So because they can't link them politically, they're refusing to see them as connected?'

'That just about sums it up. And because I keep banging on about the similarities, they've taken me off the case.'

'Does that mean you can officially talk about it now?'

Nick shrugged. 'No. I just knew that there was only one other person who would be as intrigued by these two events as me.'

'So what do *you* think is going on here?'

'I honestly don't know. There has to be a logical, non-paranormal explanation . . . And I was – er – wondering if you wanted to work the case with me?'

'But you're not on the case –'

'Exactly. Our work would have to be completely off the record. A private project . . .'

'That's pretty anarchic for a cop.'

'Blame my bad early conditioning.'

'Your parents?'

He shook his head and smiled ruefully. 'Special Ops,' he breathed. 'Trained us never to let go. So – are you in?'

He fixed her with his most disarming grin, and as he ducked his head to kiss her, all Jen's resolve evaporated.

'Oh, and by the way,' he sighed into her hair, 'I missed you.'

Jen's hands found their way to the back of his neck, and as she stroked her fingers across his razor-short hair, she was already wondering how much access Nick would be able to get to MI5's background studies. She had to admit it, she was irrevocably caught – hook, line and sinker.

16

Curse

Londinium

AD 152

It was first light. The accountant, Blandus, was walking briskly towards Cassius Malchus's chamber as instructed, two scrolls tucked under his arm. He was surprised to note that the chamber door was not attended by Cassius's terrifying elite guard. A small frisson of relief quickened his step, but an instant later caution replaced it. Where were they?

The empty doorway looked suddenly ominous. Fear prickled his spine. What could possibly have happened to Pontius and Rufus? Their third member, Otho, had recently and inexplicably vanished, and the chamber slaves' garbled stories of fever and mystical disappearance had resulted not only in their summary execution, but also a frenzy of arrests and torturings. The household was now taut with dread.

Blandus crept closer, his eyes darting around for danger. When his face was almost touching the door, he knew he had no choice. He had to knock.

No reply.

His first instinct was to run. But he did not dare. His employment with Cassius had taught him that it was better to live in perpetual fear than die face down in the river.

He knocked again, a little louder, putting his ear to the heavy wooden door. Was that a faint answer?

Tentatively, he lifted the latch and peered into the shadowy room. Thick drapes blocked out much of the light, so it was difficult to see. But he could hear . . . cracked, laboured breaths were coming from the figure on the couch. And he could smell . . . the rank sour stink of vomit filled the room. Blandus covered his nose with his cloak and crept nervously forward.

'C-Cassius?' he whispered.

The breathing stopped for a second.

'Who's there?' rasped the familiar voice of his master.

Blandus dropped to his knees by the side of the bed and stared at the man lying there. Cassius was clearly dying. His pale skin glistened with sweat, his eyes were heavy, his cheeks sunken. It was hard to believe that Blandus was gazing into the eyes of the most powerful, savage and ruthless Roman in Londinium.

'Sir, you need a physician, not an accountant –'

Cassius waved a hand impatiently. 'The physicians have no power against a curse such as this.'

'A c-curse?'

'That witch I married. Livia.'

'She did this to you?'

'Who else?'

Blandus tried not to think about the thousands of people who wanted Cassius dead. He himself would have been somewhere near the top of that list.

When Livia went missing, Cassius had not sent one man out

to look for her. So Blandus had assumed, like everyone else, that Cassius had killed her. After all, it was common knowledge that he couldn't brook dissent. And it was clear that she had not married willingly.

But maybe he hadn't killed her. Maybe she wasn't as fragile as she appeared. Was it possible that she was more powerful than he was? A witch? Or . . . a goddess – come down to deliver retribution?

'I need water. Where's Pontius?' rasped Cassius.

Blandus bit his thumbnail. Did he dare mention that no one guarded the chamber?

'I'll g-go and look,' he said, scurrying towards the door. But neither Pontius nor Rufus was there. Blandus peered along the corridor. Cassius's favourite 'escort' slave, Daria, was hovering uncertainly. She was carrying a large, heavy bowl of fruit.

'Is that for the noble Cassius?' called Blandus.

She nodded.

As she drew closer, Blandus realized she also looked ill. Her eyes stared out of dark hollows and her complexion was waxy pale. She bit her lip. His scrutiny was embarrassing her, so he shifted his gaze quickly down to the fruit she carried. He was fairly sure that Cassius's interest in food was long passed, but perhaps he had summoned it.

'I will take it to him. He has asked for water.'

She gave him the fruit and turned. 'I will fetch some directly.'

Blandus nodded. 'Daria – have you seen Pontius or Rufus?'

Daria shook her head. 'They were sick,' she said simply, then turned and slipped quickly away.

Blandus stared after her, his fears mounting. Could the curse have encompassed the entire household? Was he next?

Fighting his instinct to run, Blandus carried the fruit back into the chamber. Cassius was slumped against the silk cushions scattering his bed, his eyes shut, his breathing laboured. Blandus soundlessly placed the bowl of fruit on the inlaid ivory table next to the bed, whispered his master's name very quietly and, on receiving no response, tiptoed gratefully out. He tried to keep his footsteps measured as he passed slaves and guards, for he had no intention of discussing either Cassius's health or that of Pontius and Rufus. The household would find out soon enough. And he didn't want to be there when they did.

17

Guests

Parallon

'Who are *they*, Georgia?' asked Matthias icily.

He was glaring at the wary teenage boy and girl sitting at the kitchen table.

'Denzel and Courtney,' answered Georgia. 'They've just moved in,' she added defiantly.

'*What?*' Matt spluttered. 'They can't stay here. The palace is getting more crowded than a damned forum!'

'That didn't stop you bringing Otho back, did it!'

'Otho's my personal friend!'

'Who the hell is he, Matt?'

'What's that supposed to mean? He's a Roman from my time.'

'A gladiator, like Seth?'

'Zeus, no!' snorted Matthias. 'I said a *Roman*. Freeborn . . . some kind of guard.'

'Did you know Otho in Londinium?' asked Clare, from her perch on the edge of the table.

'No.'

'Did Seth?' she persisted quietly.

'Of course not! Seth was a *slave*. He didn't get to fraternize with the Romans. Anyway, he hated the guards far more than his enemies in the arena.'

Clare nodded. 'So Seth would be thrilled to find a Roman guard sleeping in his room then.'

'Well, Seth's not here to mind, is he?' Matt snarled.

'But when he comes ba–'

'Seth's not coming back, Clare.'

'You don't know that . . . do you?' she choked.

Matthias groaned impatiently. 'How long does he need to be gone to convince you? Just get over him, OK!'

Clare's eyes widened at the harshness in Matthias's voice. Georgia placed a comforting hand on her shoulder. 'What's happened to you, Matt?' she hissed.

'What's that supposed to mean?'

'Since you've been hanging out with Otho, you've really changed –'

'Yeah? Well, that's good. Because I was getting a little bored being Matthias-the-man-everyone-nags-and-whines-at . . .'

'What?' spluttered Georgia.

'I've finally got someone around who respects me. Someone who enjoys doing the same stuff.'

'Like rolling home drunk and stupid at 6 a.m.? Like hitting people in bars if they accidentally bump into you? Like playing around with every woman in Parallon?'

Matthias smirked. He and Otho had had quite a lot of fun on some of their nights out together.

'Matt – this isn't you –' began Clare, but Matt held his hand up.

'This *is* me, Clare. Get used to it. And if you don't like Otho, you can leave – I'm not stopping you!' Matt stood for a moment staring at them both, then turned on his heels and slammed out.

Clare's jaw dropped and her eyes filled. 'You coming with me, Georgia?' she choked, heading blindly for the door.

'I don't think I can walk out on Matt now, Clare. He's so lost. Please stay – I need you.'

'But Otho totally freaks me out. What can Matt possibly like about the guy?'

'It's obvious, isn't it?'

'Not to me.'

'He reminds him of Seth.'

'How the hell is that *animal* anything like Seth?'

'I dunno . . . They come from the same time . . . and there's something – unpredictable . . . dangerous in both of them. Look, Clare,' sighed Georgia, 'I'm sure this Otho fixation is just a phase. With a bit of luck the guy will get bored with Matt in a week or so and move on.'

Matthias walked disconsolately from the kitchen towards Seth's chamber, hoping Otho had finally got back from the bar. When he reached the door, he paused; he could hear voices inside. Otho had never brought anyone back to the house before.

'Otho? Are you in there?' he called, knocking tentatively.

No answer. Just loud, raucous laughter. Matt chewed his lip apprehensively, then pushed the door open. On the floor in front of him crouched Otho, doubled over with mirth. On either side of him squatted two more hefty men, equally helpless with laughter. When Otho spotted him at the door, he called over drunkenly, 'Matthias, my friends are here!'

Matt nodded, his throat dry. Otho had just greeted him in Latin although they'd spoken nothing but English for weeks. His eyes skimmed back over the raucous trio, and their Roman tunics confirmed his unwelcome conclusion: the newcomers were also from Londinium.

'Want some wine, Matthias?' spluttered Otho genially. Matt glanced at the jug on the floor. It was lying on its side, spilling its contents all over the notebooks and papers that were strewn there . . . Seth's notebooks and papers.

Matt gaped in horror. Without thinking, he squatted down and started carefully gathering up the books and smoothing down the pages. Otho frowned and grabbed one out of his hand.

'Matthias, this *absent friend* of yours – where's he from?'

Matt stared at Otho, his stomach momentarily clenching. But Seth's nationality was no secret and there was no point lying about it.

'From Corinth, like me.'

Otho nodded. 'I knew it – a Greek!' He threw the book scornfully across the floor. Matthias flinched and stooped down to retrieve it.

'Otho, brother, we need more wine,' roared one of the others, producing a new filled jug and slopping it into their goblets.

But Otho wasn't drinking any more. He was regarding Matthias through half-shut eyes. 'What's the matter with you, boy? Don't like us touching your friend's stuff?'

The room went silent. Matthias, who was reaching under a sofa to retrieve a couple of stray papers, instantly stilled. He could hear the menace in Otho's voice. He'd heard it before – in bars, on the street . . . Danger was always there, bubbling under the surface, waiting to erupt. He had never been Otho's target before . . . and he didn't intend being one now.

'Hey, I'm just straightening this out for you, man. I know how much you hate your chamber in a mess . . . and we need somewhere to put the banquet I'm about to produce in honour of your guests.'

Otho blinked at him for a few seconds, then grinned. 'Good thinking, Matthias. Allow me to introduce my comrades . . . Rufus and Pontius.'

But Rufus and Pontius were now lying on their backs, goblets in hand, snoring soundly.

18

Lunch

Jennifer slipped out of the office at 13.15. She scowled up at the sky. It was raining again and she'd left her umbrella upstairs. She pulled her jacket over her head and started to run. She didn't want to be late. She was meeting Nick for lunch.

She'd never have dared leave the office if Amanda had been in the building. But Amanda had boarded a plane to New York that morning. Which meant seven glorious hours of mute airspace.

Dashing along the wet pavement, the sense of freedom was delicious, and Jen was damn well going to make the most of every one of those seven call-free hours.

There it was. Café Bleu. She crossed the narrow street and peered through the steamed-up glass window. She approved. He'd picked a nice place to meet. Scrubbed pine tables and waxed wooden shelves filled with deli specialities.

She pushed open the door and was assaulted by the fabulous smell of fresh coffee blended with pungent cheeses, red peppers and . . . was that basil? Nick would probably know.

She spotted him, on a deep leather chair in an inconspicuous corner. A good place to watch from, unobserved. He'd seen her and was regarding her with a curious expression on his face – a blend of alert watchfulness and . . . pride? Like he'd just won a prize. He stood up when she got near and kissed her. He tasted of coffee.

'Hi,' she murmured, smiling.

'I knew you didn't have much time so I ordered for us. Hope that's OK?'

She looked down at the small round table. It was laden with two large steaming bowls of thick soup; warm, wrapped ciabatta; a jug of water and two espressos. Just the way she liked her coffee. Nick was earning a lot of brownie points.

Jen shook out her wet jacket and slung it over the back of the chair with her bag. Then she sat down opposite him.

Before picking up her spoon, she said, 'Nick – I'm curious. How did Elena's disappearance make it to *Crimewatch*?'

Nick raised his eyebrows. 'Why do you ask?'

'There are loads of missing people who don't hit our TV screens. Why her?'

A corner of his mouth twitched up. 'Good question. Well – as you probably know, most missing person cases aren't crimes. And on the face of it, this wasn't either. No sign of forced entry. No body. No blood. Nothing stolen. But – when we got called out to her room, there was something so eerie about it: the shape of the vacated clothes, the vomit, her bag, keys, purse, credit cards – all intact . . . It looked like a cryptic set of clues. Which made me uneasy. So I leaked the story. I wanted to try flushing out a perp. Or if there was no abductor and

Elena had gone underground, I wanted her photo out there – trigger a sighting.'

'Any response?'

'The usual crank calls. No serious leads. MI5 are checking through all the sightings again, just in case she has gone to ground. Eat your soup, sweetheart, it's growing a skin.'

Jen looked down, stirred her soup and began eating. It was good.

'Tuscan bean. Hope you like it.'

'Mmm – delicious.'

'Amanda take off OK?'

'Uh-huh,' Jen managed through her mouthful. 'Her flight was supposed to depart Heathrow at 11.14. It didn't actually leave until 11.46.'

Nick laughed. 'God, you're thorough!'

'If Amanda was your boss, you'd be too!' Jen looked at her watch. 'Hmm, she should be sitting thirty thousand feet above the Atlantic ploughing her way through my notes on Middle East oil-price fluctuations.'

'Sounds riveting,' he smirked. 'So with all that oil-price research, have you had a chance to consider any other pressing projects?'

Jen cocked her head and grinned. 'I haven't been granted a lot of time by her ladyship, so I began by checking out any news reports on unexplained disappearances. Most of them turned out to be abscondees – troubles at home, gambling debts, difficult marriages, abusive relationships. Nothing much . . . Until . . .'

Nick's soup spoon froze as he waited for Jen to continue.

'I widened my timeframe and honed the search criteria with

keywords – like sickness, clothing, etc. And I found a weird article tucked away in a local North London newspaper.'

'Go on . . .'

'A couple of teenage kids disappeared from Firs Farm Hospital in 2003. Very little information – not quite sure how it made the papers. But it was just a comment from one of the nurses . . .'

Jen put her spoon down, swung her bag on to her lap and pulled out a folder. Inside was a wad of scanned newsprint sheets. They all had highlighted sections.

Nick glanced across. 'Where d'you get those?'

'Newspaper library in Colindale.'

Nick gave her a nod. A *glad I brought you on board* kind of nod.

Jen flicked through the papers until she found the one she was after.

'Yeah – look at this . . .'

A pair of collapsed teenagers, who had been ambulanced to Firs Park Hospital, disappeared without trace from A & E yesterday, leaving behind all their personal possessions and the clothes they were wearing. Grace Okoye, the duty nurse, claims that neither of them could have possibly been fit enough to walk out as they were both unconscious with fever. A hospital investigation is underway.

Nick sat forward. 'Do you think you can find out any more?'

Jen's eyes widened. 'Nick, this was ten years ago. The hospital has probably been knocked down or amalgamated with three others since then. And the chances of getting hold of anyone who remembers anything . . .'

Nick continued to look at her.

Jen caved. 'Oh, all right,' she smiled, 'I'll do what I can. How about you? Anything?'

'I'm doing my best to find out what MI5 think they've got. I'm pretty sure they're off beam, but there must be something else triggering their interest.' He broke off a hunk of bread. 'Obviously, monitoring MI5 isn't very straightforward, but I do have an old school friend who owes me a couple of favours – his job at MI5 to name but one! Brodie's a straight-up kind of guy unfortunately, so not prepared to actually spy for me, but he will keep me loosely informed of any interesting leads.'

'Anything to go on yet?'

Nick shook his head. 'Nah. All I know is that they spent two days interviewing Elena's parents. And this morning they sent an agent to Moscow. I'm assuming it's connected.'

'I wouldn't mind a trip to Moscow,' grinned Jen. 'For research purposes, obviously.'

'You'd better join MI5 then.'

'Hmmm – what a good idea. Of course, one of the first things I'd have to do would be to mention your – er – excessive interest in one of our most sensitive cases . . . I can't guarantee how leniently we'd look on you or the mole you've placed in our midst . . .'

Nick grabbed Jen's hand and bit it lightly. 'OK – maybe I prefer you as a journalist.'

'Speaking of which,' Jen said reluctantly, glancing at her watch, 'I'd better get back to being one.' She scraped her chair away from the table and started to get up. Nick stood quickly, lifted her jacket from the back of the chair and held it open for her.

'Why, thank you, Mr Gallant,' she smiled. 'What brought all this chivalry on?'

'Just trying to make myself indispensible.'

She slipped into her jacket and turned to kiss him. 'Thanks for lunch,' she smiled, as she headed for the café door.

19

Disclosure

Parallon

Georgia stood at the kitchen window watching Matthias dashing around the garden, busy creating an elaborate shady bower for his Roman guests to relax under. They, meanwhile, lay basking on bamboo recliners, eating grapes and drinking wine.

She shook her head and sighed deeply.

'What's up, Georgie?' murmured Winston, stepping up behind her.

'Just look at them . . .' she hissed. 'They've got the whole household running around after them. It's obscene.'

'To be honest, I think we're all a bit intimidated,' confessed Winston.

'Understatement!' muttered Georgia.

'I don't know why, though. I mean, this is *our* place, not theirs.'

Georgia's eyes narrowed. 'Not any more, Winston. Elena thinks we should move out – set up somewhere else.'

'Why would we do that? They're not going to push me out. If anyone goes – it should be them!'

'I guess . . .' muttered Georgia, chewing her lip.

Just then, Matthias glanced towards the window and caught her eye. His face wore an expression of desperate mirth. Registering her disapproval, he turned defiantly back to his companions and laughed even more heartily.

The Romans weren't laughing though.

'Apollo's blood, Matthias,' snarled Otho. 'Will you *shut up*! You're drowning out every thought!'

'Or go away!' added Rufus with a wave of his arm. 'Your buzzing about is beginning to really get on my nerves.'

Matthias froze.

'I'm sick of it here,' moaned Pontius. 'I need some real entertainment.'

'We c-could go to the cinema –' stammered Matt.

'Those *flickering pictures*,' snorted Otho. 'They aren't *real*! I miss the arena.'

'The a-arena?' Matthias did his best to still the involuntary shudder that rippled through his shoulders.

'I like to *smell* the blood of the dying,' smirked Otho, licking his lips.

Matthias glanced at his expression and was instantly reminded of the faces of the arena crowd, their savage pleasure in the gruesome gladiatorial deaths.

'Maybe we should build an arena here?' Pontius sniggered.

Matthias shot him an uneasy look. An arena in Parallon? Was he joking? It was hard to tell. Matt bit his lip nervously. He needed to come up with a compelling distraction – now. But his mind flailed around, unable to supply a single suggestion. The Romans had devoured all the delights of Parallon and they were still hungry.

And then it hit him: the only solution.

'Come on! You want entertainment? I think I can give it to you.'

Matthias felt buoyant as he led the way down to the river. By the time they were standing on the bank, even Otho seemed mildly exhilarated, but as soon as Matt told them that they would be jumping into the freezing black water, their demeanour changed.

'Are you mad?' spat Rufus furiously. '*This* is your *brilliant* plan?' His anger was so intense that Matthias began to stammer.

'T-trust me . . . it is a gateway – not to Hades but to other worlds, other times . . .'

'It's a trap, isn't it?' snarled Pontius, looking around wildly for signs of ambush. 'Who are you working for?' An instant later he had Matthias by the throat and the others held his arms.

'It's no trap,' choked Matthias. 'I'll show you. I'll jump first . . . But if you follow me, think only of me – or you won't find your way back.'

He felt the Romans loosen their grip. He could breathe again. Warily, he edged his way to the riverbank.

'Stay close,' he warned, 'and jump exactly where I do.'

20

Immunity

I was finally back at St Mag's. Turned out I'd missed the entire Easter holidays languishing in hospital. But, to be honest, Easter in hospital was probably no worse than Easter at home, playing happy families. Better, in fact, because Seth turned up every morning, reminding me how good life was. And despite visiting hours and ward rounds, he'd wangled a way of spending most days there. Then when I was finally released, he also managed to persuade Rose to let me move straight back into my own room instead of the medical block. I only had one remaining problem: Dr Falana's insistence that I go on to a restricted timetable – and Seth's total refusal to use his skills to interfere.

'Just for the time being, Eva,' he argued, 'till you're back at full strength.'

'But I'm off lessons every afternoon, Seth! I'll go out of my mind!'

'You've got plenty to keep you busy,' he smiled, looking across my laptop at the virology page I was scrolling.

'Hmmm!' I snorted grumpily.

But he had a point. My research was keeping me pretty preoccupied.

'Seth, there's one thing I'm really not getting about this virus . . .'

He pulled me towards him and laughed. 'Just the one?'

'OK,' I humphed, 'one of the *many* things I don't get – is how a virus that's been around for two thousand years should be so difficult to identify. Why have there been no studies? You'd normally expect dozens of research papers. I mean, how could something so virulent and lethal have gone unnoticed?'

He nodded speculatively. 'Hmmm . . . not actually lethal in every case.'

'What do you mean?'

'Well – last night I went back into the lab.'

'You didn't wake me?' I gasped.

He sighed. 'Restricted timetable includes night-time excursions, Eva.'

I glared at him belligerently, but he just ran his thumb along my cheek and continued: 'Anyway, last night I tested my infected blood on sixteen of the teachers' blood samples.'

Despite myself, I was hooked. 'Go on . . .'

'Eight of the sixteen seemed to be totally resistant. Cell function remained completely unaffected.'

'What about the other eight?'

'I'm not quite sure. On several there were signs of cell compromise . . . but nothing very definite. So I haven't wiped the slides. I'm going to check them later.'

'Well, I'm coming too.'

'No you're not.'

'Try and stop me.'

He raised an eyebrow and suppressed a laugh, 'Ooh, tough call, Eva – but I think I may just be able to rise to the challenge . . .'

I tried to thump him on the chest, but he grabbed my wrists with one hand and carried on speaking.

'I was already sure there was an age factor from my research in Parallon. That's why I came to St Mag's. Students here would be prime subjects.'

'Really? You never mentioned that before.'

'There are no old people or children in Parallon – the average age is probably eighteen. I did find just a handful of people older than thirty – but very few.'

'You know what that proves, don't you?' I said with a sinking heart.

'What?'

'That my virus is different – or – that it has somehow mutated – or . . .' I swallowed, 'I am immune.'

'That's what I've prayed for,' he breathed.

I stared at him, willing him to understand what I had been slowly coming to terms with. 'Seth – if I am immune, I'll never be able to join you in Parallon.'

'But I'm staying here,' he murmured, squeezing my shoulder.

I decided to let it go, and forced a smile. I was pretty sure my time was running out – I wasn't going to get better. But how would it help for him to know that? I stared down at the laptop, desperately trying to think. I had to be missing something. We were looking at a highly destructive infection that could potentially annihilate a whole generation in a matter of hours, and yet it didn't officially exist. It sounded more like a covert terrorist weapon than a notifiable disease . . .

Oh – my – God! Was that it? Were we looking at some terrible form of biological warfare? In which case, of course I'd been searching for it in the wrong places. We should have been exploring secure government bio-surveillance sites. If anyone was monitoring a lethal virus, they would be.

'Seth – I know this sounds ludicrous, but I'm wondering if Professor Ambrose . . . No! It's . . . it's impossible . . .'

'Eva! We're facing the impossible every day – What are you thinking?'

'Well, do you think Ambrose could be a military scientist? Or worse – a biological terrorist?'

Seth frowned. 'I don't see how, Eva. I mean, the virus isn't exactly new! I got infected two thousand years ago!'

I nodded. Fair point. 'OK – assuming we're talking about the same virus – it could have been dormant or eradicated – like the smallpox virus . . . and then either re-emerged or was clinically reintroduced for terrorist purposes. Perhaps someone – let's say Ambrose – rediscovered it and began developing it. Our viruses have to have the same origin: same shape, same fever, same sickness and instantaneous onset . . . Although there is, of course, the one crucial difference.'

'What's that?'

'Yours ended in Parallon.'

'But, Eva, what would a biological terrorist be doing here? *In a school?*'

'It's crazy, you're right. What possible motive would he have to show *me*, a sixteen-year-old kid, such a lethal weapon? Other than . . . to kill me? And why me? I'm nobody.'

'I suppose your death wouldn't attract much suspicion . . .'

I nodded. 'So wouldn't be investigated . . . Or – worst-case scenario – pretty easy to cover up.'

Seth shook his head dubiously. 'I don't know. It feels too random.'

'Maybe I was just a trial? Maybe he's planning a bigger attack later?'

Seth shrugged.

'God,' I gasped suddenly. 'Do you think he knows that he failed?'

Seth frowned. 'What are you saying?' he asked huskily.

'I'm not dead, Seth. What if he's planning to come back and finish the job?'

There was a loud pounding on the door. I jumped a mile.

'*Eva! You in there? Let us in!*'

I exhaled with relief. I'd know that voice anywhere.

The pounding intensified. '*Astrid!* Just get in here, before you break my bloody door!'

She bounded through, closely followed by Rob and Sadie.

'Guess what, babe!' she sang.

'What?' I grinned, mystified.

'Astrid's just landed us a gig at the *Register*!' squealed Sadie, dancing around the room and punching the air.

'In two weeks!' added Rob, eyeing Seth warily.

'Wow!' I gasped, squeezing Seth's hand. Suddenly the idea of a simple life with music and gigs and no bioterrorists seemed so damned attractive.

Astrid grinned. 'No better medicine than music, babe!'

I glanced at Seth. He was clearly unconvinced, but at that moment, more than anything else, I wanted to believe Astrid was right.

'Just what the doctor ordered!' I murmured, laughing shakily.

21

Neptune's Corridor

Parallon

Matthias stood shivering on the Parallon riverbank, peering down into the water. Otho, Rufus and Pontius were supposed to have followed him straight back through the vortex. Where were they?

He glanced around cautiously. It was dark – exactly as it was meant to be. They were careful now to travel only at night – it was much less conspicuous that way. And, with luck, no more than five Parallon minutes would have elapsed since the four of them had jumped into the water. He'd learned this trick from Seth, who'd always been so careful about concealing his vortex travel.

The three Romans had taken to Neptune's Corridor (their new name for the vortex) with reckless enthusiasm, though Otho had soon devised two Corridor rules: that they would always stick together and they would *never* again return to their own lifetime.

On their first journey, Matt's efforts to get them to a Londinium arena had nearly ended in disaster as they found themselves spewed out on to the banks of the Thames, weak, shaking and scarcely corporeal. They'd barely summoned the strength to return to the vortex. But after some methodical experimentation they'd delightedly discovered that there were at least two hundred years' worth of Roman London still available to them. At last they were able to enjoy their favourite form of entertainment: the gladiatorial games.

Matt smiled indulgently at the pleasure his friends took in the bloody violence, simply relieved that they no longer talked of an arena in Parallon. And he found that he could remain peculiarly detached about the life and death of gladiators when he had no personal responsibility for their health – especially if he was sitting far enough away.

And when his friends weren't revelling in the blood of the arena, there were plenty of bawdy entertainments to enjoy, as well as raucous nights carousing in bars or taking women into shady chambers. Matt had given up trying to calculate just how many women Otho had bedded over the last few days.

It was getting cold standing by the river. He needed dry clothes. The moment the thought occurred to him, his clinging wet tunic was replaced by one of comforting soft wool. He sighed contentedly. They'd been in Londinium for so many weeks this time that he'd almost forgotten how wonderful the world of Parallon was.

'Matt! Give us a hand here!'

'At last!' breathed Matt, scampering towards Rufus as he emerged from the water. A few moments later they were hauling out Otho, then finally Pontius.

'Pontius, what kept you, man?' snorted Rufus. 'Got waylaid by another woman in there?'

Pontius frowned. 'The Corridor felt , sluggish . . .' he murmured, as they started walking back to the palace.

Otho slapped his shoulder. 'More likely you've got sluggish,' he sniggered. 'How many women was it last night?'

'Lost count!' smirked Pontius.

A moment later Otho stopped walking. 'Apollo's blood,' he groaned. 'Which one of you brought these two back here?'

A pair of disorientated Roman women stood in the middle of the street, gazing around, stupefied.

Matthias's heart sank. Not more of them. His Roman friends were so indiscriminate in their gifting of the fever – always getting into fights or accidentally infecting women they'd spent the night with. And, every time, it was his job to induct the newcomers into Parallon life.

'Matthias,' said Otho, glancing at the women briefly, 'clear up here, would you?'

'Of course, Otho,' said Matthias, leading the women quietly away.

When the Roman women were safely ensconced with a larderful of food in a small but comfortable Roman house he'd made for them, Matthias returned home.

Elena was sitting in the kitchen drinking coffee.

'You're up late,' smiled Matt, slumping down at the table opposite her.

'Your precious Romans are making such a racket, I'm surprised anyone can sleep,' she grumbled.

'They're just high-spirited,' laughed Matthias indulgently.

'They're dangerous, Matt. They treat us all like slaves. Get rid of them before it's too late.'

'Hey, you're talking about my friends, Elena,' he frowned. 'I'd better see if they need anything.' He was on the point of standing when a shadow crossed Elena's face and her features froze. He turned and saw Rufus filling the doorway, his eyes fixed on Elena, his mouth twisting into a hungry leer. It was an expression Matt knew well.

'Come here, *deliciae meae*,' he slurred.

Elena didn't speak Latin, but she didn't need to. She knew exactly what Rufus wanted – something she wasn't prepared to give. She glared at him and folded her arms. Rufus snarled and with one movement had caught her by the arm, pulled her towards him and was kissing her hard on the mouth.

'Get off me – you stink!' she spat, shoving her knee into his groin. But he anticipated the move. His hand shot out instantly, slapping her across the face with such force that she was thrown against the edge of the kitchen table.

Matthias moved automatically to catch her as she fell to the floor.

'Leave her!' Rufus warned, his voice laced with menace.

Matt froze – his instinct warring with his brain. A moment later he had control of himself and slunk helplessly from the room. He did not dare look back.

22

Ward Disappearance

North London

Wednesday 17 April AD *2013*

It was 7.15 a.m. and Jennifer Linden was sitting on a blue plastic chair in Firs Park Accident and Emergency department, feeling pretty smug. Not only had she finally managed to track down the nurse who'd been on duty in 2003 when the two teenagers had disappeared, but she'd also faked such a convincing limp that Hugo (Amanda's number two) had insisted she took the morning off to get an X-ray, giving her the perfect reason for visiting a hospital . . . albeit one fifteen miles away.

As soon as she walked into A & E she decided to drop the limp and fake the same fever symptoms as the couple she was investigating. So she told the receptionist that she'd been vomiting all night and had a high fever and splitting headache. Her goal was to be sitting opposite the large triage nurse at the far side of the room as soon as possible. But first she had to down a steaming cup of coffee so that the thermometer would register high when they took her temperature. She'd successfully used this technique as a kid on difficult school days.

The waiting room was filling out and, given her symptoms, she couldn't understand why they were keeping her waiting so long. Didn't they realize how dangerously ill she was?

When at last she got called she did her best to look ailing as she shuffled slowly towards the triage booth.

Nurse Okoye, a large Nigerian woman in her late forties, ran her eyes over Jen and picked up her pen.

'Hello, dear. What is your name?'

'Jennifer Berkoff.' She'd decided that small changes would be easier to remember.

'Date of birth?'

Nothing to give her away there, but she changed the month just to be sure.

'Address?'

She gave her own address but altered the flat number and the postcode.

'GP name and address?'

Jennifer was beginning to squirm. She realized that if she made up a GP, the name wouldn't register on the database and her cover would be blown. She stalled, wondering what to say. Nurse Okoye was waiting.

'Do you have a GP?' she asked finally.

'Er – no?' answered Jen hopefully.

Nurse Okoye nodded and sighed.

'OK, Jennifer, tell me how you're feeling?'

Jennifer tried to remember her script. 'I've been vomiting, had a high fever, awful headache . . .' She did her best to look weak.

Nurse Okoye stared for a moment, then strapped a cuff

round Jen's arm, which was attached to an automated blood-pressure monitor. She also placed a small device in Jen's ear and a clip on her finger. Jen frowned. She had no idea what they were for. She and her family were so robustly healthy that it was her first time in a hospital. She cursed herself for this lapse in her research.

'Well, your BP's normal,' smiled Nurse Okoye, checking the digits on the machine and filling in the form.

'I think I have a pretty high temperature,' said Jen, adopting her most plaintive expression.

'Actually, your temperature is normal,' responded the nurse, retrieving the device from Jen's ear.

'What?' gulped Jen. 'Th-that was a thermometer?'

Moments later the finger clip was removed. 'And your pulse and respiration are lovely and healthy . . . You've got a good colour, so I am pretty confident that you'll be right as rain tomorrow. You probably ate something that didn't agree with you, dear. I suggest you go home, drink plenty of water and get a good night's sleep.' Jen had been dismissed. As she finished speaking, the triage nurse had been recording Jen's notes on to her PC. She then placed the completed paper forms into Jennifer's brand-new hospital file and put it on the trolley beside her. She had the name of the next patient on the desk in front of her and was politely waiting for Jen to leave before she called it out.

'B-but . . .'

Nurse Okoye clicked her tongue.

'I-I need to talk to you –' Jen blurted out.

The nurse took her hand off the microphone switch.

Jen glanced round at the waiting room filling with the sick

and injured, and realized that at this point there was no way Nurse Okoye was going to talk about a couple of teenagers that went missing in 2003.

'When do you get a break?'

'What is this about?'

'It's – er – personal . . .' breathed Jen enigmatically. She figured she could just about justify that statement.

The nurse frowned and glanced up at the clock. 'I go to lunch at twelve o'clock. You can find me in the hospital cafeteria – *if* you're feeling *well* enough to stay around that long . . .' she said pointedly.

Jen chewed her lip sheepishly. 'I can wait.'

She settled into a quiet corner and pulled out her laptop. She had a long piece to edit, which amply occupied her until it was time to meet Nurse Okoye down in the basement cafeteria. She found her sipping a hot drink from a cardboard cup, and unpacking a Tupperware box from her bag.

Jen bought herself a coffee and sandwich and joined her.

Nurse Okoye eyed the sandwich cynically. 'Glad you're so much better.'

Jen didn't even bother to look chastened. 'Sorry,' she said briskly, 'I didn't know how else to introduce myself.'

'So what is all this about?'

'The disappearance of those two kids from your A & E in 2003.'

The nurse's eyes widened in surprise. 'My Lord, you haven't found them, have you?'

Jen shook her head. 'I need to know what you can tell me about them.'

'Why?'

Jen pressed her lips together, considering how much she could afford to give away.

Nurse Okoye impatiently pushed her chair back and waved at a friend across the room, indicating her intention to join her.

'Wait,' said Jen urgently. 'OK – I'll tell you.'

The nurse rolled her eyes and settled resignedly back in her seat.

'There have been a couple of other cases that sound similar. And I – er – *we* are trying to work out what the pattern is . . . so it would be great if you could tell me as much about what happened as you can remember.'

Nurse Okoye shrugged. 'I told it all at the enquiry.'

'Would you mind telling me too? It's really important.'

'Who exactly are you?' asked Nurse Okoye, eyeing Jen suspiciously.

'My name is Jennifer Linden, and I-I'm working with the City police.' Well . . . it wasn't exactly a lie, and she knew that Nurse Okoye would never speak to her if she found out that she was a journalist.

The nurse took a deep breath. 'It was a long time ago, dear.' Her eyes flicked longingly towards her friend's table and then back to Jen. She sighed. 'All right – I admit it. It has never stopped troubling me. To this day I still wonder what happened to those young people.'

'Can you tell me from the beginning?'

'They were brought in by ambulance. The girl was no longer conscious; the boy, barely. They were dangerously pyrexic –'

'Pyrexic?'

'Very high fever – over 41°, vomiting, moaning, tachy –'

'Tachy?'

'Rapid heart rate. Their situation was very acute. We had just intubated the girl and I was helping intubate the boy when it seems she – Courtney – became asystolic –'

'Sorry? Asystolic?'

'Her heart stopped beating. The registrar began compressions and called for paddles – but I wasn't in a position to get them, as I was working on the boy. It seems nobody else was available – the rest of the team were working on a family of car-crash victims.

'Then my boy also arrested – I tried compressions on him, but I couldn't get his heart going, so I dashed across to the girl's bay hoping the registrar had picked up some paddles by then . . . but neither the girl nor the registrar was there. At that point I assumed he'd moved her, but I wasn't really thinking – I was running around like a crazy thing trying to find a defibrillator.

'I finally tracked the last one down, but when I got back to the bay – the boy was gone.'

Nurse Okoye stared blankly ahead of her, reliving the scene. 'It was as though he had . . .'

'Dematerialized?' prompted Jen.

The nurse swallowed. 'His clothes, even his shoes, were still lying on the bed; the heart monitors, the intubation tube, the blood oxygen monitor all laid out as though he was still lying there . . . like . . . I don't know . . .'

As she told her story, the nurse's expression had changed from annoyed resignation to bewildered fear.

'I just stood there for a few moments, completely at a loss. Then I ran back across to Courtney's bay. The registrar was standing as still as a statue, staring at the exact same scene I had just come from. And I knew right then that nobody had taken the girl anywhere. She had also disappeared. The registrar was very disturbed by the whole thing.'

'In what way?'

'He couldn't bring himself to talk about it. Lord knows I tried. That's all I wanted to do for the rest of the day. But he just kept shaking his head, repeating over and over that nobody disappears into thin air. Because he couldn't find a logical explanation he refused to believe what he'd seen with his own two eyes.'

'But you have no doubt about what you saw?'

Nurse Okoye shrugged. 'Those kids were in no fit state to walk out. And why would they – or an abductor – strip off all their clothes and leave them lying on the beds like that?'

'Would you be prepared to go on record?'

'Look, Jennifer – if that is your name – it was a long time ago –'

'But if you and the registrar would be prepared to talk –'

'You'll never find him. He walked out of the hospital the moment the police walked in. I have no idea what he's doing now, but it isn't medicine. Terrible shame. He was a good doctor.'

'You never felt the same way?'

'I couldn't quit my job!' she shrugged. 'I have four children!'

'So what about the police? What happened when they got involved?'

The nurse's eyes darted nervously around. 'Nobody believed me, of course.'

Jen knew *exactly* how that felt.

'I was the only witness. Everyone concluded it was either a hoax or the kids had just absconded.'

'But didn't Courtney and Denzel have family – someone who wondered where they were?'

'No family showed up. Nothing about it made any sense. The police could trace no registered NI or NHS numbers – so in terms of the investigation they didn't officially exist. We had nothing but a pile of clothes and a couple of false IDs.'

'Why would they have given fake IDs?'

Nurse Okoye looked caustically at Jen, who had the grace to look embarrassed.

'They could have been runaways or just underage drinkers . . .'

Jen nodded. 'So what happened then?'

'The paperwork mysteriously disappeared and the enquiry was dropped, much to the hospital's relief.'

'So how did the press get to hear about it?'

'I have no idea. It certainly wasn't from me or the registrar. The local paper contacted me a couple of days after the registrar had left. By then I didn't know what to think or what to say. I just told the reporter as little as I could.' She sighed and started packing up the remains of her lunch. 'I have to get back.'

'Thank you so much. Er – sorry to have been so – er – underhand . . .'

'You weren't a very convincing invalid,' muttered Nurse Okoye, as she threw her empty cup in the bin and made for the door.

23

Tension

I sat in the school dining room, staring down at my toast, dread twisting in my gut. I pushed the plate away.

'Eva?' murmured Seth. 'What's wrong?'

His arm drew me towards him and his warmth was so distracting that for a moment I forgot my anxiety. But even Seth couldn't distract me indefinitely.

'The Register gig,' I gulped. 'It's tonight.'

I was truly terrified. Although I totally loved rehearsing with the Astronauts, I *hated* gigging. I still got nervous playing in the school common room on Thursdays, for God's sake. So why did I agree to do it? I could have easily got out of it on health grounds. But *there* was the root of the problem. Doing the gig was my stupid rebellion against Dr Falana and his damned restricted timetable. So I only had myself to blame.

'Hey, Eva, guess what!' grinned Astrid, pulling out a seat opposite us. 'Dr Drury's not only offered to sign the gig out as a school event – he's gonna drive us in the van!'

She'd just cleared the last hurdle.

'I know it's not exactly hardcore to turn up to a rock gig in a school minivan with a roadie in a green velvet jacket and silk cravat,' she sniggered, 'but it definitely beats sneaking out of the toilet window and lugging everything on the tube.'

'True,' I grinned. Despite everything, I had to admit that it was quite cool to see Astrid so buzzed. I high-fived her and she bounded off to tell the others.

'Eva — it's going to be great,' Seth smiled, squeezing my shoulder. 'You're ready for this. Nothing bad's going to happen.'

'You haven't seen how paralytically scared I get!'

'I've never seen you scared.'

'Well, maybe I don't get scared when you're there.'

'That's OK then. Because I'll be with you the whole time. Even in the van.'

'What?'

'I've been appointed Rose Marley's back-up.'

'Are you telling me I don't have to make my big rock 'n' roll debut with the school matron by my side?'

'No . . . just me,' he grinned.

'Hmm — I think I can live with that,' I smiled contentedly. 'But, Seth, you'll have to sit through all the sound-checks . . . and you won't get time for your run.'

'I'll run earlier. Art history can manage without me.'

'Hey, you can't bunk art his—' I started, then shut up, reading his expression. He'd clearly made his decision so there was no point arguing. He physically needed to run and we both knew Dr Lofts wouldn't give him a hard time — she adored him. So what could I say?

And just like that, the day didn't feel quite so insurmountable.

I blinked up at him, completely awed by the way he had just turned everything around. 'God, I love you, Seth,' I whispered.

I'd never said those words out loud before. Not in this lifetime. But they just slipped naturally out of my mouth. Which made it a kind of earth-shattering moment for me. I heard his sharp intake of breath and suddenly he was staring down at me with such intensity that my heart was hammering against my chest even before he kissed me.

Then the assembly bell rang and the insurmountable day began.

And it was all OK – lessons, lunchtime band practice – until it was time to leave. Astrid, Rob, Sadie and I were sitting in the back of the packed van, while Dr Drury rattled his keys impatiently.

Astrid checked her watch for the twentieth time. 'Eva, we're going to miss sound-check. Are you sure Seth said he'd meet you here?'

I nodded, peering through the windscreen into the pelting rain.

'Why the hell should Seth travel with us, anyway?' snapped Rob. 'He's not in the band!'

'Because I say so,' growled Dr Drury. 'Matron's express wishes.'

'What?'

'Get over it, Rob,' sighed Astrid. 'Seth is Rose's stand-in tonight.'

'But Eva doesn't need Seth to take care of her – we can do that!' spluttered Rob.

'For God's sake, I can take care of myself,' I erupted furiously. 'Seth must have lost track of the time. Let's just go.'

'Sorry, Eva,' said Dr Drury, 'I made a deal with Rose.'

'Does Seth know where we're playing?' asked Astrid dubiously.

'Yeah, he's run past the Register a couple of times . . .'

'He must have gone straight –' Astrid paused to retrieve her vibrating phone. 'OK . . . no . . . we're on our way . . . as soon as we can . . . yeah, see you in ten . . .'

She shoved her phone back into her pocket. 'Guys, we gotta run. The Lasers have arrived and if we want to get our own sound-check we have to leave right now.'

'We're supporting the Lasers?' I gulped. 'When were you going to tell me?'

'I'm telling you now,' she grinned. 'Dr Drury, I'm sure Seth's gone straight to the venue. And we really have to go now.'

Even teachers didn't find Astrid easy to challenge. Drury chewed his lip for a moment then reluctantly started the engine.

I took some deep breaths. The evening was spiralling out of control: the gig, the Lasers . . . a missing boyfriend. Seth didn't lose track of time. He said he'd be here. I closed my eyes. Where was he?

24
Visit

Seth hadn't had a full-length run for a couple of days, so as soon as they broke for lunch he'd slipped back to his room, changed into his gear and set off, promising himself four full hours. It was just beginning to rain, but he hardly noticed.

Sometimes his runs would take him across the bridge and he'd explore London streets he'd never visited, other times he ran along the bank of the Thames, but more often he circuited the St Mag's playing fields. This meant he could forget what his legs were doing, keep his pace consistent and simply allow his mind to drift. His body needed this exertion. Without it, the build-up of excess energy in his muscles made him twitchy and uncomfortable.

Within an hour, the scent of wet grass, the thrumming of rain on sand and the driving rhythm of his heartbeat were combining to produce that familiar, warm endorphin rush. This glorious chemical miracle gave him such a sense of well-being and power that he allowed himself to relax the tight control he'd been holding on his thoughts. But they'd been locked away for a reason, and now that they flowed unhindered, the blast of dark fear that accompanied them was something even the comforting endorphins could do nothing to neutralize.

He tried to keep his breathing even as he sifted through them.

The virus . . . He now knew that it was a hundred per cent successful on the students at St Mag's. Not one of them had immunity. The teachers, on the other hand, were a different matter. So there was definitely an age factor. Seth still wasn't sure whether increased age simply increased immunity or whether it was just the incubation period that increased. He had noted blood changes and cell deterioration on several of the samples, so it was possibly an incubation issue.

And then . . . there was Eva.

Just thinking her name caused a painful acceleration of his pulse rate. He still hadn't put his blood together with hers. He argued that she hadn't been well enough to take into the lab, which was true, but he knew he was prevaricating. There was a part of him that simply couldn't bear to find out. It was stupid, unscientific and superstitious. And yet it was the only way he knew of holding intact this magical gift of time together – because as soon as they found out one way or the other, that knowledge would change everything. But he knew that everything was going to change anyway. They were running out of time. Eva was running out of time. He could see she wasn't getting better. She had her good days, but they were heavily outnumbered by the bad. Fear for her was paralysing him. He had failed her in one lifetime and if he didn't make a breakthrough with the virus, he was about to fail her in this.

Seth glanced at his watch. His time was up – he needed to

get back and showered. He slowed down as he reached the quad and weaved his way through the end-of-class melee to his room. He had only one objective: to get cleaned up and back outside the music block within the next fifteen minutes. There was no time to stretch properly so he did a couple of lunges while he waited for his shower to heat up. When steam started to rise from the cubicle, he threw his running clothes into the laundry basket and stepped inside. Perfect. He'd loved the Roman baths, but the speed and power of a shower was unmatchable. The water massaged his neck and shoulders, and helped soothe the mounting tension re-gathering there.

But he couldn't linger. He lathered shampoo into his hair, soaped himself clean and turned off the tap. Grabbing his towel, he stepped back into his room – and gasped.

Zackary was sprawled across his bed. 'Good to see hygiene is still a priority.'

'What the hell are you doing here?'

'And awfully nice to see you too, Sethos.'

Seth felt his hackles rise, as they always did when Zackary appeared in his life. But Zackary wouldn't have come here simply to rile him; he always had a purpose. Seth's sense of unease grew, though he wasn't going to let Zack see that. He finished drying himself, spread the towel on the radiator, then rifled through his drawers for some boxers. Zackary lay with his hands behind his head and rolled his eyes. The boy was absurdly unselfconscious.

'I'm in a bit of a hurry, Zack,' Seth said pointedly, pulling on his jeans.

'Where are you off to?' asked Zackary, suddenly interested.

Seth didn't want to tell him. He wasn't sure why. Did he just want to hold on to some power in this relationship? Or was it because he didn't want Zackary to know about Eva? Zack would consider an attachment of any kind a weakness. And his love for Eva was so much more than a simple attachment. So he ignored the question and sat on the edge of the bed to tie his shoelaces.

'What brings you here, Zackary?'

Zackary pulled himself out of his horizontal sprawl and sat staring at his hands for a few moments. 'I need you to come back to Parallon.'

'What?'

'Something's shifted.'

'What do you mean?'

'It's hard to explain.'

'Try.'

'I have to show you, I think.'

'Show me what, exactly?'

'The people . . . so many people . . .'

'*I* told *you* about the influx, Zackary!' spluttered Seth. 'That was happening before I left! It's one of the reasons I came to investigate the virus.'

'Oh for God's sake, Sethos, this is far more important than your little biology experiments.'

Nobody tapped into Seth's rage the way Zackary could, and Seth knew it was deliberate. He actually caught the sly little goading glance Zackary cast in his direction. But he had dealt with worse. Igniting anger was an old gladiator trick, and loss of control in the arena meant death. So he stared coldly at Zack, taking deep, slow breaths. When he felt calm enough, he continued.

'Obviously my *little biology experiments* aren't going to prevent the influx – but that's not the point. I don't see how the influx itself should cause a problem. Parallon's parameters are infinitely flexible, as you well know.' Seth tapped the side of his head, indicating that this knowledge came directly from Zack's own head. 'Parallon can never run out of space.'

'Space isn't the issue here, Seth.'

'So what *are* you saying, Zackary, because I'd be really interested to hear?' hissed Seth.

'I have only three priorities, Seth . . .'

Seth tried not to snort while he waited for Zackary to complete his dramatic pause.

'One – the continued existence of Parallon; two – the continued existence of Earth; and three – the continued existence of myself. All three are interdependent – one shifts, they all shift.'

'So what's shifted?'

'If I knew, I wouldn't be here. All I know is that Parallon is no longer stable. The signs are indisputable.'

'What signs, Zack?' rasped Seth in exasperation.

'I need to show you, Sethos.'

'I live *here* now, Zackary.'

'Sethos, I am talking about *catastrophe* here: Parallon ceasing to exist – everyone you care about there dying . . . possibly everyone on Earth dying. And you are the only one who can help me fix it.'

'Oh, sure!' spat Seth. 'I'm the kid doing *pointless* biology experiments – how am I supposed to help fix your precious triad?'

'There is nobody else,' said Zackary at last.

'Why can't you fix it without me?'

Zackary shook his head. 'Seth, when are you going to start actually *thinking*? If you used your regrettably enhanced brain properly, you wouldn't need to ask.'

Seth stared at Zackary in frustration. This was an old game and he'd had enough of it. Zackary was never going to stop punishing him for his accidental download. It wasn't his fault the complete contents of Zackary's head now nestled within his own. He knew he had hardly scratched the surface of what was in there. Why would he? Most of it simply wasn't relevant – he was, after all, a mere gladiator slave, as Zackary had tirelessly reminded him. And right now every muscle, every tendon of that gladiator struggled against the impulse to hit Zack. Hard.

But, again, Seth controlled his impulse. He unhooked his jacket from the back of the door. 'Zackary, it was really great to see you, but I have to go now . . . I'm late.'

Long after Seth had sprinted away, Zackary walked wearily out of the building. Whatever Seth said, Zack knew his gladiator: rebellious, quick to anger but fiercely honourable – a boy who would not be able to stand by and watch people die. He was confident that Seth would be home soon.

25

The Gig

The Register, Hoxton Square, London

Tuesday 23 April AD *2013*

It was time to start. My guitar was tuned, my sound levels were checked, and I was trying not to peer through the murky gloom into the audience. It looked like everyone in the world had turned up . . . everyone except Seth. I knew I had to stop thinking about him or I would completely cave. I started going through lyrics in my head. But I couldn't control my eyes. They were defiantly scanning the room for him. Again.

I was feeling totally sick. And for once the virus had nothing to do with it. This was unadulterated fear. I glanced across at Rob, who grinned back at me. I turned to Sadie, who was tightening up one of her drum-skins, and finally to Astrid, who was giving the amps and cables one last check. *Oh God!* What was I doing here? And *where* was Seth?

I could just make out the Lasers and their entourage standing by the bar. Headline bands never normally hung around while the support act was on. Oh no, I didn't want to play in front of them. Could the evening get any worse?

Suddenly the background music cut out and it was just us facing a nearly silent room. Astrid gave the signal and, whether I liked it or not, we were launching into our first song.

There was no way I could look out there and sing at the same time: two totally incompatible actions. So I shut my eyes and forced my head back into the practice studio. A strategy that just about worked for the first three songs. I wasn't able to get right inside the music – I was way too tense for that – but I managed to go through the motions. Then about halfway through 'Crash and Burn' the tight knot of anxiety gluing me stiffly into position suddenly, unaccountably, loosened. I literally felt my shoulders relax and my heart rate slow. I was still playing the song, but I wasn't concentrating all my efforts on being elsewhere. Somehow it didn't seem so necessary any more. Tentatively, I opened my eyes.

I saw him immediately – his powerful aura opening up a path as he made his way through the crowd to the front of the stage, his eyes fixed on mine. Warmth and relief flooded through me.

The rest of the set was easy. His presence floated around me like a balm, unlocking the fear and releasing me to slip inside the music and abandon myself to it. When we finished playing and cleared the stage, I practically dived into his arms.

For a moment we just held on to each other and said nothing. But his silence was almost as unnerving as his absence had been.

'Seth?'

He just held me tight and didn't speak. He was staring at the floor, his face contorted. I couldn't read his expression at all.

'What is it, Seth?' I practically shouted.

'You're needed,' he murmured, as I felt a tug on my elbow.
'Astrid?'

'There are a couple of people you have to meet, Eva,' she announced, steering me insistently towards a corner of the room.

'Aw – Astrid, *really*?' I wanted – no, needed – to talk to Seth. I turned to glance back at him. His instincts were so acute that his eyes flashed to mine almost instantly. But there had been a moment, a millisecond, where I'd caught an expression on his face that made my blood run cold. It was pain. Raw pain.

There was no sign of it now, of course. Seth was good at control, and he'd successfully rearranged his features into a smile. But his eyes still burned too bright. I wanted to wrap myself around him, comfort him, make the bad thing go away, but Astrid was dragging me in the opposite direction.

'Eva!' she hissed.

Reluctantly, I tore my gaze away from Seth.

'Do I have your attention now?'

I nodded.

'This is Theo,' she said, her eyes willing me to look enthusiastic. 'Theo Mendes,' she added pointedly.

My expression must have revealed my complete lack of comprehension (and interest), because he coughed, stretched out his hand and said, 'I'm from Scene Music.'

OK, I'd heard of Scene Music. Anyone living within five hundred miles of Astrid would have had no choice. It was – according to her – *the* best indie record label in the UK. They'd signed an amazing list of bands, including Livid Turkey, one of her all-time favourites. I tried to look impressed.

'I liked you guys,' he said. 'A lot.'

'Thanks,' I mumbled. That was as far as my PR skills took me. I looked desperately at Astrid, who was silently begging me to keep talking. I hadn't the faintest idea what either of them were expecting me to say next. Whatever it was, they didn't get it. Fortunately, his conversation skills were more developed.

'Lucky accident, really. I was coming to check out the Lasers, but got the start time wrong, so I caught your last three songs . . . Unusual sound. Interesting melodies . . .' He was staring at me, like he couldn't quite work out what I was doing there. A sudden whine of guitar feedback announced the arrival of the Lasers onstage. 'Let's talk some more after this,' said Theo, his eyes darting towards them.

'That would be great, thanks,' grinned Astrid. I raised my eyebrows at her. Astrid did not gush. This was the gushiest I'd ever heard her.

Normally I'd have gagged to see the Lasers, but other things had taken precedence. My eyes searched the crowd. Seth was easy to spot because he was the only person moving away from the stage. In my direction. Good.

But as I watched his progress, I caught sight of another couple who weren't facing the stage either. Because they were staring straight at me. I felt a sudden jolt of panic. Their eyes quickly shifted away and they moved slightly into the shadows when they saw I'd caught them, but that just made me more scared. Were they working for Professor Ambrose? Ever since I'd started theorizing about Ambrose and his motives I'd been expecting some kind of follow-up attack. I was still alive. That had to be a miscalculation.

Seth had nearly reached me. I grabbed for his hand as soon

as he was close enough and started hauling him towards the door. He instantly picked up on my anxiety and within seconds we were standing with our backs against the venue wall in the cool night air.

'Did you see them?' I panted.

He nodded. 'They were watching you?'

'I think so,' I whispered, my eyes darting to the door. 'Let's move further away.'

Seth put an arm round me and we walked quickly across the grass towards the other side of the square. It had stopped raining now and the air felt clear and clean. Seth stopped by a bench, threw his jacket on to the wet seat and pulled me down beside him. It gave us a perfect view of the venue, and anyone who left it.

For a moment neither of us said anything. Then he pulled me in closer and kissed the top of my head, sighing deeply. 'I am sorry I didn't make it to the van. Was everything OK?'

'It was fine, Seth.' I turned my head to look at him, expecting an explanation. But he shifted his focus to the ground. There was something wrong – no question. And this had nothing to do with the two people we'd just evaded.

'Who did Astrid want you to meet?'

How long could he stall? 'Oh, just some music guy. He liked the band. Nothing important.'

'You were good tonight.'

'Oh, Seth!' I breathed, throwing my arms round his neck and kissing him. But his body was tense; his lips hard and unyielding against mine. Stung by the rejection, I began to pull away, but then his arms tightened and he shuddered – a small, insignificant movement that seemed to break the dam on an abrupt and frenzied need. His breathing was suddenly heavy and hoarse, his heart beating hard against me, his mouth kissing with a reckless intensity that reminded me of another time, a desperate time. The memory was edging its way through, threatening to take me back. And I couldn't go there. *This* was where I wanted to be . . . the taste of him now, the smell of him, the heat of his skin. I wanted to fill myself with him. Never stop. He was my everything – my world. And at this moment I knew that I was his. The power of that simple truth passed between us like a physical current. Our mouths, our bodies meshed . . . hating clothes, bench, anything that dared come between us . . . But even as we clung to each other, frantically reaffirming our connection, deep down I knew something had changed. Something *had* come between us. I'd read it in Seth's expression. I'd felt it in his body. And a dark swell of fear began to blossom inside me.

'Seth?' I choked, finally finding the strength to pull away. 'What happ–'

My phone vibrated in my pocket. Furiously, I pulled it out to switch it off.

'You'd better answer it, Eva,' said Seth huskily, glancing at his watch. 'The other band must have finished playing.' I frowned at him, but he just shrugged and looked across at the venue.

I saw the caller ID and sighed. 'Astrid,' I snapped into the phone.

'Eva, where the hell are you?' she hissed. 'I've got a record producer here, I've got the rest of the band here – I've got the Lasers heading this way, only too hungry to take our place – and my singer's missing.'

'I'm just outside – er – getting some air.'

'Well, get your ass back in here,' she growled.

I clicked my phone off and turned to Seth, who was already standing. He pulled me up and we stood silently facing each other for a moment. He smiled lightly, but the smile did not reach his eyes.

'Tell me, Seth,' I whispered.

'Tell you what?' he smiled. 'Tell you that you're beautiful and I love you? You already know that. Tell you that Astrid is going to kill you if we don't get you by her side in the next ten seconds? You probably know that too . . . so in the interest of keeping my girl alive, I think we should get going.'

I threaded my arm through his. Had I been wrong? Had I misread him? Maybe everything was OK. Maybe I was just being paranoid. I leaned against his shoulder as we picked our way carefully across the dark square back towards the club. And that's when I remembered that I had another pressing cause for paranoia.

'Just keep your eyes open for weird assassins,' I breathed.

'I didn't need the reminder,' he murmured back, pushing open the door.

I spotted Astrid and the guys almost immediately. She was the one glowering lethally in my direction.

I headed over. Rob handed me a Coke, which I took gratefully. They all studiously ignored Seth, who stood nearby scanning the crowd.

Doing my best to tear my eyes off him, I tried to engage in the conversation, suddenly aware that Theo Mendes was waiting for me to focus. He was leaning against a wall, arms folded, staring at me through narrowed eyes. I tried to look attentive.

'OK, Eva – are you with us now?' he asked with a twitch of an eyebrow.

I nodded, not entirely crazy about his teacher-style irony.

'I like a bit of attitude in band members,' he said, glancing around at us. 'But – I also like them to know when to be punctual . . . when to be nice.' He was looking straight at me. What was his problem? I frowned furiously and was on the point of turning round and walking out, when Astrid grabbed my arm.

'Eva,' she hissed, 'just listen to Theo, will you? Hear him out.'

I breathed deeply, folded my arms and waited.

'I came to see the Lasers tonight,' Theo continued, as though there had been no interruption. 'They were good, very good at times. They play well together, got a great rapport . . . but there's something missing . . . I dunno – they lack edge. They're predictable –'

I was feeling really bad for the Lasers, and my eyes flicked around the room to check they weren't anywhere near enough to hear this stuff. I saw them drinking at a corner table by the stage, trying not to look in our direction.

'You guys, on the other hand, are all edge and unpredictability. And I think that's a good thing. Actually, I think it's a very good thing. I like your bass licks, Astrid – they're sharp. Sadie, you drum like you mean it, but you've got restraint – I like that a lot in a rhythm player. Rob – you can really play that keyboard. The songs are good. They've got shape, yet they don't go where you expect. Which is pretty cool . . . And Eva . . .'

I dragged my eyes back from the Lasers' table and tried to look engaged.

'Eva – you've got that thing. That thing that makes everyone in the room want to look at you. And listen to you. I dunno what it is. And in my experience it's a gift that is often bestowed on the wrong people –' he gave me a pointed stare – 'but there you are. You've got it. Which makes the full package for me.'

I stared back at him, fighting the impulse to laugh. I hated this kind of speech. And I wasn't remotely interested in his damned package – whatever it was. I felt the pressure on my arm tighten and realized Astrid's hand was still there. This was her second warning. I tried to look polite.

'So I'm thinking about offering you the golden ticket,' continued Theo, apparently oblivious.

'The golden ticket?' I glanced at Astrid, my mouth twitching. She stared ferociously back at me. I shifted my focus back to Theo.

'A recording deal.'

We blinked at him in shock.

'Oh my God!' screamed Sadie, dashing forward and throwing her arms round Theo.

'Hey, steady!' he coughed, stepping back nervously. 'Nothing definite yet. There'd be a few conditions. I need to get you some more gigs, see the rest of your material, bring some people along . . . We'll set up a meeting at my office.'

As soon as they all got engrossed discussing dates, I looked around for Seth. He was standing pretty close, but his eyes were fixed on a point behind my head. I turned sharply and saw the pair I'd run from earlier, perched on stools at the bar. They were definitely looking in our direction . . . but not at me. This time their eyes seemed completely fixed on Theo. I glanced back at Seth, who nodded slightly. He had come to the same conclusion. Relief flooded through me, and I found my mouth suddenly arranging itself into the smile I'd been working so hard to find. Just in time, apparently, judging by the expression on Astrid's face.

So had they been watching Theo all along? Or were they interested in both of us? And why – if they were working for Ambrose – would they also be interested in Theo Mendes? I couldn't see them clearly as the light was so bad, but suddenly the woman caught me looking at her, frowned, drained her glass and stood up. The guy did the same, casually putting his arm round her, and together they made their way to the door. They had to pass under one of the angled stage lights, giving their features a snapshot moment of clarity. And it was at that point that the woman suddenly turned. Her eyes caught mine and for a split second I saw a flash of pure hatred cross her face.

26

Cracks

Nick opened the car door and Jen slipped into the passenger seat. He then vaulted round to his side, strapped himself in and put the keys into the ignition.

'Your place or mine?' he breathed into her ear, nipping her earlobe playfully with his teeth.

Jen sat frozen in her seat.

'Jen? What's wrong?'

'I just want to know what that was all about,' she said quietly.

'What?' Nick stared at her, shaking his head in bewilderment.

'Oh, sorry – I thought we were at the Lasers gig to do surveillance on Elena Galanis's ex,' she spat. 'Not check out hot girl singers . . .'

'Oh, come on, Jen, I was watching Theo Mendes all night!'

'Er – what about when he was at the back of the room and you were standing there gawping at the stage?'

'For Christ's sake, Jen, you don't think it would have been a

164

bit obvious to be looking at Mendes all through the set? Surveillance Rule Number One – make sure murder suspect knows exactly why you're there. I knew where Theo was and who he was talking to the whole evening. And when the Astronauts were playing, he was just standing by the bar, watching the band. They were good. You thought so too.'

'You weren't just watching *the band* though, were you, Nick?'

Nick exhaled furiously, flicked his indicator and released the clutch. He pulled out of the square and pointed the car in the direction of Shoreditch. Jen's flat.

Jen tried to control her breathing as she stared blindly through the windscreen. Why had she started this fight? She was hating it. Hating Nick for being fascinated by that girl. Hating herself for being so insecure. Hating the way she had managed so successfully to poison a good evening. What had she hoped to gain anyway? A confession? Would that have made her feel any better? Worse, probably. And Nick hadn't *acted* on his interest . . . had he? Surely nothing could have happened between them when she'd nipped out to the loo a while ago? Because the girl had definitely stiffened when they'd accidentally caught each other's eye just now . . . And Nick seemed hell-bent on getting out of there fast. Was he hiding something?

Hoxton Square to Shoreditch High Street hardly warranted the effort of getting into a car, so before Jen had had a chance to try and drag the evening back on track, Nick was pulling up outside her flat. He didn't switch off the engine, just sat staring ahead, his expression hard and unyielding. Clearly very angry. Well, so was she, thought Jen defiantly, as she unclicked her seatbelt and opened her door. Just before she slammed it shut she leaned in, hoping to catch his eye, but Nick didn't turn his head. Sighing, she walked to her front door. He didn't hang around to see her in, but revved the engine and drove straight off.

As soon as Jen was inside, any remnants of anger dissolved into misery, and she could barely see the stairs as she trudged wearily up to her flat. She prayed Debs wasn't home yet – the last thing she needed right now was a witness to her shame and dejection.

27

Immutable

'Good morning,' whispered Seth, softly kissing my mouth.

I blinked awake. How did he manage to get into my room so quietly?

'Is it time to get up?' I yawned. The alarm hadn't gone off.

'Nearly. We've got about ten minutes.'

I raised my eyebrows and grinned suggestively, then leaned longingly against him. He didn't resist as I expected; instead he took off his shoes, lifted the duvet and climbed in beside me. Then he pulled me into his chest, breath-crushingly close, wrapped both arms round me and began kissing me hard. His lips were everywhere, pressing my eyes shut, my mouth open, on my neck, my shoulders, my hair, as though his mouth were taking an inventory and couldn't miss any part out. Our hearts were thudding in a fast, fierce rhythm, our breathing ragged, our legs and arms an indistinguishable tangle of burning skin . . . and then the alarm went off.

Seth went still, then slowly pulled himself up on to his elbows, exhaling a deep, shuddering breath. The moment was over. He was back in control. He leaned across to switch the alarm off, and turned to face me.

'Eva –'

I lay on my side, trying to deep-breathe my pulse back to normal. Something about the tone of his voice made my stomach twist. A flash of that glimpsed expression last night at the gig passed through my head. I had been right to fear.

He bit his lower lip. I didn't touch him. I just waited.

'Eva, I love you –'

I held my breath, staring into his face.

'*But* –' I prompted hoarsely.

He looked away for a moment, at the blank wall behind me. Without his eyes to hold me, I felt instantly anchorless. I searched wildly around for something to cling on to and caught sight of his knuckles clenched, white, against the side of the bed. Oh God . . . what was going on?

And then his eyes flickered back at me, and I felt . . . safe again.

'There is no *but*, Eva. There will never be a but. I love you – I will never leave you . . . Whatever happens – this is where I belong. Here with you.'

Then he kissed the top of my head, swung his legs over the side of the bed and pulled himself up.

'Wait,' I whispered, reaching a hand out to stop him moving away.

He turned warily.

'What happened to you yesterday, Seth? Why were you late for the gig?'

He stood a moment, gazing down at me, his shoulders taut. Then he shook his head and smiled. 'I'm sorry, baby – I just lost track of time. It won't happen again, I promise. Shall I get the shower running for you?'

I stared back at him, feeling sick. Why was he lying to me? 'I can run my own shower, thanks,' I croaked, getting out of bed and stepping past him. He stood in dazed silence as I moved around the room, retrieving my shampoo and pulling my towel from the door hook. I was willing him to talk to me, but he continued to stand, frozen and mute.

'I'll see you in biology,' I sighed, heading into the shower room and locking the door.

I stood under the shower and closed my eyes. My head was throbbing, so I viciously massaged my scalp with shampoo. There was no way I could have any virus symptoms when I visited Rose Marley at lunchtime or she'd force me back in the medical block. And that was out of the question.

'Damn,' I hissed a few minutes later, as I sat on the side of the bed to pull on my jeans. My hands were trembling. I looked down at them furiously, knowing how long it was going to take to get those fly buttons fastened. But the jeans were easy compared to my trainers. By the time I'd got myself dressed and upright, I'd missed breakfast. Not good. Regular meals were one of Dr Falana's rules. And I'd skipped dinner last night. 'Since when do you care about rules, Koretsky,' I snarled, flinging my door open and slamming out.

As soon as I made it into the quad, I spotted Seth. He was leaning against the biology lab wall, his eyes fixed on me as I moved slowly towards him. God, he was beautiful. What the hell was he doing with someone like me? And my stomach suddenly clenched painfully, because I knew something had threatened us . . . and he was refusing to tell me what.

My pace was slow. I tried to speed up, I didn't want him to notice, but my legs were doing their feeble act. He moved towards me, and tentatively reached out his hand.

'Eva?' he frowned, searching my face.

Don't you dare do your mind-read thing, Leontis, I thought belligerently, and his lips quirked into a smile, which made me fairly sure he just had.

'Did you get breakfast?' he asked casually.

I ignored the question, walked into the lab and headed for the front of the room. He followed, sat down beside me and deposited a banana and a blueberry muffin on to my lap.

I stole a sideways look at him, and shook my head. How was I supposed to stay cross with him?

Then Dr Franklin was bustling through, carrying a huge box of centrifuge tubes for our catalase enzyme experiments. Just as she neared my chair, she stumbled slightly, losing her grip on the box.

'Oops!' she gasped.

I instantly jumped up to help her. Or, at least, that was the intention. But something went wrong. Everything went wrong. The whole room tipped. And then the floor tilted up at an impossible angle and hit me across the face. My last mangled thought was that floors aren't supposed to be able to do that.

28

Anomalies

Channel 7 Newsroom, Soho, London

Friday 26 April AD *2013*

After the disastrous car journey home, Jen had been sure Nick would ring to make up. But he didn't. She woke the next morning, sick with tiredness and discomfort – hating herself for the ridiculous fuss she'd made. She'd handled the whole thing wrong, and had no idea how to put it right. Her instinct was to just phone him and apologize, but she was sure that she'd blow it and end up looking embarrassingly jealous and needy. She would just have to wait for him to call her.

It was now Friday. Three days had passed and she'd still heard nothing. She promised herself that if she hadn't heard by today, she'd call him. She glanced at her phone, willing it to ring. It remained resolutely silent. She sighed and looked back at her computer. The screen was filled with rows and rows of UK rainfall and climate statistics for next week's feature. Considering how distracted she was, she'd managed to compile a pretty comprehensive dossier. But then weather was becoming a bit of a Channel 7 newsroom obsession – especially since that series of small inexplicable tornados across North London.

She glanced around the office. People were beginning to head out for lunch. Amanda was supposed to be at a meeting till 2.00, but Jen definitely didn't feel up to phoning Nick right now . . . so there was only one thing for it – she would use the time to get on with her own little research project.

She made sure she could quickly switch to a climate graph, in case of a surprise ambush, then double-clicked on the file she'd named 'Statistical Currency Anomalies'. She'd given it that title in case Amanda's beady eye ever scoured her desktop. A more accurate title would have been: 'Unexplainable Disappearances'.

Jen had now catalogued 248 significant London disappearances over the past fourteen years. She'd uncovered an additional seventeen last night, just before she put her light out. Which really bothered her. Because she'd found them on a site she'd totally exhausted the previous day. Despite her many faults (and Amanda never tired of listing them), Jen was a good researcher. Thorough. Meticulous. So why had she overlooked whole newspaper articles on disappearances?

Of the 248 subjects on her list, 221 were teenagers. She knew that statistically kids were a volatile group, and most runaways fell into the age bracket, so that wasn't so surprising. But the fact that seventy-three of them had disappeared from hospitals was seriously shocking. Why hadn't there been a national outcry? Were the disappearances being covered up? But if so, why was she able to find the stories on newspaper databases? And how could you explain the fact that last night she had revisited the 11 July 2003 facsimile of the *London Evening*

News – an edition she had thoroughly trawled less than three days previously – and had discovered a further two disappearance articles? Whichever way you spun it, she looked incompetent: either she kept missing stuff, or . . . no . . . it was preposterous. No way.

She badly needed to talk to someone about all this. Well, there was only one person she wanted to talk to. Nick. She stared at her phone.

Finally she picked it up and walked purposefully out of the newsroom. But when she got outside, all her resolve disintegrated. How could she speak to him and not mention the awful car journey? She stood indecisively for a couple of moments and then a striding figure across the road caught her attention. Amanda was on her way back.

Jen looked down at her phone and, before she could stop herself, she had sent him a text.

Just checking u got back OK? Jx

She'd deliberated over the x for a couple of moments, but anxiety about Amanda's approach forced her to press the send button.

Six hours and forty-one minutes later he texted back.

Yep.

29

Coincidence

I don't remember being moved. Just a few fragments: hands clamping on my shoulders; vomit on blue fabric; Seth's fingers in my hair; Rose repeating my name; faces coming in and out of focus; a damned annoying insect stinging the back of my hand . . .

'Eva, you're going to have to leave that alone.'

Seth's voice. Seth's firm fingers pulling my good hand away from the sting.

I tried to fight him off – like that was a battle I was likely to win.

He was laughing. I had no idea where we were. What day it was. What year it was. Was I Eva? Or Livia? I wasn't sure I was ready to find out. I opened my eyes a crack.

Medical block. Seth sprawled on a chair, grinning down at me. As scenarios went, it could have been worse.

'How long this time?' I asked, wincing. That was never my voice. Seth poured a glass of water from a jug and gently slid it between my lips. I swallowed.

'Six days,' he said, affecting a nonchalant tone. But the light-ness didn't reach his eyes.

Instinctively, I reached up to touch his cheek. 'Seth, you look exhausted. What have you been doing?'

He rolled his eyes. 'Lab work, mostly.'

I waited for him to continue.

'I've finished all the blood analysis now.'

'Everyone's been tested?'

'Well, everyone except you.'

I nodded. He was scrutinizing his hands.

'And?' I croaked.

He clenched his fists and looked up, fixing me with his clear blue eyes. 'There is absolutely no student resistance, Eva. To anyone aged between thirteen and eighteen, I am one hundred per cent fatal.'

I grabbed his hand and kissed it. He tried to reclaim it, but I clung on.

'And the staff?' I whispered.

'Not conclusive. Three young teachers responded instantly to the virus, absolutely equivalent to the student population. One secretary and two technicians reacted within twenty-four hours. But they are all under twenty-five. Two or three of the older teachers seem to have complete resistance – no cell compromise at all . . . But most staff show signs of degenerative cell damage. I'm still monitoring.'

'So you've proved a pretty clear age correlation. Any further ideas about the source, Seth?'

Seth shook his head. 'The only thing we've got really is your bioterrorism theory . . . But that hardly explains the Parallon outcome.'

I shrugged. He was right. 'Unless Parallon is an accidental by-product – some sort of a quantum error. I mean – after all – life on Earth is probably the result of an accidental random microbiological event.'

'OK – so if we ignore the Parallon element – I still have to ask why, Eva? Why conceive such a circuitous, uncontrollable viral weapon? Why would you want to get rid of whole generations of young people like this?'

I thought about World Wars One and Two – whole generations of young people mown down. And it didn't end there . . . Rwanda, Afghanistan, Iraq, Serbia. On and on – a continuous cycle of destruction and domination. Since when? The Romans, with their mass invasions? Nobody knew better than Seth about their indiscriminate killing.

'God, Seth – how can you ask that question? You can't have forgotten your home? Or the arena? The human appetite for destruction and cruelty is infinite.'

'No, Eva. The Roman destruction of Corinth wasn't indiscriminate. It was targeted and finite. They destroyed selectively. They couldn't brook opposition, so potential fighters would be either eliminated or enslaved. Yes – within that framework – their appetite for cruelty and power seemed infinite, but it was controlled.

'A replicating virus is by its very nature uncontrollable. It can travel and infect in any direction.'

'But all biological weapons work along that principle – presumably to spread fear and panic. I don't know a time that terrorists uniquely targeted their enemies. Identified targets have always been just a small percentage of the casualties. *Innocent* victims don't feature high on the terrorist list of worries.'

Seth nodded. 'I s'pose not.'

I pulled him towards me, and he perched on the side of the mattress, one arm resting lightly across my shoulders. But he remained tense. 'There's just something about it that doesn't feel right.'

I sighed into his chest. Deep down, I felt exactly the same way.

The door swung open and we both jumped.

'Eva! Welcome back!' smiled Rose, clattering a tray into the room and handing us each a mug of tea.

I winced as I tried to use both hands to take it. The back of my left hand had a damn line in it.

Rose glanced down at it. 'I think that can come out now.'

'I owe you one, Rose,' I smiled. As she unhooked me from the drip, a little blood splattered across the sheet and Seth and I stared at it, transfixed. I raised my eyebrows at him. He knew what I was suggesting. One drop – and we could find out once and for all. But he bit his lip, turned away from the sheet and sipped his tea.

'There's the new *Pride and Prejudice* film starting on TV in ten minutes,' said Rose, as she wheeled the drip stand into the corner. 'Do you two fancy watching it?'

It sounded way more appealing than worrying about fatal viruses and biological weapons. I glanced at Seth. He shrugged. 'Sure.'

We swigged down our tea. It felt incredible against my parched throat, though it tasted sort of metallic.

'Eva?' said Seth, staring at me.

'What?'

He'd grabbed a tissue and was wiping quickly round my mouth and nose.

'Seth, I'm not a kid –' I gasped, embarrassed.

He quickly threw the tissue into the bin, but not before I'd clocked that it wasn't tea he was cleaning off, it was blood. Tea had never given me nosebleeds before.

'Eeuw!' I said disgustedly. 'Sorry, Seth, that's gross!' I grabbed another tissue and held it up to my nose, horrified that he should be witnessing this. Fortunately, a couple of minutes later, it stopped.

'The tea must have been too hot,' I announced, chucking away a perfectly white tissue. 'Come on, let's go and get Darcied.'

'Darcied?' Seth asked, mystified.

'Darcy's the name of the hot love interest in *Pride and Prejudice*! Prepare to get very jealous!'

He grinned, then helped me out of bed and down the stairs. A few moments later we settled on the sofa in Rose's cosy little sitting room.

Seth had never read any Jane Austen, and I didn't get the impression that he considered it a catastrophic omission, but he sat peacefully beside me, absently twisting strands of my hair round his fingers.

For me it felt like a perfect evening. No bioterrorists. No nosebleed, no headache, no nausea. Seth breathing evenly beside me while a sweet, funny, agonizing love story played out in front of us . . . a painful story that ended happily. Could I dare to hope the same for us?

'I thought we could have eggs for supper. Would you like to stay, Seth? I can clear it with your housemaster,' offered Rose.

Wow. Seth had totally won Rose over. He grinned at her and nodded appreciatively.

'Can I help?' he asked, standing up.

'I'll call you when I need you,' she answered, disappearing into the kitchen.

He settled back beside me, and I was just reaching for the remote to switch off the news when I felt him go rigid.

He was staring at the screen.

'Elena?' he murmured.

I turned my attention back to the T.V.

It was a London News bulletin: a reconstruction of the last-known movements of a missing waitress, Elena Galanis.

A photo of an attractive, laughing girl filled the screen. Seth was transfixed by it.

'Seth?' I breathed. He didn't hear me.

His hands were balled into fists and his mouth set in a hard line of fury. He stood up and started pacing.

'Seth, tell me!' I begged. 'Who is she? How do you know her?'

Seth just shook his head, refusing to look at me.

A few minutes later Rose brought three plates of scrambled eggs into the living room and we ate in silence. Rose attempted a few light-hearted references to the film, but gave up when our non-committal grunts left her no conversational scope.

After supper, Seth wordlessly picked up the plates, took them into the kitchen and washed up. When he returned to the living room, he told us that he hadn't had a chance to run all day, and he could do with burning off some energy. I nodded.

As he lightly kissed me goodbye on the cheek, I whispered, 'See you later?'

'It's late, Eva.' His eyes didn't hold mine for even one second. 'I'll see you tomorrow. Sleep well.' And then he was gone.

I gazed blankly at the door.

'He likes to run, that boy,' chuckled Rose. 'Come on, you look wiped, Eva, I think we'll take the lift upstairs tonight.' I didn't argue.

I thought I'd be relieved when Rose finally switched out the light and left me alone, but as soon as she'd gone my stomach started to twist.

Why was Seth acting so distant? What was he keeping from me this time?

I tried to rewind the evening. He'd seemed fine until that news bulletin – or had he? Maybe he was a bit preoccupied during the movie? Come to think of it, was he watching it at all? He was facing the screen but that was probably as far as his engagement went.

So what had he been thinking about? Us? Elena?

You're overreacting, I told myself. *For God's sake, pull it together. Everything is fine. Seth needed to run. He's not going anywhere. Whatever his relationship with Elena, it is not significant. He's never mentioned her before. He loves you. We are happy together . . .*

But I wasn't so sure. Had Seth finally got fed up with me and this damned illness? He'd just had another whole week of it. Maybe he wanted a girlfriend who didn't drip blood from her nose; one who could actually do stuff with him: like go running; or into the lab and figure a virus out; or even manage to stay vertical for more than ten minutes at a time. Who wouldn't want that? Elena had looked so vibrant, so pretty, so happy.

So who was she? And what was she to Seth?

Maybe I could find out. I frantically scoured the room for my laptop, praying that Seth had brought it over at some point during the last week. He knew how much I hated to be parted from it. Then I saw it charging on the desk. I felt a sudden swell of gratitude.

It took me longer than I would want to admit to make the three-metre journey across to the desk and back, but at last I was curled on my bed again, clutching my prize.

My first job was to get online. It was after midnight, which meant circumventing the school's 11 p.m. internet curfew, but I'd done that plenty of times. Within four minutes I was online, Googling Elena Galanis. She'd disappeared without trace over three months ago. There were loads of news reports, YouTube reconstructions, appeals by her family, interviews with her friends and . . . *Oh my God!* What was *he* doing there? I was staring into the troubled face of Theo Mendes. The Theo Mendes from Scene Music. The Theo Mendes who had just talked to us about a record deal.

Theo was Elena's *boyfriend*!

Small world.

Elena had just jumped another hundred paces closer to home. And I didn't like it. She had disappeared, and both Seth and Theo knew her. What were the chances?

I never trusted coincidences. There had to be a connection.

It was late, I was tired, my laptop was getting low on battery, but I couldn't stop. I wanted more. I scrolled back through the interviews and footage again, then scanned every newspaper report I could find. I even read through reader blogs and comments. But there was so little actual information – mostly conjecture. I sighed. The battery light on my laptop was flashing. It was about to die, but there was a link I hadn't checked out yet . . . an early *Guardian* report. It displayed the usual smiling photo of Elena, and the one of her grieving parents. But underneath there was a small picture of the detective running the investigation: DI Nick Mullard.

I swallowed, recognizing him instantly from the Register. So it was detectives watching us at the gig, not bioterrorists.

My fingers immediately began Googling DI Nick Mullard. I just had time to type his first name when the screen went black. Damn. I glanced at the clock. 2.30 a.m. I leaned across to the nearest power point to recharge the laptop. The cable wasn't long enough, so there was nothing I could do but set it to charge and put out the light.

I lay in the dark, my brain whirring with images of Theo, DI Mullard, Elena and Seth. What did they all mean to each other? Were the police watching Theo because he had something to do with Elena's disappearance? But why were they watching *me*? Surely they didn't think I'd done something to her? That look the woman had given me was positively venomous.

And . . . what had happened between Elena and Seth?

I shut my eyes, trying to block out images of the two of them parading across my brain, but as I curled into a tight ball all I could feel was the cold empty space he'd left behind.

30

Weapon

Medical Bay, St Magdalene's

Wednesday 1 May AD 2013

I was already dressed when Rose arrived by my bed the next morning. I'd made a decision: I wasn't going to let this sickness dictate terms. It wasn't going to defeat me   certainly not before I'd found out what the virus was, who Ambrose was and what the hell was going on between Seth and Elena.

Rose just raised her eyebrows when she saw the jeans and T-shirt and said, 'Are you up to seeing a visitor?'

I didn't need to ask who she meant, but I was a bit thrown that he'd arrived without me hearing anything. I sat down hard on the side of the bed. To be honest, I wasn't sure if I was ready.

Rose stood in front of me, frowning – clearly questioning whether this was a good idea. And then the decision was taken away from either of us, because Seth was striding across the room.

'Eva!'

Suddenly I was in his arms, my cheek was pressed against his chest and Rose was melting away.

Then he started talking. 'I met Elena the first day I came to St Magdalene's. I'd just arrived through the vortex, I was freezing cold and soaking wet. She let me use her shower and gave me dry clothes.'

'That's it?' I asked sceptically.

He chewed his lip. 'No,' he exhaled finally.

OK – we'd got to the part I'd been dreading. I pulled away from him, opening up a gap between us. He just let his arms drop heavily to his sides.

'On my last visit to Parallon I discovered that Elena was there.'

The full implications of this disclosure hit me like a smack in the chest. Elena had contracted the virus.

'Oh, Seth,' I rasped, my heart thudding. 'What happened between you?'

He turned to me, frowning. 'Between who – Elena and *me*?' He glared at me, his eyes burning ferociously. 'Eva! What do you take me for? How can you ask that?'

I stared back at him uncertainly.

He shook his head and sighed. 'Do you remember Matthias? I think you met him briefly in Londinium. In the arena. Before the fight.'

My Londinium memories were hazy, almost dreamlike, but now that he mentioned the name, I recalled a guy about our age standing behind Seth. Holding something – a flask? He wasn't a gladiator – completely the wrong build. But the name sounded so familiar . . . I shut my eyes – feeling the whisper of another memory . . . my beautiful gladiator lying in a dark room, delirious with fever, muttering one name over and over . . . *Matthias*.

I nodded. 'Yes – I remember.'

'Matthias was like a – a brother to me,' rasped Seth. 'He arrived in Parallon shortly after I did . . . infected by my blood.' He looked down at his open palms in disgust.

I leaned across and grabbed both his hands in mine. His self-hatred was unbearable.

'I did my best to protect Matt from Zackary and the vortex – but one day he followed me . . .'

Seth paused and gazed sightlessly out of the window.

'And?' I prompted. This was clearly not a story Seth wanted to share.

'Matt started travelling with no induction. He was flailing around time really. And he . . . infected some people . . . Elena was one of them.' Seth stopped speaking, indicating the end of the story.

'Oh,' I said.

So why had that been so hard to tell? And why was Seth so angry? After all, he'd accidentally infected Matt in the first place – nobody knew better than Seth how lethal the virus was.

'It's a very dangerous virus,' I said. 'Matthias didn't –'

'It's a deadly virus, Eva, and we need to try and work out where it came from – before it's too late.'

I sighed. There was something Seth wasn't telling me, but I knew I couldn't force him. So I tried to shift focus.

'OK,' I said. 'The virus . . . Let me show you something.' I pulled my laptop up on to the bed and started revisiting some of the medical sites I'd researched.

'What are you doing, Eva?' he asked quietly, perching on the side of the bed beside me and frowning at my screen.

'I'm just trying to demonstrate the –'

'Sorry – I don't mean *what* are you doing . . . I mean *how* are you doing it? You're on secure medical databases . . .'

'Ye-e-s?' I said.

'*Secure* medical databases,' he repeated.

'Well – how else am I supposed to research?' I retaliated automatically. He was immobile next to me. I glanced up at him. 'Er – do you have a problem with that?' My voice was suddenly hoarse.

He was just shaking his head and staring at the screen. 'But how did you get *in*? These sites have seriously complex passwords and security codes. They're meant to be invulnerable!'

I shrugged. 'Well, they aren't – if you know what you're doing.'

'But you skipped through the access codes in seconds . . .'

'These particular ones were dead easy – I just used SQL injection. They shouldn't have had such big holes in their security. Some are way harder to get into – a few have taken me *days*,' I admitted.

He was still staring at me.

'Look, Seth, I know it's not strictly legal to go sneaking around other people's stuff, but I think this counts as a bit of an emergency . . .'

'Could you get caught?'

I laughed. 'I cover my tracks pretty well.'

He was looking at me sceptically. 'How?'

'Making sure I leave a clean log file . . . believe me, I've had years of practice.'

He considered me for a couple of moments, and then kissed me. 'What else don't I know about you, Eva?' he murmured against my mouth.

'You'd better hang around and find out!' I grinned. 'And, in the meantime, I suppose in the interests of science it's time I inducted my gladiator into the rudiments of basic hacking. Watch and learn, baby!'

The next site I visited, I went through the accessing process slowly, demonstrating a way to slip through leaky firewalls using a port scanner. Then I showed him how to install one of my arsenal of cunning trojans for backdoor data access.

He was a reasonably fast learner. When I was fairly confident he'd got the hang of it, I sped up again because I wanted to show him the thing that was bothering me.

We looked at site after site after site.

Finally he said, 'Eva, am I missing something?'

I smiled. 'You tell me?'

'Well, we have just trawled about fifty UK clinical sites, and one hundred and twenty in the US, and not one references anything like our virus . . .'

'Exactly,' I said. 'That's the point. It's completely invisible. Not a single clinical record. Even my hospital notes make no reference to it.'

'So what are you saying?'

'I'm asking *why*, Seth? A virus that has provenance – that has evolved naturally – will have been recorded and analysed. So running with my theory that this is a lab-made weapon – they have not only created the virus, they're testing it. And clearly have a big enough intelligence network to completely cover their tracks.'

Seth was shaking his head and frowning. 'But, Eva, the virus *does* have provenance – two thousand years of it. There is no way the Romans had the technology to develop biological weapons in AD 152 . . . And that's when I was infected.'

I sat gazing at him, waiting for him to see what I saw.

'Eva . . . ?'

'You're right, Seth. The virus couldn't possibly have been engineered in AD 152 . . . but someone could have intentionally carried it there.'

Seth swallowed slowly. 'It's a plausible hypothesis,' he finally said, hoarsely.

My heart sank. I didn't want it to be plausible. I wanted him to argue against it. I couldn't even begin speculating on the ripples a hypothesis like that would generate.

'Is it possible though?' I argued against myself.

'Well, here I stand – a time traveller. Every cell of my body carrying the lethal weapon.'

I stared at him, completely unable to think of him in that way.

'*But* – as far as I know,' he went on, 'the Parallon vortex is the only wormhole. And just three people have ever accessed it . . . Zackary, Matt and me.'

I nodded. 'And none of *you* have any terrorist intentions,' I smiled, desperately trying to lighten the atmosphere.

Seth stared into the middle distance, frowning.

'Seth?'

He shook his head slowly. 'It couldn't have been Matthias – or me – we were both victims of the virus in AD 152. And neither of us could return there – we'd have no power . . .'

'What do you mean?'

'We'd be no more than shadows . . . ghosts.'

I gazed at him, watching his mouth set into a hard line, willing him to say more.

'Seth – please tell me. I need to know this,' I said quietly.

He sighed. 'I went back once, Eva. It was a mistake I barely survived.'

'What happened?'

'I knew nothing then . . . about the vortex . . . time travel . . . the dangers.'

'So what are the dangers?'

'The distance–power correlation goes both ways.'

I clearly looked totally blank.

'You remember I told you – the further away you travel from your own time, the more intense your physical and mental power. Conversely, the nearer you approach your own time, the less powerful you become . . . maybe some sort of relativistic factor . . .'

He paused. I waited.

'The first time I entered the vortex I had no coherent intention –' his eyes darted to mine – 'and I was automatically carried to my own lifetime . . . to the time of my death.'

I took a deep breath. 'So you were at your weakest?'

He sighed, then continued huskily, 'Weakness doesn't begin to describe it. Zack has experimented and says as long as you clear your own lifespan there is no problem . . .'

'But you didn't.'

'Every second I spent in Londinium depleted the energy I needed to make it out again.'

'You nearly got trapped?'

He nodded.

'What would that mean?'

'I suppose being doomed to watch the rewind of your own death . . . locked for an eternity with no voice . . . no physical presence.' He flinched involuntarily. 'A perpetual ghost.'

I shuddered, tightening my grip on his hand. He was so warm, so alive. The idea of him that reduced and vulnerable was unbearable. He pulled me into his arms and I felt myself melt gratefully towards the steady rhythm of his heart.

'Hey, I made it out,' he smiled. 'And I am never going back – there's nothing to fear . . . Apart from the small matter of a time terrorist!'

I snorted, relieved at the subject change.

'But where's the motive, Eva?'

I shrugged. I didn't really get terrorist motives at the best of times. 'What about Zackary? Any chance he could be our terrorist?'

Seth shook his head. 'No chance.'

'How can you be so sure?'

'I just know.'

'How do you know?' I persisted.

Seth sighed. 'Zackary would never want to harm either this world or Parallon. That's why he guards the vortex so fiercely. And I can absolutely guarantee he's not interested in populating Parallon, so he's the last person who would want to go round infecting people.'

'OK,' I said slowly. 'So is it possible somebody else could have compromised the vortex?'

Seth stared at his hands for a while, then shrugged bleakly. 'I suppose anything is possible,' he said at last.

31

Reunion

'At last,' Jen breathed, leaning back in her chair. She had finished the final table for her 'Aberrant Climate' piece. She skimmed it quickly, and before she could change her mind or find anything else to edit, she emailed the document to Amanda.

She glanced at the clock – 21.30. No wonder most of the other fixers had gone. She was almost too tired to move, but she forced herself to log off and stand up. She pulled her jacket from the back of her chair and headed for the lift.

As she stepped into it, she wished it could just teleport her back to the sofa in her flat. Her stomach growled. Did they have anything at all to eat in their fridge? She tried to remember its contents. All she could picture was a dried-up garlic and a carton of shrivelled mushrooms lurking at the bottom. They didn't even have any milk – unless Debs had been shopping. Jen allowed herself a moment's optimism until she remembered her flatmate was filming in Manchester this week.

Sighing, she acknowledged that her walk to the tube would have to include the minimart detour.

'Knowing my luck, it will probably be closed,' she muttered grumpily, standing by the double doors, gazing on to the street. It was dark. Rain and wind whipped against the glass. She lifted her shoulders and embarked on her daunting journey home.

The minimart was open. She plodded in gratefully and dripped her way round the shelves, picking up eggs, milk, bread, beans, bacon and tomatoes. She also threw a couple of beers and a bag of crisps into the basket. She regretted the drinks within about two minutes of lifting the carrier bag off the counter. But the thought of frying bacon sustained her to the tube. She'd planned to start on the crisps as soon as she was on the train, but the guy on the till had wedged them under the tomatoes and eggs, and she was just too tired to dig around, so she sat with the soaking bag of food on her lap, staring sightlessly at the black cables rushing past the opposite window.

When she got to her station, she trudged up the escalator and back out into the stormy night, bumping her shopping against her legs all the way – which tonight seemed infinitely further from the station than usual. When she eventually reached her front door she groaned in relief. Before she could retrieve her key she had to unclamp her numb fingers from the bag and dump it on the wet step beside her. Which sadly turned out to be its final moment of service. As soon as she heaved it back up again, it unceremoniously split, spewing her supper everywhere. She was too miserable to even swear, and just stood staring at the food, her eyes following one of the cans as it jumped off the step and began rolling along the pavement . . . until a foot stopped its course.

Jen's eyes flitted from the can, up the black jeans and leather jacket to a face she knew. A face she hadn't seen since last Tuesday evening. It was hard to read his expression, but she didn't think she could see anger there.

'Nick,' she said quietly.

'Yep.'

He picked up the can, carried it over towards the scattered shopping, and started gathering up the rest. Jen scooped up the tomatoes and the box of cracked eggs, held open the door and he followed her upstairs. She knew the flat was a mess. She knew *she* was a mess, but she was frankly too wet and tired to care. In any case, as far as he was concerned, she was probably at rock bottom already, and she couldn't sink much lower than that. So she didn't bother to apologize when she opened the flat door on to a table littered with unsorted washing, a sink full of dirty dishes and yesterday's dinner plate still lying on the floor next to the sofa.

Nick carried the shopping into the kitchen, wiped down the counter, put the milk in the fridge, threw the desiccated mushrooms into the bin and started washing up.

Jen flung her soaking jacket on a chair and pulled out a frying pan.

'Have you eaten?' she asked.

'Is that a dinner invite?'

'Would you like it to be?'

'Yes please.'

She swallowed down the lump that was suddenly clogging up her throat, and turned quickly back to the pan.

'Just don't expect Jamie Oliver,' she muttered, as she started frying the bacon.

'Hey – you're soaking – why don't you jump in the shower? I can have this ready by the time you come out.'

Jen blinked up at him, unable to trust her voice. 'OK,' she croaked, and slipped to the bathroom.

A few minutes later, she was wrapped in her towelling robe, sitting opposite Nick Mullard and wolfing down the most delicious meal she had ever tasted.

'Mmm,' sighed Nick appreciatively, as he swallowed his final forkful of scrambled egg. 'Who needs Jamie Oliver?'

She allowed herself a smile.

He cocked his head and stared at her.

'So, what happened last Tuesday?' he said finally.

She shrugged. She wasn't exactly gagging to revisit that little episode. He sat waiting for her to speak.

'We went to a gig. We endlessly watched a guy who patently wasn't a murderer, saw a couple of bands . . . and then . . . we had a stupid row,' Jen summarized.

Nick raised his eyebrows. 'And why was it a stupid row?' he asked.

She squirmed, then shrugged again. Her throat had gone tight.

'Should I answer that?' he suggested quietly.

'OK,' said Jen.

'It was a stupid row because you accused me of something I hadn't done, and I got too angry to try convincing you.' Nick drained his glass and put it carefully back on the table. 'I'm sorry.'

'Me too,' Jen admitted, standing up and moving round the table towards him. He pulled her down on to his lap and kissed her. 'I missed you,' she murmured.

'Good,' he laughed back, biting her lip playfully.

*

Later, as they sprawled sleepily across the sofa, the late TV news burbling quietly in front of them, Jen asked him if he'd made any more headway with the case.

He pulled himself up into a more formal sitting position, and looked down at his hands.

'There've been some – er – major developments.'

Jen straightened, fixing him with her full attention.

'We're no longer treating this as a couple of isolated cases,' he sighed.

'More disappearances?' Damn – Nick must have been researching the same news sources as her.

Nick's eyes were darting around the room as though he were expecting spies to be lurking behind the doors. 'Seriously worrying ones.'

'What do you mean?'

'From Belmarsh.'

'Belmarsh – the prison?'

He nodded. 'The maximum security unit.'

'What?'

'Nine inmates have gone missing in the last three days. No sign of breakout, cell doors still locked . . .'

Jen sat mutely staring at him for a few moments. 'And their c-clothes?' she finally stammered.

He nodded, his lips a thin line of tension. 'Exactly the same as Elena Galanis.'

'*And* Winston Grey . . .' Jen added quietly. '*And* the 248 more cases I have unearthed.'

'*What?*' exploded Nick. '248? No way!'

Jen moved across the room to pick up her laptop, while fishing around in her pocket for the memory stick containing the most recent version of 'Statistical Currency Anomalies'.

Nick stared at the screen in disbelief as she scrolled through all the cases. She'd scanned in copies of the news reports because she was convinced that otherwise the stories appeared too far-fetched.

'But when we last talked you'd only uncovered a couple!'

'I know,' she answered. Could she bring herself to mention the inexplicable pattern of escalation? No. She and Nick had only just got back on track – she didn't want him to start doubting either her sanity or her competence any more than he already did. So she shifted the focus back to his revelation.

'Your inmates,' she quizzed, 'had they been sick?'

'Five of them had been transferred to the hospital wing,' confirmed Nick. 'And were reported too sick to move.'

She stared at him blankly.

'Two of them – both serial killers – were in restraints . . . effectively chained to the beds . . .' he went on.

'Were the chains broken?'

He shook his head.

Jen swallowed. 'And this hasn't made the news – why?'

Nick's eyes narrowed. He was fixing her with his gaze. 'This can't get out, Jen. We have no idea what we're dealing with, and whichever angle you take – it looks pretty damned terrifying. Either we have the mass escape of our nine most wanted criminals or there's some appalling illness that . . .' He stared down at his knuckles and couldn't finish the sentence.

'. . . entirely obliterates the body,' she finished for him.

32

Magister

Parallon

'Wake up, Matthias!' hissed Otho, shaking him hard.

'Hey!' groaned Matt, peering into the darkness. He was sprawled on the floor in the living room, the remains of last night's excesses strewn all around him. There was no sign of Pontius or Rufus.

'Clear up this mess and get straight over to the atrium.'

Matt sat up slowly.

'That means *now*!' growled Otho, striding out.

Matt sighed. Zeus – these Romans were moody. Seconds later he had willed the room to rights and was walking briskly towards the atrium. His mouth dropped open when he reached it. Flaming torches hung from the columns, casting a warm flickering light on to Pontius, who slowly paced to and fro in front of Matt's entire household. Georgia, Clare and Winston stood with the others in a straight, respectful line along the far edge, blinking blearily. There was no sign of Elena, Matt noted uneasily.

The sound of footsteps approaching along the marble peristyle prompted an ominous hush. Matt sank instinctively back into the shadows, and watched warily as Pontius, now bowing with uncharacteristic deference, greeted a stranger who strode towards them. Matthias could instantly tell that he was in the presence of an extremely powerful man. Although flanked by Otho and Rufus, the visitor dwarfed them both, and wore his Roman tunic and richly woven toga with the authority of one who was always obeyed.

'Kneel to the magister, vermin,' spat Pontius towards the bemused household. Clare and Georgia obeyed immediately, but Winston and a handful of others remained standing.

Kneel, in the name of Zeus, implored Matt silently from the safety of the shadows.

Moments later, nobody was standing. The flat of Pontius's sword was fast and brutal.

Without missing a beat, Rufus began speaking in Latin.

'The gods be praised, for our beloved magister has joined us.' His eyes respectfully followed the stranger, who was pacing around the atrium, peering between columns, disdainfully inspecting the mosaic-work.

'Naturally he needs a more magnificent palace,' continued Rufus. 'Work will commence at once. *Matthias!*'

Matt was reeling. He'd assumed the stranger was a dangerous but passing visitor. Surely, he hadn't come to stay . . . in his home . . . in his palace . . . as master of all?

Somehow Matt's legs carried him forward and he managed a shuffling bow. Unceremoniously, Rufus handed him a scroll, which Matt unrolled with shaking fingers. He stood frowning at the series of poorly executed, barely decipherable drawings, apparently diagrams of the required improvements. Matt's father had taught him to observe and draw well, so he had to do his best to conceal his scorn for such clumsy work. After several minutes of concentration he had more or less worked out what was planned: an extensive bathhouse, with sauna, steam and massage rooms; a hugely expanded atrium with two further reception rooms; an enormous master chamber on the first floor, and – tacked on to the kitchen – what appeared to be at least twenty-five single rooms. In addition, the grounds now required a Roman tavern, with tables and benches, and . . . *an arena*.

Matt stared in shock. Why would they want to build an arena here? There were no gladiators in Parallon, and they could visit the one in Londinium whenever they wanted.

'Take who you need and start overseeing the work immediately, Matthias,' barked Rufus in Latin. 'And tell the women to bring our breakfast through to the triclinium.'

Matthias stared a moment longer at the scroll and nodded, trying not to notice that he wasn't included in the breakfast invitation.

Swiftly translating the message into English, Matt sent the girls off to present appropriate Roman breakfast food. He looked down at the floor and reluctantly dragged Winston and the three other beaten boys off with him. They had already recovered enough to walk, and he needed to make sure they understood exactly how they were expected to behave.

'We'll start with the bathhouse,' he announced. This was the least controversial building, and it gave him some thinking time. They sat in the cool shade of the columned baths, studying the diagram.

'Who is this magister-bastard, Matt?' hissed Winston, rubbing the bruise at his temple.

Matthias shook his head. 'No idea. He moves like a legion commander, but clearly has the tastes of an emperor.'

'How the hell does he think he can just come in here and take over?'

Matthias bit his thumbnail nervously. 'You saw him, Winston. The magister's not a man you cross . . . unless you enjoy the flat of Pontius's sword.' He glanced at the bruise on his friend's face. 'But with any luck, he won't stay long.' Standing wearily, he gazed around his beloved bathhouse. 'Right, let's get these damned renovations started.'

The plans for the bathhouse were painfully simple, but Matt was fairly certain the magister would favour extravagant opulence. And he was determined to prove himself worthy of the task.

The writhing tail of a glorious mosaic sea monster was just shimmering into shape when the summons came: Matthias was required immediately in the atrium. He was deeply annoyed by the interruption, assuming his Roman friends were after their daily English lesson. Nonetheless, he dared not refuse.

As soon as he reached the atrium, he knew he wasn't there for a class.

'Otho?' he gasped. 'What in the name of Apollo are you wearing?'

'May I suggest that instead of standing there gawping, you change your clothes accordingly,' snapped Otho.

Matthias stared at the beautifully tailored suit and tie Otho was wearing, and hurriedly replaced his tunic and sandals for something equivalent. Seconds later, Pontius and Rufus arrived, similarly dressed.

'Where are the others?' barked Rufus.

'O-others?' croaked Matt.

'The male slaves. Get them, dress them and meet us outside.'

Matt stood motionless for a few moments digesting the words. Rufus had been unequivocal. In one sentence he had redefined the household. It was now without doubt: masters and slaves. And where did he stand? *Not with the slaves*, he vowed. He could not be a slave again.

Minutes later he was pacing quickly towards the palace's great wooden front doors, followed by the seven carefully suited boys he had managed to round up.

Just outside the entrance stood the magister, also dressed in a well-cut suit and tie, deep in conversation with Otho, Pontius and Rufus. The sight was unsettlingly incongruous.

As soon as Matt and his entourage passed through the doorway, the magister glanced round and nodded. Pontius and Rufus shifted immediately to flank him, and they started walking. Otho gestured to Matthias and the others to follow, while he took up a position at the rear.

It wasn't long before their destination became clear: the café. Matthias glanced uneasily at Winston, who wore his usual baffled expression. Emerson and Denzel were making no eye contact whatsoever. Matt gazed around warily. Why had they been brought here? He suspected it wasn't for apple cake and cappuccinos.

The café was full. It had expanded further since his last visit. Hundreds of people were now drinking and laughing around the tables. Matt found this comforting. What possible impact could four Romans make here?

A few moments later they were standing on a newly created podium, and Otho was clearing his throat.

'Ladies and gentlemen,' he announced in his heavily accented English, 'we have come to select some additional staff for the magister's palace. Kindly remain seated while we choose who to take.'

The chatter died, and the people of Parallon gaped like spectators at an interesting entertainment. They continued to watch in bemused silence while Otho, Rufus and Pontius strode around the tables, pulling individuals from their seats. From time to time one of the guards would pause and glance at the magister standing motionless on the podium, checking for his approval on a particular choice.

Within a few minutes, a sizeable number of people had allowed themselves to be herded into a group beside him.

'Guard them,' Otho ordered in Latin, and suddenly Matthias, Winston and Emerson felt heavy knives in their hands. At the same moment, the Romans were also brandishing weapons . . . and finally the people of Parallon began to realize that this was not a game. Those still seated started to melt away, but those who had been selected just looked wildly from one Roman to another. Matthias held his knife loosely, willing his captives to run. And as if he had somehow transmitted that thought, a boy in a baseball cap and baggy jeans suddenly decided to do just that. He darted between Matt and Winston and began running as fast as he could.

Pontius's knife landed neatly between the boy's shoulder blades. Everyone gasped as he gave a strangled cry and fell. Pontius nodded to Matthias and Winston, who obediently hurried to collect him. Matthias knew the boy couldn't be actually killed in Parallon, but he could be hurt, and when Winston pulled out the dagger, the boy shrieked in agony. Matt and

Winston gently lifted him and carried him back towards the others. Nobody else tried running.

'Let that be a lesson to you all,' shouted Otho in his accented English, his lip curling disdainfully at the wounded captive. Then he turned towards the magister, who cocked his head, and the entire group set off in the direction of the palace, this time Pontius and Rufus striding at the rear.

As soon as they arrived, the Romans herded their quarry into the atrium.

'Clothe them suitably and get them housed,' ordered the magister, as his own suit dissolved seamlessly into a finely woven toga.

Almost before the sentence was out, the three guards had restored their own tunics and breastplates, and began replacing their captives' colourful mix of outfits with dark, roughly woven tunics of their own. Matt watched, transfixed, willing someone to object. But nobody dared say a word. Suddenly Pontius turned to him.

'Have you finished building the new quarters, Matthias?'

Matt's stomach twisted. Of course he hadn't. He hadn't even started on them. How was he to know they would be needed immediately?

'Nearly,' he croaked, running off in the appropriate direction. He had about a minute to erect something viable-looking before they all joined him, and he needed it to be good. This was his one chance to prove himself worthy to the magister. How many rooms had they indicated? He tried to remember the plans, which he'd left on the floor in the bathhouse. He hadn't counted the rooms on the sketch, but he guessed the Romans had just appropriated about thirty new people. He quickly created a series of chambers, and ranged them around a small atrium. Each of the four pillared corridors opened on to eight identical rooms. He was in no doubt now that these were to be slave quarters, so he had to be careful not to embellish. But he couldn't bring himself to replicate the small, dark, stinking cells he and Seth had endured in their Londinium days. Instead he supplied each room with a simple window, a clean bed, a table and chair. Maybe later, once the Romans had approved the building, he could add some sort of comforting water feature in the atrium. Nodding happily to himself, he was just on the point of creating the final chair when the marching troop appeared.

Pontius had clearly been expecting to catch Matthias in the midst of building chaos – his disappointment was palpable. So he strode into the first room, determined to find fault. It didn't take him long.

'What do you call that?' he bellowed in Latin.

'A w-window?' gulped Matthias.

Pontius rolled his eyes and instantly adjusted the mistake by reducing it to a narrow vertical slit, with a series of horizontal bars ranged down its length. The space was immediately transformed from a bedroom into a dark cell. And Pontius hadn't finished. The bed shrank before their eyes, finally settling into a thin mat on the floor.

Pontius nodded to Matthias, indicating he rectify all the other rooms. Sighing, Matt obediently set about completing his first prison, guiltily thanking the gods that at least he wasn't going to have to live in it.

33

Offer

'*Eva!*'

Astrid was banging on the window of the maths room, furiously pointing at her watch. I was late for our band meeting. Euler's equation would have to wait.

'Sorry, Astrid,' I mouthed through the window, as I gathered my books and headed out to join her.

'Did you forget?' she hissed indignantly, grabbing my bag of books and slinging them over her shoulder.

'Sort of.'

Astrid would assume that meant sort-of-*yes*. Actually it meant sort-of-*no*: I hadn't forgotten. I just wasn't in quite the massive hurry to have this band meeting as she was. Maybe because it was to be in Theo Mendes's office. And he had a proposal he wanted to discuss.

'The others are waiting by the arch. You'd better sign out with matron while I hook up with Sadie and Rob. Try to be convincingly healthy for Rose. Please!'

Rose's usual inquisition meant we arrived fifteen minutes late, but Scene Music seemed pretty chilled. A beautiful, heavily tattooed blonde called Gina pointed us towards a leather couch, but we didn't sit down because we were too busy being impressed by the framed gold discs and signed photos covering the walls. I studied a picture of Livid Turkey relaxing on a striped magenta sofa and realized suddenly that the room more or less represented the Astrid Hall of Greats – all her heroes were signed with Scene Music. No wonder this was such a big deal for her.

'Theo's ready for you now,' smiled Gina, motioning us towards an imposing panelled door.

'Hi, guys,' he said, coming round his desk and shaking our hands. I took a deep breath. This felt so serious and . . . adult. My eyes flitted around the room anxiously. I don't know what I'd been expecting but this wasn't it . . . oriental rugs, dark parquet floor, deep-red walls, heavy gilt picture frames – more Toulouse-Lautrec French brothel than high-tech record label office.

'Sit,' instructed Theo, waving us over to the large striped sofa I'd seen featured in the Livid Turkey photo. The Astronauts fitted on it with plenty of room to spare.

Theo settled back in his winged office chair and sat leaning on his elbows, his fingers steepled. He remained motionless for a few moments. Playing his power. 'Do you all know why you're here?'

Silence.

Astrid cleared her throat, but before she could say anything he continued.

'You're here because I'm interested in you. And I don't get interested very often . . .'

Dramatic pause.

I felt my eyes rolling. A muscle in his jaw twitched.

'. . . and with my interest comes my time, my resources and my expertise . . . I think the Astronauts could be huge – and nobody is in a better position to make that happen than Scene Music. We are the biggest independent label in the country. We know our stuff. We don't mess about – we plan meticulously . . .'

He had started to drone, so I zoned out – I had unexplained viruses to worry about.

'. . . agreed, Eva?'

Everyone was looking at me. I desperately tried to get my brain to rewind the conversation. It categorically refused. 'Er – sorry, I think I just missed that . . .'

Astrid's eyes widened in exasperation. 'Eva – Theo just wants to be sure that we're serious . . . We're deadly serious – aren't we.' That wasn't a question. Her elbow pushed sharply into my ribs.

'Yes,' I nodded.

'Good to hear,' murmured Theo, glancing dubiously at me. 'So, to recap,' he said, typing into his iPad, 'you're good for the Register Friday-night residency . . .'

What? Every week? When did that get agreed?

'And I'll start promoting the Underworld gig.'

'Y-you're booking us to p-play the Underworld?' I choked. 'B-but that's a huge venue. We –'

'Eva, we're not messing about here.' Long, pointed stare. 'That's the gig I'll be bringing all my people to. Also I'll need you guys to get parental consents to me ASAP for the half-term week mini tour –'

Hold it! Mini tour? 'Er – isn't that meant to be A-level study leave –' I coughed.

'Oh, come *on*, Eva,' hissed Astrid. 'You're already working at doctorate level, you don't need A-level study leave!'

I looked across at Rob and Sadie's grinning faces. I was definitely on my own here.

'Good,' said Theo. 'OK, I'll get this ball rolling. Your ages make it a bit of a logistic nightmare, but nothing insurmountable.'

We had a couple more minutes with everyone blahing about how great it was to be working together, and then we were heading for the door.

I was nearly through it, when Theo suddenly called my name.

'Can I just have a word?'

I turned back, frowning.

'We'll wait downstairs, Eva,' said Rob.

When the others had gone, Theo shut the door and perched on the edge of his desk.

'OK – so what's going on with you?'

'Nothing,' I mumbled.

'Look, I've been in this business fifteen years, and I've never offered so much and received so little back. This is an awesome opportunity – can't you see that?'

I bit my lip. What could I tell him? That I had bigger things on my mind? 'I'm sorry,' I croaked.

'I know you've been sick, Astrid mentioned it – but the tour isn't for a few weeks. And the Underworld isn't till July. Plenty of time to get back to full throttle.'

I nodded. Tell that to Dr Falana.

'The band needs you, Eva. You understand that, don't you?' Subtext: *Don't mess this up for everyone.*

I nodded again.

'Great. Then I'll see you Friday.'

'Friday?'

'At the Register.'

'Oh, yeah. Friday then.' I did my best attempt at a smile, and headed for the door.

When I opened it, I saw Theo had someone waiting for him . . . a tall guy with his back to us, examining the Livid Turkey on-the-sofa photo. When he heard me emerge, he turned. I froze. I was staring into the eyes of the guy from the Register. The one I had taken for a bioterrorist hitman: DI Nick Mullard.

And he stood equally frozen, staring back at me.

34

Betrayal

'Oh Christ,' groaned Theo behind me. 'Have you found Elena?'

I stood transfixed between them, knowing I shouldn't be here; this was way too personal. But for some reason I couldn't move. Theo's voice had at least broken the freeze for the detective, who frowned and shifted his focus off me.

'No, we haven't found her, Mr Mendes. I just had a couple of things to run by you.'

He was eyeing Theo coolly. Oh my God! Of course – Theo was a murder suspect. And I knew for a fact that Seth's friend, Matt, was responsible. I glanced back at Theo, horrified to see that the confident record producer behind me had just morphed into a dejected, frightened man.

At that moment Gina bustled through the door with a mug of coffee for the detective, but when she sensed our triangle of tension she stopped moving. My eyes darted around uncomfortably.

Again, it was Theo who broke the stasis. 'OK, Eva, I'll see you Friday then.'

I had been simultaneously dismissed and released. I bolted for the door and made my way downstairs. I was panting by the time I reached the outside of the building.

'Hey, Eva, what the hell did he say to you?' asked Rob. 'You're white.'

I just leaned against the door and shut my eyes. I needed to think. A few seconds later Astrid was shoving me into a cab, and we were on our way back to St Mag's.

When I opened the door to my room, Seth was sitting on my bed waiting for me, his hair still damp from the shower. I leaned against the door frame, gazing at him. There was something so peaceful about him after he'd been running. The tension in his limbs, the wariness of his features all melted away into mellow relaxation. But as soon as he saw me, his beautiful serenity was shadowed by concern.

'Eva, what's happened?'

He was by the door with his arms round me in moments, and I was inhaling the delicious blend of shower gel, damp clean skin and the familiar intoxicating scent that was just Seth. I leaned up to kiss him. His lips were warm and soft, and his breath was indescribably sweet. God, it was so easy to lose myself, to forget everything else, when I was with him. I hardly noticed his arms tighten, or my feet leave the floor, or the movement from door to bed. I was just aware that I had imperceptibly shifted from vertical to horizontal, and the boy I loved was holding me like he would never let me go.

At last I had to break away, or pass out. I lay gasping and

smiling, stroking loose dark curls from his eyes, willing this moment to last forever. But I could tell he was waiting for me to talk.

'You remember the Register gig, Seth?'

He frowned slightly, and nodded.

'The man and woman watching us? Well, I met the guy just now. He's a cop – er – a police detective. And he thinks Theo killed Elena.'

Seth sat up. I didn't have to say any more. He understood immediately what this meant, and why I was so worried.

'There is nothing plausible we can tell the police, Eva,' he whispered, running a finger between my eyebrows and trying to smooth the furrows. 'I think we're just going to have to let justice take its course.'

'But –'

'They can have no evidence linking Theo with Elena's disappearance, so how can they convict him?'

I nodded slowly. Seth was right. What grounds could they have to convict an innocent man? And what possible explanation could we offer that could help him? I was just going to have to let it go.

And I would have, if Astrid hadn't barged into the dining room at lunch the next day, rigid with tension.

'Eva, Gina from Scene Music just rang to say Theo hasn't been able to sort out our gig at the Register on Friday because he's *helping the police with their enquiries*! What the hell do you think that means?'

Damn. I knew exactly what it meant. Nick Mullard had taken Theo into custody. I pictured the scared man I'd left the day before and my heart sank.

It was Wednesday, so the whole afternoon would be taken up with PE. Seth had already been hauled off by the athletics team for some under-nineteens' competition in Greenwich, and I had no idea what time he'd be back. I really needed to talk to him. Surely we could think of some way to help Theo?

'What do you think he's done, Eva?' badgered Astrid, as she wolfed down her lasagne and started on the pudding. 'Some sort of drugs rap, I reckon. God, I hope this isn't going to get in the way of our rise to stardom!'

I stared at her, shocked at her callousness. But then I remembered she didn't know about Elena, so I said nothing and picked nervously at my risotto.

Astrid was just about to stand up for seconds when she glanced around the dining room and groaned. People were beginning to peel off with sports kits to all their various activities. 'Aw, Eva, you're so lucky to have got – like – *infinite* Wednesday-afternoon exemption!'

I laughed. 'Maybe you shouldn't have chosen to do *assault training*! There are easier ways of passing the time!'

'Yeah,' she sighed, 'but none of them are quite so kickass!'

'Fair point,' I snorted, standing up to clear away our trays. Astrid followed at a desultory pace, clearly in no hurry to go wading through swamps, or whatever it was they got up to. We headed out into the quad and she drifted off towards the training centre, while I made my way to my room.

Rose expected me to use the time to rest – that was the deal. And to be honest I was pretty wiped out; the bed did look kind of inviting. But I was feeling too guilty about Theo. It just didn't seem right to let him fester in custody, knowing he was being accused of something he didn't do.

I grabbed my laptop and pulled it over to the bed, figuring that as long as I was there, I was honouring my commitment to Rose. My fingers started typing even before I admitted to myself what I was planning to do. Nick Mullard, DI – his name appeared instantly in the search box, and it didn't take me long to find him. He worked for the City Police and was based at Wood Street station.

Before I could stop myself, I was ringing the enquiries number.

As soon as a woman picked up, I asked to speak to him, but was told he wasn't there.

'Is there a number I could reach him on?' I asked in my most confident voice.

'What is this in connection with?'

I hesitated. 'Elena Galanis.'

'Elena Galanis?' she repeated slowly. There was a pause. 'If you leave your name and number I'll get someone to call you back.'

Damn. I definitely didn't want to talk to anyone else.

'Er – no, it's OK . . . I'll – er – catch him another time . . .' I was about to hang up when the woman on the other end said, 'I've logged your number. If you tell me your name, I'll make sure DI Mullard gets the message.'

I hesitated again, realizing how stupid I'd been to phone from my mobile, without setting an ID block first. But since they had my mobile number now, did it make much difference if I gave them my name? Probably not.

'Eva Koretsky,' I sighed, and hung up.

He rang back an hour later. From a mobile. And he didn't withhold the number. Which I guess meant we were kind of quits.

'You wanted to talk to me,' he said, voice characteristically cool.

Suddenly I didn't know what to say or how to say it. 'Er, y-yes . . .' I stammered.

'About Elena Galanis,' he prompted.

'Yes.' Big pause, as I realized just what an idiot I'd been to leave my number.

'Are you worried about talking over the phone?'

No. I was worried about talking *at all*. This was a thoroughly bad idea. Seth was right. What the hell could I actually say? *My boyfriend's friend from Parallon – which happens to be in an alternative universe – accidentally killed Elena Galanis and took her back there?* Very plausible.

'Eva? Are you still there?'

I cleared my throat. I wanted to put the phone down, but I knew that if I did he would probably ring again. God, what had I done?

'Eva, would you prefer to come and talk at the station? Or – or I could meet you somewhere? Anywhere.'

A meeting? No way. I had to bite the bullet. 'I-I just wanted to tell you that Th-Theo Mendes had nothing to do with it.'

'Theo Mendes had nothing to do with what, Eva?'

'With Elena's – er – disappearance.'

'Her disappearance.'

Why the hell was he repeating everything I said?

'You know Theo?'

'A bit.'

'And Elena?'

'No – but –'

'But?'

There – he was doing it again. Was this some sort of DI technique? Because it was beginning to get on my nerves.

'Look, detective,' I wasn't exactly sure how to address a DI, 'all I wanted to say is that it can't be legal to take someone into custody without any evidence against him.'

'I haven't taken him into custody.'

I swallowed. Why was he lying? Or had Astrid got it wrong?

'But I saw you –'

'Saw me what?' he said quickly.

My stomach tightened. I was getting out of my depth. I wanted to hang up so badly.

'So why do you think Theo Mendes is innocent?' Nick Mullard persisted.

I bit my lip. 'I just don't think a man should be taken into custody without any evidence against him,' I repeated with slightly less conviction.

'How would you know what evidence we have against him?'

'Well, if you have any evidence it can only be fabricated – because I know for a fact that he had nothing to do with it.'

'And how do you know that, Eva?'

There was nothing I could tell him, so I disconnected the call.

He tried to phone me back of course. Five times. But I obviously didn't pick up.

I decided Seth didn't need to know about this particular humiliation. It would all blow over, Theo would get released, and DI Nick Mullard would forget all about my embarrassing phone call.

The next morning I had nine missed calls and a text message from DI Mullard:

> I'd like to meet you today. Name a good place and time.

Damn. Probably if Seth had been there I would have asked his advice. But he had gone to pick us up some breakfast. I sat on the side of my bed, wondering what to do. In the end I decided there was only one option: ignore it.

At 4 p.m. I got a second text:

> Alternatively I could meet you there? I am sure your head-master, Dr Crispin, would be accommodating.

Oh God. He'd found out where I lived. This so wasn't going to blow over. I thought about my evening schedule. Seth would be running until about 6 p.m. Dinner was at 6.30 and I had a physics lecture at 7 p.m. Which meant if it was going to be today – and it didn't look like I had a lot of choice – it would have to be soon.

I punched his number. He picked up after one ring.

'Eva, I'm glad you phoned.'

'There's a Starbucks a block away from the school. I could meet you there in twenty minutes.'

'Make it thirty,' he said, and hung up.

Half an hour was better. It meant I could do my daily check-in with Rose before I left. I just caught her on her way to drop off a prescription, but she didn't seem to mind the delay too much. Temperature, normal; blood pressure, OKish; pulse –

'It's racing, Eva. Is everything OK?'

'Yeah, fine,' I lied.

She narrowed her eyes at me and said, 'Drop by this evening – after the lecture. I want to double-check you then.'

I sighed. 'Rose – I honestly don't –'

'Eva, either you drop by later, or you move back in. Your call.'

'OK, OK! I'll see you later, Rose,' I said in my ultra-sweet voice.

'Good. I'll look forward to it. Oh – and enjoy the lecture. What's it on?'

'Dark Matter,' I said, a little frisson of excitement worming its way through the thick layer of anxiety. 'We've got an astrophysicist coming from Minnesota. It's going to be awesome.'

I was about to tell her about his work on quantifying dark-matter particles, when I caught sight of the clock. I only had five minutes to get to Starbucks. Running had been out of the question for months. Even walking that distance was a challenge. Which meant that by the time I arrived there it was 4.39 and Nick Mullard was already seated and looking at his watch.

I didn't expect him to recognize me. Apart from the gig, which he probably wouldn't remember, he'd seen me in Theo's office for, like, thirty seconds.

But his eyes widened as soon as he saw me. 'God, it's you!' he breathed.

I dropped into the chair opposite him. The walk had just about finished me.

'Are you OK?' he demanded. 'You don't look so good.'

I nodded, and pressed my hands into my lap. They were shaking. Along with my legs.

'What would you like to drink?' he asked.

I wasn't sure if I could trust my hands not to slop a drink, but I was thirsty.

'Water would be great, thanks.'

He stood up and went over to the counter. I watched him, my stomach churning. I willed the girl serving to be slow and incompetent; I needed time to gather myself. Unfortunately, she was fast and efficient. He was back at the table in record time with a glass of water for me, an espresso for him, and a couple of muffins.

'Help yourself,' he said, sliding the plate over. 'You look like you could use some nourishment.'

The way I was feeling, the muffins couldn't have been less appetizing if they'd been made of ground glass.

'So, you're a singer,' he began.

'Well –'

'I saw your band at the Register . . . The Astronauts? You were good. Better than the Lasers, I thought.'

I stared at him. Why was he being nice? Was this a police technique?

'So is that what you were doing at Theo's? Has he signed you?'

'He's thinking about it,' I said, staring down at my water.

He was frowning. 'Shouldn't you be ecstatic? Isn't being signed like the Holy Grail?'

I nodded non-committally. I really wanted to take a drink from my glass, but I couldn't risk it.

He took a sip from his espresso and pulled off a chunk from the chocolate muffin, which he chewed ruminatively.

'So why are you trying to protect Theo?' he asked finally.

I shot him a startled look. 'I'm not trying to protect him – I hardly know him. I just happen to be pretty certain he didn't do anything to Elena . . . and I'm not a major fan of injustice.'

'So why are you so sure he didn't do away with Elena?'

I pressed my lips together and glanced up at him. He held my gaze, searching my eyes curiously. How much could I tell him? How much would he believe?

'Because . . . because I know where she is.'

'She's alive?'

Oh God, where was I going with this? 'Ye-es, she is alive . . . b-but she can't come back here.'

'She's being held somewhere, a prisoner?'

'Not exactly.' Not unless you counted Time as a jailor. Elena would never be able to come back to her own time.

'Eva, whatever you know you *have* to tell me . . .'

I stared at him. 'I can't,' I muttered.

'Are you frightened? Have you been threatened?'

I shook my head.

'Look, you know it's your legal obligation, right? I could have you arrested for obstruction . . . And I won't hesitate to do that if you give me nothing else.'

'Arrest me then,' I sighed, standing up to leave. I wasn't a great fan of threats either.

His arm shot out and he pulled me back down.

'Look, I don't know what it is you know, but you've got to trust me.'

'Trust you?' I laughed. 'You've arrested an innocent man, and you've just threatened me.'

'OK, Eva . . . then help me out here. You approached me, remember? Why? You're a St Mag's kid for Christ's sake – you can't be stupid. You must have known you couldn't just say

"Theo Mendes is innocent" without giving me something else? What am I supposed to do with that? I can't simply release him because a teenage schoolgirl tells me I should.'

'Sorry. You're right. I *was* being stupid. I don't know what I was thinking,' I answered shakily, trying to get up again. My head was beginning to pound.

He put a hand on my shoulder and pressed me gently back into my seat.

'You weren't being stupid, Eva. You were trying to do the right thing . . . Now you just need to follow through.'

I shook my head and closed my eyes. Maybe I could will the headache away. Maybe I could will DI Mullard away.

'What if I convinced you that you *could* trust me?'

I laughed hollowly. 'How on earth do you suppose you could do that?'

'By trading. By giving you information that would crucify me if it got back.'

'Why would you do that?'

'Because – believe it or not – I am on your side. I don't want an innocent man in jail . . . I also believe in justice. I trust you're telling me the truth, and I want to help Theo.'

The guy was so damned clever, trying to trap me with my own argument. But he had succeeded in disarming me a little. Or was it the headache? Because I seemed to be finding it harder to hold on to my convictions.

'Let's hear it then,' I sighed.

He looked down at the table for a moment, then cleared his throat. 'OK, here goes my career,' he said huskily. 'The truth is, I'm no longer working this case. I didn't have Theo arrested, MI5 did – I was there to warn him yesterday. And the reason

I'm risking my job, the reason I'm still obsessing on this case, is because I am sure there is a horrible pattern beginning to emerge, and I don't think MI5 have a clue.'

He was right. He would be crucified if that got back.

My throat was so dry that I had to risk the humiliation of the water glass. It did slop, and he did notice, but he didn't say anything.

I leaned back in my chair. I needed to lie down. I was feeling dizzy. If I didn't finish this meeting soon I'd be keeling over. I had to give Nick Mullard something. Something that would clear Theo.

I swallowed. 'There's a virus –' I began.

His eyes shot up.

'The symptoms are pretty rare.' I cleared my throat. 'I-I think I may be the only person to have survived it.'

'What are the symptoms?'

'Fever, vomiting, total organ failure, cardiac arrest and –'

He nodded. 'Go on . . .' he urged.

'– and then . . .'

'*What?* What happens next, Eva?' He was leaning forward in his chair, his eyes bright. Almost as if he *knew*. Why else was he asking that question so insistently? I was teetering on the precipice now. And I wanted to jump. Seth and I had been alone with this for too long. Surely it would be good to have someone else on board?

I took a deep breath. 'A-and then . . . Para–'

The door suddenly swung open and Seth, still in his running gear, was striding towards our table. 'What's going on here, Eva?' he said quietly, his voice tight.

I coughed. 'Er, Seth, this is D-DI Mullard.'

Seth nodded, instantly recognizing him from the night at the Register. He shifted his position slightly, so that he was standing between me and DI Mullard, one hand resting protectively on the back of my chair.

'I need to get Eva back to school now,' he said smoothly, but his eyes blazed. DI Mullard couldn't look away.

'Are you OK to walk, baby?' he asked me, momentarily breaking their eye contact.

I frowned, but stood shakily. He put an arm round my shoulders and started motioning me towards the door.

'*Stop right there*,' called the detective, hurrying after us.

The whole room went suddenly silent. Everyone was watching.

Seth stopped moving and turned round. I couldn't see his expression, but I could see DI Mullard's. His brow furrowed, then his whole face went slack. He was still standing completely motionless in the middle of the floor as Seth steered us out of the door.

The second we were on the street, Seth dropped his arm. If he hadn't, I would have shaken it off. We were both furious.

'What did you just do?' I asked through gritted teeth, grabbing on to a lamp post for support.

'Got us safely out of there,' he answered, his voice equivalently taut with the effort of keeping control.

'We were in no danger!' I spluttered.

He looked at me wildly. 'Eva, I was protecting you. Protecting us.'

'That wasn't protecting me. That was controlling me. Big difference.'

'I had no choice,' he said bleakly.

'Neither did I,' I gulped. 'MI5 have taken Theo into custody. I couldn't just let justice take its course. Justice isn't reliable.'

'So what believable defence for Theo were you about to offer?'

I swallowed. 'The virus. I was g-going to tell him about the virus.'

'And where does the virus lead?'

'To Parallon,' I whispered.

'And you were going to tell the nice policeman all about Parallon?'

I slumped against the lamp post and nodded.

Seth was staring at me like I had lost my mind. And a small, intact corner of my brain couldn't help agreeing with him. What had I been thinking? I had no more faith in authority figures than Seth did – they had consistently failed me. DI Mullard was unlikely to be any different. So why had I started spilling information to him? Because I thought it would help Theo? Because he looked so desperate? Because it felt like maybe we had an ally in him?

'Look, Seth, perhaps it's time other people knew about the virus . . . if it *is* some sort of biological weapon –'

'So how were you planning to convince DI Mullard?' he asked very quietly.

I shrugged. I hadn't got that far, but as I looked up at Seth, I instantly understood what he was saying. There was only one way to convince Nick Mullard about our virus, and that was to take him into the lab and show him Seth's blood. And then what? What would happen to Seth . . . the living carrier of such a unique and lethal pathogen? I couldn't even begin to imagine what scientists would want to do with him.

I looked down at my feet. Seth was right again. I had totally screwed up. I was just about to admit it and apologize when we became aware of Nick Mullard leaving Starbucks and running in our direction. Seth immediately stood in front of me, blocking any chance of further contact.

'Seth, let me handle it this time,' I hissed, struggling to get free.

'No,' he murmured.

So I was forced to watch the guy walk towards us, stand frozen in the middle of the pavement for a few moments, then frown, shake his head and turn in the opposite direction. When he was finally out of range, Seth moved away from me – by which time I was fuming.

'You did it again, Seth!' I exploded.

'I had to,' he shrugged.

'No, you didn't! I could have talked to him, told him I'd invented the whole thing . . . I dunno . . . I would have come up with something. You didn't need to do your mind-control thing!'

'Eva, I had no choice. You wouldn't have got rid of him. He's fascinated by you now . . .'

'Oh for God's sake, Seth! The only thing Nick Mullard's fascinated by is what I can tell him.'

'That too, yes . . .' he agreed. He was staring after the disappearing figure thoughtfully. 'I just don't understand how he managed to find you.'

There was a moment's silence. 'I phoned him,' I admitted defiantly.

Seth's eyes widened. 'You did *what*?'

'Anyway – how the hell did *you* find us?' I parried.

He looked at me then, his face a frozen mask of shock. Like I had just punched him. My stomach twisted. The words had come out wrong. I wanted to rewind, say I was sorry. But I didn't say anything.

After a couple of moments of icy silence, Seth cleared his throat. 'Are you OK to get back to school from here?' he asked quietly.

We were about forty metres from the entrance. I nodded.

'I'll – I'll see you, then,' he murmured, turning away from me.

A few moments later he was just a tiny flash of colour in the distance, and I was staring numbly after him, silently begging him to turn round and come back.

I don't know how long I stood there, unable to move. I don't know how long it had been raining when I finally realized I was soaked through and shivering. I looked down at my dripping clothes and frowned. What was I doing out here? I had to go and find Seth. Apologize. My legs were so unsteady that it seemed to take forever to drag myself back to school. When I finally made it through the arch, I headed straight for Seth's house. Rain hammered relentlessly down on the empty quad – nobody wanted to be out in this. Surely Seth wouldn't still be running? But his room was empty. I sat on the chair at his desk to wait, staring out of the window at the water thudding against the glass, praying he was OK, and hadn't skidded and fallen. When the light began to fade and he still hadn't returned, my stomach was a tight ball of fear. I forced my legs back across the quad and over to the running track. It was floodlit as usual, but the lights picked out only the glistening needles of rain and the deserted track.

I turned away. There was no point staying here. If Seth was still running he could be anywhere, the whole of London was his running track. And I knew he could run indefinitely. So where should I go? I looked at my watch. The physics lecture was about to start. Was it possible Seth could have gone straight there? He'd been as excited by it as I was.

When I arrived, it looked as though the whole school had turned up for the lecture. I scanned the faces desperately until I could pretend no longer. He wasn't there. Unable to face returning to my room, I spent the rest of the evening sitting on the edge of one of the big planters in the quad, watching the rain and willing him to return.

35
Force

Parallon

'How many more?' Georgia whispered to Winston. They were crouched behind a peristyle column staring out at the practice arena, where Otho, Rufus and Pontius were training up their newest recruits.

Georgia had counted twenty of them out there. Which brought the total number of new guards up to sixty-five.

'Issuing discipline' was this evening's training task. They'd watched with growing revulsion as a succession of newly acquired slaves were brought before the trainee guards for a variety of punishments. Rufus would choose the slave, Pontius would choose the guard, Otho would choose the punishment.

Winston and Georgia were about to witness the fifteenth of the evening. It was a flogging. The victim was tied to a post and the selected guard was given a long whip and told to lash the man fifty times.

By the seventeenth stroke the man's back was in ribbons; by the twentieth he was unconscious; by the twenty-fifth Winston and Georgia had seen all they could stomach. Not one of the guards had asked what the slave was being punished for. Not one had flinched at the task he was given – whether it was kicking a man into a bloody heap or hanging him by his feet.

Georgia signalled with her eyes, and she and Winston crawled silently through the shadows back towards the atrium. 'Come on,' she breathed, heading further along the marble passage.

'Where are you going, Georgia?' hissed Winston in alarm.

'Where do you think I'm going?' she snarled, knocking quietly on the closed door they now faced.

The door opened and Matthias stood on the threshold. When he saw them he looked around wildly and beckoned them quickly inside. 'In the name of Zeus, what are you doing here?' he rasped.

'Where are they getting the bastards from, Matt?'

'What are you talking about, Georgia?' Matt swallowed.

'The new guards – I've never seen guys like them around Parallon.'

Matthias shrugged. 'People are always arriving here.'

'Yeah – but these guys look like they've been specially selected for their brutality. Have you *seen* them?'

Matt didn't answer. Of course he'd seen them – although he was doing everything in his power to stay out of their sight lines.

'What the hell are the Romans up to?' hissed Winston. 'They virtually control the whole place: they've posted guards on most street corners; if they see more than three people talking they systematically break them up; they've shut down the café . . .'

'They've even started replacing all the buildings,' said Georgia.

'*Enough!*' snapped Matthias. 'You shouldn't be here.' The last thing he needed was for slaves to be found in his chamber.

'Matt, for God's sake, how can you be on their side?' gulped Georgia. 'You've seen what they've done to Parallon. You've seen how they treat us. I thought you were our friend – how could you desert us?'

'I don't have to listen to this!' snarled Matt, flinging the door open.

What right did she have to judge him for being on the side of the masters this time round? And it hadn't been easy. He'd had to work really hard for the position he now held. Thankfully the magister was very pleased with his palace renovations – so pleased that he had started giving Matt prestigious building remodelling projects all over Parallon. But the Romans were volatile. He couldn't afford to be found with two slaves in his room. He had to get rid of them.

'Just *get out*, Georgia!' Matt snorted, shoving her through the door.

'Seth would never have abandoned us,' she sobbed, as she pulled Winston out. 'Seth would have stood up to them.'

Matt slammed the door behind them, willed himself a large cup of wine and gulped it down. He was breathing so hard he could barely swallow, but as soon as he'd finished that cup he willed himself another. How dare Georgia talk to him about Seth? How dare she idolize him like that?

Seth had abandoned them all.

36

Capitulation

St Magdalene's

Early Friday Morning, 10 May AD *2013*

Seth stood next to Eva, watching her sleep. Her breathing was soft but a little hoarse, and there was a worrying rattle in her chest. He scrutinized her face for signs of developing fever. Her skin was pale, almost bloodless, except just beneath her eyes – where the colour deepened, appearing slightly bruised. He lightly brushed a strand of hair away from her face. Her cheeks were hot. Too hot. He pushed the duvet back from her body, hoping to cool her. She stirred slightly, but didn't wake.

By the time he had finally stopped running, the St Mag's curfew had come and gone; and the clock next to Eva's bed read 1 a.m. Yet he still hadn't found the peace he sought. His thoughts – no – his feelings remained a mess: vacillating between fear, jealousy, betrayal and self-hatred. And they all centred – as ever – around the girl he was gazing at; the girl he loved more than life itself. Her eyelids fluttered. He held his breath, willing her to wake up. He wanted to talk to her so badly . . . to find his way back to her. But what could he say?

He was still reeling from her revelation . . . still unsure which hurt the most: the fact that she had phoned the detective without talking to him first, or that she had been on the point of telling the man *everything*.

No . . . he wasn't being honest with himself. It was neither of those things. What really hurt, the real knife in the gut, were her words. They had been the rhythmic chant fuelling his marathon-length run . . . '*How the hell did you find us?*'

He had played them around his head, trying to extract a meaning that would feel less like a betrayal . . . but there wasn't one. The meaning was absolutely clear. She hadn't wanted him there.

How *had* he found her, anyway? What strange instinct had stopped him during his normal running circuit and compelled his legs to carry him there? He hadn't understood it, but he'd always followed his instincts, they'd never failed him before. This time, though, they'd let him down spectacularly.

He took a shuddering breath, reached out and ran a finger lightly along her cheek. She flinched and he quickly took his hand away. He shouldn't have come. He was tormenting himself and disturbing her. And she needed to sleep.

His watch alarm vibrated – 2 a.m. He frowned at it for a moment, until he remembered that they'd been planning to go into the lab tonight. She'd finally convinced him that he could stall no longer – they *had* to put their blood together.

He laughed humourlessly. At least that was one painful experiment he wouldn't have to put himself through right now. He really hadn't relished the thought of watching his blood cells annihilate hers.

With Nick Mullard she would be safe, a harsh voice in his

head taunted. *Mullard's blood isn't laced with a lethal virus. Maybe Eva would even start to get well if you were out of her life.*

His heart hammered against his chest. *No.* He and Eva belonged together. They loved each other. Nobody could come between them. In the morning they would talk and everything would be all right. Cautiously, soundlessly, he sank down on to the mattress beside her. A heavy lock of hair had fallen across her face. He was gently smoothing it back when he noticed the thin stream of blood trickling from her nose.

His stomach twisted. Not good. He reached across the bed for a tissue and gently dabbed it away.

Please get well, baby, he silently begged. He had faced daily fear in his life as a gladiator, but he had never known dread like this. The terror of losing her was choking him. He looked down at the blood-stained tissue clenched in his fist and took a long shuddering breath. It was time. He had to do it.

He tenderly touched her lips with his own and eased himself up from the bed. He pulled the biology lab keys from his sports bag and shoved them in his pocket, then curled his hand round the tissue. It was time to face his fear.

37

Persuasion

St Magdalene's

Early Friday Morning, 10 May AD 2013

Seth shivered slightly as he surveyed the quad. It was raining. And dark. And . . . something didn't feel quite right. He glanced across towards the biology lab – his destination. It looked exactly as it usually did, but Seth remained uneasy. He felt watched.

He couldn't ignore his instincts, so he stood a moment longer, deliberating. Then he turned nonchalantly back towards the doorway he'd just come through and sat on the edge of the stone urn beside it to retie his shoelaces. The urn stood just under the porch and housed a miniature fir tree surrounded by waning primroses. By the time Seth had finished on his shoelaces, the urn also concealed the biology lab keys and a newly acquired blood sample.

Seth straightened and began a couple of leg stretches. As he practised his lunges, he listened. Yes. Behind the rain, he could sense something else. Someone was definitely here. Before he'd completed his quad stretches, he knew exactly where.

It was possible that the intruder was just an opportunist thief, who had no agenda other than to grab a few PCs and some hard drives. But Seth didn't think that was likely. If Eva's bioterrorist theory was correct, then it was simply a matter of time before someone turned up and targeted her, and his instinct to protect her was all-consuming: any danger had to be eliminated.

He glanced quickly around the dark quad on the off-chance of finding some sort of useable weapon – a discarded baseball bat, a spade – anything. But he could see nothing at all. He would have to rely on his own strength and speed.

The moment Seth adjusted his weight to run, the balance and shape of his entire body realigned and he moved so quickly that he was at the archway with his hands around the intruder's throat before the man had even registered his predicament.

Less than a second later, Seth's hands had dropped. 'Zackary! What the hell are you doing here?'

Zackary was too busy coughing to answer.

'I could have killed you!' Seth ranted. 'What were you thinking, coming here in the middle of the night?'

Zack swallowed cautiously. 'What are you doing, randomly attacking strangers, Seth? Missing the arena?'

'How many random strangers do you think we get at St Magdalene's?' Seth spat back.

'Someone's rattled your cage, haven't they?'

Seth didn't answer.

'I was expecting you to come home.'

'*This* is my home.'

'Oh, please! A boarding school? Are you reliving some childhood idyll?'

'What kind of childhood do you imagine I had, Zack?' said Seth dangerously.

Zackary leaned wearily against the wall of the archway and took a deep, shuddering breath. 'Don't make me beg, Sethos.'

'I'm staying here,' said Seth firmly.

Zackary stared impassively at him. 'What's keeping you here, Seth? It has to be more than your little research project.'

'Oh, excuse me for believing that an escalating, decimating virus is worthy of attention. Clearly there are far more pressing things to consider.'

'There are,' said Zackary quietly.

'Oh yes – a population explosion in Parallon! Why do you think I'm here, Zackary? We both know the virus is the key.'

Zackary nodded. 'You're right, Seth. The virus is the key. But the door isn't here.'

'For God's sake! When are you going to stop talking in bloody riddles and give me some useful information?' exploded Seth.

'As soon as you come back to Parallon.'

'I told you. I'm staying here.'

'Why here, Seth? What's so great about here?'

'You wouldn't understand,' muttered Seth, walking away.

Zack grabbed his shoulder. 'Try me.'

Seth paused for a moment, staring down at Zack's hand. It was covered with cuts and bruises. He frowned. He'd barely touched Zack, hadn't he?

Seeing where Seth's eyes fell, Zack quickly pulled his hand away. 'Look, Seth – whatever you have here – whatever you're protecting –'

Seth turned away furiously. How had Zack picked up on that?

'– whatever you think it is you're guarding . . . it won't survive. Everything is threatened. In this world. And in Parallon. The dequilibrium is escalating . . .' Zackary's voice shook with intensity. 'We're out of time, Seth.'

Seth frowned at Zackary, searching for the sarcasm; the game; the hostile condescension. But Zackary wasn't playing. He was deadly serious. And because Seth had so much knowledge of Zackary from the inside, he also knew how much this would be costing him – to have had to come here twice; to have had to appeal to Seth of all people . . .

He glanced involuntarily towards Eva's room.

Zackary sighed. 'If you don't come, this world will be lost anyway . . . everything that you care about will die. But if you come now, and we get this right, you can return to this exact moment and you will have lost no time here at all.'

Seth nodded slowly. If he were accurate in his intention, he would not actually need to leave Eva for more than a few moments. She would never have to know he'd gone.

He breathed out heavily, staring reluctantly at her door, every particle of his body longing to return to that room.

'OK,' he said finally. 'We'd better get going.'

38

Rewind

St Magdalene's

Friday 10 May AD 2013

'Seth?'

I reached out for the delicious warmth of his body . . . but he wasn't there. I sat up and blinked blearily around at my chilly St Mag's bedroom, desperately trying to hold on to the comfort of my dream: our grassy summer meadow, Seth leaning over me . . .

But the image evaporated as memory slammed into me: the argument; my stupid, stupid words . . . *How the hell did you find us?*

I had been genuinely curious to know how he'd worked out where I was, but I'd been so angry and ashamed that my words had come out totally wrong. God – the look in his eyes . . .

I stared at the clock. 6.30 a.m. He must be back by now. I *had* to find him; had to tell him I was sorry. I threw the duvet off, but the room was so cold, my body began to shudder in horrible uncontrollable waves. How could it be so freezing in May?

I squeezed my eyes shut and tried to concentrate on holding my limbs still. The alarm suddenly shrieked, sounding more strident than the fire bell. What had happened to my clock? I thrust an arm out to silence it, but now my hand was shaking so much the alarm was flung to the floor, where – thank God – it stopped. Had my head been pounding before that awful noise? I tried to remember. Another wave of intense shivering swept over me.

A hot shower. That would do the trick.

I pulled the duvet round my shoulders and looked across towards the cubicle. It had done the old *Alice in Wonderland* trick of retreating – and was miles away.

Get a grip! Rooms don't change shape. The shower hasn't moved.

I shut my eyes again. Maybe I was still dreaming. Yes – this was some weird nightmare. I just needed to go back to sleep. Everything would be OK when I woke up.

'Eva!'

Someone was shouting. Right in my ear. Not helping the headache.

I groaned. Tried to respond. Tried to shape words in my mouth. Nothing came out. The shouting started up again.

'Eva? Can you hear me? Wake up, Eva!'

I could feel hands on my shoulders, shaking me. *Let go!* Did I say that or did I just think it?

'Eva, you're burning up. Eva! Eva! Please –'

I tried to place the voice. I was sure I knew it.

Come on, open your eyes, I told myself. What had happened to my eyelids? Why were they so heavy?

The shouting had stopped. Thank God. My shoulders were free. I could hear someone panting. Really close. Too close. A distant tapping, a beeping. I had to open my eyes. What was happening? Oh no. That voice – it was shouting again.

'*Rose – you'd better come quick –*'

Rose. That name rang a bell. But it wasn't the right name. I searched around for the one I was missing . . .

Footsteps . . . banging . . . *Hey, please keep it down – I've got a headache.*

'*There's blood everywhere, Rose –*'

'It's OK, Astrid. Spilt blood always looks worse than it is.'

'Christ, the pillow's soaking –'

'She's just had a nosebleed, Astrid. And she's sweating. It's the fever. Get the duvet off her, open the window . . . I'll get her cleaned up a bit. I wonder where Seth is – I would have expected him to ring me . . .'

Seth. That was it. That was the name . . . Where was he?

I felt my body go rigid. Panic. *Seth?*

'Eva, breathe!' Rose's voice was shouting at me. I flinched. I felt my chest vibrate. Oh yes. In. Out. In. Out. That was better.

'Eva?'

Why did she have to shout so loud? I wasn't deaf.

'Eva, can you hear me?'

Of course I could hear her. She had a voice like a foghorn. I tried to laugh, but couldn't remember how.

And then the word *laugh* got all mixed up . . . and kept sliding around my head blending with other words, confusing me . . . laugh . . . love . . . live . . . lie . . . line . . . lying . . . lyre . . . kith-kitha – kithara – words . . . jumbled, messed-up words . . . that had me clawing around the murky darkness for their meaning . . . an endless wading, punctuated only by sudden sharp noises that would make me jump, interrupting the swirling tangle . . .

And as I crawled around this buzzing swamp, I listened. I was waiting to hear something . . . a voice . . . but I couldn't catch it . . . I would just have to go and find it. I was on a mission. Searching for this thing . . . But it was so hot – crawling through this swamp. Why was it so hot? I just had to keep going . . . my mission . . . Mission? What mission? I couldn't remember . . . Needed to rest . . . Couldn't stop – had to find something . . . but I was so tired . . . so tired of crawling around in the heat . . . maybe if I just lay down for a moment . . .

'Eva, stay with me!'

Stay where? Where was I? Pain everywhere . . . shoving me . . . throwing me . . . panic . . . fear . . . *Cassius?* . . . *Oh God, please not Cassius* . . . screaming . . . no sound . . .

Let me go! . . . Please let me sleep . . .

'I think she may be stabilizing.'

Beeping . . . a rhythmic, comforting, familiar sound, a memo to my errant organs, reminding them of the necessary pattern . . . in, out, in, out . . .

I opened my eyes. Bright lights, machines . . .

I knew where I was. I knew what the suffocating mask over my mouth meant, I recognized the weight and tightness on the back of my hand, the raw throat and the punched-in-the-chest ache . . .

My eyes took a moment to adjust to the light, the faint memory of the headache still whispering around my temples, but I felt like me again. I understood who I was and where I was. I had survived the dark swamp, and the unfathomable mission, and lived to see another day . . . only someone was missing.

'Seth?' I croaked, pulling the mask off my face.

The nurse who was adjusting the drip peered down at me and gave me a big patronizing smile.

'Hello, dear! Glad to have you back!'

I blinked at her.

'Do you know where you are, sweetie?'

I don't care where I am. 'Seth?' I said again, more urgently this time.

'Hey, hey,' said the nurse soothingly, reaching down and touching my shoulder. 'Don't get excited! Your best friend's right here. She's hardly left your side.'

The nurse's eyes glanced at the chair next to my bed, where a girl was curled up, eyes shut, lightly snoring.

'Astrid?' I rasped.

Astrid jerked awake, and when she saw me peering at her, jumped up, grinning. 'Bloody hell, Eva! I was beginning to think you were never going to wake up. Nobody needs that much sleep!'

'Sorry,' I sighed. 'How long have I been here?'

Astrid shrugged uneasily. 'Oh, I dunno – a few days, I guess.'

'Oh God, Astrid! You shouldn't be wasting time here – what about school?'

'Got exemption!' She grinned smugly. 'Special circumstances. Brilliant, really. I mean – I managed to get out of that philosophy seminar – you know, the one that *someone* was s'posed to be priming me for?'

'Oops,' I muttered.

And that was about all I managed on that conversation. I found my eyelids shutting, and I couldn't seem to stop them.

'Eva? Eva!'

I frowned. Was nobody around here going to let me get some sleep?

I huffed grumpily and opened my eyes. About ten people were gathered round my bed. I glanced across at the chair Astrid had been sitting in. It was empty.

'Good morning, Eva,' said a familiar voice.

'Dr Falana,' I sighed.

'Back again so soon?'

'Must be your magnetic personality . . .'

Dr Falana chuckled and turned to his students.

'Eva Koretsky. You have all seen her notes. This is her fourth admission, and the most severe. She arrested in the ambulance and twice more in A & E. When defibrillation, adrenalin and atropine failed to stabilize her, we had to resort to transcutaneous pacing. It was touch and go there for a while.'

Great. Just what I wanted to hear.

'On none of Eva's four hospital admissions have we been able to identify any specific viral or bacterial trigger; and lymphocyte reaction again doesn't suggest any standard viral response. However, we did detect some unusual signs of neutrophil toxic granulation. Any ideas about what this could mean?' Dr Falana stared round the group with raised eyebrows.

Blank silence.

'OK, toxic granulation? Anybody?'

No response.

Dr Falana sighed. 'Dark, coarse granules found in the white

cells – the granulocytes to be precise. And to be super-precise, in the neutrophils.'

Dark, coarse granules? Was that what Seth and I saw under the microscope?

'Er – do they look like faint dark clusters, Dr Falana?' I asked.

The consultant cocked his head. He'd forgotten about the annoying interloper in the bed. 'Yes – they do sometimes cluster . . .'

'So what does granulation signify?'

'Well, Eva, it indicates some kind of inflammatory response, which would be consistent with a fever like yours . . . But, again, inflammation can be caused by any number of infection triggers – viruses . . . bacteria, prions . . . We ran a few PCRs for some potential identification, but couldn't get any kind of match.'

Surprise, surprise.

'But I'm OK now?'

'For now – yes. Organ function is pretty good, your blood oxygen levels are passable – not perfect, but reasonable – and your heart rhythm seems to be stable. But – your history suggests it likely that this won't be the last episode. You need to be prepared for that, Eva. Do you understand what I am saying?'

'That the next time my heart stops – you might not be there to kick-start it up again?'

Dr Falana nodded, chewing his lip uncomfortably.

'Maybe Eva would be a good candidate for a heart transplant?' suggested one of the students perkily.

I knew what Dr Falana was going to say before he said it.

'It's not simply Eva's heart that's the problem here . . .' he said quietly.

There was an awkward silence and everyone did their best to avoid any eye-contact with me. I decided to put them out of their misery by closing my eyes and pretending to go to sleep.

When I next opened them, the room was empty.

I lay gazing up at the ceiling with a knot of anxiety building in my stomach.

This was all happening too fast.

Nothing Dr Falana had said was exactly a surprise, but I had been banking on more time.

Time at St Mag's. Time with Seth.

I clenched my fists.

Seth.

Where was he?

39

Mission

Parallon

Seth was doubled over, dripping wet and panting, beside the Parallon Thames. He couldn't quite believe he had made it through alive. He looked wearily across at Zackary, who was shaking vigorously, his clothes all shredded and torn. Glancing down, he realized his own were in no better shape, and the skin underneath was slashed with cuts and dappled by bruises.

'What happened?' Seth finally gasped. 'What the hell was wrong with the vortex?'

Being sucked through water and time had never been exactly pleasant, but the journey they had both just endured could only be described as harrowing.

'I told you, Seth. It's no longer stable – the vortex has been compromised. But that's the worst it's been.'

Something had definitely shifted, Seth was in no doubt now. Despite his complete clarity of intention, the vortex had felt unresponsive – no – chaotic. He and Zack had been tossed against each other, against the great pulsing wall of water and . . . other travellers? 'Zackary – it felt like there were th-thousands of people in the vortex with us.'

Zackary stared at the ground. 'You felt that too?'

'Have we somehow intersected another wormhole or were those people actually travelling through ours?'

'They were on our space–time trajectory,' said Zackary bleakly.

As Zackary spoke, Seth was staring at the strange prisms of light shimmering off the surface of the river. The smooth sparkling water totally belied the turbulent chaos beneath. It was simply a breathtakingly lovely sight. For a moment he pictured Eva standing right here beside him, sharing the view. It was the first time he had ever tried to picture her in this world. With him. And the thought filled him with a painful longing.

In that instant Parallon ceased to be the barren prison it had always seemed and he was able to see its beauty . . . the magical city that Zackary and Matthias loved so much. It was a revelation. And suddenly its present vulnerability really mattered to him. He no longer just wanted to save Parallon for Zackary and the others, he wanted to save it for her.

'So you think the vortex has been breached?'

'At first, I assumed – as you did – that it was some kind of anomaly: a crossed line . . . or vortexual intersection. Then I wondered if it was just an oscillating space–time echo . . . but its behaviour convinced me that neither theory was likely.

'I started a round-the-clock watch on the river – which left me in no doubt. It is our vortex that has been located, compromised and . . . undermined. I saw the people using it.'

Seth's mouth went dry. *Matthias?* He swallowed. 'What sort of people?'

'Seth – quick!' Zack was pulling him into the shadows of the nearest building.

Seth ducked down next to Zackary, hurriedly creating some warm, dry clothes. Dusk was beginning to settle around them, but as he peered through the murky light he could make out a pair of tall, sturdily built men pacing along the road just beyond their hiding place.

'Zeus!' he breathed through clenched teeth. 'What are Roman guards doing patrolling here?'

'What do you think I've been trying to tell you, Seth? Parallon has changed. Irrevocably.'

They crouched in silence as the guards marched past, then Zack gestured for Seth to follow him quickly across the exposed stretch of road towards his house.

'Zackary – your building! It's gone!' choked Seth.

'It hasn't gone, it's just . . . disguised. Quick – through here.'

Seth followed Zackary as he darted between a pair of marble Ionic columns and through a large doorway. Once they were safely inside, Seth saw that the place looked exactly as it always had. Despite the heavy wooden doors behind them, they continued to step carefully, creeping soundlessly upstairs. On the first floor, they moved across to the window and stood, shielded by curtains, monitoring the street below.

Seth shook his head in disbelief. It was as though he were watching a version of Londinium playing out in front of him, filtered through the Parallon prism of light.

Gone were all the tall glass buildings he had found so strange when he'd first arrived in Parallon. It was as if they'd never existed. The skyscape had been lowered and now replicated the classical proportions of Rome. Marble columns lined the street.

There were no cars. The shimmering pavements and tarmac had been replaced with straight stone Roman roads, flanked by gutter channels. But more disconcerting than all of this was the constant marching of guards.

'What the hell's happened here?' asked Seth.

Zack inhaled deeply. 'As Parallon's only Roman gladiator, I have to assume this has something to do with *you*, Seth.'

'*Me?*'

Zackary raised his eyebrows and shrugged, as though nothing further needed to be said.

'How could *I* have done this?' choked Seth. 'I went back to Londinium only once and – as you know – I was completely powerless there. In any case, I've been in twenty-first-century London for months.'

'You've been absent a little longer than that.'

'How long?'

'At least two Parallon years, I would estimate – give or take . . .'

Seth nodded slowly: that would make more sense of such a momentous change.

'So if – as you say – you haven't revisited Londinium since that accidental return to your death,' continued Zackary, 'we need to go further back. Could you have infected anyone in Londinium before you died?'

Seth stood in silence. Of course he could have. He did: Matthias – the same Matthias who had clearly been travelling through the vortex like a bull in a china shop. What on earth had he unleashed?

Seth started to pace, trying to work out what he could do. Despite everything, whatever Matt had done, Seth couldn't betray him to Zackary. After all, he himself had inadvertently brought Matt to Parallon, and then accidentally led him to the vortex. He had to take some responsibility.

'Seth, sit,' commanded Zackary, placing two cups of coffee and a plate of chocolate cookies on to the low glass table in the centre of the room.

Seth obediently sat on the cream and chrome sofa.

'Before we can begin to restore Parallon,' said Zackary, sipping from his coffee, 'we have to fix the vortex.'

'What's wrong with it?'

'I'm not certain – but I think the sudden influx of traffic has overloaded the gravitational intensity.'

'That doesn't sound so bad. How do we repair it?'

Zackary's face was a mask of exasperation. 'Seth, we're talking instability on a catastrophic scale.'

'What do you mean?'

'Think excessive negative density . . .'

Seth snorted with frustration. Why did Zackary have to make everything a test? He took the cup of coffee from the table and began drinking, trying to apply his mind to the clues he'd been given.

A sudden cold chill ran down his spine. 'Excessive negative mass energy would mean some sort of powerful g-gravitational pull . . .' he gasped hoarsely. 'Zack, are you telling me that the vortex could transform into a black hole?'

Zackary continued to gaze at him, his mouth a taut, thin line.

'S-surely not?' rasped Seth.

'A mass that could consume anything – everything . . . you, me, Parallon, Earth . . .'

'W-what can we do?'

'I don't know . . . maybe nothing,' Zack answered bleakly. 'Or . . . maybe we could try to seal it off . . . Re-site it . . .'

'How in Hades do you move a wormhole?'

'Absolutely no idea, Seth. Not my specialist field. I studied wormhole dynamics for a couple of years under Louis Engelmann – until he got offered a job in Washington with NASA. After that I moved on to – er – other research areas. But if anyone has any idea how to seal and re-site a wormhole, Engelmann will.'

'So – you need to talk to him,' said Seth.

'Of course I need to talk to him!' exploded Zack. 'But as I just mentioned, he exists in my time, so popping back there for a quick chat isn't an option. Which is where you come in.'

'Me?'

'Obviously, you'll have to go instead of me.'

'Zack, you're joking.'

'I don't joke, Seth. I need you to travel across to 2043 and meet Engelmann.'

'2043,' murmured Seth thoughtfully. The date rang a bell, but the closest Zack had ever taken him to that time on their travels was 2016.

'Of course, convincing Engelmann that you travelled through a wormhole to speak to him could be an interesting challenge,' continued Zackary, 'because – as far as I know – he's only ever achieved one physical demonstration of his traversable wormhole theory, and that was microscopic –'

'But, Zackary,' interrupted Seth, 'even if I manage to make it through the vortex to your time, how do I get access to Engelmann? Why would a NASA quantum physicist talk to *me* – a random eighteen-year old – about a complex theoretical area of his research?'

'He will talk to you if you are with me.'

Seth stared at Zackary. 'Go on.'

'Engelmann comes to London for a conference on 7 September 2043. On 9 September – my birthday – I book a table in a restaurant and he, along with a couple of other colleagues, joins me for dinner. You will join us too.'

'How? Just turn up at your table and ask to sit down?'

'Facetiousness doesn't suit you, Seth,' snarled Zackary. 'Now pay attention. You will need to get a job in my lab. It won't be easy, I only take on exceptional lab assistants and most people bore me –'

Seth rolled his eyes.

'– but you will have two advantages over most people: first, the enormous amount of knowledge I've invested you with; and second, the time-amplification factor.'

Seth nodded. His ability to influence people's thoughts would definitely help. But still it wasn't going to be easy.

'Anyway,' continued Zackary, 'once you've met Engelmann, you will need to act fast. He will only be in London for two more days. You'll have to make sure you rendezvous with him the next day . . . whatever his other commitments.'

'And what if he has never considered the proposition? I mean – why should his exploration of wormholes include the theoretical chances of sealing and re-siting them?'

'If that is the case, then you'll have to bring him back to Parallon so that he *can* consider it.'

Seth's head jerked up. 'You're suggesting I *kill* him?'

'Oh, come on, Seth, it's what you *do*!'

'It is *not* what I do, Zackary,' hissed Seth furiously.

'Christ,' muttered Zack. 'Why did I have to get landed with the only gladiator across two worlds who is squeamish about a bit of blood!'

'I don't want to gratuitously kill your friend and mentor, and you call me *squeamish*? Maybe if *you*'d been a bit more squeamish, we wouldn't be in this mess!' shouted Seth.

'Me?' choked Zackary. 'Do I need to remind you that it's the *Romans* destroying Parallon and the vortex – not *me*! I've done everything in my power to preserve it! And I don't suggest bringing Engelmann here lightly . . . The risks of doing so are enormous.'

'Risks?' snarled Seth. 'Risks to who? I'm guessing you're not counting Engelmann in your risk assessment?'

'Oh, Seth, when are you going to start using that brain I generously enhanced? Engelmann's life is totally insignificant compared with the enormity of what we're contemplating. I don't suppose *time anomalies* ring any bells?'

Seth breathed out furiously. Of course 'time anomalies' rang bells. Sort of. Zackary began explaining in his 'patient' voice.

'Every time we travel through the vortex we are risking time anomalies – you *know* this. Just by interacting with events that have and will take place we are causing small history shifts. Normally time heals itself with corrective overwrites, but when you factor in an unstable vortex . . . and an interaction with someone as influential as Engelmann . . .'

'How influential is Engelmann?'

'In 2046 he will rewrite and reinterpret the theory of exotic matter and tachyon waves, leading to a completely new strand in quantum exploration. On the back of that work, four young scientists will find a way to start harnessing dark matter. Try and imagine the consequences to that pattern of events if Engelmann suddenly disappears. The ripples across time would be infinite.'

'So why suggest it?'

'Obviously because the alternatives right now are so much worse. If we can't stabilize the vortex, we won't be talking about little ripples across time, we'll be talking bloody great tsunamis. Tsunamis that neither Earth nor Parallon could survive.'

Seth knew Zackary was telling the truth, but he couldn't dispel the feeling that the Parallon Zackary valued and sought to preserve was a very different world to the one he would wish for. And Zackary had made it clear that he wasn't remotely squeamish about his methods.

'But presumably if Engelmann was your teacher, he isn't in the sixteen to twenty-five age bracket?'

Zackary's eyes narrowed. 'Of course not, he's –'

Suddenly Zack recognized the implications of the comment. Engelmann's age would almost certainly give him virus immunity. He couldn't be brought across.

'The truth is, Seth,' he retorted, 'if you don't get the answers we need from Engelmann, his world is doomed. He'll die anyway. We all will.'

'Then I'll just have to make sure I do,' said Seth grimly.

40

Absence

St Magdalene's

Saturday 18 May AD 2013

Everyone avoided mentioning Seth's name to me in the hospital.
Whenever I asked about him, there'd be some excuse or an instant
subject change. At first I was too dazed to notice. I was dreaming
of him so much, my waking-dreaming states were so blurred and
there were so many drugs that I was permanently confused.

But when they eventually said I could leave, the realization
hit me. I'd had visits from *everybody* else (even my mum and
Colin) and the niggling anxiety I'd been suppressing swelled
into a churning dread. All the way back in the car I sat in
clenched silence as Rose chatted breezily through random bits
of St Mag's news.

She had just settled me on to the sofa in the medical block,
and was checking the pile of pills the hospital had prescribed,
when I finally caved.

'Where is he?' I whispered.

She carried on counting, as though she hadn't heard. I
waited. Maybe she really hadn't heard.

'Rose –'

'Would you like a cup of tea or some hot chocolate?' she asked. 'I'm dying for a cuppa.'

'Rose, please –' I could hear my voice sounding shrill.

Rose had disappeared into the kitchen to put the kettle on.

I got up from the sofa and padded after her. My legs had started shaking. I steadied myself against the wall.

'Eva! What are you doing in here?' spluttered Rose, slopping the mug she was holding on to the counter and bustling towards me. 'Hey, let's see if there's anything good on TV.'

'Rose, I need to know where Seth is,' I said quietly. 'Please tell me.'

She propelled me back to the sofa and sat down beside me. Then she took my hands in both of hers.

'Eva, we don't know where Seth is. We thought – maybe you two had . . .?'

She paused, leaving her sentence hanging in the air between us. I was staring at her, trying to assimilate what she was saying.

'Eva – did he tell you where he was going?'

'How long's he been gone?' I breathed.

'Nine days.'

'And nobody thought to tell me?' I choked.

'Did he say anything to you about heading off for a few days?'

I shook my head. Surely – surely my words hadn't been enough to drive him away completely? Had they? I felt my chest begin to heave.

'W-we had an argument, Rose.' I shut my eyes, trying to dispel the image of his shocked expression. Hot tears forced their way through my eyelids and I leaned my head back against the sofa cushions, unable to bear the weight of what I'd done. 'It's all my fault.'

'Hey, Eva, I can't believe Seth would walk out on you and his school just because you had a silly argument –'

'He had every reason to walk out,' I said listlessly. 'I was really stupid.'

'Oh, Eva! You're incapable of being really stupid,' snorted Rose.

I stared at her. 'You have no idea.'

She was frowning at me, obviously trying to work out what the hell I'd done to drive someone as amazing as Seth away.

'Well, he'll be back soon, I'm sure,' she said brightly. 'Though I think he may have some explaining to do to Dr Crispin.'

'Did they call the police?'

'Of course. They had to. I just find it so hard to believe that Seth would be irresponsible enough to –'

'Don't blame him, Rose,' I gulped. 'I did this. It's the one thing I'm really good at.'

'What?'

'Driving people away. My speciality.'

'Eva, you don't drive people away,' argued Rose. 'You draw them to you like moths to a flame. Seth's completely devoted to you. I don't think –'

'Whatever you think, Rose, you're wrong.'

'Nonsense. Wherever he's gone, I know he'll be back. It'd take a lot more than an argument to push him away.'

I shook my head. I'd seen the look in his eyes. He'd finally figured out who I really was . . . the dysfunctional, unlovable girl that everyone gave up on in the end.

41

The Vortex

Parallon

The night was inky black and eerily quiet. Seth stood on the edge of the Parallon Thames contemplating the journey ahead. He had watched and waited all evening for this moment, meticulously monitoring the guard changes and their circuits, absolutely determined that nobody was going to follow him on this particular crossing.

As he gazed down at the heavy, still water below him, preparing his mind and body for what was to come, his treacherous brain suddenly distracted him with an image of Eva waking up without him . . . opening her eyes and looking for him. It was an unbearable thought. He ached so badly for her that he groaned.

'I promise I'll be back before you wake,' he whispered. But he knew that if he was ever going to see her again, he had to concentrate on what lay ahead. Zack's plan was a dangerous, maverick one, but Seth had reluctantly acknowledged it was the only one they had.

He needed to arrive at Zack's at least a week before the birthday dinner. This would give him a few days to get

London – Zackary to offer him a job and then trust him enough to take him along to meet Engelmann. There was little room for error.

Seth was aiming for 2 September – exactly seven days before the dinner.

He stared once more into the dark water and took three slow, centring breaths. Yesterday's vortex injuries had now fully healed, so he had no further distraction. He cleared his mind, channelling his focus in the same way he had always done in the arena. Below him, the vortex lurked like another vicious opponent he was determined to vanquish.

As soon as his heartbeat was slow and steady, his mind clear of all extraneous thought, Seth unlocked his knees and jumped.

The water closed around him and the inexorable pull began tugging him downwards. For one brief moment, the familiarity of the motion made him wonder whether the vortex had miraculously repaired itself . . . but then it started. Instead of the stomach-dropping tunnelling cyclone, dense walls of water began smashing into his body like an army of tanks. His breath was pummelled out of his lungs, his body was flayed from all directions and his limbs felt they would be ripped from their sockets, but he knew he had to cling on to that one corner of consciousness . . . a date . . . 2 September 2043.

An agonizing screeching sliced through his head, merging with the intolerable, throbbing cacophony of relentlessly crashing water and screams of agony. He wanted to shut down, disappear, relinquish his mission, abandon his intention, but the gladiator in him could not surrender. He battled against himself, against the water, against the tossed, broken, ephemeral bodies that crashed into him as he journeyed ever

259

forward . . . just one thought leading him on: 2 September 2043.

And then there was stillness. And silence. And darkness.

Where was he? Lost in time? Dead?

But would he feel this much pain if he were dead?

Gradually he became aware that his lungs were filling . . . in and out . . . So he could breath then. Now he could feel water lapping against his body. He was floating. He opened his eyes and found himself staring up into a cloudless sky. Clear and blue – apart from three aeroplane vapour trails drawing straight white lines across it.

He rested for a few minutes, too exhausted by his journey to do anything else. But as further sounds began to penetrate his consciousness, he realized he had to move. He could hear people, the rumble of traffic, the clank of hammers on metal . . . He couldn't afford to be noticed.

Turning his head, he registered the bank of the river towering above him. He'd need to locate some steps. Yes – there they were – just adjacent to the bridge. He began the painful task of swimming towards them. Forcing his arms to arc into a slow crawl, he wondered briefly if he had any broken bones. His ribs felt crushed and his right leg wasn't working at all.

He couldn't afford injuries. They wouldn't heal here as they did in Parallon, and nothing could compromise his mission. So, using the bruised muscles in his arms, he hauled himself through the water, fighting his body's contemptible longing to stop, using the pain of each stroke to help him focus his mind. As he swam, he tried to make sense of the skyline. This was definitely twenty-first-century London: the tall, multilayered, sculpted glass buildings proclaimed it . . . but which year?

At last his body bumped against the steps and he began hauling himself up. When he came face to face with the gated barrier at the top of the steps, he almost gave up. It was not so tall, but at that moment it looked insurmountable.

'What kind of a man are you?' jeered a scornful voice in his head. 'One that allows a simple gate to defeat you?'

He groaned wearily and, cursing Zackary, the Romans and the vortex, he summoned a final vestige of strength and forced his jangling body over the gate. He lay panting on the other side and shut his eyes, willing the pain in his ribs and his leg to subside. His journey couldn't end here, in a bedraggled heap on the riverbank. He had to move. He was too exposed in this position; anyone passing this way would spot him. He knew he didn't have the strength to stand, so gritting his teeth, he dragged his protesting body a few metres along the uneven ground into the cover of shadow. And only then did he surrender himself to the merciful oblivion of sleep.

42

Distraction

'Eva, this has got to stop!'

'Stop what, Astrid?' I'd been zipping up my guitar case, but my fingers froze.

'This – this – I dunno – *vacancy!* It's like the lights are on but nobody's home. And I've – *we've* – had enough!'

We were packing up after another two-hour rehearsal, and I was pretty tired and definitely not looking for a lecture. But the rest of the band had sort of gathered round me and seemed to be preparing for a group assault.

'Look,' Astrid went on, 'men are all bastards – no offence, Rob – they walk out – leave you stranded – but life goes on! More importantly – the band goes on! And *zombie chic* is not the vibe we're going for here. Now Theo was cool about us bailing on the mini tour, mainly because he was kind of preoccupied with all that cop stuff, but he's back on it now. Big time. We've got to pull it together for the Underworld gig, so please, Eva – you have to get back in gear. We can't do this without you.'

'But I *am* with you,' I protested. 'I'm totally with you.'

Astrid shook her head. 'Yeah, you're turning up. You're going through the motions. But it's like you've left the vital bit at home. And we need it back.'

'God, Astrid,' hissed Rob, 'Eva's not well. She can't be expected to –'

'Oh, come on, Rob, Eva's been sick for months,' she snarled, 'but this is completely different. Look at her! I mean – *nothing* touches her. She could hardly even manage to raise a smile when I gave her the special edition live Livid Turkey DVD for her birthday last week! Now that is not normal!'

'Hey, I loved that present,' I argued listlessly.

'I'm sorry, Eva, but I for one have had enough. It feels like you've . . . abandoned ship.'

Astrid was wrong. I hadn't abandoned ship – though God knows I'd thought about it. It was just so hard taking breath after breath, when the crushing weight of Seth's absence gnawed at my chest like a solid thing . . . And it was even harder acting like everything was OK. And I really thought I'd been doing a pretty good job of it too. Clearly, I was wrong.

'Astrid –' I interjected.

She put out a hand to shut me up and just ploughed on. 'So – I've devised a programme . . .'

My heart sank.

'. . . Mourning period is officially over. From now on every minute of your day will be accounted for . . .'

'Astrid – you can't be serious?' I gasped.

Ignoring me, she pulled out a scrappy piece of paper and started reading out a timetable.

Bloody hell. She'd totally honed her Gestapo tendencies. The new plan was watertight. I couldn't skip breakfast or lunch. She'd inserted daily group exam revision sessions, so there was no sloping off after school, and I wasn't granted any *alone* time until 10 p.m.

I was seriously crabby with them for about two days, but by day five, I kind of realized Astrid had a point. Nobody needed a zombie around the place, sucking the fun out of life . . . I owed it to them to make an effort. And though I hated to admit it, the distraction turned out to be a bit of a relief. The time-table gave me considerably less time to acknowledge the great gaping hole in my chest.

And there were fringe benefits too. Astrid finally learned some Latin vocab, and the band got pretty damn good because the programme dictated we rehearse every night. But the thing Astrid couldn't have predicted – and I certainly didn't expect – was that I suddenly remembered how much music meant to me. She was right, I had been going through the motions – turning up, hitting the right chords, singing the right notes – but I'd completely forgotten the reason I was there.

The one major drawback with Astrid's programme, though, was that it made me more afraid than ever of solitary, Seth-preoccupied time. At 10 p.m. when she finally released me, the sudden surge of grief would hit me like a tidal wave. So I devised an additional distraction programme of my own: searching for Professor Ambrose – bioterrorist.

I started off by assuming Ambrose wasn't working for any *elected* government. Maybe it was naive, but I didn't think that any legitimate power would sanction taking a lethal weapon into a school and letting it loose on students. And, anyway, it had been illegal to develop biological weapons since 1975. So, could Ambrose be working for an illegal organization or – more scarily – for some rogue state?

Seth and I had spent weeks trawling through registered and non-registered chemical and biological research labs but found absolutely nothing useful. It was definitely time to change tack, which was why I suddenly started considering biodefence. It wasn't illegal for military scientists to be working on neutralizing biochemical threats – and how would you be able to work out how to neutralize something you didn't have access to? So I could only assume that even though military agencies weren't officially *developing* biological weapons, they would still be doing everything in their power to monitor developments.

The US were surprisingly open about their biodefence research programmes, and although I had to worm my way through state-of-the-art security blocks, I didn't hack into a single site that showed any sign that they'd encountered anything like our virus.

I moved on to UK biodefence sites and found even less. UK policy seemed to prioritize the mobilization of troops and vaccine administration and storage rather than biochemical research.

So I was – as usual – hitting dead ends. No virus. No Ambrose. But I refused to give up. I drove myself night after night through firewall after firewall, fruitlessly cracking multi-layered security codes and trawling one unproductive site after another.

Lying in bed, after a particularly frustrating trawl, I couldn't help wondering whether Nick Mullard was having any more luck than me. Was he still working away on his own or had he started sharing with MI5? I cursed myself for allowing my mind to drift in his direction. I devoted *a lot* of energy into *not* thinking about Nick Mullard. Which wasn't easy because since our disastrous meeting he had been phoning several times a day. And every single call I ignored was ratcheting up my guilt. Guilt for avoiding him, guilt for the way Seth had treated him, guilt for the way I'd messed everything up by contacting him. It was just one big guilt fest.

Get on top of it, Koretsky, don't you dare wallow. You've got a job to do.

With a supreme effort, I dragged my mind away from Nick and Seth, and forced it to rewind a couple of steps . . . back to MI5 and the information they might be working with. And then it hit me. If MI5 were investigating Elena Galanis, they might have got wind of the virus by now. I really needed to find out what they knew.

Maybe I'd be able to set up my own surveillance on them?

I could hardly wait to get started the following night. But worming my way into their system proved tough . . . much tougher than I expected. After eight frustrating nights I found there was no way of hacking it remotely – they used two-factor authentication across the entire network. Which meant that all access required an encrypted swipe card key, plus biometric ID. So I'd have to physically get entry into Thames House and import some biometric ID on to their hard drive. Yeah, easy: a seventeen-year-old turning up at the front door and blagging her way in, accessing one of the securest networks in the world and then importing her own pass codes. And even if I had the nerve and the skills to do that, how could I get away from Rose for long enough? She was checking my damned blood pressure every few hours.

I badly needed a breakthrough.

Time was running out.

43

Date

Amanda was preparing for another big summit, and naturally expecting the usual 24/7 diligent devotion from her minion, Jennifer Linden.

Why couldn't that woman get a life? Jen was sure her boss hadn't been home the whole week. The only time Amanda ever seemed to leave the office now was to fly off for a conference or to set up a shoot. It just wasn't healthy . . . at least, it wasn't healthy for Jen. But there was respite ahead. Amanda would be leaving for Helsinki in the morning, though until that plane took off Jen would get absolutely no chance to go on any secret rummages through missing person databases.

And Jen's list of disappearances was growing. She was now up to nearly 700 cases – *700!* Practically an epidemic!

The problem was that every day she was finding it that bit harder to keep it a secret. Nick had given her a window on to the biggest news story of the century and then sworn her to silence. And she was a news journalist. It was like waving a bottle of fine brandy under the nose of an alcoholic. How could she possibly resist? She knew that with the full resources of Channel 7 behind her she could really begin to investigate this. But she had absolutely promised Nick that she would leave the case to him, Scotland Yard and MI5.

And though storms and hurricanes blasting across the UK, Europe and Scandinavia were pretty big in news terms, she knew that hundreds of disappearing people would be bigger . . . would be massive. And how the hell would she feel if the BBC suddenly got hold of the story and broadcast before her?

But – she had to keep reminding herself – she really only knew about all this because she had a boyfriend on the force; a boyfriend who trusted her. She tried not to dwell on the fact that he was also a boyfriend who had been too busy to speak to her properly for the last four days.

She sighed and checked her watch. All being well, she would be meeting him at the bar round the corner in forty-five minutes. She glanced back at her screen. The report she was working on had to be on Amanda's desk in twenty-eight minutes. And it had to be good. Amanda would kill her if she messed this up. Because when Amanda started asking questions of governments on Monday, the eyes of every nation would be on her.

The recent clusters of tornados were becoming a world issue. Not just because the damage had been so extensive, but because these land masses normally maintained consistent, stable weather profiles.

Jen had gone back 200 years, methodically researching and cataloguing any pattern that could have predicted the current spate of extreme weather. And there was nothing.

The implications were huge. Climate change appeared to be

not simply escalating but also flouting its anticipated course. It had gone rogue. Random. Chaotic.

Jen finished the final prediction graph and checked the numbers on each axis carefully. Then she meticulously read through the other twelve pages of the report – double-checking all the references and footnotes. She glanced up at the clock. 19.59. She had one minute to email it to Amanda. She hurriedly saved and sent it. And took a long, deep breath. She now had twelve minutes left for Amanda reaction time. Then she was out of here. Whatever.

Assuming Amanda wouldn't react immediately, Jen ran quickly to the loo, brushed her hair, put on some mascara and hurried back to her desk. She'd just sat down when the click of her boss's heels announced her imminent arrival. Jen had seven minutes.

She adjusted her seat and her screen and did her best engrossed-in-work act. Amanda's heels clicked towards her. Jen didn't look up until the clicking came to a deliberate stop at her desk. Amanda stood in her coat, laptop bag over one shoulder, small suitcase in her hand, gazing contemplatively at the rain and wind hammering the window. When Jen glanced up at her, Amanda reluctantly tore her eyes away from the weather and spoke.

'I've had to change my flight, Jennifer. I'm off tonight. I should be back on Thursday. Hugo will brief you till then.'

'OK,' mumbled Jen, but Amanda was already out of the door.

Jen now had three minutes to get to the bar.

'No problem,' she thought gleefully, grabbing her coat and umbrella, and running for the lift.

She got there dead on 20.15 and scoured the lounge for Nick. He wasn't in their usual corner and, as the table was empty, she assumed she'd managed to get there before him. Triumphantly, she headed to the bar and bought a beer for him and a white wine for herself. She took the drinks over to their table and waited, sipping her Chardonnay and beginning to relax.

An hour later she was on to her second glass and Nick's bottle still stood untouched. She had texted him twice and rung him five times, but had got no answer. She was now hungry, a bit drunk and very cross. She would never have kept him waiting an hour without a phone call – whatever she was doing. She had just started putting her jacket back on when she saw him at the door. Her first instinct was to simply stride haughtily past him and walk out – but then she saw his face. He was bone white. And his hair was plastered to his forehead. Was it still raining? She glanced out of the window. No.

She raced towards him. 'Nick? Are you OK?'

He opened his mouth to speak and then crumpled to the floor.

44

Double

The River Thames

Seth woke to find his body shivering uncontrollably. The shadows he'd crawled inside earlier had lengthened and a fierce wind lashed his wet clothes, which now clung to his skin like cold clammy fingers. He had to get moving. He was on a crucial mission and had no time for prevarication. He hauled his aching limbs towards the riverbank gate, then spreading his hands firmly across the top bar, levered himself upright. He stood swaying for a moment, trying to assess his condition. Not good: his breathing was hampered by the pain in his ribs and his right leg would hold no weight. But if the vortex's instability hadn't drastically undermined his intention – and this was indeed Zackary's time – the building should be no more than fifty metres from here.

He and Zackary had discussed the best arrival strategy. Zack had urged him to beg, steal or borrow some dry clothes because he was absolutely certain that London-Zackary would have no time whatsoever for some insane-looking guy arriving soaking wet. But Seth knew he wasn't going to be able to get hold of any dry clothes. He was too injured to wander around searching, and too cold to spend much longer outside. Right now, trying to convince Zackary that he wasn't a crazy hobo seemed the least of his worries. His first task was to establish whether this was even Zackary's London, let alone if he'd arrived in the right time frame. So, grabbing on to the riverbank wall, he began limping painfully towards the building that – Zeus willing – would be Zack's.

As soon as he'd passed an incongruous cluster of trees next to a multistorey charge port, Seth saw it. Zack's place. Exactly as it had looked when he'd first encountered it in Parallon.

'Well – good. It exists,' Seth breathed, gazing up at it. A part of him just wanted to assume this was 2 September 2043 and knock on the door. He was in pain, cold and thirsty . . . desperate to get inside. But unless he was in the right time frame there was absolutely no point. He'd be better off presenting at a hospital, getting fixed up, heading back to the vortex and trying again. The thought of repeating that journey sent a sickening shudder through his body.

He looked around for someone to ask, and only then registered what a mess the street was. It was littered with debris . . . shards of graphene, battered sheets of perspexalene, broken glass and household rubbish . . . as though some sort of riot had taken place.

Must be way off the time frame, he thought miserably. Zackary had definitely not said anything about riots. It seemed that whatever had happened was clearly over now, because a troop of fluorescent-suited men with robotic debris collectors were systematically loading all the detritus on to two huge hovertrucks. Seth limped painfully over to the nearest man, who looked at him in surprise.

'Blimey – did you get caught in the hurricane, mate?'

Hurricane . . .?

The man was waiting for an answer, so Seth nodded non-committally.

'Looks like you need to see a doctor . . . Seen the state of this guy, Dougie?'

'Er – could you tell me what time it is, please?' asked Seth.

'2.30, mate.'

'What day?'

The workman rolled his eyes. 'Wednesday.'

'And the date?'

'Blimey – you definitely need a doctor! Ninth of September, mate.'

'What year?'

'You some kind of joker?' he grunted crossly, turning away and picking up a huge sheet of cracked perspexalene and chucking it on the truck.

Seth was getting impatient, but he stood motionless, and when the man glanced at him again, fixed him with clear blue eyes.

The answer came immediately. '2043,' the man stammered.

'Thank you,' answered Seth, limping away.

That left him only five hours to meet Zackary and get him to trust him enough to take him along to his birthday dinner tonight.

Great.

45

Helpless

A Bar in Soho, London

Friday 28 June AD 2013

'*Nick!*' Jen screamed, kneeling down next to the convulsing body on the bar floor. But he didn't respond.

She pulled her bag off her shoulder and started rummaging for her phone, but when she found it, her hands were shaking so much it slipped through her fingers and landed on the floor by Nick's jerking arm. She put her hand out to steady him.

'Nick,' she whispered, willing him to open his eyes and smile at her.

His eyes did open briefly, but they just stared blindly up at the ceiling. Then he turned his head and vomited all over the carpet. His skin was white, sweat was glistening across his forehead and he was unconscious again.

'Oh my God,' Jen gasped, scrabbling once more for her phone. She had to call an ambulance.

People had started to gather. 'Blimey, he's had one too many,' observed one woman.

'Can't you see he's sick?' Jen screamed back at her. 'Is there a doctor here? *Anybody?*' she wailed, looking wildly around at the blurred faces surrounding her. Nobody answered. She was struggling with her phone, trying to unlock the keypad. She didn't see herself as someone going to pieces in a crisis. But here she was. Going to pieces.

'Who are you trying to ring, love?' called the guy behind the bar.

'999,' she gasped, 'ambulance . . .'

'OK, let me do it,' he said, picking up the landline. A few minutes later he crossed the room and, skirting the pool of vomit, squatted down next to Jen. 'They'll be here soon – the hospital's only five minutes away.'

'Thanks,' Jen answered absently, taking one of Nick's shaking hands in both of hers and holding on tight. He was freezing. She took off her jacket and put it across his chest, tried rubbing his arms, anything to warm him up. But he was shaking so hard, her jacket was instantly thrown off him.

And then time stood still. She stared at him – so far away now – and wanted to tell him that she was sorry. Sorry that she hadn't trusted him enough to get there tonight. Sorry that she was angry with him for not phoning. Sorry, sorry, sorry. She promised him that she would never doubt him again. Just as long as he got better . . .

The sirens screamed outside, and then Nick was being strapped to a stretcher and carried out. Jen followed numbly. Minutes later the ambulance wailed to a halt outside University College Hospital. Jen hurried behind the paramedics as they wheeled Nick's stretcher quickly towards a team of waiting staff.

She needed to be close to him, so pushed her way forward,

craning to see through the wall of medics around him. But as soon as she caught sight of him she gave an involuntary cry. The resemblance to her handsome energetic boyfriend was barely perceptible. This man was chalk white and convulsing. He had a tube down his throat and various wires attaching him to bleeping machines.

A nurse beside her gently touched her hand. 'Would you like to sit down over here while I fetch you a cup of tea?'

Jen felt herself being led to a chair across the room. Her legs were shaking so hard that she couldn't resist the nurse's gentle pressure, and she found herself slumping down gratefully, though her eyes remained fixed on the green-clad group working on the jerking body that was Nick. She hardly dared blink – a stupid, superstitious part of her brain was scared that if she allowed herself to stop looking at him she would lose him.

The clattering in her hands alerted her to the cup of tea the nurse must have brought. She frowned at the saucer dripping with spilled liquid. It was almost cold. How long had she been holding on to it? Her eyes darted quickly from the teacup to the bed. She'd allowed her focus to drift for too long.

The cup was clattering again. Why couldn't she control her hands?

He'll be OK! she assured herself. *He's so healthy. And strong.* She gulped down what was left of the tea. *Of course he'll be OK! We'll be laughing about this tomorrow.*

Jen put the cup and saucer down on the floor beside her; it was a relief to get rid of the noise they'd been making. But almost as soon as she had resumed her watchful vigil on the bed, the pace of activity around Nick changed.

'He's crashing,' shouted a doctor.

That didn't sound good. Her brain was just trying to work out what it meant when the same doctor shouted, 'Adrenalin – now!'

Jen found that she was moving forward, her voice croaking, 'Is he OK?'

Nobody answered. Nobody heard. She knew then that Nick definitely wasn't OK.

The beeping on the monitor had changed into one continuous note. The spiky lines on the screen had gone crazy. Someone started slamming electric charges through pads on Nick's chest. Again and again.

The long note didn't change, but suddenly the manic spiking on the screen settled into a single flat line. They increased the power.

Twice. Three times. Four times.

And then the doctor shook his head, switched off the machines and looked at his watch.

'02.32,' he said simply, and glanced momentarily in her direction.

Jen stood numbly, staring at them all.

What had happened? Why had they stopped working? Why weren't they looking after him?

The doctor walked over to her, touched her lightly on the shoulder, and said, 'I am so sorry. I've never seen a body fail so fast. Are you his wife? I'd like to take a full history from you, if that's OK?'

Jen tried to make sense of what he was saying.

'Er, I think she might need a few minutes alone with him, doctor,' coughed one of the nurses tactfully. Then she pulled a chair up to the bedside and helped Jen into it. As she left, she drew the curtains round the bed, saying softly, 'You stay there as long as you like, love.'

Jen felt the sobs begin deep in her chest and explode upwards. A part of her brain registered the awful sound coming from her mouth, but it was a small, detached part. And it appeared to have absolutely no control over the rest of her. She grabbed Nick's hand and held it up to her lips.

'Don't go!' she hiccupped. 'Please don't go!'

She tried rubbing his cold hand between hers, desperate to warm his skin, but it remained limp and icy. Hardly a hand at all: just bone and muscle and skin.

'Where are you, Nick?' she choked, searching his lifeless body for some sign that he was there. But it was obvious, even to her, that he was gone.

Her running mascara was making her eyes sting and her vision blur. She rummaged in her jacket for a tissue and furiously wiped her face.

But her vision didn't clear. Nick's body remained blurry. She blinked. She blinked again. And then she gasped. 'Nick? Nick? What the hell's happening . . . Nick? *Nurse!*' she screamed. '*Nurse!*'

Two nurses and a doctor arrived in the cubicle, just in time to witness Nick's body transform from a solid dead thing . . . into a translucent echo of a solid dead thing . . . His hand in both of hers had become weightless, barely perceptible. Jen stared mutely until her fingers were cupped around nothing but air. All four people stood, utterly transfixed. They had just witnessed a phenomenon that was completely inexplicable. The body of Nick Mullard had entirely disappeared.

46

Birthday

Seth stood in front of Zackary's door and prepared to knock. He had hammered on this door many times in Parallon, and he'd been greeted in a number of ways – usually with irritation or sarcasm.

Though the situation was dire, something about it made Seth want to laugh. He knew Zack fairly well now, but this Zackary wouldn't know him at all. For once he held the power – and he even had Zackary's own permission to exploit it!

His fist reached out and he knocked.

No answer. As he expected. Zackary had warned him that he'd be unlikely to answer the door – he hated interruptions while he worked and he was bound to be working. So Seth knocked again. And again. He knocked until he could hear muttered swearing proceeding along the hallway towards him.

He smiled to himself. Definitely Zackary.

The door opened and Seth's eyes widened. Zackary looked

so young. And then he remembered what day it was . . . Zackary's twenty-seventh birthday.

Zack was staring back at Seth, his eyes narrowed. 'Who the hell are you?'

Seth had been primed with a convincing backstory: Professor Brandon from Oxford had suggested he come to him as a research intern, blah, blah, blah. But he decided to abandon it. Given the condition he was in, it felt implausible and pointless.

'My name's Seth. I – er – got caught in the hurricane,' he began. 'I could really use a hot shower and some dry clothes.'

Zackary stared at the bedraggled, bleeding stranger before him. Not only had he disturbed his work, but clearly he wasn't here to deliver the replacement reflection, either. Yet the moment the boy started talking, Zackary's self-righteous fury dissipated. There was something so compelling about the directness of the request and the intensity in his eyes that Zackary found himself standing aside and ushering him in.

'Looks like you might need a doctor,' he observed, as Seth stumbled along the hall.

'I think I'm OK. J-just a bit cold.'

Zackary pulled a couple of towels out of a cupboard and supported Seth up the stairs to the bathroom. He activated the steam shower and then began helping Seth out of his wet clothes. He tried not to broadcast his shock when he saw the state of Seth's body, but was defeated by the massive gash on Seth's leg. Congealed blood plastered the fabric fast to his skin, and Zackary couldn't bring himself to pull the material away. Seth was leaning back against the wall, wincing with pain.

'Please – just do it!' he rasped. So Zackary shut his eyes and, ignoring Seth's choked cry, ripped away the jeans. He tried not to look at the blood gushing down Seth's leg as he steadied him into the shower.

'You all right?' he asked.

Seth nodded, so Zack left the room and went straight to his v-com.

'Anton?'

'Hey, Zackary! Happy birthday! Still on for dinner tonight?'

'Of course! But I just wondered if you could swing by here first . . . with your medidock?'

'What's up, Zack?'

'Oh, nothing serious! Just – er – a friend of mine – er – got caught by the typhoon . . . Needs a bit of patching up and maybe an ABV shot?'

Zackary was frowning as he commed off. What was he doing? He didn't give a damn about this boy. Wondering what on earth had come over him, he headed back down to his lab. He'd been in the middle of setting up rows of incubators when the knocking had distracted him. He now rechecked their source-flow and thermostats. But he couldn't concentrate. There was a stranger in his bathroom and he didn't like strangers in his building. Especially given the sensitivity of the work he was doing. What if the boy had been sent to spy? His body was bashed around but incredibly muscled. Could the whole injury thing just be an elaborate cover? Zack glanced around his lab as though it had already been violated, and stepped out, reactivating the digital keypad behind him.

Then he mounted the stairs.

For a moment, he waited outside the bathroom door, listening. He could hear the steam hitting the tiles but little else.

Had he opened the door and glanced in, he would have seen

Seth propped up against those tiles trying to summon the energy to turn off the steam jet and get out. But the water was soothing, so he slid down the wall and crouched on the shower floor, closing his eyes for a second. He was too spent to stop his treacherous mind slipping away from Zackary's bathroom, to another set of tiles . . . a bottle of shampoo on the shelf . . . her shower gel fallen to the floor . . .

He could not allow his thoughts to drift. He had a job to do. In just a couple of hours, he needed to be on perfect form. He reached up, groaning involuntarily, and turned off the shower. Then he gingerly wrapped a towel round his battered body. Some of the pain was familiar. The smashed ribs. He knew if he took shallow breaths, and avoided large movements, he could live with that – he'd lived through worse. But the leg was a problem. It was swelling fast and the skin around the gash was heating up. He could barely touch it. He couldn't afford to be crippled. Not with the amount he had to get done in the next couple of days. Not with a return journey through the vortex to negotiate.

There was a light tap on the door and before Seth could rearrange his features Zackary had come in.

One look at his visitor's wretchedness convinced Zack that he wasn't going to be doing much spying tonight.

'Hungry?' he asked, throwing Seth the grey silk dressing gown that had been hanging on the back of the bathroom door.

Seth shook his head. 'I'd love a glass of water though.'

He tried not to wince as he pushed his arms through the sleeves of the robe, and was grateful that he didn't have to put his jeans back on – yet. He knew he had that pleasure waiting for him in a couple of hours.

Zackary helped Seth into the room he introduced as his library. Seth shivered. It was an exact replica of the room in which he'd paced away most of his last night in Parallon: the wall-to-wall bookshelves, the two comfortable sofas, the huge dining table and the tall windows. He glanced tentatively through one of the windows now, half expecting to see an endless stream of marching Roman guards. But he simply saw the street he had walked through earlier today, almost clear of debris; the two trucks gliding away in a slow convoy, humming past the oval, metallic green car rounding the corner towards them. That car . . . he was sure he'd seen it before – so sure that a man's name started to form itself in his mind. But then Zackary handed him a glass of water and he turned back to the room.

'Sit,' said Zackary. And Seth, using both hands, stretched out his painful leg and sat, trying to play the role of total stranger . . . not a man who had sat in this exact spot on the previous night, talking to a Zackary who knew him; a Zackary who looked at least twenty years older than this one.

Seth had just touched the glass to his lips when a knock at the door startled him enough to send half its contents on to the floor. His brain instantly assured him that the Romans couldn't have found their way here yet, but his body was taking a moment to catch up. He took a couple of deep breaths to resettle himself, an action that only added to his discomfort by flaring the pain in his ribs. Wincing, he closed his eyes and did his best to focus on the steady steps of Zackary heading down the stairs to open the door. He still had his eyes shut when Zackary returned.

'Seth . . .'

His eyes opened.

'. . . I'd like you to meet a friend of mine . . .'

Seth didn't need Zackary to name him. He recognized the man. Or at least the part of his brain that contained Zackary's memories recognized him. This was someone Zackary trusted. Anton. His was the green car.

'Hi,' croaked Seth.

Anton moved towards him, carrying a large, translucent, rigid bag.

'My friend's a doctor, Seth. He's just going to check you over.'

Anton made Seth stretch out on the sofa while he began a careful inventory of his injuries.

'How did you sustain these?' he asked.

'The hurricane,' mumbled Seth.

Anton frowned, but said no more. He pulled the glass coffee table closer and carefully placed his bag on top, then clicked open the pull-down front flap, unhooked the scanner and set it to power-up. While they waited, he gave Seth a shot of something that he promised would make him more comfortable. Seth tried to protest – he couldn't afford to get too comfortable, he had work to do – but a few minutes later he couldn't remember what that work was, or why it was so important. And a few minutes after that he couldn't remember how to keep his eyes open.

He jerked awake. Totally disorientated. He stared straight ahead for a couple of moments, trying to work out where he was. He sat up quickly and swallowed back the gasp of pain.

'I'd avoid sudden movements if I were you.'

Seth turned his head and blinked. Anton, Zackary, an older man and two women, one dark, one blonde, were sitting round the dining table at the other end of the room. The table was lit by candles and there was a delicious smell of spices.

'Care to join us for dinner?' asked Zackary. 'My birthday dinner, actually.'

The birthday dinner: 9 September 2043. But it was supposed to be in a restaurant. Why was it here?

'Damn,' murmured Seth under his breath. They'd rearranged it – because of him. He'd been here a couple of hours and had already precipitated a time anomaly. But the company was blissfully unaware of the situation.

'Happy birthday, Zackary,' Seth mumbled guiltily.

Anton stood up from the table and strode over to Seth's couch.

'If you rest up properly, your fractured ribs should start to feel a little better tomorrow. I've elsonned the trauma areas, which will have accelerated the bone fusion, and should help with the swelling and bruising. Your leg trauma was more serious – the tibial fracture is quite severe. Again, the elsonning will have begun the fusion process but for best results you'll need at least eight more treatments – one each day. My surgery is close by, so I'm happy to drop in on my way home. In the meantime I've nugrafted the gash, so scarring should be minimal. I've also splinted your leg to prevent displacement, but you'll need to keep your weight off it until all the treatments are finished. Other cuts and abrasions have been lazonned, so with any luck they – at least – will be healing well by tomorrow.'

'Thank you,' said Seth quietly. Anton's prognosis, and the

glow of well-being from the painkiller, helped to blanket his unease about the time-scale. They also gave him the strength to pull himself up to standing, tighten the dressing-gown sash and, with Anton's support, shakily limp his way over to the dining table.

As Anton pulled out a chair for him, Zackary regarded Seth through distrustful eyes. Seth grinned. This was the Zack he recognized.

'Some chicken pasanda – before they all finish it?' offered the dark-haired girl now sitting directly opposite him. She was holding a spoonful over his plate.

'Sure,' Seth answered. He'd never eaten that before, but it smelled pretty appetizing.

'Wine?'

'Please,' he smiled, holding out his glass.

As he took his first mouthful of food, he was acutely aware that the whole table had gone silent and was watching him.

'Mmm – that's good!' he announced, loading another fork-ful. He was suddenly starving.

Zackary refilled the wine glasses and the general table conversation started up again.

Seth ate and listened, quickly picking up that the older man was indeed Louis Engelmann, and the grey-eyed blonde was Lauren Baxter, a young NASA colleague. The dark-haired girl, Rana, was a doctorate student who had worked in Zackary's lab on a six-month internship last year.

Engelmann had spent the day at the astrophysics conference and was sharing some of the symposium topics with the table. Zackary had a ticket to go and hear Engelmann lecture the following day.

'What will you be speaking about?' asked Seth, seizing his opportunity.

Engelmann just laughed and looked at his plate. 'Oh, I don't think my specialist subject is likely to be of any interest to you!'

'Try me,' responded Seth, fixing him with his most disarming smile.

'W-well – my presentation tomorrow concerns relativistic time dilation effects on exotic matter . . . Glad you asked?' Engelmann chuckled.

'Very,' said Seth quietly. 'Are you talking theoretically or do you have direct knowledge of wormholes?'

Engelmann looked a little startled – as did Zackary, whose expression had transformed suddenly from sceptical to hostile.

Seth realized instantly that as far as Zackary was concerned, he had just crossed over from hapless, injured victim to science spy. This Zackary was clearly as paranoid here in London as the Zackary he'd left behind in Parallon. And Seth hadn't forgotten how ruthless Zack's paranoia made him. He would not hesitate to kill Seth if he saw him as a threat.

Seth calmly surveyed the suspicious faces ranged round the table, and considered his options. He had two: blast them with his intense will; or talk his way out. If he could talk convincingly enough, it would be much easier to complete his mission. His time-amp powers were expedient, and had instant impact, but they relied on proximity, which meant they gave him limited control.

So – if he was going to try and talk his way out of this, he clearly wasn't going to get away with being a random stranger with a particular fascination for wormholes. He was going to have to pull out the backstory Zack had given him.

'Zackary, forgive me – I never got a chance to explain . . .
Professor Brandon, at Oxford, suggested I got in touch with
you – just before he went off on his sabbatical.'

Zackary's eyes narrowed. 'Now, why would he suggest that?'
he asked icily.

'Well,' continued Seth, ignoring the obvious distrust in
Zackary's voice, 'I've been working with him on my doctorate
in the molecular biophysics faculty . . .'

'What's your subject?' Zackary quizzed aggressively.

'DNA topology,' Seth answered casually, then continued with
his narrative. 'Professor Brandon mentioned that you were
complaining about losing a good intern . . .' Seth's eyes darted
to Rana, who smiled and flushed. 'And knowing *I* needed a
placement . . .'

'Why didn't he v-com me?'

'He tried – you didn't pick up . . .' In Parallon, Zackary had
told Seth he hardly ever looked at his v-com – it was just another
interruption.

'So – how did you wind up on my doorstep in such a mess?'
Zackary's voice was marginally friendlier.

Seth shrugged. 'Not sure really. I just got out at London
Bridge subport, and there was masses of stuff blowing around.
I suppose I must have been hit by something . . .'

Anton regarded Seth quizzically for a few moments, but Seth
flashed a smile at him, and he simply murmured, 'Unlucky
timing.'

'We had a couple of typhoons in Washington last month,'
sighed Engelmann. 'I'm just grateful I wasn't still in the air
when this one struck,' he added, staring out of the window
with a mournful expression.

'I'll get some coffee,' announced Zackary, standing and moving towards the kitchen.

'Do you need some help?' asked Rana, also standing.

'Watch and learn, Seth,' laughed Zackary, and Seth knew then that he had just landed the lab job. He also realized he had Louis Engelmann almost to himself for a few minutes. So despite the wine and painkiller haze, he had to make the most of the time.

'Professor, is your wormhole analysis all theoretical or have you done any practical experimentation?'

'Practical experimentation is what I do now, Seth. Well – what we do,' he corrected, smiling at Lauren.

'Pretty full time,' she nodded.

Seth's spirits lifted.

'You can create wormholes?'

'Oh yes,' agreed Engelmann. 'Once you can harness exotic matter, you can construct wormholes . . .'

'Traversable wormholes? Really!' gasped Anton. 'Wormholes people could travel through?'

'Ah –' Engelmann paused. 'No. I am sorry, Anton. The only wormholes I have managed to keep successfully open are microscopic. We've been trying to build a larger scale one, using negative mass and cosmic string . . . but the negative energy densities lose stability . . . though theoretically, mathematically, it is possible, and we get closer each year . . .'

Seth's heart sank. Theoretical success was not going to help him. Unless . . .

'Do you imagine there could be naturally occurring traversable wormholes?' he asked.

'Oh yes, of course. We have identified countless numbers of

black holes, many of which could be wormholes. Why shouldn't some of those be traversable?'

'Though in theory,' interjected Lauren, 'they are more likely to be pathways to alternative universes than time corridors within our own.'

'So,' ventured Seth, 'if you were to find a naturally occurring, large, traversable wormhole – would there be any possible way to divert it or re-site one end of it?'

Professor Engelmann gazed towards the window, deep in thought. Lauren just stared straight into Seth's eyes, frowning.

Seth held his breath and waited.

'Theoretically,' murmured Engelmann, 'I suppose you could try diverting the mouth of the wormhole, electromagnetically . . . but the Casimir power required to effect that kind of diversion would be massive – and the chances of the wormhole remaining intact extremely low . . .'

'Would it be easier to do that than build a new one?'

'Not necessarily . . . but the trick would be to try and preserve the corridor. And I think that would be difficult.'

'Anyway, at the moment neither is an option,' smiled Lauren. 'At least, on any scale larger than microscopic.'

Seth tried not to look too dismayed. He had one further question, but it would be a difficult one to ask.

'Supposing – theoretically – you had a traversable wormhole that had become unstable . . . would there be any way of repairing it?'

'When you say unstable, Seth, do you mean erratic or intermittent?'

'Erratic, I suppose, Professor. Functional but not reliable.'

Engelmann was contemplating Seth through narrowed eyes.

Seth shifted in his seat. Had he given too much away? Fortunately, the awkwardness of the moment was suddenly eclipsed by Anton's frantic attempts to clear a space on the table. Rana was clattering towards them with a tray of steaming mugs.

'Oh, Rana, you angel!' grinned Anton. 'I'm so glad you got involved in the coffee proceedings – Zackary's brew can be lethal.'

'Well – I hope you all like your coffee black,' she smiled, 'because he's run out of milk . . . Note to new intern: "Keep the fridge stocked – keep everyone happy."'

Seth nodded and laughed, more grateful for the diversion than the advice.

As the table conversation shifted from interns to the price of milk, Seth's attention began to wane, especially as his injuries were starting to trouble him. He shifted on his chair a couple of times, trying unsuccessfully to find an easier position. He was on the point of standing up and attempting to walk off the pain when Rana cleared her throat. 'Anton, I think Seth could probably use another shot.'

Anton glanced at his watch and said, 'Of course. Sorry, Seth, it's been hours since I gave you any pain medication. Let's get you back on the couch.'

Seth considered refusing. He knew that the medicine knocked him out, and there was still so much he needed to know, but Engelmann was yawning – it was likely the party was about to break up anyway and he could do with some sleep. So he gratefully accepted, and a few minutes later he was out cold.

47

Threat

Jen sat numbly on a grey plastic chair, trying to remember what it was like to feel connected to her thoughts. She was staring vacantly across at the flimsy blue curtain that a nurse had pulled round Nick's bed. How long had she been sitting here? How long since she'd been bustled unceremoniously out of his bay and told to sit there until the forensics team arrived?

She'd completely lost track of time. She gazed blankly at the nurses and doctors moving purposefully between bays as though this was just another ordinary night. But it wasn't. Nick was gone. She said it over and over again. Trying to make sense of it. But it just didn't make sense. And nobody had given her a chance to make sense of it. They'd shoved her out of there so fast that she'd barely had time to register it.

Anger suddenly flared inside her. How dare they push her away from him like that? She hadn't even said goodbye. She needed to get back in there. Really needed to.

'Sod the forensic team,' she muttered under her breath, and

293

as soon as the corridor cleared, she darted quickly across the floor and through the curtain.

The bed was covered in a thin white sheet. An oxygen mask along with a tangle of wires and cables still attached to various machines and equipment seemed randomly strewn around the bed. But she knew that there was nothing random about the scene she contemplated. Nothing had been touched. The shock of the disappearance had kept everyone at a terrified distance.

But she wasn't terrified, she was desperate. She reached out a hand and gently shifted the sheet, gasping as she revealed Nick's jeans. She slid her hand along them, caressing them, picturing his body back inside. But they were empty and flat. Her hand moved along the bed until she felt the edge of his leather jacket. Soft. Worn. She buried her fingers into his pocket, remembering how on cold evenings she would slip her hand in beside his, and they would walk along, fingers warm and entwined. She felt for his hand now. And the image of it disappearing between her fingers sent fresh shudders through her aching body. She thought she had cried herself out, but she hadn't. Tears were running down her face again, plopping on to her lap.

'What happened to you, Nick? What the hell happened?' she choked.

She looked accusingly at the crumpled white sheet, willing him back. Willing him to help her out here.

With an effort she forced the numbness away. Nick had lost his life trying to find out what was going on . . . Now it was up to her.

She took a deep breath, looked furtively behind her, and then pushed her hand further back into Nick's jacket pocket. Were there any clues there?

His iPhone. She pulled it out quickly. He stored his contacts, his diary, even his emails on it. She ran her fingers to his inside pocket . . . and pulled out his ID wallet. She opened it. A concrete affirmation that he had truly existed: an unsmiling photo of Nicholas Mullard. She knew she had to return it, but she wanted to hold on to it so much. Did she have any pictures of him? Maybe there was one on her phone – she couldn't remember. She quickly took out her phone and photographed the card, then slipped it back in his pocket. She was just about to move round to the other side of the bed when she heard urgent voices and footsteps striding through the corridor outside. She hurriedly pulled the sheet back in place, dropped Nick's iPhone into her bag and, slipping quickly through the curtain, hurled herself back on to her chair.

Her heart was pounding. Especially when she saw how many people were heading her way.

No! This couldn't be the forensic team. *All twelve of them?*

The doctor who had called the time of death was leading them quickly towards the cubicle. He glanced at Jen uncomfortably. 'Er – this is – the girlfriend . . .' he stammered.

One of the men stopped in his tracks.

'What's your name?' he snapped.

'Jen,' she croaked. 'Jennifer Linden.'

'And you were with Mullard the whole time?'

She nodded.

'Could I have a word, please?' he asked, waiting for her to stand. He was tall, slightly greying at the temples and bony. He wore a shirt and tie, but looked as though he'd be equally comfortable in a tracksuit. He was tapping his foot impatiently.

Reluctantly, Jen got to her feet, and he instantly grabbed her elbow and began trying to steer her away.

Jen stood her ground and cleared her throat. 'W-who are *you*?'

'Does that matter?'

'Yes, of course it matters,' she answered sharply.

His eyes darted towards one of his colleagues, who shook his head imperceptibly. At that moment, Jen knew they were MI5. The police weren't evasive. Not like this.

'What do you want?' she asked guardedly.

'Just a word,' he said quietly. 'I know this has been hard, but there are a couple of things I need to ask you.'

For some reason Jen didn't trust this guy. He was refusing to give her any information and wanted to lead her off God knows where.

'I'm happy here, thank you,' she asserted, planting her feet. 'What would you like to know?'

A muscle in his jaw twitched. He clearly wasn't used to dissent.

'All right then,' he replied. 'I'd like you to tell me what you saw tonight.'

'Oh,' Jen answered frostily, 'that's an easy one. I saw my boyfriend get sick and then – disappear. Is that all you wanted to know or was there something else?'

The man took a deep breath and frowned impatiently.

'Flippancy is hardly appropriate –'

'Actually, I am feeling far from flippant,' snapped Jen furiously. 'In fact I have a couple of little questions of my own.'

'Oh, do you?' he asked coldly.

'Yes, I do . . . Like – what the hell's going on? Like – where was Nick working today? Like – when are you going to wake up and notice we're looking at a bloody epidemic?'

Jen realized her voice was now quite a lot louder than the whispered hiss she'd planned. The expression on her companion's face was thunderous.

'Ms Linden,' he snarled, 'whatever you think you saw tonight – you didn't. And whatever you think you know – you don't. So I suggest you go home, make yourself a nice cup of tea, phone a friend and try to get on with your life.'

'Get on with my life? What kind of life do you think I have now?' she retaliated hoarsely.

He stared at her for a few moments, appraising her.

'This is about something a whole lot bigger than you and your boyfriend,' he answered coolly. 'And if you know what's good for you, you will do as I suggest.'

Jen's eyes widened. Had he really just threatened her? It sounded like a line from a bad movie. But he was still standing there, arms folded, staring her out. She was not going to give him the satisfaction of looking scared. So she just shook her head in disbelief and strode out.

Her legs were trembling by the time she found the hospital main entrance. She stepped outside and leaned wearily against the wall. It was still dark and she was grateful for that. She wasn't ready to face daylight. How was it possible that her whole world had imploded in just a few hours?

Nick. Where are you? She stared into the velvety blackness, searching for him. Maybe he was there, somewhere? Would she ever find him? How the hell did you mourn a man who had vanished into thin air?

48

Arena

Parallon

'The magister will see you now,' announced Rufus coolly.

Matthias nodded, smoothed the folds of his toga, lifted his head and moved towards the open door. He suppressed the small flutter of vestigial fear. He was chief designer and architect now, he reminded himself proudly; responsible for most of the extensive Parallon renovations. He wore a toga. He'd been given his own slaves. The magister favoured his work . . . But he had been summoned unexpectedly. It was unnerving, even though he had a pretty shrewd idea why he was there.

Matthias strode through the spacious columned hall, unable to suppress the shiver of pleasure in its perfect proportions. He had surpassed himself in here: three large glazed windows cast rectangles of shimmering, prismatic light across the polished marble floors, creating the ideal setting for the opulently carved maple furniture. Yet surprisingly the magister's delight in the room seemed to derive almost entirely from the handful of delicately painted swans and parakeets decorating the cool grey plastered walls. Noting this, Matthias had made sure to include bird motifs on all his state buildings.

'Ah, my architect,' boomed the magister, looking up from his desk. 'What have you to report?'

'Magister,' responded Matthias, bowing low and walking briskly towards him. 'In the last four days I have completed the temples of Apollo, Mars and Neptune, as well as repaving and re-siting the main road from the bridge and those perpendicular to it. I have re-fronted the buildings in that section and –'

'I'm no longer interested in temples and roads, Matthias,' interrupted the magister impatiently. 'I want to know about my arena. Otho tells me work has still not begun on it.'

Matthias glanced at Otho, who stood behind the magister, gazing impassively ahead. Matthias wasn't surprised by this betrayal. He had been aware of Otho's resentment for some time.

'Forgive me, master . . . but work has begun.'

Otho's eyes flared.

'Are you suggesting Otho is a liar?'

'Jupiter, no, magister – Otho isn't lying. I have not yet had the opportunity to show him . . . m-my fault entirely. I started work on the area marked out for the arena a while ago, but felt it was too meagre a space, and could not support the majestic construction I had in mind. So I took the liberty of re-siting it – to the location of our Londinium one, where, when complete, it can stand as a glorious tribute to you and that great city.'

The magister cocked his head thoughtfully.

Matthias held his breath.

'Very well, Matthias, take us to this glorious building.' He pushed back his chair and started striding towards the door.

Matthias, flanked by the elite guard, followed him out of the palace.

The magister did not need directions. He knew exactly where the Londinium arena had been sited. When Matt's still-unfinished construction loomed against the horizon, the magister stopped and stood in silent contemplation. Matthias hardly dared breathe.

Otho, seeing that there were only five seating tiers completed, spluttered with rage. 'Matthias, you dare to present the master with this pitiful effort? Magister, I will see that the architect is punished –'

'Hold your temper, Otho,' interrupted the magister, raising a hand. 'It is true the arena is not yet ready for my eyes – but visiting today was my choice . . . And,' he added, pacing across the huge sanded floor and peering into the spaces Matthias had created underneath the seating tiers, 'the design is thoughtful and elegant. I like it. When will it be finished?'

'Er – t-tomorrow, magister,' stammered Matt gratefully.

'Very well, we shall return tomorrow at noon,' agreed the magister, striding briskly away. The guards followed swiftly behind him, but when Otho turned and glared silently in his direction, Matt knew that he would find a way to exact vengeance.

49

Warning

Shoreditch, London

Saturday 29 June AD 2013

'Jesus, Jenny! What the hell happened to you? Where have you been all night?'

Jen fell through the front door, collapsed into Debs's arms, and the dam broke.

'Has somebody hurt you, Jen? Do I need to call the police?'

Jen took a deep shuddering breath and shook her head.

Debs held her friend tight until the sobbing subsided and then steered her gently into the bathroom. 'Jennifer Linden, I am prescribing you a hot bath laced with my Jo Malone bath oil . . . Yeah, yeah, I know I've been saving it for, like, years, but clearly the occasion warrants it . . .'

Jen allowed her friend to undress her and help her into the warm scented water. Then she lay back and shut her eyes. At some point Debs must have helped her out of the bath and into her towelling robe, because that's how she found herself eleven hours later, under the duvet curled up in her bed.

Debs was shaking her gently. 'I'm making some soup. How does that sound?'

Jen blinked awake and for a moment couldn't identify the reason for her swollen eyes and aching throat. Then last night's horrors slammed through her sleep-hazed brain.

She squeezed her eyes shut, trying to find oblivion again, but there was no escape. She was right back in her messed-up life.

'Jen, your soup's getting cold. Come on now!' Debs pulled her unceremoniously out of bed and sat her down in front of a steaming bowl of minestrone and a pile of buttered toast.

'Tell me, Jenny,' she breathed, squeezing her hand.

Jen gazed into her friend's anxious eyes, and swallowed. 'Y-you know I told you about Nick – er – the guy I was seeing –'

'I *knew* he'd done this to you!' exploded Debs. 'I'll *kill* him!'

Jen's head jolted up at these words and her hands began to shake again.

'What, babe? What did I say?'

Jen shook her head and, lifting her red, swollen eyes, whispered, 'I'm afraid someone got there before you, Debs.'

'*Christ, what the hell does that mean?*'

But Jen laid her head on her arms, shut her eyes and refused to speak any more.

'Jenny, your phone's vibrating!' whispered Debs, shaking her gently.

Jen winced. 'I'm asleep,' she mumbled.

'I think it may be urgent. It's the twelfth call.'

Jen sighed and stumbled across the living room to pick up

her bag. By the time she got there the vibration had stopped. Good. She didn't feel like talking to anyone. She was about to slump down on the sofa, when the phone started up again. She groaned and began rifling through her bag. It had better not be Amanda.

It wasn't. It wasn't even her phone. It was Nick's.

She stared at it for a moment, her heart hammering. She'd forgotten putting it in her bag. The caller ID was Brodie Covington. She couldn't place the name.

'Hello?' she answered.

There was a pause. 'Er – sorry, wrong number.'

'This is Nick's phone,' Jen said quickly.

'Ah. Is he there?'

This time it was Jen who went silent.

'Hello? Could I speak to Nick, please?' he repeated.

'No,' Jen whispered.

'I'm sorry?'

Jen swallowed. What could she say?

'Look, what's going on? What are you doing with his phone?'

'I'm – er – looking after it,' she said finally.

'Why? Where's Nick?' Brodie's voice was starting to sound uneasy.

Brodie! Jen suddenly remembered who he was – Nick's MI5 friend: His man on the inside.

'Brodie,' she said urgently, 'are you alone?'

'Yes . . .'

'I think we should meet.'

'Now?'

'Sorry – is it too late?' Jen asked, looking at her wrist. She'd left her watch in the bathroom.

'Are you in London?' asked Brodie.

'Shoreditch.'

'I can be there in twenty minutes.'

Jen gave him the address and hung up.

Debs was standing in front of her, hands on hips, mouth hanging open. 'Tell me you haven't just invited a complete stranger round to our flat at –' she glanced at her watch – '11.45 p.m.?'

Jen pressed her lips together. She wasn't yet ready to tell Debs the full circumstances of Nick's death. She said simply, 'Brodie is – was – a friend of Nick's.'

Debs snorted with frustration and stomped off to the bathroom. When she emerged, she took one look at Jen, sitting slumped on the sofa clutching Nick's phone, and melted.

'Do you think maybe you should put some clothes on, then?'

Jen looked down at her old towelling robe and frowned. 'Oops,' she nodded, and allowed Debs to propel her into her bedroom. A few minutes later she'd thrown on a pair of joggers and a vest top. Debs handed her a hairbrush, which she obediently pulled through the tangled mess on her head. She straightened her duvet, picked up Nick's phone again and returned to her sofa vigil.

The doorbell rang.

'Would you like me to stick around?' hissed Debs, suppressing a yawn.

Jen shook her head and stood up to press the ground-floor door release. 'I'll be fine, thanks, Debs. You go to bed!'

Brodie wasn't quite as quick on the stairs as Nick. But maybe he didn't challenge himself with speed tests the way Nick did. Used to do. When he got to Jen's open front door, he stood uncertainly for a moment.

'Come in,' she said quietly. In another life she might have found him appealing: broad-shouldered, mid-brown hair, easy smile. She watched as he shut the door behind him and made his way across the room. Then she slumped back down on the sofa and he pulled up the wicker rocking chair opposite her.

'OK . . . Would you mind telling me who you are and what's going on?' he asked.

God, she hadn't even given him her name! 'Sorry. Jennifer Linden . . . I'm – er – I was Nick's girlfriend.'

Brodie's head jerked forward. '*Was?*'

Jen was staring at him, looking for clues. He had to know more than she did, surely? He was MI5, for God's sake.

But Brodie was just shaking his head wildly. 'What are you telling me, Jennifer?' he asked.

'Haven't you heard?'

'Heard *what*?'

'That Nick's . . . disappeared.'

Brodie breathed a sigh of relief. 'Oh, thank God, for a moment there I thought . . .' His voice tailed off, realization dawning.

'D-did Nick get sick?' he stammered.

Jen nodded. 'His heart stopped last night . . . and then . . .'

Brodie stared at her and let out a deep uneven breath. 'I told him not to –'

'Not to what?' asked Jen quickly.

Brodie shook his head. 'I am so sorry, Jennifer. It's – confidential. I can't talk to you about it.'

Jen's eyes flashed. 'You and your bloody spy games! People are dying and disappearing and you're so damned worried about keeping your secrets that nobody is doing anything! I

305

was investigating this too, you know. Nick and I w-were doing it t-together.'

Brodie was staring at her, stunned. 'Investigating what exactly?'

Jen shrugged and moved across to open her laptop. 'I was researching unexplained disappearances . . . and Nick had just started on the whole Belmarsh prison lead.'

'Nick was in Belmarsh?' Brodie's face had gone white. 'I told him to leave it alone. I told him it was too dangerous . . . He is just so damned stubborn.'

They both flinched at Brodie's accidental tense slip, but neither said anything.

'What exactly is going on in Belmarsh?' asked Jen, her voice cracking.

'I have no idea,' answered Brodie. 'But what I do know is that everyone is in on it now . . . the military, special branch, MI5, MI6 – even the CIA.'

'Are we talking biological weapons here?' whispered Jen.

Brodie didn't answer. He stood up slowly, picked up his jacket and headed for the door.

'Jennifer, Nick was my friend. I can't believe he's dead. I can see you want answers, but for God's sake don't try looking for them. Let this go. Nick would tell you the same. Get rid of your research, wipe your hard drive, leave London if you can. For your own sake, forget you ever knew him . . . Oh, and please don't contact me. Get rid of my number. Get rid of Nick's phone.'

Jen was staring at him numbly.

'Do you understand?' Brodie asked, frowning. He waited until she nodded slightly. Then he left.

50

Library

Light fingers gently touched his shoulder, and Seth smiled sleepily. 'Mmm – so beautiful . . .' he murmured.

'Seth?'

He opened his eyes and blinked, momentarily confused by the figure standing over him, silhouetted against the sunlit window.

'What were you dreaming?' she asked shyly.

Seth didn't answer. He was working too hard at dealing with the crushing disappointment of being dragged away from the cool blue room, where Livia had been lying in his arms. He shook his head and glanced around, trying to get his bearings. He was on the couch in Zackary's library. 10 September 2043.

Rana was standing over him.

'Did you stay here last night?'

'No,' she laughed. 'Zackary asked me to come over this morning.'

'Where is Zackary?'

'Gone. He left for the symposium about half an hour ago.'

'Damn, what time is it? I wanted to go along.'

'Seth, you can hardly move –'

'Of course I can move,' he grimaced, hoisting himself up.

His ribs were tender still, but bearable. Holding on to the back of the sofa, he tried to put some weight on his bad leg.

'Hmmm,' he winced.

'Anton left you these,' Rana smiled, handing him a couple of yellow capsules and a glass of water.

'What are they?' asked Seth dubiously.

'Painkillers.'

'Are they going to knock me out?'

Rana checked the container label. 'Proketolorac. Should be fine.'

Seth glanced at her face and saw she was telling the truth.

'So why did Zackary ask you to come over?' asked Seth, swallowing the pills.

'To check you were OK,' she answered nonchalantly. But her tone of voice telegraphed to Seth that this wasn't entirely accurate.

'Zackary didn't trust me in his house, did he?' he chuckled.

Rana just rolled her eyes and grinned. 'He's very – er – careful about his stuff.'

When Zack had v-commed her that morning, she couldn't believe her luck. She'd lain awake half the night wondering how she was going to engineer another meeting with Zack's unbelievably gorgeous dinner guest. And now she had him to herself for the whole day.

'I really need to get to that event –'

'It's ticket only and sold out,' she shrugged. 'Why do you want to go so much?'

'I just – I just need to see Professor Engelmann again. We – er – started talking about something last night –'

Rana tilted her head to one side, considering. She was eager to please this man in whatever way she could. 'Well, maybe we can catch him afterwards?' she suggested. 'Anton's coming round this afternoon to elson your fractures, but the symposium doesn't finish till 18.00. We might persuade him to give us a lift!'

Seth tried to suppress his impatience. Rana's plan meant spending a whole day hanging around waiting, and Engelmann was leaving for the States tomorrow. He didn't have time to waste . . . But if he didn't play this right, he could end up with nothing at all or, more significantly, risk another time anomaly. So he forced a smile and said, 'Thanks, Rana, that sounds perfect.'

'Good,' she answered happily, bounding over to the bag of shopping on the dining table. 'I've collected some supplies for breakfast. Are you hungry?'

He actually felt pretty nauseous – probably a result of the cocktail of drugs and last night's rich food – but he started limping slowly over to the table. It was good to get upright, and he needed to flex some muscles, his body was so stiff. Rana rushed over to take his arm, but he refused her help.

'Thanks, Rana, but I have to be able to manage alone.'

Stung, she dropped her hands. 'Anton doesn't want you putting weight on that leg,' she argued.

'Oh, it's much better this morning,' Seth lied. 'And I can't afford to get all needy,' he added with a grin.

Yes, you can, thought Rana longingly, but she let it go and strode off to make the coffee.

Seth's progress to the table was slow. His leg was so painful and unreliable that after only seven steps he was forced to pause for a moment against the bookshelves. Cursing, he calculated his chances of surviving the vortex the following day. Not good. But the sooner he could get back to Parallon, the sooner he could return to Eva. He was determined not to delay – the distance between them was becoming intolerable.

'Seth, are you OK?' asked Rana, depositing the breakfast tray on the table.

'Fine,' he answered hoarsely.

'Checking out Zack's passion for obsolescence?' she smirked.

'What? Oh – you mean – his books?'

'Well, it's pretty weird that someone at the vanguard of new thought should still cling to such an antiquated system of communication, don't you think?'

'Er –actually, I still quite like books myself,' admitted Seth, running his fingers along the spines affectionately. 'That's weird . . .' he murmured.

'What?' she asked, pouring coffee into mugs.

'Every single book here is on bio-nanotechnology . . .'

'Of course! That's Zack's obsession,' she laughed.

Seth frowned. Not the Zack he knew. The Parallon library contained hundreds of books – on art, literature and science – but he'd never seen any on bio-nanotechnology. He pulled one off the shelf and flicked through the pages. It contained no memory triggers for him. Normally when he opened one of Zack's books he was flooded with a sense of recognition . . . So what could it mean?

'Come on, Seth, your coffee'll get cold,' urged Rana.

He nodded absently and returned the book to its shelf. Then

he turned back towards the table to resume his hobbling journey. He found Rana's watchful gaze unnerving. He needed to distract her. 'Rana, what were you working on with Zackary?'

She pressed her lips together and looked down at her plate. 'I'm sorry, Seth, I'm not allowed to talk about it.'

That sounded like a Zack directive. Seth's curiosity, already piqued by the library changes, now fired a little harder. So when Rana next lifted her eyes from her plate, she found herself drawn straight into the intensely compelling blue gaze of Zackary's new protégé.

'I'll take you into the lab after breakfast, if you like,' she found herself offering.

'Thank you, Rana, that would be wonderful.'

51

Stowaway

Parallon

Matthias was putting the finishing touches to his arena as the sun finally sank on to the horizon. He stood in the centre of the sanded floor and gazed around, satisfaction swelling in his chest. It was beautiful: towering; majestic. He was particularly proud of the classical frieze depicting a sequence of combatants – beautiful athletes wielding spears, shields and tridents; exquisitely rendered, frozen in action. The magister should be pleased with it.

Desperate to share the excitement of his achievement, he headed straight for the palace kitchen. Winston, Clare and Georgia were huddled together in a corner of the larder.

'I think I've surpassed myself this time!' Matthias crowed.

'Doing what?' asked Georgia, turning to face him, her voice strained.

'The arena, Georgia! It's perfect. I think the magis–'

'What sort of arena?' asked Clare, backing away from him to stand next to Georgia.

'A huge one!' Matt grinned. 'Circular, with seating going up layer after layer – and I've used carved columns and friezes and –'

'Yes, but what's it for?' Clare pressed.

'For entertainment . . .' swallowed Matthias.

'What kind of entertainment, Matt?' asked Winston.

Matthias hesitated. 'Well – it probably won't come to it –'

'Come to what?'

Matthias sighed. 'G-gladiatorial games,' he said finally.

'*What?*' gasped Clare.

'I was asked to build it,' protested Matthias. 'It wasn't my idea. Why are you looking at me like that?'

'So . . . who are the gladiators?' asked Georgia quietly.

The exact question Matthias had been avoiding since he'd been given the first drawing.

'I have no idea,' he snorted angrily.

How had three lowly slaves managed to completely undermine his good mood? He frowned at them, standing so motionless, staring at him stiffly. What was he thinking, coming here, honouring them with his news?

'Thanks for the support,' he hissed, slamming out of the kitchen.

Georgia and Clare followed him with their eyes until the door shut. After a couple of moments of frozen silence, they exhaled.

'It's OK, you can come out now,' breathed Clare.

Winston quickly moved the baskets of fruit and sacking they'd been masking, and helped their newly arrived stowaway crawl gratefully out of his suffocating corner.

'What are we going to do with him?' whispered Georgia anxiously. 'How will we keep him safe?'

'Safe from who?' croaked the stranger crouched on the floor.

The three of them stared down at him.

'I should never have brought him here,' breathed Clare, biting her lip anxiously.

'I can think of one or two safer places,' sighed Georgia, squatting down next to the man. 'Do you have a name? I'm Georgia, by the way.'

'Nick. Nick Mullard,' rasped the stranger, gazing around the Roman kitchen. 'Christ – where the hell am I?'

'Parallon,' answered Winston quietly. 'Otherwise known as *Hell*.'

Nick's eyes darted from one face to another, hoping to see some sign of humour. But he saw only fear and misery.

52

Resolve

Shoreditch, London

Early Sunday Morning, 30 June AD *2013*

Jen was sitting cross-legged on her bed staring at Nick's phone, thinking over what Brodie Covington had told her. Well – virtually nothing . . . except if she valued her life she should get out now. She considered that option. Her mother lived in Suffolk; she could conceivably spend a few days with her, clear her head, get her feelings sorted out . . . or . . .

She could try and find out what the hell happened to her boyfriend. If anything, Brodie's warning had only strengthened her resolve. She'd always had a tendency to do the opposite of what she was told. She glanced at her watch. 1 a.m. Why did she feel so awake? Oh yes – she'd slept through most of the day. She padded out to the kitchen, made herself some coffee and sat down with her steaming mug and Nick's iPhone. She stared at it for a moment. It contained a mine of information: contacts, emails, text messages . . . but it was Nick's. The only thing she had of his. She pressed it to her lips tenderly, fought the sudden tightness in her throat and took a deep breath. Better make a start.

She crossed the room briskly and pulled out her laptop, found a notebook and pencil, and settled herself back at the dining table. Then she began her trawl.

She started with his emails, but after an hour of meticulous scouring had to acknowledge that Nick had been frustratingly good at covering his tracks. He had deleted regularly, and kept absolutely no mail trail of anything pertaining to the disappearances. She could tell because the message she'd sent him three days previously with a couple of missing-person news story attachments wasn't in any of his folders. Just in case, she did a quick name search for Winston Grey and Elena Galanis, but found no matches. Which meant either he'd given them code names or had the information stored somewhere safer.

Sighing, she moved on to his contacts – there were hundreds of them. Name-searching all of them would take weeks . . . unless she could find out who he'd been in contact with recently . . .

'Please don't have wiped your call register, Nick,' she silently begged, as she keyed in the search.

'Oh, thank you, sweetheart,' she breathed, kissing the screen, when a complete log of dialled, received and missed calls over the past two months scrolled down. She picked up her pencil and started jotting down the numbers that appeared more than once. Most were listed as the Wood Street station desk; Brodie Covington's cropped up a few times; and her own appeared with comforting regularity. But when she came across her flurry of missed calls on that last evening, her breath caught. She stared unseeingly at the phone, remembering her distrust and misplaced anger. Why had she wasted so much of their time together acting paranoid? Her hands shook slightly as she reached for her mug and she gulped down the cold remains of her coffee. Then she forced herself back to the job and was rewarded almost immediately by spotting a mobile number Nick had dialled eighty-seven times. Jen wrote down the name and number, then scrolled through the rest of the call register. Finding nothing else particularly interesting, she moved on to his text messages. He wasn't an epic texter at the best of times – one word where possible – and again it looked like he didn't keep messages hanging around on his mobile for very long. The most historic text listed had been sent sixty days ago. Jen pictured her own message box – she had thousands of texts dating back at least eighteen months. Anyone scrolling through it would have a pretty good idea about her day-to-day life. Nick's was unlikely to give much away, but at least she'd be able to work through it reasonably quickly.

Suddenly her fingers froze . . . two texts sent to the name and number she had just jotted down:

I'd like to meet you today. Name a good place and time.

Sent at: 07.30 a.m. Thursday 9 May.
Followed by:

Alternatively I could meet you there? I am sure your head-master, Dr Crispin, would be accommodating.

Sent at: 3.58 p.m. Thursday 9 May.
The recipient of both text messages and the eighty-seven calls was Eva Koretsky.

Jen underlined the name three times and then glanced at the clock: 4 a.m. She'd better get some sleep if she was going to be able to talk to anyone coherently on the phone tomorrow. And Eva Koretsky would definitely be getting a call.

53

Classified

Zackary's House, London

Thursday 10 September AD *2043*

'Are you OK in there, Seth?' called Rana, rapping on the bath-room door.

'Well – it looks like I'm going to need to borrow some clothes,' answered Seth with irritation. 'I can't get my jeans over this brace, and my shirt is –'

'Your shirt's what?'

Sighing, Seth wrapped a towel round his waist, opened the bathroom door and held it up for her.

'Bloody hell – it's in shreds.'

Rana tried to keep her eyes focused on the shirt, but Seth standing there half-naked was a bit distracting. God, he was well-toned – but his skin was patterned with hefty cuts and bruises.

'Seth! What did that hurricane do to you?' she gasped, wincing.

He frowned, momentarily mystified, then he followed her gaze. 'Oh! They're nothing,' he shrugged nonchalantly.

'B-but I thought Anton had lazonned all your injuries,' she persisted.

'He did – I'm great now,' Seth laughed, 'apart from the lack of clothing.'

Rana didn't entirely agree with the negativity of that statement, but she managed to hold her tongue.

'So do you think Zack has got anything I could borrow?'

Her eyes shot up, and Seth realized he'd sounded way too familiar. Officially he'd only just met Zackary.

'Zackary's pretty possessive about his stuff,' began Rana, anxiously biting her lip. But then her eyes caught Seth's and she suddenly wondered why she'd been so cagey. 'Of course he won't mind,' she smiled confidently. 'I'll run up and find you something.'

'Thanks, Rana,' answered Seth, catching sight of Zack's razor. He smiled at the thought of Zack's face when he told him he'd used it.

By the time Rana returned with clothes, Seth had shaved and found a spare toothbrush. But getting dressed proved less straightforward. His body rebelled against every movement. At least in his gladiator days, he hadn't had to force his injured limbs into T-shirts and trousers. Tunics were much simpler, and he'd usually had Matt to help.

'Are you OK?' asked Rana dubiously, when he finally emerged in one of Zack's tracksuits. His complexion was chalky white.

'Fine,' he replied quickly.

'Seth, Zackary's lab is on the ground floor – that's two flights of stairs to get down. I'm not sure you should . . .'

'It won't be a problem,' said Seth firmly. He had to see inside that lab, and he needed to get this leg working better. He took a deep breath and began the painful descent. But by the time he'd reached the bottom step, he was so light-headed he had to lean on the banister and shut his eyes for a few moments.

Rana was uneasy. Anton had told her specifically that Seth was to put no weight on the leg, and yet she'd somehow allowed him to completely override those instructions. And now he looked terrible – like he was about to pass out.

'S-Seth?' She reached out to touch him, but before she could make contact, he straightened, opened his eyes and fixed her with his dazzling smile. 'So, let's take a look inside this famous laboratory.'

He watched carefully as Rana's fingers flew across the entry code pad.

'Zackary has always been dismissive of DNA-recognition key entry systems,' she smirked.

'Aren't they more secure?' asked Seth.

'He doesn't think so. He reckons it would be harder for a data thief to work out and memorize a long sequence of symbols than to grab a stray hair from his jacket and use that as an access key.'

'Put like that – he's probably right.'

'Zackary likes to store all his information in his head.'

Seth nodded, inwardly wincing at the ironic result of Zackary's flawed security conviction. Because now most of that guarded information resided in his own head too . . . if only he could access it.

The door swung open and Seth gasped in surprise. The lab looked so different . . . not to mention significantly smaller.

Zack's Parallon lab was a massive, open-plan space, spanning the entire ground floor. Although much of the equipment was the same – the banks of terminals, the quark marker, fluorescent and phase contrast microscopes – even the chrome incinerator – there were some significant disparities, like . . . *incubators?*

What was Zack doing with them?

And where was the huge central monitor screen that dominated his Parallon laboratory?

Rana looked at Seth and smiled. 'I know! I was blown away by it when I first came. Zackary has got some wild hardware, hasn't he?'

Seth nodded absently. He had just realized why the lab looked so much smaller. There was a partition wall about two-thirds of the way in. He stared at the unfamiliar doorway. It had another keypad lock beside it. So – another section of lab behind that door. Naturally, Seth was drawn straight to it.

'What's through there, Rana?' he asked, limping towards it.

She shook her head. 'Nobody goes in there except Zackary. That's his inner sanctum.'

'*You* must have seen inside though?'

She shook her head. 'No,' she shrugged.

'Haven't you wondered what he's got in there?' persisted Seth.

'No . . . not at all,' she answered honestly. 'I was just so over the moon to be working here. Professor Brandon must have warned you – Zackary hardly ever offers placements. He's not known for his sociability. So to actually work with such a great scientist . . . I mean, he's a total genius – everyone wants to work with him.'

'Really?' asked Seth sceptically.

'Of course! I mean, he's terrifying and kind of sarcastic, but he's always doing something groundbreaking – who wouldn't want to be part of that? For me it was enough to be able to contribute in whatever way I could. Even if that meant making sure there was milk in the fridge.'

Seth nodded, trying to add 'groundbreaking genius' to his other less flattering list of Zackary character traits.

He had obviously known that Zack was a scientist. And Zackary had made it pretty clear that there was nobody in the world quite as clever as he was. But he'd told Seth virtually nothing about his work – even when Seth had pressed him for information about the lab job he'd be applying for. Apart from the Professor Brandon background story, the only thing Zack had offered was, 'I suppose you could mention the Pascal Project.'

'The Pascal Project?'

'Just something I was trying to get funding for. James Pascal was a colleague – a biomedic-researcher working on post-trauma memory regeneration – and I had some ideas that I thought might be worth exploring.'

'So how am I, a stranger off the street, supposed to know anything about the Pascal Project?' Seth had said.

'You won't be a stranger off the street – you'll be posing as a student of Professor Brandon.'

'And how does that help?'

'Pascal, Brandon and I were all at Oxford together . . . Brandon was the only other person who knew about the Pascal Project.'

So was that what Zackary was working on behind that locked door? There was a quick way to find out.

'Rana – does the Pascal Project mean anything to you?'

'You know about the Pascal Project?' she gasped.

Seth waited.

'That's what I was working on . . . writing funding application letters, ordering lab chemicals and materials, transcribing columns of data . . .'

'And was Zackary working on it here with you?'

'Some of the time. If he wasn't in this lab, he would be in there.' She nodded towards the locked door. 'But we really shouldn't be talking about it. I mean, it's going to be such an incredible breakthrough for neuroscience and everything . . . but it's completely classified until his patents and funding come through.'

'It must be,' said Seth, nodding as though he knew exactly what they were talking about.

'Zackary made me sign a twelve-page non-disclosure agreement.'

'Don't worry, Rana, you haven't told me anything I didn't know already,' smiled Seth encouragingly.

But actually she had. She'd just told him that Zackary was spending most of his time working in a secret lab on something that was *beyond* classified. And Seth needed to know what that was.

54
Games

Parallon

Matthias stormed blindly out of the kitchen, through the atrium and towards the gardens. He needed to get as far as possible from Georgia, Clare and Winston. How had the three of them managed to undermine his good mood so thoroughly?

Matt didn't slow down until the soothing scents of rosemary, lavender and basil filled his nostrils. He'd reached the beloved herb garden – his most potent reminder of Corinth . . . and Seth. The two of them used to sit here on summer evenings, drinking honeyed wine and losing themselves in the unique blend of fragrances.

But thinking about his former friend caused Matt's gut to curl uncomfortably. How would Seth feel about his latest building project? He couldn't help picturing the outrage on his face. Yet the thought made him bristle with self-righteous anger. Seth would have no right to disapprove – Matt had had no choice.

Before the Seth in his head was given the chance to argue his position, Matthias heard heavy footsteps behind him. Footsteps he instantly recognized.

'Matthias,' greeted the magister genially, 'just the man.'

Matt's heart thudded and he bowed low. 'Magister?'

'So – how's my arena?'

'F-finished, my magister!'

'Excellent. In perfect time for the celebration.'

'C-celebration?' stammered Matt.

'To honour my accession here . . . I intend to preside over the best gladiatorial games in the empire. We shall start our Accession Games in five days.'

'But, magister – you have no g-gladiators –'

'Of course I have gladiators. They will begin training in the arena tomorrow.'

The magister took a long draught from the golden goblet he carried, and smiled. 'And the beauty of my gladiatorial games is that we need never stop.'

'M-magister?' gulped Matthias.

'My fighters are immortal,' said the magister, his eyes glinting with pleasure. 'However hard they beg, they simply cannot die!'

55

Memories

'So is there anything else you want to know?' asked Rana, logging out of the labcom.

She had just shown Seth the lab equipment and talked him through all the material logs and sponsorship accounts. Seth's eyes flicked over to the locked door, but he knew Rana wouldn't be able to help him with that.

'Well – I'd really like you to fill me in on some of the Pascal Project background.'

'W-what do you want to know?'

'Who exactly is Pascal?' smiled Seth.

'Oh, he and Zackary go way back,' shrugged Rana, perching on the edge of a table. 'And, as far as I know, James Pascal spent maybe eight years working on post-trauma memory loss . . . with a fair amount of success. He found that if he extracted stem cells from brain-trauma victims, and then used them to generate new nerve cells in lab cultures, he could reintroduce the freshly grown cells directly into the hippocampus.'

'Did that work?'

'In seventy per cent of trauma cases it would be enough to trigger significant memory regeneration.'

'All kinds of trauma?'

'Sudden trauma – stroke, head injury – that kind of thing . . .'

'But not if the memory loss was caused by disease?'

'God – you think just like Zackary!' Rana gasped. 'That's exactly what he was interested in . . . You see, Pascal wasn't having much success with chronic memory loss. Within weeks, the disease would cause nerve cells to die again, so stem-cell generation ceased and memory loss recurred.'

Seth nodded. As Rana spoke, he realized everything she said was familiar to him – clearly she was triggering more Zack-memories he hadn't been previously aware of. He listened attentively as she continued.

'So Zackary began developing his biotachyon implant.' Rana paused nervously and bit her lip. This was highly classified stuff.

'Go on . . .' urged Seth, catching her eye and smiling encouragingly.

'Well – the implant is a microscopic transmitter that can be placed just under the skin at the temple, and is able to send neuro-impulses directly into the hippocampus . . . impulses programmed to trigger stem-cell regeneration. So – *at its most basic* – once stem-cell regeneration begins, the implant can offer full short-term memory restoration. It works for epilepsy, dementia . . . even normal age-related memory loss.' Rana smiled proudly. 'No toxic drugs, no repeated invasive surgery – and a permanent solution. Just one tiny implant can completely eliminate one of the most significant, universally debilitating aging factors. The medical and commercial value of such a device is off the scale.'

Seth nodded again. But he could tell by the way Rana was staring at the floor that there was more.

'OK. So at its most basic it can restore short-term memory loss. What can it do at its most sophisticated?' he prompted.

Rana shook her head and licked her lips nervously. 'To be honest, I think Zackary is more fascinated by the idea of *irretrievable* memory loss; memories that can't be recovered by stem-cell regeneration because the pathway damage is too extensive. He's been disappearing for weeks, studying people who can't remember their own names, how to talk, who their family members are. I think – if he could get funding – he would be exploring the possibilities of uploading virtual memory on to the implant . . .'

Seth's eyes widened at the implications. 'You mean uploading fabricated virtual memories?' This was all completely new to him.

'With the help of family and friends – to build up a memory bank and upload it . . . Fill in the gaps . . .'

'But they would be *false* memories,' persisted Seth. 'Wouldn't that be potentially very dangerous?'

'You mean – if the technology fell into the wrong hands?'

'Well – yes. But even at its most benign, you are consigning people to walk around with a fictitious, distorted past.'

'Better than no past, surely? Imagine sitting in a room, terrified of everyone who comes in because you don't recognize them.'

Seth shook his head. He could see the attractiveness of the idea, though it made him very uneasy.

But Rana's eyes were sparkling with excitement. 'And look at the potential applications,' she continued. 'You could implant all sorts of other stuff directly into the brain: how to speak Chinese, the history of Western art – *whatever!* Just imagine a world where *any* kind of information could be transferred directly into the hippocampus. Who'd need to dedicate years and years to learning and study, if you could simply insert infinite knowledge? Let's face it – it'd be literally *mind-blowing!*'

'Wow,' said Seth slowly. He had not failed to recognize that Zackary's hypothetical research had clearly become a reality: he himself was walking around with uploaded information from Zackary's computer terminal. Which meant that Zackary had presumably not only cracked this research, he had also managed to come up with an alternative method of neurotransmission.

So why did he have no recollection of this work? Surely if he had all Zackary's memories, he should know about this? Normally his Zack-memories were instantly accessible. Now – although there was a whisper of familiarity in the research she described – he couldn't locate it. He scanned the lab for memory triggers. The far wall was shelved out with stacks of empty glass cases . . . another anomaly – there were no glass cases in the Parallon lab. He stared at them, willing his brain to remember.

And suddenly he shuddered . . .

Rats. He was picturing a wall of rats. One in each case. Row upon row of black rats.

Rana noticed what he was staring at.

'Used to contain fifty lab rats,' she said. 'All dead now.'

Seth frowned, waiting for her explanation.

'There was something wrong with the first-stage implants,' she shrugged. 'Zack thought it may have been the casing? I think he's working on different materials now . . . It's just a matter of time.'

She glanced at Seth's face. It was white and drawn. 'Oh, Seth, I'm sorry. You really need a break – I've had you standing around for hours. Come on – it's way past lunchtime.'

Seth didn't argue. The rats had stirred a memory, but it was incomplete; he just couldn't reach it. And the effort was making him feel almost dizzy. Or was the dizziness coming from the throbbing pain in his leg? Whatever the source, he definitely couldn't stand here for very much longer. Leaning heavily on the banister, he heaved himself up the two flights of stairs to the library and stumbled on to the couch.

'Stay there. I'll fix us some eggs,' Rana said, heading for the kitchen.

She had just put butter in the pan when her v-com vibrated and Zackary's face appeared on the screen. 'Hey, Zack,' she called over to it.

'Hmm – has my house guest got you slaving away in the kitchen?'

Rana smiled. 'Hardly! I'm just throwing something together for lunch. How's the conference going?'

'Good.' Zackary's eyes were darting around the kitchen.

'Looking for Seth?' she chuckled. 'He's resting in the library. His leg was giving him a bit of trouble.' She couldn't quite bring herself to admit that it was because she'd had him limping around the lab all morning. 'Er – Zackary, did you have plans for later?'

'This evening? Why, what did you have in mind, Rana?' he grinned.

Rana suddenly felt awkward. She and Zackary had had a

brief, humiliating fling a while ago, which she'd allowed herself to temporarily forget in her enthusiasm to set up Seth with his chance to talk to Engelmann. She tried to cover her embarrassment. 'Oh – er – I just thought maybe we could *all* catch some dinner later?'

There was a moment's hesitation. 'Well – I was planning to take Louis out – make up for last night . . .'

'Oh, right,' said Rana. She felt alarmingly disappointed. Her desire to please Zack's house guest was verging on the unhealthy.

'But,' Zackary continued, 'Engelmann did mention that he and Lauren had something they wanted to talk to that boy about – which intrigues me somewhat . . . So, why not? Is Seth mobile?'

'Sort of. Don't worry, I can get him there.'

'Why don't we meet in the conference centre dining room at 7 p.m.? They're doing an excellent menu.'

'Great! That's a date.'

Damn, mouthed Rana silently as Zackary's v-com disconnected. Why had she said the word 'date'?

She finished cooking the eggs and carried the plates into the library. Seth was stretched out on the couch, one arm across his forehead, his whole concentration fixed on blocking out the jangling pain shooting through his broken leg.

'God, Seth, I am so sorry,' she gasped, catching sight of his expression. 'I was supposed to give you more painkillers too. Ages ago.'

She picked up the tablets, poured him a glass of water and darted across the room to his side. But he barely noticed her. His pain had dragged him to another couch, in a blue room, where soft footsteps meant instant salvation . . .

'Seth?'

He opened his eyes and frowned. Wrong room. Wrong footsteps. Once again, he had to struggle to fight the crashing dismay.

'Rana? Sorry. I was – er – miles away.' He smiled apologetically and gratefully took the pills from her.

'You'd better eat something quickly. You aren't supposed to swallow those on an empty stomach.'

Seth nodded dutifully. But he wasn't hungry, just tired. He closed his eyes briefly, summoning his resolve. He was in danger of being sidetracked and nothing could get in the way of his objectives: sort out the vortex and get back to Eva.

56

Contact

Running along the hot sand. Laughing. Hand in hand. Our paces perfectly matched . . . The sky a brilliant blue and the sun glinting off the waves lapping at our bare feet. Empty beach, just Seth and me; white sand, blue sky, sparkling water.

Suddenly his face turned to mine, his eyes dancing. 'Let's swim, Eva!'

Our clothes thrown in a pile on the beach, hurling glittering, arcing sprays at each other, jumping and twisting in the water. And then his arms round me – singing and dancing to the rhythmic motion of the waves.

My face lifted to his. 'I love you, Seth. I'll always love you.'

Seth kissing me, long and warm and tender. The waves nudging our glistening bodies, twined round each other, melting together, two bodies, one beating heart.

Wide blue eyes. 'Look!'

A beautiful island in the distance, bright with heavy fruit trees and colourful birds flying from branch to branch.

'Do you think that's Paradise?'

'No, Eva, it's Parallon. Come on, I'll race you.'

*Swimming towards it, our strokes synchronized and even.
Stroke after stroke, breath after breath, but the island always
distant. Never any closer.*

*'I can't swim any more, Seth, let's go to Parallon another day.'
Panting, turning to face him. Facing only a restless, empty ocean.*

'Seth?' Screaming. Choking. 'Seth, where are you?'

*The sun suddenly shrouded. Ominous heavy clouds growing,
darkening – the whole sky one seething black mass, spewing
out sharp needles of rain . . . falling in great sheets, pounding
me, pushing me further and further down into the water.*

*Spectacular streaks of lightning ripping through the pulsing
black sky, crashes of thunder filling the leaden air, and me drifting away from it all, down . . . down . . . down . . . away . . .
untouchable . . . Seeing nothing, hearing nothing but thunder . . . crashing on and on and on . . .*

'Eva!'

Oh – not crashing thunder . . . banging. On my door.
Relentlessly.

I groaned and was just on the point of hauling myself out
of bed when Astrid burst in.

'We're gonna be late for breakfast, Eva. Didn't your alarm
go off?'

She was staring down at me, frowning. 'Are you OK, babe?
You don't look so good.'

Probably because I'd been up till 4 a.m. trying to find the
elusive Professor Ambrose and his killer virus.

'Yeah, I'm fine,' I said quickly, throwing the duvet off. I sat up carefully. The hammer was going in my head again. I sank back down against the pillow and shut my eyes. Damn Ambrose – this was his fault . . . Everything was his fault.

'You'd better stay put – I'll pick you up some breakfast. But, honestly, you could have chosen a more convenient day . . . you swore to sit next to me in the Latin test. Now what am I supposed to do?'

'You'll be fine, Astrid. You know this stuff. We went through it yesterday.'

She snorted and left.

I had a brief visit at some point from Rose, but spent most of the morning either trying to swim to Parallon or following Ambrose through murky corridors. I guess it could have been worse. Cassius could have joined the party.

I was just about to open the final door in the final corridor when my phone rang. Rose had put it right next to the bed, in case of emergencies, so I reached out and answered it, without checking the caller ID. Big mistake.

'Is that Eva? Eva Koretsky?'

I wanted to say, 'Who wants to know?' like the tough guys always did in cop films, but I settled for a wobbly, 'Yes.'

In my defence, I had been asleep. Plus she did have the kind of voice that you had to obey.

'I need to talk to you. *Urgently*.'

'What?' I had a sinking feeling.

'*Today*.' Could she sound more assertive?

'Er – I don't think so.' Could I sound less?

'At 4.30? I've checked – your lessons should be over by then.'

Who *was* this woman? How the hell did she know my time-table?

'I'm s-sorry, I'm sick today. I can't –'

'I'll come to you.'

Oh God. She knew where I lived. 'Look, who the hell are you?' I finally managed to snap.

'Jennifer Linden,' she said, and hung up.

I closed my eyes again.

'Lunch, Eva!' Astrid bellowed in my ear.

I sighed. What I wouldn't give for a bit of peace and quiet.

'How was the Latin test?' I asked her, as she settled herself and a tray of food on to the bed next to me. She gave me a withering look, then started sharing out a mound of mushroom risotto between the two plates.

'By the way – no need to worry about the band rehearsal tonight,' she sprayed through a mouthful of grey gunk. 'I've decided we could all do with a night off.'

'Great – that should give you plenty of time to check out that Latin verb list I wrote out for you,' I smirked. She was not amused.

When she'd gone, I managed to get myself across to the shower and into some clothes . . . If I hadn't dreamed up the terrifying Ms Linden, I definitely didn't intend facing her in my pyjamas. To further distract myself, I sat at my desk and tried tackling some chemistry homework. But my head was still pounding, so I picked up my laptop and got back into bed. I shut my eyes for a moment or two, and when I jerked awake, Rose Marley was looming over me with her damn blood-pressure kit.

The good news was that she gave me something for the head-ache. The bad news was that she was stressing about my blood pressure and threatening to come back in an hour. I looked at my watch. It was four o'clock. If I could get Rose to hang around for another half hour, maybe she could get rid of the Linden woman?

But Rose was packing up her stuff and heading for the door. 'I'm just popping over to the pharmacy, Eva. I'll be back at five.'

Opportunity lost.

As soon as the door had shut behind her, I grabbed my laptop. I needed to see if I could dredge anything up on Jennifer Linden. Forearmed was forewarned.

One simple name search later, I was staring at a YouTube news video report. I instantly recognized the reporter. It was the woman who'd been with DI Mullard at the Register that night . . . watching us. Now, though, she was standing with a microphone, next to a smashed-up motorbike by the side of the road. I stared in fascination as the camera panned the scene, then paused at a man in leathers sprawled across the ground a few metres away from the bike. There was blood everywhere. *God, that's a bit voyeuristic*, I thought disgustedly. Then I suddenly realized that it wasn't a dead man. It wasn't even an injured man. The clothes were empty. They had been placed there to look like a man lying dead on the ground . . . Some horrible practical joke? I started paying attention to what Jennifer Linden was actually saying . . .

I was on my third play of the video when there was a knock at the door.

I glanced up in shock and noticed that my clock said 16.30 exactly. Surely, surely, no one would let her come and find me in my bedroom? This was a school, for God's sake. There were rules! It had to be Rose, come early.

'Hey,' I said, and the door opened.

It wasn't Rose. It was the woman I had just been watching on my screen. The one who had looked at me in the Register as if she'd like to see me burn in hell. Which was exactly the way she was looking at me now.

'*You!*' she breathed venomously.

I stared back at her, frowning. I could so do without another person hating me right now. Especially when – as far as I knew – I hadn't done anything at all to alienate this woman. But I guessed two could play the aggressive card.

'Who the hell do you think you are – barging into my room?' I demanded. Problem was, my voice came out all cracked and a bit pathetic sounding, so the sentence didn't carry quite the power I might have hoped for.

'We had an appointment,' she said in a clipped, cold voice.

'We didn't have a venue,' I parried.

Her eyes narrowed. Why was she looking at me like that? I wanted to ask her, but instead I mumbled, 'Who told you where I was?'

She shrugged. 'One of the kids in that square out there. Lucky I got somebody who knew.'

Traitor. Bet it was Ruby.

I thought we had some sort of security? Could a stranger literally come right through the gates and into my bedroom? My hands began to shake. Not cool. I hid them under my duvet. But I'm pretty sure that the lovely Jennifer Linden noticed. She had these hawk eyes that kind of darted all over the place, taking everything in. If I hadn't just seen her doing a news report I would have assumed she was another detective. That – or a Rottweiler.

'So – Eva Koretsky – I'll get straight to the point. What were you doing with DI Nick Mullard?'

I suppressed the familiar wave of guilt at the mention of his name, and glanced at my phone. At least he hadn't called for the last couple of days. I did my best to keep my face neutral; I couldn't afford to give anything away to this woman. Anyway, weren't they supposed to be working together? They certainly had been on the night at the Register. So hadn't he told her about our meeting? He couldn't have. Did that mean I could genuinely trust him? Or that he didn't trust her? Or that he was so shaken up by Seth's little mind readjustment that he was too embarrassed to mention it? The only honourable thing I could do was cover for him.

'I don't know what you're talking about.'

'I think you do,' she snorted.

Jennifer Linden had so met her match. I'd had years to develop my blocking skills and I could do teenage recalcitrance better than anyone. The secret was to refuse any eye contact with the person haranguing you and gaze at an object in the middle distance. You had to fix on it and never flick your eyes away, however blurry it got.

Everyone gave up and walked out in the end. Which is exactly what Jennifer Linden did twenty minutes later. But by that time my head was pounding again, so I slid down on my pillows and shut my eyes.

I groaned when I heard the door handle rattling. Surely she wasn't back? But it was only Rose.

'Eva?' she frowned, as she tightened the BP cuff. 'You look feverish. You haven't been out, have you?'

I shook my head. 'If only,' I sighed.

She tutted. 'Your blood pressure has dropped even further. I'm sorry, but I think you're going to have to move back in with me.'

'I'm fine, Rose –' I began. The thought of getting out of bed and making my way across the quad felt like way too much effort. 'I just need to sleep a while.'

I closed my eyes. Much better. I vaguely felt her hand on my forehead, but it was nice and cool, so I didn't mind too much. The next thing I knew, I was propped up in a wheelchair riding in the medical centre lift. Rose on one side, Rob Wilmer on the other.

Great. I shut my eyes again. It made the humiliation just that bit more invisible.

The next morning the headache was gone and my brain felt less fuzzy. Good. I wouldn't have to stay here. I had some stuff I needed to find out . . . about Jennifer Linden and DI Mullard. What exactly was their relationship? A DI and a reporter – a bit unusual, wasn't it? And why had DI Mullard kept our meeting confidential?

I swung my legs off the bed and pulled myself upright. The room stayed still. I'd take a quick shower and be dressed before Rose got here, I promised myself, as I headed for the bathroom. But by the time I'd squirted a handful of shampoo into my hair, I didn't feel quite so motivated. I dried myself slowly and stretched out on the bed. I just needed a short rest before completing that task.

'Some breakfast, Eva?'

Rose was standing next to the bed with a tray of food.

I was still wrapped in a towel, covered in goosebumps.

I grinned sheepishly at her. 'I'm a lot better today, Rose,' I said. 'I was just about to get dressed.'

Rose nodded, plonked the tray on the bedside table and handed me my pyjamas. I scowled and put them on.

'Er – thanks for – you know – taking care of me again, Rose,' I mumbled.

'It's what I'm paid to do, Eva,' she shrugged, pouring some orange juice.

'I don't think you reckoned on it being quite so full-on.'

'Neither did you.'

'Yeah, but I don't get a choice – I'm unfortunately stuck being me. You could walk away.'

She laughed. 'Why would I do that?'

'Because it's not going to get any better,' I said quietly. 'You know what Dr Falana said . . .'

She looked up sharply. 'Doctors are always getting things wrong, Eva.'

'He's not wrong, Rose.'

'Nonsense. Now would you like jam or marmalade on your toast?'

'Have you told Astrid?' I persisted.

She frowned. 'Why on earth would I talk to Astrid about your health?'

'B-because the band is the most important thing in her life, and I don't know how much longer I can –'

'Nobody knows what lies ahead, Eva. We all have to take each day as it comes. So my advice to you is to simply enjoy today and stop worrying about tomorrow . . .'

I nodded. I really wouldn't mind a day off worry.

'. . . and once you've tasted my sister's special recipe straw-berry jam,' she added, waving the jar under my nose, 'the only thing you'll be worrying about is whether there's enough in there for your second slice of toast.'

Hmmm. It did smell delicious. 'OK, then,' I smiled, settling back against my pillows. Maybe enjoying today wouldn't be such a bad idea.

As Rose deemed me out of immediate danger, she went off to join the school doctor in surgery while I slept the morning away. She woke me up for lunch and then had some prescriptions to fill and samples to drop off. She left me with her mobile number and a list of other emergency contacts, but I knew I'd be OK. I was feeling much better.

I looked around for my laptop. Damn. It wasn't here. Must still be in my room. I was just contemplating dragging myself over there, when there was a knock on the door.

I glanced at the clock. 2.30 p.m. Everyone was at lessons.

For one unguarded moment, that sealed-off corner of my heart started beating . . . *Seth*?

'Hello?' I croaked. Damn. Why did my voice have to sound so awful?

The door opened slowly and a head appeared. Jennifer bloody Linden's head.

'What?' I spluttered, disappointment and anger fighting for supremacy. Then suddenly fear joined the party, as I realized how alone I was. The medical block was set away from the other buildings, and was currently completely empty, apart from me – and Jennifer Linden.

She walked into the room slowly, skirting me like I was a

343

dangerous animal she needed to be wary of. Then she cleared her throat. 'I think we started off on the wrong foot . . .'

I didn't speak.

'I – I can see you're not well –'

Congratulations on your observation skills, Ms Linden. Glad they finally taught you something *in reporter school.*

'It's just that I've had a lot on my mind, and I didn't handle myself well yesterday. I-I'm sorry . . . I d-did the same thing to Nick – and he f-froze me out too.'

I frowned. What the hell was she talking about? Oh God, she wasn't . . . she was . . . she was crying.

I passed her a tissue and she blew her nose.

'I saw them carrying you and putting you in a wheelchair – and for a while I thought that maybe you'd caught what Nick had. And suddenly – I wasn't jealous any more. I just wanted it to stop.'

My head shot up. 'Is DI Mullard sick?'

She looked up at me with such an awful expression, I felt a chill go through me.

'Not any more,' she whispered.

57

Fusion

Zackary's House, London

Thursday 10 September AD 2043

'Seth, Anton's here to check out your leg.' Rana was gently shaking his shoulder. He jerked awake, one hand grabbing defensively on to Rana's and the other locking round her forearm and twisting it sharply behind her body. She let out a small cry and he instantly let go. She was staring at him in bewilderment.

'I'm so sorry, Rana,' he mumbled. 'Er – bad dream.' He frowned. He hadn't responded like a gladiator for a very long time. Why was he suddenly doing so now?

Anton breezed through the taut atmosphere and set up his medidock. He helped Seth peel off Zackary's joggers and began examining the fractures. Seth had been barely conscious the day before when Anton had scanned the injuries, so he watched the images on the monitor with interest.

'I don't understand . . .' murmured Anton. 'The tibia crack should have started fusing by now. Surely you haven't been moving around on it? I made it absolutely clear that the next few days were critical. If the bone begins to knit when it's out of alignment, it'll have to be reset. Rana? What's he been doing?'

Rana turned pink and began stammering a response, but Seth interrupted.

'I fell, Anton . . . in the bathroom. Sorry. Don't blame Rana – she's been a perfect nurse.'

Anton shook his head. 'If you value your mobility, Seth, you're going to have to be a lot more careful.'

'I do value my mobility, Anton. A great deal. And I need to get moving now,' Seth answered urgently, staring hard into Anton's eyes. 'Is there no way of speeding this process up?'

Anton blinked. 'No . . . well . . . apart from – No, there isn't.'

'Anton, talk to me.'

'No – it's experimental, and I would never recommend it.'

'Go on,' demanded Seth, staring directly into Anton's eyes.

Anton licked his lips anxiously. 'Protracted, full-power elson. But it can only be done under general anaesthetic and the risks are high. Whereas our way, there are no risks – apart from some mild skin irritation. The healing process is relatively fast, and total mobility guaranteed. It is the only safe option.'

'So tell me about the risks,' persisted Seth.

'Tissue damage: LcG waves of that intensity can't be focused without burning surrounding skin and muscle. Also, there's a high risk of severe bleeding; as well as infection, of course. Really, Seth, it's no contest. The only gain is time . . . a few days at most. What could possibly be that urgent?'

For a fleeting moment Seth envied Anton his ignorance. Then he took a deep breath, gazed impassively into Anton's eyes and said, 'OK, then. We'd better get on with it.'

'No, Seth – you misunderstand,' laughed Anton. 'I said it

could only be done under a general anaesthetic. At a hospital. In sterile conditions. It would take weeks to set up – by which time you'll be fine!'

'You gave me some pretty good medication yesterday, surely that'd be enough?' asked Seth.

Anton snorted. 'What I gave you yesterday was a mild sedative. I assure you, you'd need a lot more than that for this procedure.'

'It'll be enough. I'd like you to do the elsonning now, Anton,' said Seth quietly, his eyes still fixed on Anton's face.

Anton stared at Seth and then nodded slowly. 'All right then. I am warning you though, it won't be pleasant.'

Seth knew he could deal with unpleasant. He'd endured a world of injury without the luxury of anaesthetic.

'You can't be serious?' gasped Rana. 'Anton, Seth's not –'

'We'll have to take him to my clinic. At least I can do sterile there. Rana – does Zackary have a bottle of whisky around here?'

'Whisky?'

Anton flicked his eyes towards Seth. 'There's no way Seth'll get through this sober.'

But Seth shook his head. 'No whisky, Rana.' He couldn't afford to get drunk. He had to talk to Engelmann later and he'd need a clear head.

'You're insane,' breathed Anton. 'Rana, bring the bottle, he'll be begging for it in no time.'

Anton packed up his medidock, and he and Rana helped Seth down the stairs to his car.

Although Seth had never travelled in Anton's car, the memories Zackary had given him meant that the sensation was neither strange nor unnerving. So when he saw the streamlined shape, the curved bench sofa seating and the absence of steering wheel, he didn't blink. As soon as they were seated, Anton clipped his medidock in place, then announced their destination, and the car slid quietly into motion.

The clinic was a large glass building a couple of kilometres north of the river. The car pulled up outside, they disembarked, and Anton programmed it to wait in his parking bay. Then he pressed his thumb to the clinic keypad, the door slid open, and they were standing in a large bright reception area.

'Come, my surgery's just through here.'

They followed him along a spotless glazed corridor, through a suite of rooms, into a white airy space containing a hospital bed and banks of bleeping equipment.

Anton v-commed Nadia, his nurse, who arrived via a door at the other end of the room.

'Nadia, Tori isn't around too, is she?' asked Anton. 'I could really use two assistants for this procedure.'

'No, she was on early shift, I'm afraid, Anton.'

Anton turned to Rana. 'So – how would you feel about helping out here?'

Rana narrowed her eyes. 'I'm not a medic, Anton. What would I have to do?'

'I'll give clear instructions,' he smiled. 'While we decon, Seth, I'll need you to strip down to your underwear. Here, you can put this on,' he added, passing him a gown.

Seth looked at it and frowned. Why would he put that strange garment on?

He just shook his head and did his best to take off Zackary's clothes without any obvious signs of pain. He didn't want to give Anton any reason to cancel.

Rana tried to keep her eyes off Seth as he limped across to the bed, but she couldn't deny herself a small furtive glance. She was slightly annoyed to catch Nadia doing the same thing.

As soon as they emerged from the decon chamber, Anton and Nadia prepared a trolley with dressings, antiseptic swabs and sealed hypodermics. As Anton inserted a cannula into his hand, Seth was suddenly reminded of Eva, in her hospital bed. He shut his eyes for a moment, praying she was OK. *I'll be with you soon, baby*, his mind called, and his resolve was strengthened by the thought.

'I'm going to introduce the sedative now, Seth, along with some ABV.'

'ABV?'

'Infection prevention. Afterwards we are going to feed fluids into your system from this sachet here to try and keep you nice and stable.'

Seth nodded, and moments later he felt the drug beginning to seep through his veins. He shut his eyes, barely aware of the small sting in the crook of his arm.

'I have just inserted a small electrode that will keep monitoring your blood pressure and oxygen levels,' said Anton. 'And now I'm attaching pads to your chest.'

'What are they for?' asked Seth sleepily.

'Just in case I have to restart your heart,' he replied. 'Still want to go through with this?'

Seth nodded.

'Chin up, Rana,' grinned Anton, seeing her blanch. 'By the end of today, you'll be deeply grateful to me for reminding you why you chose a career in research rather than medicine.'

'Very reassuring, Anton,' she muttered caustically.

'OK, I think we're just about ready to begin.' Anton unfastened Seth's leg brace, then touched a keypad on the full-sized elsonnator, which slid into position over the bed. He released the base plate, placing it carefully under Seth's damaged leg, and secured the leg tightly in position. Then he switched on the monitor screen so that he could watch the fusion as it took place.

'Nadia, stand by with oxygen, atropine, adrenalin and blood. Rana, you will be monitoring the fluids and blood pressure. If these numbers change from green to red, let me know.'

The elsonnator hummed into action and Seth closed his eyes. His head felt comfortably detached and the sensation of the elsonning was not unpleasant . . . a gentle glow of warmth. He felt himself drifting off, wondering if Anton's dire warnings had been some sort of joke.

For the first time in ages Seth's drowsy mind took him back to the arena. He could hear the braying crowd, smell the blood of the fighters who had fallen, and now he could see the sand scuffing beneath his feet. He ran his hand along the smooth stem of the trident in his right hand and flexed his fingers round the net in his left. He was walking towards his opponent, who was standing facing the crowd, his back to Seth.

'Unusually confident,' he thought. He had never encountered a gladiator before who flaunted such reckless audacity. But maybe he knew that Seth would never strike a man from behind.

His opponent waited until Seth was no more than a metre away and then he turned; his face was concealed behind a heavy iron helmet, his chest encased in armour. He wasn't tall, but the armour gave him breadth. There was something about his stance that was familiar, but Seth couldn't place why.

Suddenly his opponent raised a heavy sword and began to roar, lunging towards Seth with all his force.

The crowd cheered.

Seth darted out of range and danced around his opponent, planning his strike. He saw immediately that the man was all bluff; he had no serious strength and was slow to react. For a second he felt an unexpected rush of pity, his instinct to survive and win momentarily eclipsed. But an instant later he had possession of himself again, and began taunting his quarry – a ploy the lanisters encouraged because audiences loved it. He leaped in and out, forcing his clumsy, cumbersomely armoured opponent to make costly, ineffectual lunges. Before long Seth could feel his enemy's hot fury, and his slowing responses told Seth the man was exhausted.

'Enough,' he thought. 'Time to end this.'

The next time the armoured gladiator thrust out his sword, Seth netted him and drove his trident hard under the man's arm. Blood gushed instantly from the deep wound. His enemy screamed in pain and fell heavily on the sand. Seth heard the crowd roar with delight, but he felt no pride or sense of victory. Instead of raising his hand in acknowledgement of his win, he stood gazing down at the man dying at his feet.

Some impulse made him bend and lift the man's head. Gently, he removed the iron helmet and gasped in horror.

'Matthias?' he choked.

'He's dead,' jeered a voice behind him. Seth turned, knowing immediately who would be there. Who was always there at the centre of everything dark: Cassius.

'This time,' gasped Seth, 'this time it finishes. This time you die.'

But Cassius shook his head and laughed. 'Not this time, slave.' He raised his sword, which was suddenly made of flame instead of iron, and then plunged it deep into Seth's leg.

'No,' cried Seth, twisting away from the snapping flames.

'There's no escape, gladiator scum! I will burn you till you die.'

And Cassius thrust again, and again Seth screamed, but there was no respite. The flames burned into his flesh, deeper and deeper, until his body was on fire, his mind flailing to find comfort.

'Livia,' he screamed. 'Livia, where are you?' His chest heaved as the agony of the blade seared him again.

'Seth, it's nearly over.' A cool hand on his forehead.

'Livia?' he choked.

And then the flames drove deeper and he screamed and jerked and tried to get away, but Cassius had him pinned down. He had beaten him again. Adrenalin coursed through him. No. Cassius couldn't win. If he died, Cassius would kill Livia next. He had to fight. He tried to turn, to face his oppressor, but he felt his limbs growing weak. He couldn't make his body move. Perhaps he had no body any more. Perhaps he was no more substantial than ash. And yet he burned on and on. The screams that echoed round his head . . . Were they his? Or Matt's? Or the arena crowd? Screaming for blood. Blood everywhere. He could taste blood. He could smell it. He was lying in a pool of blood and flame, sliding into it, sinking deeper, falling through blood into the pit of flame. Consumed by it, until there was nothing left of him, nothing but darkness.

58

Pathways

Seth could hear someone moaning.

'I think he's coming round. No, don't decrease the oxygen yet, Nadia.'

'Thank God,' said a shaky voice. A voice he knew. A cool damp cloth on his skin . . . but it didn't mask the pain. The scorching. His leg was on fire.

'Flames,' he gasped. 'Burning . . .'

'It's OK, Seth, it's all over now. The bone is fused.'

Seth opened his eyes and squinted against the bright light. He tried to sit up, but Anton held him down. 'I think you need to lie still for a while, Seth. We have to get your oxygen levels up and your body fluids are still low. You coped remarkably well, considering. Not something I would put myself through.'

Rana's face loomed into view. 'Hi, Seth.' She was paper-white.

Seth forced a smile. 'Hey – you look terrible! Are you OK?' he croaked.

'Am *I* OK?' she spluttered.

'What time is it?' Seth murmured, trying to remember why it was important.

'Relax, Seth, for God's sake. You've just undergone a major procedure. You need to allow yourself some recovery time.'

'I . . . I have to meet . . .'

'Engelmann?' interpreted Rana. 'You've got to be joking!' she gasped.

'Have to,' Seth answered, gritting his teeth as he tried to pull himself up.

'Settle down,' ordered Anton, 'or I'll call security. You're not in any fit state to go gallivanting –'

Seth jolted forward, pushing Anton's hand away. 'I've got to get there –' he rasped.

'Hey, calm down!' interrupted Rana crossly. 'Zackary just v-commed. The conference is over –'

Seth doubled his efforts to get off the bed.

'Hey! It's OK, Seth! Zackary is taking Engelmann and Lauren out to eat, and then bringing them back to his house for coffee. All being well, you can see them there.'

Seth stared at her for a moment or two. She was telling the truth. He nodded and lay back again, closing his eyes. He was just drifting off when Rana cleared her throat.

'Who's Livia?' she asked in a determinedly casual voice.

Seth pretended not to have heard.

Three hours later, they were sitting down to a light supper at Zackary's house. Seth had refused Anton's offers of whisky, but accepted another shot of analgesic, and had managed to walk out of the clinic unaided. He could now put his full weight on the leg, and no longer required a brace, but it didn't feel good. He'd simply traded one kind of excruciating pain for another: the bone was healed but the injury site was now a mangled mess of blood and charred skin. Anton had done his best with nugraft, but the area of damage was large, and the bleeding had been difficult to control. The nugraft's thin transparent layer could do little to disguise the gore underneath. But Seth could move now. Which was the point.

Rana had laid out a meal of cheeses, olives and salad. Seth looked at the table in surprise. He could have been back in Corinth. Or Londinium. Or the early days of Parallon, when it was just him . . . and Matt.

Oh Zeus – Matt . . . Matthias lying on the sand, covered in blood. Seth's stomach twisted painfully. He shook the image away. He had to pull himself back to the present and focus. In less than half an hour, Engelmann would be here. He needed to find out everything he could so that he could head back to the vortex before morning.

He stared down at his plate. Rana had piled it with food, but the pain was distracting and he couldn't summon an appetite. Anton, on the other hand, was eating voraciously, so while Rana was refilling the water jug, Seth managed to offload most of his food on to him.

They were just clearing away the dishes when Zackary breezed in with his guests. 'Is that coffee ready, Rana?' he called into the kitchen.

Rana rolled her eyes and started measuring out scoops, and a few minutes later they were all settled back in the library with coffee and Florentines . . . a speciality biscuit that Rana had bought, knowing how fond of them Zackary was.

The atmosphere was benign, but it was clear by the way Engelmann's eyes kept resting on Seth that the previous evening's conversation had intrigued him.

At last Lauren Baxter offered them a conversational opening.

'Louis and I were talking about your wormhole premise last night, Seth.'

Seth held his breath. 'And?'

'You were asking how we would *hypothetically* go about restabilizing an erratic space–time corridor, weren't you?'

Seth nodded.

'Well, if this hypothetical unstable wormhole existed, I personally don't think you'd have a hope in hell of restabilizing it,' laughed Lauren. 'Unstable exotic baryons are so unpredictable that any kind of control is unlikely. But Louis disagrees, don't you?'

Engelmann was staring at Seth through narrowed eyes. 'No, Lauren, I don't disagree,' he smiled. 'You are entirely right about our hypothetical wormhole *if* it occurred in a vacuum or even a low-density gas . . . but if it existed in a dense fluid with suitable dielectric properties . . .'

'W-what kind of dense fluid?' rasped Seth, his throat dry with tension.

'Well – water, possibly,' shrugged Engelmann. 'Then there might be some sort of chance . . .'

Seth swallowed. 'What would you need to do?'

Engelmann frowned. 'If it were me, I'd try blasting within the fluid using a high intensity three-dimensional electric field. By exploiting the surrounding stability of the denser medium, there might be a way of restoring some semblance of equilibrium through the corridor itself.'

'So, if the wormhole was in – say – water, how would you generate and target the power?'

The professor nodded. 'Good question. You'd need to calculate the size of the target area, and position and pulse the three-field generators precisely. A microscopic wormhole would require significant power to effect such a change, so the equation to determine the scale of generation might challenge your resources.'

Seth nodded thoughtfully. Resources didn't pose a problem in Parallon. They could build anything there – just as long as the Romans didn't find out. But would Parallon-Zackary know how to construct an appropriate generator? Because Seth definitely didn't.

'Given the parameters, how would you calculate the power required?' he asked.

Anton yawned. 'This is getting a bit specialized for after-dinner chat. And I'm sure Louis and Lauren don't want to spend their last night in London talking shop.'

'On the contrary –' protested Engelmann.

'Anyway,' continued Anton, 'I've got to give Seth another ABV shot and some analgesic or he's going to have a miserable night. Then I must go home . . . I've got an early start in the morning. We can do this over by the couch, Seth.'

Seth did his best to swallow his frustration and followed Anton to the other side of the room.

As he stretched out along the couch, he glanced across at Louis and Lauren, who were both staring at him speculatively. Their hungry expressions told him that they were now pretty certain Seth wasn't talking about a hypothetical wormhole. He'd given too much away. Damn. Would he still be able to get more information out of them or was it too dangerous?

Suddenly Anton shifted the nugraft on his injured leg, and wormholes and field generators slipped instantly from his mind as pain overwhelmed him. He groaned.

'Blast,' complained Anton. Blood was gushing from the wound on to the couch.

'Oh for God's sake, Anton,' moaned Zackary. 'That's going to stain, isn't it?'

When Seth saw the blood, he froze. The virus . . . Anton's life was now in grave danger.

'Get away from me,' he shouted huskily, glaring at Anton, who instantly dropped the swab from his hand and stepped away.

'Anton's just trying to help, Seth,' murmured Rana, cautiously making her way over to the couch.

Seth gazed at her and said slowly, 'I am going to clean up the sofa and my leg, and nobody is going to help. OK?' He looked around at everyone, making sure he had eye contact. They all stopped moving.

He wrapped his leg in a clumsy bandage, limped over to the kitchen where he soaked some cloths in water, and came back to clean up the couch. As he scrubbed he realized that Anton, Rana and Nadia must have been exposed to his blood that afternoon. He had been too sedated to consider it. But that was hours ago now, so the gloves must have been adequate protection.

When he'd finished, he looked down at the bloody cloths in his hands and said, 'I'm going down to the incinerator in Zackary's lab, and I don't want anyone to follow.'

They remained fixed in place.

Seth had memorized the door code, so a few moments later

he had powered the incinerator and was loading it with the cloths. He leaned against the wall, panting – the sprint downstairs had left him exhausted and jangling. He glanced down at his leg to check the bandage was holding. Blood was seeping under it and on to the floor. He needed more padding, but a quick visual scan around the lab revealed nothing useable. His eyes rested on the door to Zackary's secret room. Zeus, he wanted to know what was in there. Maybe he'd even find bandages inside. It was an excuse of sorts and gave him all the justification he needed to look at the entry keypad on the door.

What could the code be? He shut his eyes. The answer had to be somewhere in his mind. If Zackary's memory bank was in there, the code had to be. He forced himself to focus on the pad. A series of sequences danced across his brain. Old ones . . . discarded ones . . . then suddenly a code that felt right presented itself to him. Cautiously, he keyed in the series of numbers, letters and symbols, and waited. He instantly recognized the small hiss as the door lock released. The Zackary-in-his-head knew that sound intimately.

The lights came on automatically as he moved into the room. He was facing a huge dark monitor screen, the exact replica of the one he had touched in Zack's Parallon lab. He also saw several more glass cages, some containing live rats, others empty. Against one wall was a bosonoscope – an instrument much more powerful than the quantum particle microscope at St Mag's. Seth had seen one in the Parallon lab, but Zackary had never drawn much attention to it. It was clearly integral to the work he was doing in here. Why?

He continued to explore the room. In the centre was a complex maze with jumps and tunnels that Seth assumed

Zackary used to trial rat memory. Which meant the research he was doing in here was definitely connected to the implants Rana had worked on.

So why was it so secret?

He glanced again towards the big monitor screen. Just below it on a small shelf were two small wireless electrodes. Instinctively, Seth placed one on each of his temples. He frowned. What impulse had made him do that?

Then he reached a finger out to touch the screen and a burst of colours spread from the centre.

'Good evening, Zackary.'

Seth flinched, because he knew he hadn't actually heard the voice, the sound had come from inside his head. But the part of memory that was Zackary's recognized the greeting.

'Return to file PLZA2043?' asked the voice.

'OK,' croaked Seth.

As he stared at the screen his heart started to pound. The colours were assembling to form a word he recognized: *Parallon.*

Underneath appeared a subheading: *ZA2043*

Then the letters and numerals dissolved into a three-dimensional street – exactly replicating the one outside Zackary's building. Only this street shimmered a little with prisms of light thrown off all the surfaces. Zackary's building itself was visible in the distance. Seth wanted to see it more closely, and the moment the thought had occurred to him, the street before him began to adapt, shifting perspective as though he were actually moving towards Zackary's house. He reached the closed front door and before he was even aware of the desire to go inside, watched it open and felt himself moving through it into Zackary's central hall. The door to his lab appeared on the left of the screen, exactly as it would have in the original building. Again he wished to enter, and again he was instantly inside, looking around the replica room, with its lab equipment flashing and buzzing exactly as it did here . . . only the virtual lab was bathed in a shimmering glow. The same glow that he'd come to identify with the Parallon he had just travelled from.

Seth's pulse raced. He suddenly wanted to leave Zackary's computer-generated house and see if he could find Matthias's palace. No sooner had the thought occurred to him than the perspective changed again, and he was heading out through the front door and moving quickly through familiar streets until he was staring at the exact image of the sparkling white marble palace he had walked out on all that time ago.

Which could mean only one thing. His brain was controlling the images he saw, in exactly the same way his intentions controlled the environment in Parallon.

So he was looking at what? A prototype?

He wondered if he could will Matthias to appear at the door of the palace . . . No. The palace door remained firmly shut, and nobody appeared. Did this mean people weren't incorporated into the programme or the people had to be ones Zackary was familiar with?

He willed Zackary to appear at the door, but again, nothing happened. The threshold remained empty. Anton? No. Rana? No.

Seth played around – adding trees, paths, shrubs, additional rooms. Yes, they all appeared instantly.

He stared at the screen. What was this? Had Zackary already been to Parallon and somehow installed a recreational version of it here?

Unlikely. If Parallon already existed, why would Zackary want or need to make a virtual version? He wasn't remotely interested in recreation, and he was far too clever and egotistic to bother creating a virtual, brain-operated world as a game. In any case, Zackary would have been unable to travel from Parallon back to his own time. So what was this?

There had to be more information to find.

'I'd like to see my other files,' he said firmly to the screen.

The Parallon window disintegrated and a desktop of files appeared.

Seth looked through them: MemPat2041, MemColl2043, ImpR2043, ImpH, PL2043, TCYV2043. None of them had names that meant anything to him at all. He had no idea which one to choose, so he shut his eyes and randomly touched the screen.

'TCYV2043, Zackary?' asked the voice in his head.

'Yes, thank you.'

Seth stared at the monitor as tables and text began scrolling across it. He scanned the pages as they moved across the screen, hoping that something would trigger his interest. And suddenly something did. One word: *virus*.

It was repeated again and again, usually accompanied by another word: *unidentifiable*. That sounded way too familiar. He touched the screen, highlighting one of the repetitions, and the window immediately changed and began a new document scroll.

The new file was entitled 'Tachyoviridae' and it documented a series of 112 rat implant trials, detailing their maze success rate followed by host death.

He had just reached the table of symptoms when the door

behind him swung open and Zackary and the others burst through it.

'Seth, what the hell are you doing in here?' hissed Zackary in a terrifyingly calm voice. He had heard the tone before in Parallon – just before Zackary had tried to kill him. The others were all staring at him in various postures of bewilderment.

Seth had forgotten all about them. He knew his mind control had a limited time span; he should have returned to them sooner. And now he felt guilty that he had been caught in this act of betrayal.

His mind began planning. He could easily fend them off if he needed to. None of them were fighters . . . but he didn't want to hurt anyone. Which left only one option – to try and control them again.

Zackary was heading straight for him and the others' attention was divided. For his influence to work, he needed eye contact. So all he could do was to try and convince Zackary that he meant no harm, then maybe the others would relax. But Zackary's entire focus was on the computer screen behind him, and it was impossible to catch his eye.

'How did you get in?' Zack asked icily.

'You gave me the door code,' said Seth deliberately.

Zack glanced up at him in furious denial and Seth grabbed his opportunity. 'Tell me about the virus, Zackary.'

Zackary blinked at him and shook his head. 'I don't understand the virus . . . Some sort of tachyon mutation. No discernible virus on the hard drive, no virus on the memory data, but the moment implantation takes place . . .'

'But what does memory implantation have to do with the Parallon simulation?'

'Parallon was conceived as the interface on which to build and test the memory data . . . Virtual visual data banks.'

'How could the Parallon simulation work on rats?'

'It's not for *rats*! I'm building individualized Parallon worlds for the human subjects. When their virtual memories are completed they will be ready to implant.'

'So how does this virtual Parallon connect with –'

Suddenly the rest of the group surged forward, knocking Zackary out of the way, and charged Seth. Lauren grabbed him round the neck and Anton restrained his wrists, while Rana and Engelmann held his arms.

'Who the hell are you?' Engelmann's voice came from behind his shoulders. 'Where have you come from?'

Seth considered. They were all scientists; it seemed only reasonable to tell them. But Parallon-Zackary had made him swear to say nothing of his mission or where he came from. And Seth could not break his word. 'I can't tell you,' he said at last.

It was definitely time to go. Although they held on to him tightly, Seth could feel the weakness in their grasps. He knew the element of surprise would be enough to break their hold, so he suddenly brought his teeth down hard on the arm that was thrust round his neck. Ignoring the blood and the scream of pain, he fiercely pushed his bound hands apart. Twisting his body in a sharp right angle, and bracing forward, the holds on both arms were instantly broken apart. As soon as he was free, he fixed them with his unwavering blue gaze and said in a commanding voice, 'Wait here.'

Then he darted for the door, momentarily losing his footing on the trail of blood his injured leg had dripped along the floor.

No wonder they found me, he thought furiously, *I provided them with a damned trail.*

He cursed the leg for slowing him down as he moved swiftly towards the doorway into the larger lab. When he got there he turned briefly to slam the door shut behind him, but Lauren Baxter was already there, blocking the way. Now she was slipping through behind him.

How had he failed to make eye contact with her?

With one hand he slammed the door on the rest of them, and with the other he caught her arm, pushing her away from him as he continued running. But when he heard the crash and her gasp, he stopped and turned. She must have skidded, because she was now sprawled across the floor.

'Are you hurt?' he asked.

'Only where you bit me,' she hissed, waving her injured arm at him. 'Seth, please tell me what's going on. I know you're not –'

But she suddenly couldn't speak. She'd begun to convulse. Seth's eyes darted from her arm to his blood spattered all over the floor and his heart sank.

A few moments later, Lauren Baxter began to vomit.

Seth stood for a second, torn by indecision. How could he run away and leave her to die of his virus in Zackary's lab? He needed to warn her of what was in store . . . plus he had to keep her infection from the others.

He took off his sweatshirt and did his best to wipe up the rest of the blood, then picked her up and carried her out of the front door and into the night.

Running with Lauren writhing and shaking in his arms wasn't easy, and her additional weight put massive strain on his injured leg. He had to bite hard on his lip to stop himself groaning with pain. She was completely gripped by fever and Seth had no idea how long she would be sick, but he was determined to stay with her until the end. It was the least he could do.

They had arrived at the edge of the river. He was going to have to face the vortex already injured, and if they both made it back to Parallon, he would need to be able to protect Lauren from the Romans.

He laid her down next to the river. There was virtually nobody down here at this time of night, and it was dark enough for the two of them to remain unnoticed.

'Lauren,' he whispered.

She was no longer conscious. Her breathing was shallow and hoarse. Her skin was burning. He found a windblown plastic cup and jumped down the steps to the Thames to fill it with water. He sprinkled her burning face and wiped the vomit from her mouth.

He sat vigil over her until her convulsing body was still and her breathing had stopped. He had no oil with which to anoint her, but he felt uneasy affording her no funeral rites, so he offered a short prayer, using water. His stomach twisted when he realized he had no coins to place in her eyes for Charon the boatman, but then he shook his head. Surely Lauren would have no need of Charon? She was bound for Parallon, not Hades.

It was still dark. He obviously couldn't make a pyre or bury her, as he would have done in Corinth, but he didn't want anyone to discover her here. There was only one thing he could do – take her body into the vortex with him. He was halfway down the steps to the water when he realized it was no longer a struggle to carry her. She had become virtually weightless. He looked down and blinked. She was almost . . . transparent. He stopped moving and stared. Moments later he was gazing at nothing more than her empty clothes. Lauren had completely disappeared.

Of course. He'd seen this phenomenon before. On the virus-infected cells under the microscope at St Mag's. Did all virus deaths end this way? Had *he* just disappeared from Londinium? And Matthias? The more he thought about it, the more sense Lauren's disappearance made of the lab slides.

Seth gazed at the clothes in his arms for a few moments, then crouched down by the water and let them drop. As they slowly sank, anger began to build in his chest. 'Zackary!' he snorted. He must know *everything* . . . must have always known everything. He'd been playing him all this time, watching him flail around in the dark, seeking answers, sending him on dangerous missions . . . while holding on to his secrets like a miser hoarding gold.

Fury pumped through him as he waded into the water. Dawn was beginning to lighten the edges of the horizon: he had to leave. But he vowed if he ever made it back to Parallon, he was going to tear Zack apart.

59

Gladiators

Parallon

'Matthias!'

The voice was barely a whisper. He turned and peered into the shadows.

Georgia's eyes glowed out.

'What are you doing here?' he hissed, looking around nervously.

Matthias had just arrived at the arena, where he would shortly be joining the magister on the podium at the gladiatorial games. He couldn't be late.

Georgia's eyes burned accusingly. 'What are *you* doing here, Matt? Hanging out with your powerful new friends?'

Matthias's jaw twitched with irritation. 'What do you want, Georgia? I'm in a hurry!'

'Winston needs your help.'

Matthias frowned. 'Winston? What kind of help?'

'Maybe you were *too busy* to notice when he was taken to fight in the arena?' snarled Georgia.

'Winston?' croaked Matthias in surprise. He hadn't had time to watch many tournaments and had assumed all the gladiators had been selected from the later Parallon arrivals. 'Where is he?'

Georgia pulled him by the arm and, keeping to the shadows, skirted the main walls of the arena.

'We need to get down there,' she breathed. She was pointing towards a guarded staircase. Matt knew exactly where it led: the underground holding area for waiting gladiators. He knew because he had built it.

Matthias stepped towards the guard and said in Latin, 'I am Matthias; Parallon designer and architect. I am meeting the magister shortly, but before I do I need to inspect the holding bay below.'

The guard nodded and stepped aside.

Matt couldn't help grinning to himself as he followed Georgia down the stairs. He took enormous pleasure in wielding his small amount of power.

The moment he reached the bottom step, his smile disappeared. He was suddenly hit by the appalling stench of blood, vomit and sweat. He froze for a moment, reeling back into his former life of butchered limbs and ugly injuries. But this was Parallon, not Londinium. People didn't bleed here . . . not for long anyway. And they were never sick. What in Apollo's name could it mean?

Keeping to the shadows, Georgia led him past the guarded gladiators waiting by the doors, into a dingy corner.

'Georgia, how can you expect me to see anything in this light?' muttered Matt, creating himself a flaming torch and holding it high. A moment later he wished he hadn't. Nothing could have prepared him for the scene he'd illuminated: men lying with half-severed arms, blood pumping from open wounds, flayed, blistered skin, exposed bone and suppurating sores.

Matt had to stop himself from retching. 'Why aren't they healing?' he whispered to Georgia.

'They don't want to be healed, Matt,' she answered quietly.

Matt turned to her, frowning. 'Why not?'

'Oh, Matt, you just don't get it, do you? Come on.'

He followed her towards the furthest end. When she stopped moving and stood by a groaning heap on the floor, Matthias squatted down and found himself staring at the mangled body of Winston. The familiar eyes were open, but no flicker of recognition registered in them.

'What's wrong with him?'

'He's had enough, Matt. He wants to find a way to die.'

'B-but, Georgia – I can give him salves and medicines. We can heal him . . . He doesn't need to lie here –'

'Matthias – for God's sake *open your eyes*!' spat Georgia. 'Winston doesn't *want* medicines and salves. He doesn't want to be made well enough to go back into the arena – to perform for your precious magister. That monster *enjoys* watching them bleed. He *relishes* their pain, and is grateful they don't die, so he can watch them fall again and again, hour after hour, day after day. His appetite for torture is . . . infinite. And Winston's had enough. He would rather lie here making himself bleed than go into the arena against anybody else . . . But h-he's in agony, Matt –' Georgia's voice broke. 'His mind refuses to let himself heal . . . and . . . I c-can't stand it . . . I can't watch it any more. Parallon is a living hell for him . . . So – I-I just want to know . . .' Georgia grabbed Matt's hand and forced him to face her.

'What, Georgia?' he sighed. 'What do you want to know?'

'Is – is there any way out?'

'What do you mean?' he rasped nervously.

Georgia drew him further into the shadows. 'Seth isn't in Parallon any more, is he? He had to have escaped somehow.'

Matthias glanced around him. 'I don't know what you're talking about,' he hissed. 'Now I've really got to go.'

And he strode quickly away from her accusing eyes and Winston's groans and the terrible stench.

60

Declaration

St Magdalene's

Thursday 4 July AD *2013*

I was trying to focus on the band rehearsal, but my phone was vibrating in my jeans pocket. Again. Probably another text from Jennifer Linden . . . asking me to meet her later.

And the reason I hadn't answered was because I couldn't decide what to do about her. A part of me was desperate to see her again. She had information I wanted, and clearly thought I could help her. But did I trust her?

No.

Surprise, surprise . . . Did I trust anyone? A year ago, the answer would have been a resounding 'no'. I wasn't good on trust. But – I guess I did trust a few people now . . . Rose . . . and Astrid. And maybe Rob and Sadie. On the other hand, I had trusted Se–

'Eva, helloo!' Astrid was waving her arms in front of my face.

'Sorry, Astrid – missed that. What did you say?'

Astrid growled. 'First chorus – the band will drop out on "*Where d'you go? I need to know . . .*"'

I nodded.

'. . . then two bars vocal and drums, and everyone in for the second chorus. You all got that? OK, let's try it again. Rob – pass Eva that stool, would you? She's got her pale look on.'

I didn't bother to argue. She was basically right. It was getting harder for me to get through rehearsals standing up. Rob leaped across the room, grabbed the stool and plonked it behind me. Then, before I had time to get myself on to it, he gently pushed down on my shoulders, effectively forcing me to sit. And, as usual, his hands stayed in position.

'You sure you're OK to keep going?' he whispered.

'I'm fine, Rob,' I said, manoeuvring myself out of his grasp. 'Thanks.'

'OK – final three songs,' announced Astrid.

I groaned. These were the three I'd written. And I found them almost impossible to sing now. 'Aw, please, Astrid. We've got twenty-one awesome songs. We really don't need these.'

'Sorry, Eva. Theo likes them so we can't drop 'em.'

'I don't think –'

'Look, Eva, I know you wrote them for *the bastard*' – her new name for Seth – 'but you're just gonna have to detach, babe.'

Detach. Yeah, right. Like Seth wasn't in my head . . . *all the time*. And the truth was, I wanted to keep him there. And protect him from Astrid's attacks. I really hated her calling him that. Every time she said it, I felt like hitting her. But I never did because I knew that basically her motives were pure. For some reason she still hadn't got it – that it was totally my fault he'd gone. I tried to tell her, over and over, but . . . well, Astrid was Astrid.

So I had to suck it up and sing the damn songs.

'OK – that's a wrap,' she grinned as we hit the final chord. 'Get an early night in, guys – we've got a busy week!'

I tried to slip out unnoticed, but Rob insisted on walking me all the way to my door, and then hovering.

'Thanks, Rob, see you tomorrow.'

'Are you sure you're OK, Eva? You look kind of . . . feverish.'

'No, I'm fine,' I said quickly. 'Just – er – really tired. Look –' I said, holding up my mobile, 'I've got you on speed dial – I'll ring if I need anything.'

'Eva –'

Oh *no*! I knew that look. 'Rob, please –' I began fumbling with my door handle.

'Eva,' he persisted, grabbing my hand. 'I – I don't want to be just a number on your speed dial. I want to be here with you. Always. You – you know how I feel about you, don't you?'

'Rob . . . I can't . . . Seth –'

'*Seth walked out, for Christ's sake!*' he snorted. 'He doesn't care about you. But I do. So much. Eva, I l-love you –'

Suddenly his hands were round my waist and he was pulling me towards him.

'Rob, please don't do this,' I gasped, as his lips pushed against mine. I struggled ineffectually against him, his arms gripping tightly round me. And a tiny part of me wanted to respond, craved the contact, the warmth . . . But everything about him felt so wrong: wrong arms, wrong lips . . . wrong boy. My chest suddenly heaved and I started to cry.

He froze. 'Eva?' he whispered, drawing away, his expression a mixture of bewilderment, guilt and hurt.

I just slumped against the door, wiping my face on my sleeve.

'I'm sorry, Eva,' he choked. 'I shouldn't have done that. I know you're tired and –'

I reached out and touched his hand. 'I'm not worth this, Rob.'

'What?' he spluttered, grabbing my fingers.

'I mean it. There are so many girls . . . *Please* give up on me. I can't love you . . . I can never –'

'You just need time, Eva. I can wait.'

I shook my head sadly and pulled my fingers from his grip. 'Rob, look at me! I'm a mess . . . Broken. Empty.' I banged my chest angrily. 'There's nothing here. There will never be anything here. Whatever I had, I gave it all to him.'

Rob's jaw clenched. 'I don't care, Eva. I don't care how little he's left. It's enough for me. I can love enough for two. I can give you everything I have. What did *Seth* ever give you?'

'His love,' I choked.

'Yeah, right!' spat Rob. 'He must have really loved you to walk out so spectacularly.'

I blinked at him, doing my best to get some control over my features.

His eyes softened. 'God, I'm sorry, Eva. I didn't mean to say that. The last thing I want to do is hurt you.' He reached out his fingers to wipe away the tears that were now spilling down my face, but I stepped back.

'You're right, Rob. He did stop loving me. But I – can't stop loving him.'

'You're wasting your time loving someone who isn't here!' he said.

'So are you,' I sighed, backing into my room. 'Goodnight, Rob. Thanks for bringing me back.' He didn't try to follow me inside.

I slumped wearily down on to my bed and nearly had a heart attack a few moments later when the door creaked open and Jennifer Linden crept in.

'You OK?' she asked, staring at my messed-up face.

'What the hell are you doing here?' I demanded, grabbing a tissue from the bedside box.

She was frowning at me dubiously. 'You didn't answer my calls . . . And we've got to talk.'

I shoved my keys in her hand and she went over and locked the door, while I propped myself up against the pillows.

She pulled my desk chair over to the bed.

'Eva,' she began, 'I need to know why Nick wanted to see you.'

'Look, Jennifer, we've been here before. I haven't changed my mind. How the hell can I trust you? You're a *journalist*, for God's sake. At least Nick was interested in uncovering the truth.'

'And you think I'm not?'

I shrugged. 'All I know is – journalists have a tendency to manipulate the truth. The truth serves the story. The story serves the programme. The programme or newspaper has to be your priority. Nick had no conflict of interest.

'Listen, I'm really tired. It's been a long evening and I don't have the energy for another argument . . . so are we done here?'

She hesitated. 'OK, Eva, how about an information trade?'

I closed my eyes. Why wouldn't she just go? 'Do you have anything worth trading?'

Her mouth twisted as she deliberated. A part of me really hoped she'd decide the trade wasn't worth it. But as I watched her straighten her shoulders and take a deep breath, I realized that part of me was out of luck.

'Nick and I have been investigating mysterious disappear-ances for several weeks now . . . starting with Winston Grey – who literally disappeared after a motorbike accident. But neither of us saw any kind of pattern until Elena Galanis's body vanished in a similar way. Once I started really looking, I began uncovering more and more unexplained disappearances, some going back decades. And as well as the whole – er – vanishing thing, a lot of them had something else in common . . . an intense fever.

'According to an eyewitness, even Winston Grey, the crash victim, began convulsing just before he died, which – which is exactly w-what happened to N-Nick . . .'

'So – how do you think Nick got the virus?' I said.

'You think it's a virus?' she asked quickly.

I nodded. 'Where do you think he picked it up?'

'Belmarsh.'

'The prison?'

'The secure wing. From which the most dangerous, violent criminals are disappearing in droves.'

'*What?*' I spluttered. I put my head in my hands. None of this made sense. Were all these dangerous criminals now in Parallon? And . . . were they being taken there on purpose?

'MI5, MI6, Special Branch, the Met – everyone's in on it . . . but Nick was convinced they are on completely the wrong track . . . Please, Eva. You have to tell me what you know.'

I leaned against my pillows and stared at her. She was seri-ously frightened.

'Has someone threatened you?' I suddenly asked.

Her eyes flicked down to her hands.

'Who?'

'MI5.'

I nodded. Not so surprising. She was a journalist. A story like this one would not go down well with the public.

'What do *they* think is going on here?'

'Bioterrorism of some sort . . . and from what I've put together, they reckon Elena was some kind of double agent —'

'No.' I spoke before I could stop myself.

'Eva, what do you know?'

'I do know something about Elena. That's why Nick wanted to talk to me. But — but I couldn't tell him.'

'Why?'

I shook my head. 'It's complicated.'

But I suddenly knew I was out of options. Maybe if Seth was still around, I would have felt differently . . . maybe if I had made any more headway with Ambrose and the virus . . . maybe if I thought I had a lifetime ahead of me to try and figure this stuff out . . . but I didn't have any of those things. Time was running out on me. I was going to have to pass what I knew on to someone else. But . . . Jennifer Linden? A journalist? I glanced up at her crumpled face.

'Why did Nick Mullard trust you?' I asked suddenly.

She pressed her lips together and shrugged. 'Maybe because I was all he had?'

I shook my head. DI Mullard was shrewd. Even I could tell that.

Jennifer inhaled. 'He wanted the truth. His team had been shut down, so he needed someone to do the legwork. I'm a damn good researcher and I was already interested. But I think he only trusted me because I promised I wouldn't spill. And — and he believed me.'

I nodded. 'Can you promise me the same?'

'If I have to.'

I took a deep breath. 'OK, then.' My stomach twisted. This felt like such a betrayal. Of Seth. Of us. But I honestly didn't think I had a choice.

'Elena was killed by mistake . . . She wasn't targeted by Russians or bioterrorists . . . She was accidentally exposed to the virus – and –'

'And N-Nick? Was *he*?' choked Jen. 'He was only twenty-eight. He was a great d-detective . . . and I – I didn't have long enough with him.'

'Jennifer,' I said, my hand reaching out involuntarily and touching her shoulder, 'I d-don't think Nick is dead.'

She shook her head. 'I saw him, Eva,' she hiccupped. 'I saw him die.'

I passed her a tissue. 'And then you saw him disappear,' I said. 'Elena isn't dead either. I know someone who has seen her.'

Jen was staring at me, her eyes round and brimming. 'W-where are they?' she gasped.

I sighed. 'A place called Parallon.'

'Can I go there?'

I shook my head mournfully. There was nowhere I wanted to go more. 'No. Not unless you catch the virus.'

'But what about you? Don't you have the virus?' she whispered.

I laughed bitterly. 'Yes and no. I don't know what I've got. I was infected just like the others, but – I didn't die . . . and I'm not a carrier. I may have a mutated version, I just don't know.' There was only one person who knew. 'There's a guy I've been

379

chasing for months. I think he's the one everyone should be looking for.'

'What's his name?'

'He calls himself Professor Ambrose. I don't know who he's working for – but I'm pretty sure he could answer a few of our questions.'

Jennifer was writing his name in her notebook. 'I'll see what I can find out.'

I looked at her and smiled. 'I'm reasonably good at research too,' I said quietly, 'and I promise you, there's only one place left to look.'

She raised an eyebrow. 'And where is that, Eva?'

'MI5.'

61

Summons

Parallon

Matthias dragged fresh air into his lungs. He couldn't let his encounter with Georgia and Winston spoil the evening. He hurried away from the holding bay towards the arena and was soon gratefully climbing on to the magister's podium.

He was flanked as usual by Otho, Rufus and Pontius.

'Ah, Matthias, come and sit,' waved the magister graciously.

Matt bowed and crouched on the bench at his feet.

'One of my guards mentioned you've been visiting the gladiator holding area . . . Find anything interesting?'

Matthias swallowed. Who had been watching him? He cleared his throat.

'No – nothing really. Er – I was – er – thinking about putting up a partition wall – dividing the gladiators – so that those who have been fighting and are recovering from injuries are kept separate from those about to go on – but . . .'

The magister nodded ruminatively. 'Might not be such a bad idea . . . don't want our fresh meat tainted – do we, boys?' he laughed.

Matthias tried to suppress the small curl of revulsion the comment triggered. Even in Londinium the gladiators were valued a little more highly. He regretted the thought the moment it had slipped through, because an image of Seth preparing to fight suddenly filled his mind and the uneasiness in his belly grew into a painful ache. He had hated watching his friend walk through those doors into the screaming arena. And here he was about to witness a whole troop of barely trained men do exactly the same.

His eyes turned to the sand of the arena below him. He had just missed the music and parading, which the magister tended to keep short, so the four pairs of gladiators were already making their way into their combat positions.

The crowd was roaring, but Matt suddenly wondered how appreciative they sounded. How many of them had been forced into their seats? He looked around at the numerous guards marking each seating area. They'd formed a very different pattern in Londinium. Nobody had needed to coerce a Roman audience to the arena. They'd clamoured to get in.

Matt's mind drifted to his childhood in Corinth, and the stadium there. He vividly remembered the excitement of being taken to the Isthmian Games with his family. But those games had been a celebration of stamina, strength and courage, not savage violence. The Roman appetite for entertainment was very different.

He sat now at the magister's feet, trying to watch the fighting, trying to see it as a celebration of physical skill. But there was little skill on display below. Just desperation. He gazed in dismay at the half-naked retiarius clumsily wielding his trident in a wretched attempt to block the thrusts of his opponent's sword. And Matt's mind wandered inexorably to that other retiarius: fast, furious, mesmerizing, sublimely gifted, and winner of nine wreaths – Sethos Leontis.

He squirmed uneasily, as he imagined what Seth would make of him sitting here with the Romans while Winston lay bleeding in the dungeon below. But what in Jupiter's name was he supposed to do about Winston? He was sure Seth wouldn't have an answer if he was in his position. But Seth would never be in his position, admitted Matthias reluctantly.

Someone was shoving him on the shoulder.

'The magister is talking to you, architect!' barked Rufus.

Matthias turned quickly. 'S-sorry, magister, I was –'

'Engrossed in the combat? I find that hard to believe! This has to be the least entertaining gladiatorial games I've ever witnessed.'

The magister lay back and yawned languidly. Matthias was sensing an ominous change in atmosphere. He darted a look at Otho, who appeared to be trying not to laugh.

'There was a retiarius once who *was* worth watching,' the magister continued. 'I'd give a significant reward to watch *him* fight again.' He raised his eyebrows and fixed Matthias with a cold reptilian stare.

Matthias licked his lips nervously.

'The slave went by the name of . . . now what was it? Ah yes . . . Sethos Leontis.' Matthias froze.

'I believe he was a *friend* of yours, Matthias?'

Matt's eyes went straight to Otho, who raised an eyebrow and smirked in silent victory. What had Otho told the magister? And what was that book the magister was now ostentatiously flicking through? It looked a bit like . . . Seth's notebook.

Matt watched in horror as the magister suddenly stilled and stared down at the front cover, his lip curling up in disgust. The source of his displeasure was a single word written there, in Seth's bold and steady hand. Even from here Matt could read it. He shut his eyes.

'*Livia*,' spat the magister through gritted teeth.

A deep foreboding filled Matt's chest.

'How many deaths does it take –' snarled the magister in a dangerously quiet voice.

'M-magister?'

'– before I am finally rid of that adulterous pair?'

Matthias's eyes widened, realization finally dawning. 'You are C-Cassius Malchus?' he croaked.

'Who else would have the strength and power to build this empire here?' he roared. 'Down on your knees, Greek scum!'

'Hail, Magister Cassius Malchus!' instantly chorused the guards, throwing themselves to the ground.

'Matthias,' Cassius's voice was heavy with menace, 'it is time for you to bring Sethos Leontis back to me.'

'B-but I – I don't know w-where h-he is!' stammered Matthias.

'Well, you'd better do your best to find out. Because until he returns,' Cassius smiled, nodding to a guard nearby, 'I'll be expanding my gladiatorial troop.'

Six guards strode towards them, dragging Georgia, Clare, Tamara, Courtney and Elena between them.

Matthias stood gaping, but Otho struck him hard across the face.

'On your knees, slave!' he commanded.

Matthias gasped in pain and bowed his head.

'You have my leave to go now, Matthias,' said Cassius dismissively. 'I suggest you make reasonable haste. These women won't take long to break. But I will enjoy every moment.'

62

Arrival

Parallon

Seth was staring up at a velvety black sky, too weary to ask himself where he was. His body was bobbing gently in water. Faint sounds reached his ears, but he couldn't force his mind to focus, so he drifted.

Suddenly light glared against his eyelids; someone was pulling him, whispering his name. His body was no longer bobbing gently – he could hear panting, feel friction on the backs of his legs. His eyes flickered open in confusion. He was being dragged along the ground.

'Thank God you're awake, Seth, you weigh a ton – and the guards are just about to circuit.'

Seth blinked and tried to pull himself upright. Zackary was dragging him towards the shadows. A second later he was on his feet and silently following him through the Roman facade into Zackary's building.

'What took you so long?' hissed Zack. 'I thought you'd absconded.'

'How long was I gone?'

'Weeks.'

Seth's eyes widened in shock. Zack pushed him through the front door and started up the stairs. Seth padded after him.

'Did Lauren make it here OK?'

Lauren's face peered over the banisters. 'I did,' she said.

Seth looked up at her, his throat suddenly dry. He was entirely responsible for her arrival in Parallon. 'I'm so sorry, Lauren –'

'What are you apologizing for, Seth? Lauren's probably the only reason you made it back at all,' said Zack, continuing up the stairs. 'She's been working on stabilizing the vortex.'

Seth followed him wearily into the library.

'Before you sit down, Sethos, I'd appreciate it if you did something about your wet clothes,' remarked Zackary. 'Anyone for coffee?' he added, disappearing to the kitchen.

Seth glanced distractedly down at the torn, dripping remains of his clothing – London-Zackary's joggers – and quickly willed on a pair of dry jeans and T-shirt. Lauren was standing by the dining table watching him. He toyed with his trainer laces, trying to delay the moment when he would have to confront her. But in the end he had to meet her gaze.

'So – how are you?' he asked, his throat tight.

'Could be worse,' she answered quietly. 'I could be dead.'

He nodded. 'There are a few compensations. Zackary has probably shown you?'

'Oh yes – he has,' she smiled bitterly. 'I don't have to apply for funding to produce state-of-the-art field generators, but I can only leave the building at 4 a.m. to try them out – or risk being chained and carted off by legions of thugs dressed as Roman soldiers. What a fabulous new world you've brought me to, Seth.'

Seth slumped down on to the sofa and sighed. 'It was the last thing I meant to do, Lauren.'

'Oh, come on, Seth,' she snorted. 'The generators? How were you planning to design those without guidance from Louis or me?'

Seth's head shot up and he stared at her. 'What do you take me for?' he choked. 'You got infected because you tried to stop me leaving.' He stood up and walked over to the window. 'Do you think I'd deliberately bring anyone else back here?'

He stared out at the Roman facade opposite, then darted away from the window as his eye caught movement on the street below . . . a trio of guards marching towards the river. A couple of minutes earlier and he and Zackary would have been caught.

Lauren moved to the window beside him.

'It wasn't always like this,' sighed Seth. 'Did Zack tell you?'

'Sort of. He's not very good at disclosure,' she answered. 'But he's excellent at getting what he wants.'

Seth nodded. 'So – he got you to fix the vortex?'

'Well, it's just about functional, but I wouldn't call it fixed. We'd need to blast it with a continuous pulse to effect genuine stability – and the Roman patrols make that impossible. We got you back though.'

Seth took a deep, shuddering breath. At some point he'd lost consciousness in the vortex, but by then he'd given up the fight. He looked down at his arms. They had been ripped to the bone in there, lashed by water and rock. Now they were already healing. He suddenly remembered the mangled flesh on his leg and rolled up his jeans . . . just a faint scar.

Lauren smiled wryly. 'OK, I get it. One of the compensations.'

Just then the door banged open and Zackary clanked in with a tray, balancing a pot of coffee, mugs and a large chocolate cake. He deposited it on the low glass table between the sofas, sat down and started pouring coffee into the mugs. Lauren and Seth joined him on the sofa opposite.

'So – tell me, boys,' said Lauren, as Zackary handed her a mug. 'How much chocolate cake do you have to eat in Parallon before you start getting fat?'

Zack and Seth exchanged looks and they all started to laugh.

'I think in the interests of science, it's time we found out,' said Zackary, cutting three large slices.

Zackary made good, strong coffee. Seth took his mug and sipped. He rested his head against the back of the sofa and closed his eyes. He needed to think. What were his priorities now? He had unexpectedly succeeded in his mission for Zackary – the wormhole was operational again.

But understanding wormhole stability now seemed insignificant compared with the snatches of information he had acquired in Zackary's lab. He had finally begun to realize just how powerful this man was. And secretive. And duplicitous. No wonder Zackary was so scornful about Seth's virus research at St Magdalene's. It was all totally pointless. The answers lay here. With Zackary.

Seth's mind flashed to the St Mag's biology lab . . . the neatly stacked slides of blood samples. Then his thoughts turned inevitably to Eva. And all his questions fell away as a great wave of anxiety and longing filled his chest.

The questions could wait. He knew there was no way Zack was going to volunteer any information unless it served his purpose in some way, and Zackary's immediate purpose had just been served: the vortex was working – mission accomplished.

So Zackary, Parallon and the Romans were no longer his priority . . . Eva was. And as soon as he could, Seth was going back to her.

63
Fall

Parallon

Matthias made his way from the magister's podium towards the arena exit. As he passed the guards at the gate, he was certain he saw one of them smirk condescendingly in his direction. Did they already know he had fallen from grace? Or had he *never* been in favour? Had Cassius been playing him all along? His chest heaved with bitterness, but he strode out with his head high. His legs started carrying him towards the palace, but as he approached, he realized there was little sense going there – it was hardly home. It hadn't really been home since . . . Seth left.

So where should he go? And what in the name of Apollo was he going to do? How could he consider delivering Seth straight into the hands of his enemy? They had not parted friends, but – a betrayal of that magnitude . . . On the other hand, how could he leave the girls to their fate? Cassius wasn't bluffing. He would throw them into the arena with savage delight.

Matt couldn't think of a single way out.

If only he'd left with Georgia and the others before his

meeting with the magister. They would have been safely away by now. How was he to know that the magister was Cassius Malchus? Or that Otho would find a way to betray him? What was he to do when the fates continually conspired against him?

Although he told himself he was simply walking to clear his head, his legs carried him swiftly to the bank of the river. He gazed down at the water speculatively. He was actually fairly sure he knew where to find Seth . . . at that school with the quantum particle microscope . . . St Magdalene's. Seth was probably with that damn girl too, he reminded himself bitterly. The girl who'd brought back all the Livia insanity. By Zeus, he cursed her for that. Seth would probably still be here if it hadn't been for her. What did she call herself? Something close to Livia . . . Eva? Yes, that was it. Eva.

64

Messenger

St Magdalene's

Friday 12 July AD 2013

'Hey, Eva – Rob doesn't need help loading the van, so can you coil the cables, babe?' Astrid was pushing me on to a bench and shoving a pile of leads into my arms.

'Sure.'

I'd given up arguing. They all played the game now: pretending they needed me to do sitting-down jobs; that it was easier for three people to carry gear than four. But, to be honest, I was kind of grateful. Especially tonight. I needed all the help I could get. Theo had just phoned Astrid to remind her that he was bringing a load of industry people to the gig. As if playing the Underworld wasn't pressure enough.

Deep breaths, I told myself. It would be OK. I could do this. As I coiled cable, I glanced around at the others. None of them seemed worried. How could they be so chilled? Would I be feeling less scared if Seth was here? *No*, I told myself firmly. *I didn't need Seth. I was fine without him.* But I was lying to myself. He'd centred me. He *was* my centre. He made everything OK.

I gritted my teeth and firmly pushed his image away, doubling my cable-coiling efforts.

'Great, Eva,' said Rob, striding over and taking the last lead out of my hands. 'We're good to go.'

He had been carefully avoiding eye contact for days, and I didn't know what to do or say to make things better between us.

'OK,' I said, easing myself to my feet. I grabbed the back of the chair for support until the wave of dizziness settled, and then followed him out of the music block and across the quad. I was supposed to drop by the medical centre to get my blood pressure checked before setting off, but the dizziness told me that Rose would never let me play this gig if I went to her now. And I couldn't pull out. It would kill Astrid if we cancelled. I glanced furtively across at the building and moved decisively in the opposite direction, towards the van.

Rob was walking just ahead, trying to slow his pace to match mine. Sweet Rob. A familiar wave of guilt threatened to swamp me. To distract myself I put my head down and started humming through song lyrics. Which may have been why I nearly ploughed straight into a guy standing right in my path.

I stopped dead and stared up at him. He was soaking wet and dressed in a Roman tunic . . . and he looked vaguely familiar.

'What have you come as?' sniggered a Year Ten girl from across the quad. The gang of kids she was with all started laughing. We both ignored them. I was busy trying to work out who he was, while he was perfecting a kind of frowning scowl.

'Livia,' he sighed finally. 'It is you.'

'Eva . . . Livia . . . w-whatever.' My mouth was suddenly dry. 'Who are you?' I croaked.

'Matthias,' he answered warily.

Yes, I knew that name. And I had seen him before . . . in Londinium. Standing behind Seth in the arena. Seth's friend . . . The friend who'd given the virus to Elena . . . What the hell was he doing here?

My heart was pounding. 'Is he here?' I breathed. 'Is Seth with you?'

I scanned frantically around the quad, but Matthias's expression told me he had come alone. He was just on the point of speaking when Rob and Astrid strode over, and within moments stood flanking me, facing Matthias like he was the devil himself.

'Come on, Eva, we're going to be late,' said Astrid, taking a firm grip on my elbow.

Rob had a hand on my shoulder and was applying equivalent pressure. But I refused to move.

'I'll be there in a sec,' I promised, without taking my eyes off Matthias. 'Meet you at the van in five.'

'Really?' frowned Astrid, her eyes glinting dangerously in Matthias's direction.

I nodded, and they moved a couple of metres away. They seriously didn't trust this guy.

'So,' I said huskily, 'why are you here?'

'I'm looking for Seth.'

'H-he's gone.'

Matthias was frowning. 'Where?'

I began to shake. 'Well – P-Parallon.'

'No. He's not there.'

What? He had to be. Oh God, if he wasn't there, where was he? 'W-why are you looking for him?'

Matthias licked his lips and stared down at the ground. 'I've been sent . . .'

'Who sent you?' I whispered.

He took an unsteady breath. 'Cassius.'

The ground seemed to fall away suddenly and black shadows started edging across my vision. I was choking, trying to remember how to breathe, trying to remember who I was, where I was . . .

'Give her some air, for Chrissake . . . she's coming round. Eva? Are you OK, babe?'

Oh God, where was I now? I kept my eyes closed while I tried to remember. My hands were clenched into fists. I opened them and pressed down . . . Gravel . . . I was on the ground . . . Astrid's voice . . . St Mag's.

I opened my eyes tentatively. Heads were swimming above me – Astrid, Rob . . . and – Matthias. I sat up and found I was shaking. Rob was crouching beside me. 'Shall I get Rose, Eva?'

I shook my head. 'I'm OK,' I croaked. But I wasn't. How could I be? *Cassius* was alive . . . and he was looking for Seth.

'It's time we got this guy off the premises,' hissed Astrid, jerking her head towards Matthias.

'*No!*' I gasped. Then I turned to him. 'D-did Cassius come with you?'

'No . . .' he answered bleakly. 'He sent me to take Seth back.'

So at least Cassius didn't know where Seth was – that had to be good. But then *nobody* knew where Seth was. Was he hiding out somewhere?

I just couldn't picture the Seth I knew hiding out. Though

how well did I really know him? I bit my lip. Obviously not well at all.

'Eva –'

I jolted back to St Mag's quad. Astrid jiggling from foot to foot.

'The gig,' I muttered. Just what I needed right now.

'D'ya think you're OK for it?' she asked, doing her best to conceal her total desperation.

How could I let her down? 'Yeah, I'm fine,' I said.

'What about *him*?' she frowned, jerking her head at Matthias.

I couldn't let Matthias leave. He was my only link to Seth. 'Do you want to come to a gig?' I smiled tensely.

He looked completely bewildered.

'Rob, have you got some clothes you could lend him?' I asked.

'But why's he –?'

'Long story, Rob – I'll tell you later.'

'You wanna bring him in the van with us?' spluttered Astrid. 'Are you crazy, Eva? How are we s'posed to explain him to Dr Drury?' Astrid was not happy.

'Please, Astrid?'

She rolled her eyes and groaned. 'Get going then, Rob,' she snorted finally. 'I'll deal with Drury – but if we miss our sound-check slot, Eva, you are so dead.'

65

Romans

Parallon

Seth had been watching the window all afternoon. He was monitoring the guard circuits around Zackary's house and along the river and had learned that three armed guards patrolled on the hour, every hour.

He hadn't told either Zack or Lauren that he was returning to the vortex that night. Although he had no qualms about keeping this information from Zackary, he felt uneasy about abandoning Lauren. He'd brought her to a hostile, alien world, with no friends and little idea of who to trust. So he devoted the afternoon to inducting her into the ways of Rome and Parallon, as well as teaching her some basic Latin vocabulary and how to dress herself inconspicuously as a Roman. But as evening drew nearer, and his desertion became imminent, he suddenly made the decision to run to Matt's palace and talk to Georgia and Clare. Maybe Lauren could move into the palace with them? They'd be a lot friendlier than Zackary.

'Where the hell are you going?' asked Zackary, as Seth moved towards the door.

'I need a run,' he answered smoothly. 'And I thought I'd check out my house.'

'Don't be a fool, Leontis. Do you have any idea what it's like out there? The place is a military prison! If you get caught, they'll haul you off and throw you in the arena!'

'The *what*?' asked Seth, his voice barely audible.

'Oh, you are behind the times,' snorted Zackary. 'Parallon now hosts a huge amphitheatre. Every day our noble citizens are forced to watch gladiators mutilate each other until they drop. *You* would be quite a catch, I daresay, as someone who actually knows how to fight.'

Seth gaped at Zackary. An arena in Parallon? People had allowed this to happen? The Romans now wielded this much power?

'I'm going to take a look,' he said, ignoring Zackary's outraged expression. He quickly replaced his jeans and T-shirt with a tunic and slipped out of the front door. The guards had circuited about five minutes earlier and he knew the immediate vicinity was safe, but he had no knowledge of patrols elsewhere, so he kept to the shadows. And he suppressed his intense need to run. It would be foolish to do anything that might draw unwanted attention.

As he skirted familiar streets, he realized just how much Parallon had changed. It had been entirely converted into a Roman city, although it was nothing like the Roman city he had actually lived in . . . because this one was perfect. All the buildings were clean, matching and equally proportioned . . . unnaturally uniform. He was tempted to shift something . . . ruin one of the vertical lines, change the colour of a facade. But he resisted. He didn't have much time, it was beginning to get dark and he'd planned to be in the vortex the moment the sun set.

To reach Matthias's palace, he needed to cross through the centre of Parallon and head west. He wondered if the arena was sited in the same place as the original Londinium one. If so, it was more or less on his way.

He hadn't gone far before the unmistakeable circular walls filled the horizon. And even from this distance he could hear the crowd, shouting for more. His heart began to thud as his brain flooded with grim memories. But it didn't fundamentally shock him to see the arena here. Unlike Matthias, he had never really believed in a world where the arena didn't exist. His years in Londinium had taught him about the human appetite for power and cruelty – he had little faith in a world without it. Which was why he'd spent day after day practising his skills; remaining in a state of readiness.

He was so close now he could smell the blood. The violent gladiator screams and harsh clash of weapons were so evocative that a swell of bitter anger suddenly flared in his chest. How dared the Romans invade Parallon as they'd invaded Corinth? He had been a boy then, and had not known how to fight, but he was a man now. A part of him wanted to hurl himself at the guards flanking the arena entrance and pummel them to the ground.

But he hadn't won nine wreaths in the arena by being reckless. So he continued to stand in the shadows; watching and thinking. Then he slipped away to look for Matthias's house.

From a distance it looked much the same – white reflective marble shimmering against the dusky sky. But as soon as he was close, and could see the facade more clearly, his uneasiness grew. Matt's beloved fruit trees had been replaced by ostentatious ornate extensions, each fronted by columns supporting golden statues of the gods. And the double-doored main entrance now flaunted a portico with . . . a large golden eagle on either side.

Seth's stomach turned. Eagles?

No!

He knew only one man who decorated his palace with eagles . . .

Cassius? Here? This couldn't mean he . . . but how? Why now – after all this time?

Seth backed away, his heart pounding. He had to get back to Eva. Now more than ever.

Shady dusk meant his return journey to the river could be fast. He shrouded himself in a long black cloak so that he could run silently in the shadows. And with every footstep he berated himself for all the times he'd spent trying to convince Eva that her nightmares and fears were unfounded and couldn't hurt her. Because suddenly he wasn't so sure.

66

Pressure

The Underworld, Camden, London

Friday 12 July AD 2013

Fortunately I was spared The Wrath of Astrid. We made it to the Underworld just in time for our sound-check. As soon as we were done, I squinted around the room for Matthias. The venue was pretty murky, and he wasn't quite so easy to spot now that he was wearing a pair of Rob's jeans and a T-shirt.

'Why don't you go and sit over there, Eva? I'll get some Cokes,' said Astrid. 'Theo'll be here soon.'

It seemed as good a plan as any. But as soon as I was in my seat, fear began clawing at my stomach. *Get a grip*, I told myself sternly. I pulled out the crumpled sheets of song lyrics from my back pocket and stared at them, willing them to distract me from the rising panic.

Cassius doesn't know where Seth is, I reminded myself. *If he knew he wouldn't have sent Matthias to look for him. Seth is safe.*

But was he? What if Professor Ambrose had taken him? Or Jen's Belmarsh prison time-terrorist?

Seth wasn't taken. He left. You drove him away, remember?

I froze, suddenly realizing that by driving Seth away I may have just saved his life. The tight knot in my stomach, the one that had been sitting there for weeks, the knot that contained all the pain and loss and guilt, seemed to slacken a little. And for the first time I realized that my love for him was bigger than any of those things. I could live with pain and loss and guilt, but I couldn't live with the thought of anything happening to him.

'Hey, Eva,' hissed Sadie, shaking my shoulder. She was breathless with excitement. 'Theo's just arrived – and he's got about ten people with him. In suits.'

My eyes darted to the door where Theo and his entourage were gathered. And they weren't the only ones who'd just got here. The venue was packing out. When Astrid said she was inviting everyone she knew, I didn't realize she'd meant it so literally. Well – if I messed up tonight, it was going to be on a pretty grand scale. But, somehow, messing up a gig suddenly felt like the least of my problems. I scanned the crowd for Matthias. I had so many questions for him – but they would have to wait now, because Theo was heading our way.

'All set?' he smiled, slopping his glass of beer on the table.

'Yep! We're gonna blow you away tonight!' grinned Astrid.

Glad someone was confident.

'Good, because if you impress, I may have an interesting proposal to discuss.'

That sounded ominous. I ducked my head and sipped my drink. Thank God, the support act was mounting the stage: no conversation would be able to compete with them – I'd heard them sound-check.

By the time they'd finished their set, Theo had wandered back to his colleagues and Astrid was hauling me on to the stage. Ah, well . . . The sooner we went on, the sooner it would be over.

Our guitars were lined up against the back wall. I picked mine up and made sure it was in tune. Then I checked my foot pedals and mic. Astrid was stomping around the stage, furiously trying to readjust the settings on her bass amp, because the previous band had messed with it. I glanced across at Rob – he smiled and nodded. He was ready. Sadie was tightening her cymbals, but she gave me a quick thumbs-up. I licked my lips and glanced out at the audience, scanning for Matthias. There was a guy by the door that could have been him, but it was hard to tell with the lights in my eyes. I was just jerking my head back to check how Astrid was getting on with her amp, when I spotted Jennifer Linden standing near the stage. She raised an eyebrow at me and gave me a little wave. Was she here because she'd found something out? Could she possibly have managed to crack MI5 security?

Suddenly the bass riff from our first song erupted on to the speakers, I darted an exasperated look at Astrid, found the right chord, and the show had begun. We'd rehearsed the set so tightly that there was no room to panic or think or worry about lyrics . . . I just had to zone out, thrash guitar and sing. Sixteen songs later we were stumbling off the stage after two encores. The gig had gone well. Theo looked kind of pleased. I felt kind of exhausted. I was looking around for Matthias and Jen, when Astrid's firm hand propelled me towards Theo and his guests.

'Focus, Eva,' she hissed behind me. 'Theo's got that glint in his eye. Something's going down.'

Theo didn't just have a glint in his eye. He was practically glowing.

'Awesome, guys,' he beamed. 'What can I get you to drink?'

'Just water for me,' I said, wondering how long I'd be able to stand. I was beginning to feel dizzy again. We were all congregating near a pillar, so I edged my way over and leaned against it. Astrid darted me an *are you OK?* look. I pretended not to have noticed. Theo's guests were introducing themselves. Three of them were American. From LA. And the rest were from here. But that was as far as I got before zoning out. My head was aching, I was feeling sick and I was desperate for some fresh air. But I didn't have the physical strength or the emotional courage to leave. And, anyway, I couldn't do that to Astrid. So instead I slid down the pillar until I was sitting on the floor. I pulled up my knees and rested my head down. That felt better. I could vaguely hear the conversation going on above me – Astrid trying to cover for my weird behaviour – one of the Americans joking about bad-boy rock stars – Rob laughing nervously. I closed my eyes, wishing Seth was here. He'd never given a damn about protocol. He'd have no problem leaving the room.

Something cold was nudging against my fingers. I opened my eyes. Theo was squatting down next to me, shoving a glass of water into my hand.

'Eva,' he hissed. 'For God's sake, get up! You don't mess with people like these.'

I stared at him and shook my head. 'Don't think I can,' I whispered.

'You can and you will,' he breathed back icily.

Then he grasped my elbows and hoisted me to my feet. I swayed for a couple of moments, then grabbed on to the pillar for support.

The room was pulsating.

'Eva,' Rob was saying, his face close to mine, his voice sounding strangely echoey, eyes willing me to participate, 'we've just been invited to do a tour of the States. This summer! Isn't that fantastic?'

I tried to get my mouth moving. Get the corners to turn up. Smile. That was the least I could do. But I couldn't. I needed air.

I pushed blindly through them all, my eyes fixed on the door. I might have heard Astrid's voice calling my name, but I had only one objective: to get outside. Somehow I reached the front of the building. The door was open and moments later I was stumbling out into the cool, clear night.

67

Notes

The Underworld, Camden, London

Friday 12 July AD 2013

Matthias was standing at the back of the room when she began to sing. And instantly he understood how losing this girl had broken Seth's heart. There was something about her, about her voice, that made him catch his breath. It shifted unpredictably between a pure kind of sweetness and a rough, breathy edginess, in a way that was simply mesmerizing.

He hadn't forgotten the two fleeting moments when he had glimpsed her at the arena, and conceded that she was genuinely beautiful – but here, under the constantly changing lights, her loveliness seemed ephemeral and fragile. There was something so vulnerable about her, something that made him want to protect her. Yet only hours ago he had literally hated her, resenting her for the endless suffering she had inflicted on his friend.

He leaned against the back wall, listening to song after song, hoping he would tire of her voice, that his fascination would wane. But it didn't. He found himself wanting to get closer, wanting her to see him when she next lifted her eyes. He glanced around at the rapt faces of the audience and realized he wasn't alone.

When the band finished playing, the crowd appeared momentarily stunned. And then the place erupted – screaming, cheering, stamping feet. At last she stepped in front of the microphone and looked into the audience as though there was someone she was hoping to find. The room went silent. Watching. Waiting. She closed her eyes and very quietly began to sing a love song. And Matthias could tell that every person in there felt that she was singing that song for them.

When the final notes faded away, the audience exploded. She glanced out at them and smiled in a bewildered kind of way, as though she wasn't expecting to find them there. Then suddenly the band started playing again, only this time it was really fast, and everyone was dancing and clapping and singing along. After three choruses, and resounding cheering, the spell was finally broken and the band were allowed to leave the stage. Matthias pushed through the crowd towards her, but she was already being propelled away to the other side of the room, and was soon surrounded by people. He would have to wait.

Now that she was no longer singing, he realized how hot and airless it was in the room, so he fought a path to the front door and pushed his way outside, where he found a low wall to sit on.

People began spilling out on to the pavement behind him, with cigarettes and glasses of beer and wine. He watched them, thinking how similar this place was to the taverns of Londinium. Then his mind drifted fleetingly to the café in Parallon. The café where he and his friends had spent so many happy hours . . . before the Romans came and spoiled everything.

68

Key

When Eva had ruefully mentioned that the Astronauts were playing the Underworld, Jen had had absolutely no intention of going. There was no way she was going to be joining the Eva Koretsky fan club. She'd seen the way everyone was around her . . . God – she'd seen the way her own boyfriend had watched her.

Her relationship with Eva was purely professional – based entirely on mutual need. Eva was the one positive witness Jen had to the bizarre sequence of events she was researching, plus she'd revealed herself to be pretty damn good with a computer – which made her a useful accomplice.

Then at 19.13 that evening Jen had accidentally found the key she and Eva had both been looking for.

Jen stood smiling up at the stage as her fingers curled round the innocuous plastic card in her pocket. She couldn't believe she'd found it. And if she hadn't been so bloody clumsy she never would have. Her smile turned into a silent snigger as she realized that in a small way she could thank her horrible boss, Amanda, for its discovery.

At 19.09 that evening Amanda had left the office with a bunch of papers in her hand – probably off to talk to Adrian, Head of Input. That gave Jen a few clear minutes to slip off the radar. She picked up Nick's phone and headed for the ladies' toilet, planning to phone his old friend, Brodie Covington, one more time. She'd tried him six times since their meeting, and on each occasion her call had gone straight to voicemail. He hadn't phoned back, but Jen was nothing if not persistent.

As soon as she'd locked herself in the cubicle she started scrolling for his number. She'd just selected his name when the outside door swung open and Amanda and Portia McDowd (the one other seriously obnoxious woman on the team) crashed in, mid-argument. Suddenly Jen was stuck in a cubicle, the only witness to a major clash of the Titans. Her hands stopped moving, but it was too late, Nick's phone had connected and the call was going through. The ringtone sounded . . . not loud – nothing like as loud as their voices – but loud enough. Where was the damned silence button? In her panic to shut it off, the phone slipped out of her hands and on to the tiled floor with a resounding crack.

The two women stopped shouting at each other, immediately aware of the locked cubicle door. Jen sat frozen to the spot, staring down at the floor, where Nick's iPhone had now split into three pieces.

Someone pushed at her door. Amanda. Jen could see her shoes through the gap. She lifted her own feet off the ground. The tension in the room was so taut, Jen wondered if they could hear her heartbeat. Then suddenly both sets of shoes clicked purposefully out, the door slamming hard behind them.

Jen took a deep breath and looked down. Nick's phone – the only thing of his she had left. And she had just broken it. With shaking fingers she retrieved the pieces – and realized that the phone was actually intact. The impact had simply forced the cover away, along with whatever had been wedged inside it.

At first she assumed it was a credit card – same shape and size. Then she realized it was some kind of ID . . . black, with a photo embedded into it: Brodie Covington's photo. Along with a shiny square biometric panel. How did Nick get hold of this? And what was he planning to do with it?

Jen was a good researcher, but she wasn't a hacker. She was prepared to bend the boundaries of legality a bit in the pursuit of information . . . but this was on a whole new scale. And she knew only one person she could consult. Eva Koretsky. She quickly dialled her number and as usual went straight to voice-mail. Then she remembered. It was Friday. The night of their big Underworld gig. She popped the phone and card in her pocket, ran back to her desk, logged off, then picked up her bag and slipped out of the building.

Normally she wouldn't be wearing a dress and jacket for a rock gig, but she didn't have time to go home and change. She grabbed a box of sushi on the way into the tube and thirty-five minutes later she was squeezing her way through the venue.

The support act were on their last song – thank God. They were loud, derivative and monotonous. As they cleared the stage, Jen eased her way nearer. By the time the Astronauts had set up, she was pretty close to the front. Close enough to catch

Eva's eye. And Jen smiled when she recognized the spark of interest reflected there.

By the end of the set, she had to admit the band had something . . . especially the damn singer. Jen's mouth twitched with irritation, watching ruefully as Eva left the stage. She didn't look so good though . . . sort of droopy and pale. Certainly didn't seem interested in playing the star. In fact she looked like she wanted to find a hole and hide in it. Jen followed her, but hung back when she saw the bass player grabbing her and hauling her towards a big group of people. She'd have to bide her time. Jen edged her way nearer, and realized that Theo Mendes was one of the group. Had he signed them?

She eased herself into a position where she was standing directly in Eva's eyeline. As soon as Eva glanced her way she would give her a signal to meet her outside. But Eva was leaning against a pillar with her eyes shut . . . Hang on – *no* – she was now sliding down the pillar and crouching on the floor . . . much to the obvious annoyance of the group she was with . . . *God, she really didn't care, did she?* Now Theo was hauling her to her feet. Christ, she looked terrible . . . her eyes were kind of glazed and she seemed to be shaking. Jen frowned. Whoa – she was leaving . . . pushing through the crowds and heading for the door. Jen wrestled with the crowd to follow her out.

69

Chase

London

Seth hauled himself on to the riverbank, praying the vortex had thrown him accurately into Eva's London. His intended time destination was 2.20 a.m. Friday 10 May, just about the time he'd met with Zackary in the St Mag's quad. He was cautiously optimistic as he ran through dark streets towards the school. By the time he was sprinting under the archway of St Magdalene's, despite his clinging, wet clothes, he was sweating hard.

The quad was empty. That was a good sign. He raced straight to Eva's room. Locked. Hmmm . . . when he'd left her asleep he hadn't locked the door. He knocked quietly. No answer. He put his fingers along the top ledge where she always left a key for him, and smiled when his hand curled round it. He opened the door. She wasn't there. Neither was the guitar she always propped against the window corner. He looked at the clock – 10 p.m. That had to be wrong. He must have arrived too early. He peered again at the clock, staring at the date. No. *Impossible.* How the hell could it be . . . *July?* His heart started to pound as he sprinted from the building towards the music department. If her guitar was missing, maybe she was rehearsing. But the music block was empty. Maybe a gig?

Seth stood in the middle of the quad trying to work out how he was going to find her, when a couple of girls emerged from Isaac Newton house. He ran towards them.

'Ruby?' he panted.

She stared at him with her mouth open. 'Seth!' she gasped. 'You're back! What happ—'

'Ruby, where's Eva?' Seth demanded.

Ruby's eyes narrowed and she shrugged.

'Ruby,' said Seth quietly, looking her straight in the eye, 'I need to know where Eva is. Right now.'

Ruby blinked. 'The gig at the Underworld – probably over by now, though.'

'Where's the Underworld?' asked Seth patiently.

'Camden. You can't miss it – just opposite the tube.'

Of course – he'd passed it on one of his runs . . . about three kilometres away, ten minutes' hard run – if he remembered the way.

70

Darkness

I leaned against the front wall of the venue and shut my eyes. The ground, the wall, the air – everything felt like it was tipping. Or was it me?

I sighed. I couldn't do this any more . . . I couldn't be the Eva they all needed me to be. Whatever I did now, it was never going to be enough – I would always be letting someone down. It had to stop. I was tired: tired of fighting the virus; tired of struggling against my own physical limitations; tired of all the effort. I was ready to let go.

And the thought of letting go filled me with a peculiar kind of peace. I impatiently blinked away a couple of stray tears that had squeezed their way out, and looked up at the stars. They always put everything into perspective. Me and my worries were not even a speck on the huge canvas that stretched around us.

Was Seth out there somewhere? I prayed he was. However

vast it was, I couldn't bear to think of a universe without him in it.

A sudden movement at my elbow forced me back to the present. I turned, expecting to see a random stranger jostling past. But it wasn't a stranger.

'Greetings, Livia.'

No!

This couldn't be happening. It wasn't real. Another nightmare. *Please* . . . I needed to wake up . . .

'What a pleasant surprise.' His cruel mouth quirked into that smile . . . the one that constantly haunted my nightmares.

'*Cassius!*' I choked.

He had a hand pressed against the small of my back and was using it to propel me firmly away from the Underworld, away from all the people . . . away from the light. And I had neither the energy nor the will to resist.

As we moved towards a dark and narrow side street, I didn't think about screaming for help or trying to run. A strange, detached part of my brain wondered vaguely if he was using the same power Seth had used on Nick Mullard . . . if this was what it felt like. Or was it just that I'd already given up? My body was barely mine any more . . . it had been claimed by the virus . . . and now here was Cassius to take what was left. Only this time I wasn't fighting – I had nothing left to lose.

We had stopped moving. Cassius turned me round to face him, and took my chin in his hand. I didn't struggle, just stared back into his dark, hooded eyes. For the first time ever, I faced him without fear. I didn't even feel bitterness or anger – because this time he couldn't take anything from me that I hadn't already lost.

He frowned. 'So beautiful,' he breathed, his mouth millimetres from mine.

I flinched away. His fingers tightened on my jaw.

'You know I'm going to kill you properly this time, Livia,' he murmured smoothly.

I planted my feet and shrugged.

'You're not afraid?' Disappointment flitted across his features.

It was a small victory – but it made me smile.

He slapped me across the face, his heavy gold ring slicing through my cheek. I gasped and lost my footing, but his hands clamped down on my shoulders, steadying me. I tried to shake them off – revolted by his touch – but he held on tight. I took a deep breath, silently acknowledging how stupid I'd been. There were no victories with Cassius. Only pain. I had just needlessly extended my own death.

'So – where is he, Livia?'

'Who?' I hissed. As if I didn't know.

'The gladiator.'

'I have no idea,' I snarled.

'Well then, I'll wait,' he smiled.

'W-what?' I gasped. Was this some kind of weird reprieve?

'I wouldn't want him to miss seeing you die . . . again.'

And then, God help me, I laughed. Long and hard.

Rage contorted his face and he grabbed me round the neck and pressed his thick thumbs into my throat.

It's over, I thought gratefully, as blackness swum across my eyes. But then his hands slackened. I staggered back into a lamp post and slumped against it, trying to drag air into my lungs.

But Cassius was looming over me again. 'I'm going to ask you one more time, Livia. And this time I would like an answer. *Where is he?*'

'*I don't know!*' I screamed . . . only my throat was so bruised my voice came out hoarse and cracked.

He hit me again, knocking my head hard against the lamp post. I sank to my knees. I could feel blood running down the back of my neck.

'You can wait forever, Cassius . . .' I gasped. 'Seth isn't coming.'

'There's no point playing this game, Livia. Matthias led me here.'

'*Matthias?*' I choked. Seth's *friend* betrayed us? But it didn't matter . . . I was already dead . . . and this time Cassius wasn't going to get Seth.

'Matthias knows nothing,' I gasped. 'Seth's gone, Cassius . . . He – he stopped loving me. He's not coming back.'

Cassius was glaring at me through narrowed eyes . . . trying to determine whether I was telling the truth. His lip curled in disgust.

'The pitiful slave *stole* you from me and then *discarded* you?' he roared.

'*I was never yours, Cassius!*' I cried. 'Seth stole *nothing* from you.'

'By the gods, Livia,' Cassius snarled, his dark eyes burning, his breath coming in sharp, hoarse bursts, 'you will pay for your defiance!'

He was going to kill me now; I read it in his eyes . . . But I had won. Cassius didn't have Seth. This time Seth would be safe. And that was everything – the only thing I cared about.

I smiled triumphantly into those ruthless black eyes and watched them dilate as the crushing blow hit my chest. Then my head was crashing against concrete. Bright lights, pain. Darkness.

71

Message

Jennifer Linden had fought her way to the main doors of the building, but when she got outside she could see no sign of Eva. She gazed around, perplexed. How far could the girl have got? She'd looked ready to drop.

Suddenly Jen caught sight of movement across the road. A boy stealthily following a couple . . . weird. But something about the couple was wrong. The guy was big, but he carried himself like he was huge. And his posture was so stiff, so purposeful, it almost looked like . . . like he was pushing the girl. Jennifer peered into the darkness . . . God – was he wearing some kind of dress? Her eyes shifted to the girl. Long dark hair. A flash of white T-shirt. She swallowed. Eva had been wearing white. Jen's heart started to thud. Eva had told her that she had enemies. MI5 had warned her to keep off this case.

With trembling fingers she got her phone out and dialled 999.

'I think I may be witnessing a kidnap,' she whispered into

the phone. She gave the address. She took her eyes momentarily off the pair to slip her phone back in her pocket, but when she looked up again, the couple had disappeared. She desperately scanned the streets around her and was on the verge of panicking when she spotted the boy who had been tailing them, ducked behind a wheelie bin and staring into a dark, narrow street. Jen crept over and soundlessly crouched down beside him. He turned to her, his eyes wide with fear, and put a finger to his lips. Jen peered round the bin and gasped in horror as the girl, blood pouring from her face, crashed to the ground.

'Oh my God! *Eva!*' she breathed, moving to dash forward.

But the boy grabbed her. 'Don't be an idiot,' he hissed. 'Do you want to end up like her?'

'We have to stop him!' Jen gasped. 'Come on!'

'He's got a knife –'

'For God's sake – I *know* her! And there are two of us! Help me!' Jen cried, pulling the boy by the hand.

Eva was lying motionless on the ground, but Jen could see movement in her chest. The heavy-set guy was standing over her, breathing hard.

The boy had been right. In the man's right hand was a long curved knife.

He turned when he heard them.

'Ah, Matthias! Just in time to take a message to the gladiator.'

'Magister,' gasped Matthias, kneeling. 'I couldn't find –'

'You *will* find Sethos Leontis,' commanded Cassius. 'And you will give him this message from me.'

'*No!*' screamed Jen, as the man pulled Eva to her feet and, holding her limp body with one hand, plunged the knife deep into her stomach with the other. Eva gasped and then slumped against her captor.

Matt held Jen back as Cassius pulled the knife out and wiped it carefully against Eva's jeans. He held her body against his for a moment, then kissed her harshly on the mouth and let her crumple limply to the ground.

Jen stared in dumb horror as Eva's T-shirt turned from white to red, but before she could react, her attention was caught by the sound of footsteps running towards them. 'The police!' she gasped. 'The police are coming!'

Cassius looked up lazily, threw down the knife and started striding away.

'They'll get you for this!' she screamed.

'Let them try,' he laughed, disappearing into the darkness.

72

Blood

Seth flew through the door of the Underworld and ploughed across the crowds towards the stage. No band was playing, but he caught sight of three familiar faces – Astrid, Rob and Sadie – and headed straight for them.

'Seth!' gasped Astrid, as he got close. 'What the hell are you doing here?'

'Where's Eva?' he panted.

Astrid was on the point of telling him that he was the last person she would talk to about Eva, when she suddenly found herself saying, 'She went outside a couple of minutes ago. I was just about to check she's OK.'

Seth turned and ran back towards the door. Astrid followed close behind. Rob darted quickly after them, his shock and fury at seeing Seth totally eclipsing his desire to ingratiate himself with Theo's guests.

As soon as he was through the main door, Seth paused,

scouring the area for Eva. There were too many people standing around.

'Did you see a girl with long dark hair –?' he began.

Astrid had arrived next to him. 'The singer – anyone see her?' she bellowed.

'Took off with a big guy – down there!' gestured one of the bouncers.

Seth sprinted away, Astrid and Rob close behind. Seconds later, Seth had arrived at the corner of the dark narrow street the bouncer had indicated.

Two people were standing in the middle of the road ahead, gazing down at the ground. Seth's heart began to pound as he hurled himself forward.

'*Eva!*' he choked, falling to his knees and pulling her lifeless body towards him. She was wet with blood. He could feel it pumping over his fingers. He laid his hand over her heart and felt a faint beat.

Wildly, he glanced up at the two figures standing like frozen statues.

'Matthias?' he rasped. '*Help her!*'

Matthias was shaking his head. 'I'm sorry, Seth . . . Cassius –'

'*Please, Matthias!*' Seth sobbed. '*I c-can't lose her . . .*'

'An ambulance is on its way,' breathed the woman. 'A-and the police.'

Matthias crouched down next to Seth. 'They'll be too late, Seth. She's dying, brother. You need to say goodbye.'

'*Eva!*' Seth howled, pressing her body to his. '*Don't leave me!*'

Suddenly Matthias threw himself across the road and grabbed Cassius's knife.

'Give her your blood, Seth,' he gasped. 'There may be a chance . . .'

'She's had the fever, Matt. She didn't go to Parallon. My blood won't –'

'*Try it*, man!' shouted Matt.

Seth snatched the knife and slashed it along his wrist. As soon as the blood started flowing, he ripped Eva's shirt apart and squeezed his blood deep into her knife wound. But her limpness appalled him. Frantically, he began slashing a second cut into her neck, determined to flood her body with his virus. But the instant the knife touched Eva's skin, Astrid and Rob barrelled towards him.

'*Seth! What the hell are you doing?*' screamed Astrid, forcing the knife away from Eva's neck.

'*Get your filthy hands off her!*' yelled Rob, grabbing the knife and pointing it at Seth.

Seth's body tautened, and a moment later he was on his feet, Astrid and Rob were thrown clear and the knife was once more in his hand.

'*You want to watch her die?*' he snarled, his eyes blazing into theirs. 'Or can I try and save her?'

Without waiting for an answer, he turned and crouched down again next to Eva.

Astrid and Rob stood frozen, but Jen and Matthias moved behind them, ready to hold them back if they made another move.

'You have to trust him,' murmured Matthias. 'He would give his life a hundred times to save hers.'

They all watched helplessly as Seth gently pushed Eva's hair away from her neck and ran the knife along her skin. As the thin line of red appeared, he squeezed his cut wrist across it, but his blood flow had slowed. Furiously, he cut a second, deeper incision into his other wrist, and as the wound began to gush, he painted Eva's neck red with his blood. Then he shifted slightly and tenderly cut a thin line into the crook of her arm, squeezing fresh blood into that. He continued to make small incisions across her whole body, forcing his blood into each of them . . . until she started to shudder.

'Eva!' Seth sobbed into her unresponsive lips. 'Please don't leave me . . .'

He didn't hear the sirens. His eyes were fixed on the shaking girl in his arms.

And then she was still.

'*Eva!*' wailed Rob, twisting out of Jen and Matthias's grasp. '*You've killed her, you bastard!*'

Seth just crouched, motionless, waiting, not daring to breathe. Matthias squatted next to him, and together they watched as she slowly began to disappear.

'Eva?' rasped Astrid, running forward. 'What the hell have you done with her, Seth?'

Seth didn't turn, he just continued staring down until the faint outline of the girl he loved faded into air. Then his head jerked round wildly.

'*Cassius!*' he choked, jumping up. 'I've got to get to Eva before he does!'

'The gods be with you, brother!' breathed Matt, touching his shoulder.

Without another word, Seth fled swiftly towards the river, leaving Matthias, Astrid, Rob and Jennifer Linden to face the ambulance crew and two police cars pulling up at the other end of the street.

'Er – I'd better be going,' stammered Matthias, as he saw them arrive.

'No way,' hissed Jen. 'What on earth are we supposed to tell them?'

Matthias shook his head and shrugged helplessly as he followed Seth into the night.

He knew he was heading back to a savage, cruel world. He knew that he could be called upon to fight. He knew that he might have to confront his own weakness and fear . . . But now that Seth was coming home, he suddenly felt anything was possible.

And he ran towards the river with hope swelling in his chest.

TO BE CONTINUED . . .

Acknowledgements

Thank you to my two stellar editors – Shannon Cullen and Anthea Townsend – who deftly steered the dangerous path between firmness and encouragement . . . a delicate recipe which they conjured with immense care and expertise. Boundless thanks are also due to my dazzling copy editor, Karen Whitlock, whose attention to detail has been a wonder to behold. It's been a privilege to become a member of the Puffin/Penguin family, and working with such a dynamic team has been an inspiration. Thanks especially to Sam Mackintosh for her powerful editorial support and kindness; Katy Finch for her wonderful cover designs; and Zosia Knopp, Susanne Evans, Joanna Lawrie and Camilla Borthwick for their incredible enthusiasm and amazing foreign rights successes. Thank you also Fi Evans and Hermione Lawton for so heroically spreading the Fever!

There were several times during the writing of *Fever* and *Delirium* when I asked myself why I'd chosen to write a story set in three time zones, across two universes, and necessitating shockingly difficult-to-grasp quantum physics. Fortunately, I wasn't on my own! Thank you so much Kevin Walsh for your generous input, and for helping me coherently hyphenate the science with the fiction. And thank you Ian Cockburn for talking electromagnetic pulses and still managing to drive fast along winding Spanish roads! Thank you to my amazing sister Caroline for tirelessly fielding my medical questions, and reading the manuscript with such care. And I couldn't have managed without my brother-in-law Ed either, as his expertise on hospital protocol and procedures both current and futuristic was invaluable. Thank you also to the computer gurus, Richard Hindley, Duncan McNeil and Max Sulley, for offering such coherent and precise IT insights. Enormous thanks again to my friend and supreme classicist Andy Mylne for throwing up all sorts of unaddressed questions about Roman hinges, doors and costume embellishments. I am indebted to the wonderful Chris Shaw for showing me around the Channel 5 Newsroom and then checking the relevant sections for authenticity. Thank you Martha Kearney and Nicola Gooch for generously chatting to me about TV and news at parties and dinners without a single sign of ennui! Thank you so much Nicola Kumaran for taking me round Hendon Police Academy, for introducing me to the DI world and for reading the Nick Mullard sections with such meticulous attention. Thanks also to the kind anonymous DI at City Police for answering all my queries.

I'd also like to offer an enormous thank you to the promo film and website team: Chris Barton, Addison Axe, Zackary Falls, Max Barton, Shannon Cullen, Katy Bulmer, Jamie Dorman, Becky Waters, Emma Sulley, Tom de Freston, Eve Hedderwick Turner, Zora Bishop and Jessie Wilde.

And as ever I have to thank my family for their continued forbearance and immense contributions, particularly: Axie – for being my Eva inspiration, for building the website, for playing Eva in the promo video, for giving me all that first-hand gigging insight, and for making sure I was accurate about my sound-checks! Max – for providing me with the boy angle, for playing so many roles on the website and in the promo, and for writing the soundtrack music. And above all, thank you, Chris, for story-boarding, directing, shooting and editing the promo, for being an endlessly patient ear to my Parallon ramblings, for having the courage and energy to challenge my narratives and adverbs, and then staying up night after night reading through the final drafts with me. As ever – I couldn't have done any of it without you.

PASSIONS BURN
IN
AFTERLIFE

THE FINAL INSTALMENT
in the thrilling Parallon trilogy

THE STORM IS COMING . . .
SPRING 2014

WWW.FEVERBOOK.CO.UK

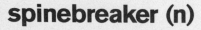

SIX SPINE-TINGLING BOOKS

as chosen by the Spinebreakers crew

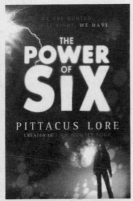

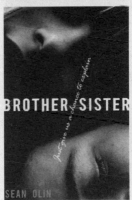

The list continues at www.spinebreakers.co.uk

DO YOU WANT TO JOIN US?

If you are a story-surfer, word-lover, day-dreamer, reader/writer/artist/thinker . . . BECOME one of us.

spinebreakers
spinebreakers.co.uk

GET INSIDE YOUR FAVOURITE BOOK

He just wanted a decent book to read ...

Not too much to ask, is it? It was in 1935 when Allen Lane, Managing Director of Bodley Head Publishers, stood on a platform at Exeter railway station looking for something good to read on his journey back to London. His choice was limited to popular magazines and poor-quality paperbacks – the same choice faced every day by the vast majority of readers, few of whom could afford hardbacks. Lane's disappointment and subsequent anger at the range of books generally available led him to found a company – and change the world.

'We believed in the existence in this country of a vast reading public for intelligent books at a low price, and staked everything on it'
Sir Allen Lane, 1902–1970, founder of Penguin Books

The quality paperback had arrived – and not just in bookshops. Lane was adamant that his Penguins should appear in chain stores and tobacconists, and should cost no more than a packet of cigarettes.

Reading habits (and cigarette prices) have changed since 1935, but Penguin still believes in publishing the best books for everybody to enjoy. We still believe that good design costs no more than bad design, and we still believe that quality books published passionately and responsibly make the world a better place.

So wherever you see the little bird – whether it's on a piece of prize-winning literary fiction or a celebrity autobiography, political tour de force or historical masterpiece, a serial-killer thriller, reference book, world classic or a piece of pure escapism – you can bet that it represents the very best that the genre has to offer.

Whatever you like to read – trust Penguin.